Treasure Uncovered

Diane Greenwood Muir

Cover Design Photography: Maxim M. Muir

ISBN-13: 978-1490939285
ISBN-10: 1490939288

CONTENTS

ACKNOWLEDGMENTS

This has been a crazy few months. I finished my Master's Degree and wrote another book. It would have been impossible without the love, prayers and support of my family and friends.

A special thank you to Ralph and Sue Storm, whose barn graces the cover of this book. I am safe out here in the middle of rural America because they keep an eye on me. Ralph plants trees, plows my driveway in the winter, mows when the grass in the meadow is too overwhelming and they take moments to chat just to check up on me and ensure I'm doing alright in my solitude.

My editor / proofreaders / readers all encourage me and at the same time press me with questions and recommendations so that I write a better story. Any errors you find in the text are my responsibility, though. They've done their best to keep me on track.

Thank you to Rebecca Bauman, Tracy Kesterson Simpson, Linda Watson, Carol Greenwood, Alice Stewart, Fran Neff, Max Muir, and Edna Fleming for all they do to make these books happen.

It terrifies me to put raw, unedited text out there for anyone to read, but this group finds humor in my ridiculous mistakes, reminds me that my errors don't define my writing and then each of them focuses on something different as they read so that I can clean the manuscript and prepare it for publication.

CHAPTER ONE

Polly stood on her stepstool beside Nat's left shoulder, brushing him down. She rested her head against his body as they enjoyed a rare moment of warmth in the sun. Of the four black Percherons she had rescued, Nat had been in the worst shape and trusted her the least in the beginning. Little by little though, as she kept showing up every day, ensuring that he had the food and care he needed, as well as a whole lot of attention, he soon began to respond. When the four were in the pasture, it was Nat who came to her voluntarily for nothing more than affection.

She smiled as she thought about the last couple of months. When the horses arrived at Sycamore House's brand new barn, Mark Ogden, her friend and the local veterinarian, not only had to help bring them back to health, but teach Polly how to care for four immense animals. Her crazy idea to build a barn last January had come with the hope of finding one normal-sized horse who would be patient and kind and let her learn the ins and outs of being a horse owner. What she'd gotten were four badly neglected draft horses in need of a strong-minded owner.

That was the first and most difficult lesson Mark had taught her. No matter how sorry Polly felt for the horses, he reminded her that she had to be in charge from the beginning or she would never be in charge. Seven thousand pounds of horse could get out of control in a hurry, so she listened and learned. At some point in late March when the horses began to show outward signs of recovery and as Polly's confidence increased, Mark finally stopped showing up every day to check on them.

When Polly opened the Dutch doors to the pasture for each of the horses this morning, it was as if they sensed the sunshine. After breakfast, Nan had taken off for the end of the pasture and skittered around a little as Obiwan chased a butterfly. The dog had grown quite comfortable with the horses and knew enough to stay away from their feet, but he did love running with them whenever they could be convinced to play. Demi and Daisy were on the west side of the pasture sniffing over the fence at something in the trees by the creek. The day felt a little pastoral and Polly decided to enjoy it for as long as it might last. She had finally stopped wondering if spring was ever going to arrive and was grateful for the warmer temperatures.

She picked up her stool and moved to brush Nat's other side and saw Jeff standing at the gate.

"Good morning!" she called. "It's a beautiful day. Do you want to come out and play with us?"

"You know better than that," he laughed.

"Did you need something from me?" Jeff Lyndsay, her assistant and manager and a self-proclaimed city boy, wasn't fond of large animals, so he preferred not to associate with them if possible. They'd finally figured out that since she was spending a lot of her day with the horses, it would be easier for him to call her cell phone, so it was a little surprising to see him standing at the gate to the horse's pen.

"Not really. It's a beautiful day and I thought I'd enjoy the view."

"That doesn't sound like you!" She jumped off her stool and led Nat to the gate.

"Yeah. The truth is, I'm avoiding Harry."

They were having the worst luck finding a good custodian.

Harry Bern was the fourth person they'd hired in the last two months and all he did was whine and complain. He whined about the price of gas, the price of milk and the price of bread; he whined about the President and the mayor and the elementary school principal. He whined about the weather and people who drove too fast or too slow; he whined about the color of the sky and the way water tasted. If he caught you sitting or standing in one place for too long, he would get wound up and twenty minutes later, you hoped for the world to end soon, there was nothing left to live for.

So far, only one of their guests had said something to Jeff about Harry's behavior. It had taken everything in Polly to find an easy way to tell poor Harry that he couldn't bother their guests with his whining and complaining. He'd taken it fairly well, but it was getting old.

"What do you think we should do?" she asked.

"I don't know. Maybe we buy a cork to fit his mouth. I keep hoping that he will stay away if I shut my door, but he very politely knocks and lets himself in."

"And you wonder why I'm outside all the time."

"Not really, though I don't think it's fair."

"I'm never coming back in, you know. The rest of the blacktop from that old playground should be cleared out soon and then I'll rent a tiller so I can start a vegetable garden. Between these guys," she patted Nat, "and the gardens, I'm planning to stay out here away from all of you."

"Gardens? Plural?"

"Plural. Lydia and Andy and their garden club want to put some sort of waterfall or pond and heirloom garden with a walking path and benches. It sounds like there will be a beautiful park in the front corner of the lot."

"And the sycamore trees? When are those coming in?"

"Over the next couple of weeks. The grounds are going to completely transform before your eyes," she said.

"You really aren't coming back inside to work, are you?"

"Not if I can help it. I'll see you next winter."

Nat nudged her and she laughed. "Apparently, I'm allowing you to distract me from what's important. You can stay here and watch, but I think he knows it's Daisy's turn to exercise and he's ready to be let loose."

She and Nat walked to the gate leading to the pasture and she opened it, then took his halter off. After a moment's hesitation, she saw the glimmer in his eyes as he leapt forward and ran to the other end, nickering to Nan. Daisy was next and when Polly picked her halter up off the fence, the horse came closer.

"That's my good girl, Daisy," Polly said, setting the step stool on the ground. She chuckled. It couldn't have been neglected ponies; it had to be immense Percherons. She had never known such exhaustion in her life before those first couple of months with them, but she could feel her muscles toning and she hurt less now than she had at the beginning. There had been one morning she was sure she might need to be hospitalized. When she had tried to sit up in bed, her muscles had refused to respond to commands from her brain. She had finally rolled over and off the bed and after standing under the hot shower and flexing her limbs, she was able to restore enough movement to get through the day. Polly was grateful for the months she had spent running and walking with Obiwan. Those had been a start to the hard work she was doing now, but it had no comparison.

Jeff watched as Polly began moving Daisy around the pen.

"When is Henry getting back?" he asked.

"He called last night and said they were finishing today and he would start driving back home by the weekend. I think he's tired of Arizona."

Henry's mother had called him about a month after the barn raising. The driver of a delivery truck had lost control and run into a corner of their home. As if that hadn't been enough stress, his father experienced a heart attack the next day, so they called for help and Henry packed his truck with everything he thought he might need and took off for southwest America. His father was going to be fine, but insisted that Henry was the only person he trusted to do the work to repair their home.

4

Lonnie, Henry's younger sister, had spent the week of her spring break helping her mother, but for the last month, he'd been alone with his parents and was ready to be back home.

"You'll be glad to have him back in town. You haven't had anyone around to build things for you!"

Polly nodded and turned her attention back to the horse. Every day she was out, the touch and commands made a little more sense to her. She was thankful these horses had been well trained before they got to her. Their former owner had purchased the Percherons and then named them after characters from one of his wife's favorite book series by Louisa May Alcott. After he died, his wife couldn't bear to sell them, so continued to pay for their food and care. The woman was much too old to spend any time with them and when the drought had put pressure on the caretaker's funds last year, he slowly began neglecting them until the day Polly and her friend Sylvie, discovered the horses and called Mark Ogden for help. The very next day, Mark arrived at Polly's new barn with four horses and Polly's life had changed one more time.

"You're right. I do have things for him to build. I hope he's had enough vacation for a long time," she said, laughing. "It's about time to get started on a new project."

Jeff shook his head and began to turn back toward Sycamore House. "You just miss having all the action around here."

"I suppose I do!" she said and then repeated to herself, "I suppose I really do."

She also missed having Henry around. They talked for a few minutes every evening, but it wasn't the same as having him here. Polly smiled. Maybe the old adage was true and that's why it was an old adage. Maybe absence really did make the heart grow fonder. She'd gotten quite comfortable spending time with Henry and his sudden departure had left a fairly large hole in her life.

Polly slowed Daisy back down and pulled out her phone.

"I was thinking about how glad I am that you're coming home this weekend," she texted and slipped the phone back in her pocket.

She finished with the horses and desperately wanted a nap, but Lydia and Andy were stopping by with several plans for the large northwest corner of the property. Lydia Merritt was the lifeblood of Bellingwood. A woman filled with love and grace, she had taken Polly under her wing as the self-appointed welcome committee and they had become fast friends. Andy Saner and Beryl Watson were two more of Lydia's close friends, a group that continued to grow.

Polly checked the gates, stood for a few moments to watch the horses as they grazed in the pasture, then whistled for Obiwan, her German Shepherd / Labrador mix. He came bounding through the barn to meet her and they went inside and up to her apartment. She took a quick shower and settled in on her sofa to check her email. The subject line of an email from her friend, Sal Kahane, read, "I'm coming to Iowa!" and Polly clicked it open.

She and Sal had been college roommates at Boston University and remained close friends while Polly lived in Boston. Since she'd moved to Iowa, they maintained contact but Polly missed their regular lunches and movie nights.

"Hey, sweetface. Is Iowa ready for me? To be more concise, are you ready for me?

Do you remember Ardyce, the idiot? She was supposed to be going to a seminar next week at the University of Iowa. She 'remembered' this morning that she is also supposed to be giving a lecture on how to read James Joyce's 'Ulysses' at your old library here in town! So, when she asked us this morning who wanted to take her place, I jumped out of my chair, flailing my arms. I probably surprised them and looked a little silly all at the same time.

Anyway, I looked at the map and Iowa City is a bit of a drive from you, so I can't stay with you while I'm at the seminar. I'm flying in to Des Moines, though. Can we make this work? I'll take some vacation days if you have time for me.

I miss you girlfriend!"

Polly shouted out loud, disturbing the dog and the cat, "Sal's coming to Iowa!"

"Sal, you glorious gal, you! Of course I have time for you! Do you want to come up here before or after you go to Iowa City? If it's after, you could return the rental car and I'll pick you up there and then deliver you back in time to fly home.

I'm so excited! I can't wait for you to see what I've done here and meet my animals and my friends!

I love you and I can't wait!"

She pressed send and sat back on the sofa, smiling. She leaned back to make noises at Luke, one of her two cats. He nudged her cheek and promptly returned to cleaning his shoulder. His sister, Leia, was perched on the ledge of their cat tree in the bedroom, too busy to join the rest of them.

Her phone buzzed and she checked it, *"Sorry I missed your text earlier. We're done. Mom and Dad say they're tired of me and I should go home. I'm on the road tomorrow,"* Henry's text said.

"Good. How much rest do you need before we get started on another project here?"

"You're a pushy lady. Will you at least take me out for dinner and a movie? You owe me one, you know."

The last time she had attempted to take Henry out on a date, it had been interrupted by a threat to one of her guests at Sycamore House. They'd ended up eating takeout and watching a movie in her apartment that night. He was right. She still owed him a nice evening out.

"I'll take you anywhere you want to go, but I want you in Bellingwood first."

"I miss you too. I'll talk to you tonight."

"Be good today!"

She scratched Luke's head and closed her eyes. When Polly had proposed building a barn and that led to a barn-raising, Jeff Lyndsay had accused Polly of having a menagerie. He might have been right.

Her front doorbell chimed and Polly came awake, startled. "You let me fall asleep," she admonished Obiwan, who was curled up on his blanket at the other end of the sofa. Luke must have also settled in because he stood up, arched his back, then stretched his front paws out.

Polly ran to the front door and saw that Lydia and Andy were standing there with two women she didn't recognize.

"You weren't down in your office and Jeff said he saw you come upstairs. Did we wake you?" Lydia laughed.

Polly glanced around her apartment. Other than her bedroom, everything looked fine. "I'm sorry," she said. "You're right. I sat down and fell asleep."

"Should we wait for you in the conference room?"

"No, that's alright. Come on in." They followed Polly into the entryway. She winked at Lydia, who nodded.

"Go ahead," Lydia assured her. "We'll get comfortable at your dining table."

Polly swiftly closed the door to her bedroom and checked the bathroom. She folded the towel and hung it up over the heated rack, closed the shower door and scooped everything on the counter into the top drawer. The room had been wiped clean yesterday, so she nodded at herself in the mirror, fluffed her still damp hair and went back into the main room.

"Can I get anyone some coffee? I could put water on for tea," she said.

Though they all declined, Polly drew water into her teapot and put it on to boil. The women were spreading papers and plans out on the table and she watched as they shuffled things into some sort of order.

"We have some wonderful ideas, Polly," Andy said. "And we have the labor to make it all happen."

Polly stood beside Lydia, looking down at the first layout.

"Oh!" Lydia said. "I should introduce you. This is Nancy Burroughs, the president of our local garden club and Deb Waters, whose gardens win prizes every year."

Nancy Burroughs' hands were strong and Polly could feel callouses on them when they clasped her own. A woman in her early sixties, Nancy had shoulder length grey hair, a face filled with laugh lines and green eyes that smiled even when her mouth was at ease. Deb Waters was a blue-eyed blond, whose bouncy curls were held back with bright pink barrettes. Her well-worn jeans, black t-shirt and work boots seemed at odds with the curls and perfectly made-up face.

Deb pointed to a map of the space and when she spoke, Polly thought she'd never heard such a beautiful speaking voice. Maybe it was because of her last name, but to Polly it sounded fluid, like water rushing through a river. She wrenched her attention back to what Deb was saying.

"If we get started now, we can build the basic structures, then fill out the gardens as temperatures warm up."

"Deb's husband, Louis, is a carpenter, Polly," Lydia said. "We figured Henry would be busy with other things and this would get someone else involved in a Sycamore House project. There are a couple of other husbands who have dug up their yards for ponds and waterfalls and are willing to help us."

"That's great!" Polly said.

"This corner has been so boring for such a long time, I think it's wonderful that you are going to do something with it," Nancy Burroughs said. "There are a lot of us who look forward to it being a pretty little park."

The corner of Polly's lot was nearly as big as one of the town's blocks and the women had come up with an attractive design, complete with a walkway, which included a pond and a bridge, as well as several spots for benches. They had even planned for a trellis covered entrance leading to Sycamore House.

"It's lovely," Polly said. "Now, what's this?" She pointed to a blocked out area at the far corner of the park.

Andy dug underneath a stack of papers and pulled out a sketch. It was a brick monument sign which read, "Sycamore House."

"We thought you might like this," she said.

"I love it!" Polly laughed. The concrete over her front door was engraved with "Bellingwood Public Schools" and she didn't plan to erase that connection to the building's origins, but this sign would identify the property for at least the next fifty years.

"Oh," Polly said, "This is all amazing. Every step we take makes things more wonderful around here. Thank you for initiating this!" She couldn't wait to tell Jeff. This garden area was going to be a terrific draw for brides as they looked for a place for weddings and receptions.

As the ladies began talking about flowers and plants, Polly quietly pulled out mugs and saucers and placed them on a tray. She had made lemon shortbread cookies yesterday after school with Jason and Andrew, the sons of her friend and Sycamore House's chef, Sylvie Donovan. Arranging them on a plate, she set everything on the peninsula. When she handed the basket of teabags around the table, no one said a word. They were engrossed in their plans and allowed her to serve them. However, Lydia winked at her and nodded before jotting a note on the plans where the dahlias would be planted.

Polly jumped at another knock at her front door. Harry was standing there with a chunk of concrete in his hands.

"What is this, Harry?"

"I found this broken off the back step by the storeroom door. What should I do with it?" He tried to step into her entry way, but Polly stood firmly in the door.

"Go ahead and write a note telling me exactly where it was that you discovered the break and put it and the piece of concrete on the main office desk. I'll deal with it when I'm downstairs."

"I could describe the whole thing to you now," he pressed. "If I could come in and chat with you ..."

"No, I have people here right now, Harry. Go ahead and write it up and I'll be sure to take care of it."

"I'm only worried about people trying to get in that door and hurting themselves. With all of the rain and mud, it wouldn't do to have someone trip on it. Can you believe all the rain we've been having? I feel as if I'm going to drown just coming to work. You know that creek is going to flood and will probably destroy your lawn and I'll bet when it does your horses will be in trouble. Last year it was a drought and this year we have all of this dreadful rain."

He took a breath and Polly stepped back inside, pulling the door toward her. "Thank you, Harry. Please put it on the desk downstairs and I will take care of it."

She pushed the door shut and stepped back into the living room.

CHAPTER TWO

One more time. It figured. Custodian number four wasn't here for the second day in a row. Polly was tired of scrubbing toilets and began to think that somehow the job description was a curse. Harry Bern hadn't shown up at all yesterday and he wasn't here yet today. She slammed her hands down on her desk, stood up, and stomped into Jeff's office.

"I don't have time for this crap," she said, dropping into a chair.

He grinned. "I think I'm going to write a book called 'The Curse of the Custodian.'" They had talked about this after the third person they'd hired for the job called to tell them he was moving to Florida because he'd met a wonderful woman online and was going to live in peace and harmony with her and three other couples on a farm. Their second custodian had lasted longer than their first, Shawn Wesley. He held the record. He hadn't lasted a day before Polly kicked him out. John Bennett had lasted three days. He walked in one morning to give fifteen minutes notice because he'd gotten the job he had been hoping for as a waiter in Ames. Polly began to think Jeff was right. Maybe the job was cursed.

"Do you think there's anything wrong with Harry?" she asked.

"He's here every morning at 9:45 to have coffee before starting to work at ten. And when he has had to be late for any reason, he calls. Let me try to reach him. I tried yesterday and didn't get an answer, but figured if he was skipping work, he was ignoring me," Jeff replied. He dialed and listened.

"Nope. Voice mail," he said. "Yes. Maybe we should worry. Do you want to drive or shall I?"

"I'll drive," she sighed. "If he's doing something strange in that house though, you're dealing with it, not me."

Polly had taken Harry home one afternoon when his car had been in the shop, so she knew where he lived. They pulled into the driveway of his small house and went to the front door.

She stopped as she raised her hand to knock on the door and sniffed the air. "Damn it. I hate to tell you that I recognize this smell."

Jeff wrinkled his nose and sniffed, then grimaced and asked, "Really?"

"Really."

She looked at the door, drew her sleeve over her hand and said, "Don't touch anything," and pulled the screen door open. With a gentle push of the front door, she opened it into the living room. Lying on the floor in a pool of blood from a head wound was their fourth custodian, Harry Bern. That was all she needed to see.

"I'm not going in there," she said.

"Yeah. If he was alive, we wouldn't be able to smell it clear out here," Jeff agreed.

They walked back to the front yard and Polly pulled out her cell phone, dialing a very familiar number.

"Hello, Polly. Don't tell me you've found another body," Aaron Merritt, the sheriff, said. Aaron was Lydia's husband and the two of them had taken care of Polly through many a mishap. She could have called the local police, but knew that Aaron would tell her what to do next.

"Why do you ask me that every time I call you?" she asked.

"Because you call my wife unless something bad has happened.

You've found more bodies than any one person should," he responded. "But, how can I help you today?"

"I found another body." Polly's voice was flat.

"No kidding!" Aaron laughed at her and then apologized. "I'm sorry. I shouldn't laugh. Oh, Polly. You can't be serious!"

"No," she whimpered. "I wish I were. This morning Harry Bern didn't come in to work for the second day in a row and when Jeff and I came over to his house to check on him … well, he's very dead."

"How do you know he's dead?"

"I opened the front door because I smelled something rather familiar. Aaron, I can't believe that I have that scent in my memory. Don't worry, I used the sleeve of my shirt and didn't touch anything. He's in a pool of blood in his front room. I didn't go in to check, though. See, watching police shows is good for me and you, right?"

"Polly, I'm sorry I laughed. I'm calling Ken and he'll have someone over there right away. Do you mind staying until they arrive?"

She sighed. "We'll be in my truck."

"I'll talk to you later. I'm sorry about this Polly," he said, but she heard him chuckling as he hung up.

"We wait?" Jeff asked.

"Yes. We wait. Someone should be here pretty soon." They got back into her truck and she backed out onto the street. She knew if she didn't, the locals would come in with multiple police cars, a fire truck and the EMTs and she'd be trapped. She wanted to be able to get out of there as soon as possible. She put the truck in park, sat back and closed her eyes.

"You know this is going to increase my infamy, don't you?" she asked, with her eyes still closed. "Henry isn't going to believe this when I tell him."

Jeff started laughing. "I know this is a tragedy," he said, "but you have to admit, it's over the top funny. There is no one other than you who could have walked into this situation."

Polly started to chuckle and then snorted through her nose. "I know!" and pretty soon she was laughing so hard she couldn't breathe. "How in the world does this happen to me?"

She opened her eyes, turned her head toward Jeff and said, "And crap, we have to hire another custodian!"

They were both laughing when Ken Wallers, Bellingwood's police chief, pulled up and into the driveway. He walked over to her truck and Polly rolled her window down, trying to maintain a straight face.

"I saw you laughing," he said. "I guess you know about the pool at the Elevator." Polly did know about it and she didn't like it much, but knew that it had nothing to do with her feelings. After skeletons had fallen out of the ceiling of a bathroom they were remodeling at Sycamore House and then when she and her friends had discovered Madeline Black's body in her home, several jokesters thought they would begin a pool as to which body Polly Giller might find next. Her friends all knew about it and knew that it drove her batty, but it was still in place. After today's events, she was sure that it would grow.

"Oh no!" cried Polly. "Who won this time?"

He chuckled, "I'm not sure, but this is certainly going to have the town buzzing. Aaron said you had been inside the home?"

"I only opened the screen door. The front door's lock had been broken and I was able to push it open. Harry's body is right there in the front room."

"And you're sure he's dead?"

"Well," she said. "I didn't touch him so I could check for a pulse or anything, but I remember that awful smell from Madeline Black's house."

At that, the fire truck and EMTs pulled in.

"You two can go back to work if you like," Ken said, "but don't leave the country, alright?"

Polly tilted her head at him in confusion.

"I'm kidding. I'll be over later to talk to you both about Mr. Bern."

He patted the hood of her truck and walked to the house as another police car pulled up. Polly recognized the two EMTs.

They had rescued her the night she had gotten hit on the head by a couple of goons from Chicago who were there to kidnap one of her guests. Sarah waved at her and then turned to follow them all inside.

Polly pulled out and Jeff said, "Well, now that the initial shock has worn off, I'm a little freaked out by this. I've never seen a dead person before. Hanging around with you has its own special benefits."

"Stop it," she scowled. "I can hardly believe this has happened again. Am I some strange sort of dead body magnet?"

"Well, whatever you are, this is the last damned time I get in a vehicle with you to check on someone. From now on, you go by yourself or I'm sending the Sheriff."

"I hate to be callous about this, but now what am I supposed to do about a custodian? It seems tacky to advertise for a new employee when this one has just died, but I can't sit around and wait until his body is in the ground." She smacked her fist on the steering wheel and snapped, "I don't have time for this."

"I'll call the paper when we get back. There is time to get an ad in this week's edition. You call your pastor friends. I met the Standard Manufacturing's Human Resources manager last week at the Chamber of Commerce luncheon. I'll give her a call and see if they have any good leads."

They pulled into the parking lot in front of Sycamore House as Lydia was getting out of her Jeep. She waited while Polly parked.

"Aaron called. Are you two doing alright?" she asked.

Polly chuckled and shook her head, "I'm fine. We've already found the humor in this. Now I'm annoyed that I have to find another custodian and before long I'm going to feel really guilty about having these feelings and about the fact that I didn't like the guy all that much. So yes, I suppose I'm fine. Are you here to check up on me?"

"Yes, and to show you sketches for the garden. I also wanted to show you some ideas I had for the middle room upstairs."

"Have you had lunch yet?" Polly asked.

"Not yet. Do you want to run uptown? I'll bet I could talk you into a pork tenderloin."

"I could really use that. I've been running since I got up this morning and it looks like I'm back to scrubbing toilets this week," she said.

Jeff had continued walking to the front door of Sycamore House without them.

"Jeff?" Polly called out.

He turned around, "Yes?"

"I'm running up to Joe's Diner with Lydia. Do you want me to bring something back for you?"

He thought for a minute, "Just bring me a club sandwich and chips. Thanks."

"I'll see you later!"

Lydia got back in her Jeep and quickly grabbed the stack of papers from the passenger seat. She held onto them as Polly got in, then handed them over after Polly was settled.

"Alright, Lydia. What are the odds that people are already talking about Harry Bern's death by the time we get to the diner?" Polly asked, cradling the pages on her lap.

"Even money. If they don't know about it by the time we get there, we can watch as the news begins to filter in. People will have seen the activity at his house and it won't take long for speculation to occur."

Polly shook her head. "I can't believe it happened to me again. There are nearly fifteen hundred people in this town and I was the one who knocked on his door."

Lydia patted her leg, "At least I wasn't involved this time. That gave Aaron no small amount of satisfaction. Is it wrong of me to tell you that he was still chuckling when he called me?"

"A little bit," Polly grimaced.

Lydia pulled into a parking place and took the papers from Polly. She stuffed them into a bag she pulled out of the back seat and they went inside and found an empty booth.

Their waitress's nametag read "Anna," and she placed two glasses of ice water and menus in front of them, "Will there be anyone else joining you today?" she asked and pulled out her receipt pad.

Lydia responded in the negative and asked for coffee. Polly touched her cup, nodded and began looking over the menu.

She laughed, "I'm not sure why I'm looking at the menu. Of course I'm having the tenderloin. What about you?"

"Probably the Cobb Salad. You know us older women, we have to keep watching our weight and I don't have a zoo to keep me running around all day long." Lydia laid her menu on the table and asked, "How are you doing with those horses? I haven't heard much from you lately."

"They're good and I'm doing fine," Polly said. "I think I'm finally past the full-blown exhaustion every night, but I'm still pretty weary." Her face fell. "Honestly, Lydia. If we don't find someone to work at Sycamore House pretty soon, I'm going to get on Demi and ride away into the sunset. I can't keep this up."

"Is Jeff helping?"

"As much as he can, but he's so busy with all of the events coming up and taking care of the guests and their needs and activities, I hate to ask him to do any more," Polly sighed. "And as much as Harry drove me nuts with his whiny running commentary, at least he did his job."

"What can I do to help? I can scrub toilets and wash down bathtubs. I can do laundry and sweep floors," Lydia said.

"Oh no, it's fine. I'm only complaining," Polly responded.

"Well, I certainly don't mind. I'm glad to help."

"Thank you. I appreciate it. But, I'll be fine. And besides, I know you have a million other things to do every day, including the park and garden on my corner."

Anna came back with a pot of coffee and took their orders. She gave Polly a sideways glance as she walked away and Polly rolled her neck, sighed and said, "She knows, doesn't she."

"It's a small town, Polly."

Polly tapped the bag Lydia had carried in with her. "What do you have for that middle bedroom upstairs? I'd really love to finish that room and quit thinking about it."

Lydia pulled a folder out of the bag and opened it so Polly

could see what she had printed out. The bed itself was incredible. It was a gorgeous maple sleigh bed with a sweep at the base on the sides and a tall headboard with wings on each side. The bedside table was opulent with inset cherry panels on the front and a marble top. The dresser had three drawers in the front and the rounded doors on the side opened to smaller drawers. A small chest and an arched mirror which would fit over the dresser were both available. A matching storage bench rounded out the set.

"I was thinking we could do the room in golds and whites with lots of color as small accents," Lydia said.

"You amaze me, Lydia Merritt. You absolutely amaze me. But, we need to find a desk as well."

"What about a simple cherry writing desk. It won't be an exact match, but will be elegant on its own. A leather blotter on top will protect it from most scratches."

"And that will also look pretty cool," Polly agreed. "Alright, do it. I'm excited!"

Lydia smiled, "It is so much fun to work with you. And it's even more fun knowing that a lot of people are going to see my creations. I never thought I'd get hired as an interior designer. Jill thinks it is a riot."

Jill was one of Lydia's daughters and as Beryl told it, Lydia had encouraged all of her kids to decorate their rooms using as much or as little color as they liked. She'd taught them to never be afraid of color in their lives. Lydia's tastes were classic and beautiful, but that didn't stop Jill's from becoming an ode to the color pink when the kids were young.

Polly's phone buzzed in her pocket and she pulled it out. She had a text from Henry, *"You did it again, didn't you."*

She showed the text to Lydia. "How did he find out so fast?" she asked.

Lydia burbled with laughter. "I have no idea! You don't suppose Aaron told him, do you?"

"It's not fair!" Polly whined. "It's just not fair!"

Before she could respond, another text came in, this one from their friend Beryl, *"You're getting a reputation. I'm going to have to go to the Elevator and get in on this pool."*

She showed that one to Lydia as well and they laughed again.

"Apparently the story is getting around," Lydia said. "By the way, when is that boy of yours supposed to be back in town?"

"If by boy, you mean Henry, he said he'd be back sometime this weekend. He left yesterday from Arizona."

"You're going to be glad to have him back, aren't you?"

"I am. Having him gone for two months was probably good for me. It made me realize how important he is to me."

Lydia opened her mouth to speak and Polly held her hand up to stop her.

"Don't think for a minute that I'm ready to settle down into marriage. I'm not ready for anything like that. But, I might be willing to state that the rest of the single men in Bellingwood are safe for the time being."

"We haven't had a chance to really talk about this," Lydia said.

"No. I'm not talking about it at all. The universe can let me do what I'm doing without interfering. Right?" She pursed her lips and looked at Lydia, as if daring the woman to challenge her.

"So, you decided that Doc Ogden isn't your cup of tea?"

Polly giggled. "Don't get me wrong, the man is gorgeous, and I love having him around to help with the animals, but no, we don't feel right together." Polly leaned over to stage whisper to Lydia, "And besides, I think Sylvie has a little crush on him."

"What?" Lydia said, "Our Sylvie?"

"Yes. Our Sylvie. He danced with her several times at the hoe-down and I think her heart might have gotten a little trippy about him. She denies it, but when she picks up the boys and he's in the barn with us, she makes a point of talking to him. So, yep. She might be crushing a little on the vet."

"Has she ever told you about her ex-husband?" Lydia asked.

"No. She gets all sad-eyed when it comes up and then she avoids the topic. In fact, she refuses to talk about it."

"Alright. Well, I'm not going to say anything. It's her story to tell. But, suffice it to say, she's probably a little wary of men, especially since she's working so hard to raise good young boys."

Polly realized that Lydia wasn't going to tell her anything more and that was fine. When Sylvie was ready to talk about her past, Polly would listen. For now, it was enough that her friend was starting to come alive.

Anna startled Polly when she came up behind her and set the plates on the table and pulled a bottle of ketchup out of her pocket. "Can I get you ladies anything else?" she asked.

"In about twenty minutes, would you mind putting in an order for a club sandwich to go?" Polly asked.

The girl scratched a note on her pad and said, "Sure!"

After she walked away, Lydia pulled out a pile of papers. "We spent time working out a plan for the garden after we left you the other day. I think you're going to like it and I think it's going to be a perfect little spot for the community, too."

Polly had no idea what some of the abbreviations meant, but they had drawn a winding pathway through the space and then began building the design from there. At the back of the space she saw they had placed a pond and assumed that 'wtfl' meant waterfall.

"This looks pretty cool," she said. "I don't know what all of it means, but you are the ones who will be doing the work, so I'm going to let you have at it."

"You aren't very good at micro managing people, are you Polly?" Lydia asked.

"Oh," Polly shuddered. "That sounds horrible. I have so many things to worry about that if someone wants to do something and I trust them, I'm glad to keep my hands off it. I don't know anything about gardening like this and I'm fairly certain I would kill everything I touched. Are you planning to put koi in that pond?"

Lydia laughed and said, "Where in the world did that come from?"

"It looks like it is big enough, so I was just wondering."

"No, I don't think we will. There is a lot of traffic that goes past it and since it is so far away from your house, I don't think it would be safe for the poor fish."

"That makes sense."

They talked about the garden a little more and Polly asked some questions about the vegetable garden she hoped to put in her back yard. Anna brought Jeff's lunch over with the check and Lydia took her back to Sycamore House.

CHAPTER THREE

Leaving a trail of filthy clothes from the entry way into the living room, Polly flopped down on her sofa, too tired to even crawl in the shower. She'd grabbed a long hoodie from the coat tree and made a beeline for the first soft spot she could find. Since Jeff's busiest times were the weekends, she'd taken to completely cleaning the stalls and barn on Friday nights so she could be available to help out around Sycamore House on Saturdays if necessary. She leaned back, dragged her computer from the coffee table onto her lap and logged in so she could be ready for the evening call from Henry. He planned to stop one more night and be back in Bellingwood tomorrow, but even on the road, he called before they both crashed. She turned the television on and after scanning through some channels, landed on an old Cary Grant movie. It only took her a few moments to realize it was *North by Northwest*. Perfect.

Obiwan jumped up and wriggled his way in between her legs to curl up at the end of the couch and the cats paced back and forth until Leia settled in beside Polly's head and Luke planted himself just past Polly's reach. She opened up a couple of browser tabs, checked email and the rest of her online world, found nothing that drew any more attention than necessary, lay her head back on the cushion and decided she needed to rest her eyes for a few moments. A shower and supper could come later.

The horses had been unusually skittish this evening. She'd had trouble getting them all to come back into their stalls and couldn't figure out what was going on. She hadn't done things any differently than before and was even beginning to feel fairly proud of herself for getting things down to a science. She checked their water, everything was fine and they had plenty of feed and hay. They'd all had great days outside and seemed happy until it was time to come in for the night. She'd give Mark a call tomorrow and see if he had a clue what she might have done to upset them. She was going to have to go up in the hayloft again before Monday morning, her main level supply was getting low. Oh, how she hated dropping bales out of the loft and then hauling them around. Her shoulders and back ached every single time she had to perform that task.

She chuckled. If only her friends in Boston could see her now. Museums and cafes, bookstores and nights at the theater had given way to online shopping, quick swipes at the coffee pot downstairs, random lunches at Joe's Diner and big shopping excursions to the grocery store in Boone. Going all out meant a trip to Ames for bagels or frozen yogurt with one of her friends.

Obiwan sat straight up and the cats came to attention. Polly startled out of her nearly asleep state and listened. She didn't hear anything.

"Stop it. You scared me to death!" She turned the sound off on the television and still heard nothing, but the animals were alert.

Then she heard a knock at her door and leaped off the couch. She wasn't dressed enough to have someone show up and her apartment was a disaster! She ran into the bedroom and found a pair of sweats in the middle of a pile of clothes on her chair. Pulling them on as she tripped her way back to the front door, she shoved her dirty jeans and shirt out of the way and said, "Who is it?" as sweetly as possible.

"The boogieman," the voice said.

She flung the door open. "You're home early!"

Henry stepped in and hugged her. "I got up early and drove straight through." He held her at arm's length, "Ummm, why do you smell like a barn?"

"I'm sorry!" she laughed. "I scrubbed down the barn and haven't taken a shower yet." Polly put her right hand on his chest and pushed him back into the hallway. "And my apartment is a dump. I can't tell you how much I don't want you to see it like this."

Henry removed her hand from his chest, pulled her in for another hug and said, "I can't tell you how much I want to see you any way I can. I don't care about your apartment. Surely you aren't going to send me away when I've driven all the way from Arizona to look at your cute face."

It felt good to have him hold her. "Alright, but if you say a single word about the state of my home, I'm going to do something awful to you."

She turned around, bent over and scooped up the clothes she had dropped in the entryway, rolled her eyes at the messes she could identify through the apartment and ran to the bedroom, picking up errant clothing and shoes. Dropping things on the floor, she pulled the door shut and stood in front of it with her hand still on the doorknob. Henry watched and smiled.

"Not a word," she repeated.

Obiwan was standing in front of him, wagging his tail and panting for attention. Henry knelt down and rubbed the dog's ears while Polly cleared off the sofa and coffee table.

"Get comfortable," she said. "I'll be right back." She ducked into the bathroom, picking towels up and tossing them into her bedroom. She opened the top drawer beside the sink and swept everything into it, ran back into the bedroom and picked up a towel. Running some water across it, she scrubbed the countertop and sink clean, then flung it back into the bedroom. She hung a fresh hand towel on the rack beside the sink and shook her head. "I'm such a slob," she muttered to herself before walking back into the living room.

Henry was sitting on the sofa, with Obiwan on the floor in front of him. Luke had curled up beside Henry, while Leia had jumped to the floor and was rubbing her face on his left boot.

"It looks like the animals missed you, too," Polly said.

Henry laughed, "I had no idea we were all such close friends."

"I've heard that we should trust animals when it comes to who they accept or reject. I'm glad they like you," she said, then asked, "Have you even been back to your own home?"

"Nope. You're my first stop. I couldn't wait to see you." He reached his hand out for hers and she sat down beside him, pushing the cat out of the way. Luke meowed and headed into the bathroom.

"I've missed you," Polly said.

"Me too," he agreed and pulled her close. Then he said, "Okay, whew. Your hair stinks."

Polly sat straight up. "I'm sorry." She thought for a moment, then said, "Have you eaten supper yet?"

"No, I drove straight through."

"I'll make rice. I have chicken and leftover vegetables and can toss it into a fried rice after I take a shower."

"You don't have to work that hard tonight. I showed up unexpectedly and you've had a long week," Henry protested.

"I don't want to go out to find something to eat, do you?" She got up and walked into the kitchen,

"No, you're right. I don't. But, don't you have something simpler than that?"

"The longest this is going to take is boiling the rice and if I set the timer and you promise to check it if I'm not back out here when it dings, we're good."

"I can do that. Do you want my help with anything else?"

"In the shower or the kitchen?" she teased.

"Well, I've really missed you, so ...," he started.

"Stop right there. Keep an ear out for the timer and I can handle my own shower." She shook her head at herself. What was she thinking? She'd missed him terribly, but that was a little forward, even for her.

The water came up to a boil, Polly waited and then turned it down to simmer. She set the timer and when she walked past the coffee table, handed the remote to Henry. "Here, occupy yourself."

When she got to the bathroom door she stopped and turned around. "It's good to see all of you. Video chats were great, but it's nice to have you here."

Polly hurried through the shower and dug into her dresser for fresh clothes. All she had left were well-worn shorts and a t-shirt. She giggled and thought, "Bad Polly," but pulled them on and went back out into the living room. Henry whistled.

"I've never seen that much leg on you before!" he leered.

She picked up a stray sofa pillow and tossed it at him. "I'm out of clean clothes. I can't believe I let things get this far out of control!"

He followed her into the kitchen and stood behind her, pulling her in close again. "Now you smell really good." He turned her around in his arms and kissed her.

"I've missed you," he said.

"I've missed you too." She leaned her head against his chest and they held each other until the timer rang on the stove.

She broke away and turned the heat off under the rice, then went to the fridge to forage for additional ingredients, bumping Henry out of the way.

"What can I do to help?" he asked.

"Nothing. I've got it. I'm only going to whip this together." She moved everything over to the cutting board beside the stovetop and cracked eggs into her cast iron skillet, scrambling them while she cut up green onions and chicken.

Henry looked around the kitchen and began filling the sink with sudsy water, gathering up dishes, mugs and pans.

"What are you doing?" she asked.

"Helping. It seems like you might have lost control around here."

"This has been a long week," she sighed. "I've cleaned every other inch of this building and the barn, but ran out of caring when it came to my little hovel."

"I know you told me you were fine with finding him dead, but how are you really doing with all of this?"

"I feel awful. He drove both me and Jeff out of our minds." She said conspiratorially, "If I tell you that at some level I'm relieved to not have to fire him will that make sense? I can't say that to anyone else."

Henry chuckled as he rinsed out a mug and set it in the strainer. "It makes sense to me. You're terrible at firing people." Then, he looked at her and caught her eye, "but apparently, you're not terrible at finding dead bodies!"

"Stop it!" she cried. "I'm scared people around here are going to start whispering and pointing at me whenever I walk downtown."

"As long as you aren't actually killing anyone, I think you're fine. I wouldn't worry too much about it," he laughed. "Do they have any idea what happened to him?"

"Not yet," Polly replied. "Ken stopped by yesterday to get some more background information from his employment file here. I didn't have much, but gave him what we had."

"I didn't know him," Henry said. "He wasn't here very long and I don't think anyone ever mentioned a family."

"I don't know anything about that."

"Have you found anyone to replace him yet?"

"No and it's driving me crazy. Jeff has some temp agency providing help for the weddings, but I told him I'd take care of the guest rooms and the classrooms downstairs."

Once the eggs were done, she poured them into a dish, added some oil to the skillet and sautéed the onions, then added frozen peas and carrots. She tossed in the chicken and egg, followed by the rice, adding ginger, garlic, butter and soy sauce, sprinkling a few sesame seeds in.

Henry dried two plates and set them down beside her.

"Thanks," she said, then put the wooden spoon in the skillet, turned the heat down and reached out to pull him close. "Wow, I've missed you."

She felt tears come to her eyes and buried her face in his chest.

"Don't go away for that long again, okay?"

"If this is the reception I get when I return, I might go away a lot more often," he teased.

"Hmph," she said and dished the rice up to their plates. "I'm going to keep you so busy around here that you won't have time to go anywhere else, how about that?"

"That sounds fine," he agreed. "Now, can I have one more before we eat?"

"One more what?" Polly was confused.

"One more of these." He took the plates out of her hand and put them on the peninsula, then wrapping his left arm around her waist, he threaded the fingers of his right hand into the hair at the base of her neck and tipped her back, kissing her. Polly quit thinking.

When he released her, she swayed and he helped her stand back upright. She stood still for a moment and said, "Oh my. Welcome home."

They pushed papers and books away from a corner of the table and sat down to eat. She pulled out one of the larger sheets of paper from the pile and set it in front of him.

"What do you think?" she asked, showing him the sketch that Lydia had given her of the garden area.

"This is for the corner of the lot?"

"Yeah. I told you about that, didn't I?"

"You did. Who is doing the work on this?"

"Louis Waters is going to do some of it and Lydia has lined up people to do the digging and concrete work. I think it will take them all summer to get it where she wants it, but it's going to be beautiful!"

"It won't take that long. Louis is as good as they come, Polly. Someday you should go by their house. He and Deb have created a garden fairy land. If they're involved in the project, you are really lucky."

"Nancy Burroughs is the other person Lydia has helping her. She mentioned that they've wanted to do something with that corner for years. I don't know what else I'd do with that space and if we can keep from mowing it, all the better."

"Nancy used to teach home economics here at Bellingwood before they closed the school. She retired after that, but I think she's still involved with the garden club in town and maybe the Farmer's Market too."

Henry put his fork down and said, "So, how are things going with the horses?"

"Oh, Henry, I can't wait for you to see them! They are so much healthier!"

"Are you having fun with them?"

"You know, it's been fun learning how to take care of them and I have loved watching them come back from where they were. It's a lot of work, though."

"But, are you having fun with them? Are they yours yet?"

"I think Nat and Daisy are all mine. Both of them come looking for attention and affection when I go out there. I don't know what to think about Demi. He's a bit of a brat. Sometimes I think that he's messing with me like a brother would. He'll ignore me and then the next thing I know he will sneak up behind me and blow air at my head. Whenever we work, he's really good about it, though."

"What about Nan? You said she was the alpha of the group."

"I think she likes me, but she spends a lot of time wandering around the pasture and travels back and forth in and out of the barn. It's almost like she can't believe it is really going to be okay. If I were giving her human emotions, I would say that the neglect upset her because there wasn't anything she could do about it. When she isn't wandering the pasture, she keeps a close eye on Nat and Demi. Mark says that one of these days she will relax and feel like this is her home."

"So," he drew the word out, "how are things with him? You haven't mentioned him too much in the last few weeks."

Polly scowled. "That's because he isn't here all that often. You do know there's nothing between us, don't you?"

Henry heaved a sigh. "I should say yes, shouldn't I."

"I'll be honest with you, are you ready for that?"

He braced himself, "I'm ready."

"It was fun being all flirty when I first got to know him. He's gorgeous and it was nice to have someone like him pay attention to me, but Henry," she put her hand on his forearm, "I'm not interested in him and he's not interested in me. There's nothing there."

"You're kidding yourself if you think he's not interested. He's definitely interested," Henry said.

"Then the only thing I'm sure of is that I'm not. Now, can we declare this conversation to be in the past and not fret over it any longer?"

"I'll try. It was really hard for me to be gone, knowing that he was here all the time."

"Oh, for Pete's sake, Henry! Why would you be concerned? I talked to you every single night and texted back and forth with you during the day. He was only here to take care of the horses and show me what to do out in the barn and then he left. He comes less than once a week now unless I have a problem. You have to stop worrying about this."

"I'll try. I promise. I'll try. It's not easy, though."

"The good stuff never is, right?" She sat back in her chair. "Now, I'm going to change the subject completely. When are you going to be ready to start on the next project? I'm dying for this garage and with all of the events Jeff is scheduling, we have to get that back parking lot finished."

"Can I at least have the weekend?" he laughed.

"Well, you can have part of the weekend," she said. "I was hoping we could drive down to Des Moines tomorrow night. I have tickets to a show at the Civic Center. I wasn't going to say anything if you didn't get back until tomorrow, but I'd like to finally take you out for a nice evening."

"You can leave? What about the horses?"

"Saturday is an easy day for all of us. I'll make sure everything is ready to go and Jason is pretty good with them. Mark said he would come over and watch Jason bring them in for the night. All I have to do is call and say it's on."

"I'd love to go to Des Moines with you, then. Shall we take the Thunderbird?"

"Really?" Polly remembered her first date with Henry. He'd driven the Thunderbird and taken her to Ames. A first kiss, him tentatively touching her shoulders. All the feelings of burgeoning romance happened that night. "That would be terrific!"

"How about you let me take you out for dinner since you got the tickets," he said.

"This was supposed to be my night, though."

"Let me?"

"Alright. But, we're dressing up, right?"

Henry winked at her, "I like it when you dress up, Polly. You're stunning."

"I notice that you didn't say that when you first got here tonight. I'm sorry about that." She stood up and took their plates to the kitchen. The water had turned tepid, so she emptied the sink and refilled it. Henry followed her in and picked up the pan filled with leftover fried rice. She pointed at the cupboard with plastic ware and he pulled a container out.

"It's alright," he laughed as he scooped the rice. "I've discovered that you have a lot of different sides to you. They're all interesting. Some smell better than others, that's all."

Polly flicked suds from the filling sink at him and he ducked, allowing the splatter to reach the cupboard behind him, leaving a mark in the dust and grease covering the door.

He looked up at it and Polly grimaced, "I need to scrub this place down soon, don't I!"

"Don't worry. It doesn't bother me. I'm so glad to be back here, nothing bothers me."

He leaned in and gave her a quick peck on the nose. "I'm glad to be here tonight with you, no matter what. Thank you for not kicking me to the curb."

CHAPTER FOUR

Looking out over the door into the pasture, Polly smiled at the horses who were happy to be out in the sunshine. She had gotten up early in order to get her day started. Once the fencing had been finished around the pasture, Obiwan had the run of the place and they didn't have to put his leash on every morning. He obediently followed her through the gates and then bolted into the pasture every morning as she headed for the barn.

Henry was coming in this morning to go over plans for the garage and apartment addition on the north side of the building as well as a future addition on the south side to make four more rooms available for guests. Polly wanted to get started on things before she could talk herself out of the projects. They'd been going back and forth with the plans for the last two months while he was in Arizona, and now it was time to dig in and go.

She hauled feed into the stalls for breakfast and smiled as she thought about her weekend. She and Henry had arrived in Des Moines early enough for a wonderful dinner downtown. After the show, they had driven through Saylorville and stopped to look at the bright moon and the stars. They hadn't gotten back to Bellingwood until long after midnight and then Henry had come over early Sunday morning to help with the horses. They'd spent the entire day together watching movies and napping on the couch.

Sylvie and her assistant, Hannah, had been on site Saturday evening preparing dinner and she had spent a few minutes gossiping with them about the worst of the Bridezillas, but managed to regain some control of her living space and her clothing. It felt wonderful to have a closet full of clean clothes again and she wondered why she always let it get so out of control.

When she went into the feed room to get hay, she was confused. She thought the horses had used more than this. It looked as if she had a full room. Polly shook her head. She must have brought more down from the hay loft on Friday evening than she realized. She filled the old tractor tires outside with hay and opened the stall doors so they could head out when they were finished eating, then pulled the wheelbarrow to Demi's stall and began the task of cleaning up the floor.

Obiwan dashed into the stall from outside, sniffed at Demi's droppings, shook his head and walked over to Polly and nudged her leg. "I know, Obiwan. I'm working on it, I'm working on it." He nudged her leg again and she stopped to rub his head. He went on to greet each of the horses and then went tearing back out into the pasture as Nan finished eating her feed and sauntered out. Polly watched her ears flick as she considered chasing the dog, but she settled into the hay and began to munch. One by one the horses left the barn and Polly finished cleaning up.

"Come on, Obiwan! Let's go in!" she called and waited for him to catch up. Polly stopped at the main gate, turned around to look at her horses and smiled. They were a lot of work, but she was falling in love with each of them.

She turned the coffeemaker on in the main kitchen and pulled cereal, fruit, and muffins out onto the counter for her guests. There were only two people upstairs and they didn't require much in the way of attention. The photographer in the front room was generally out most of the day. He told her he was shooting a series for a book he called "Iowa's Spring to Life." He hadn't shown her much, but was gone from morning until evening every day. Another young man was staying in the Walnut Room. She wasn't sure what it was he was writing, but he always had his laptop with him and wrote in his room or in the auditorium, the front steps, in a lawn chair outside if it was warm enough. Polly had found him sprawled out in the hallway upstairs and when she'd asked if he'd lost his key, he assured her that he only wanted a different location to work. She was never certain where he'd show up next, but he found a way to write at all hours of the day.

After getting things set up, she went back to her office and found Obiwan watching as Jeff worked at his desk.

"Good morning!" she said.

"Good morning to you," Jeff said, looking up from his computer. "Is that your new look for the day?"

"Hush. I've been working."

He laughed. "I know. Obiwan's never down here unless you've come in from being with the horses. You're a little late this morning."

Polly scowled. "I am not! In fact, I'm early."

"Maybe it's because I'm here before my normal hour," he laughed.

"Why are you here so early this morning," she asked, "and why are you dressed like a professional?"

"I have to be in Fort Dodge this morning. Didn't I tell you about the summer events?"

"Oh, that's right," she interrupted. "Don't let Obiwan get near you then with your fancy duds. He and I need to spend some time with the brush."

"That's why I have these," he laughed and pulled his drawer open. He took a dog treat out and Obiwan stood up on his back legs, placing his front paws on Jeff's desk. He took the treat out of Jeff's hand and then sat back down, keeping a steady eye on the drawer as Jeff closed it.

"Alright, you beggar butt, let's go upstairs and get some real food in you," she laughed. "I'll be back before you leave and thanks."

She got upstairs, fed the dog and cats, took a shower and was back in Jeff's office within the hour.

"How did things go Saturday night?" she asked.

"It was smashing, just smashing," he said. "I spoke with two girls who were there and have set up meetings with them and their wedding consultants next week. And Sylvie? She was a hit!"

"That's awesome," Polly said.

"No, I mean she was really great. The aunt of the bride decided to come in and start making a scene about something she didn't like. The poor bride was near tears and her mother wasn't much better. This woman was the older sister of the bride's father and a complete bitch. After all the work we had done, as well as the work the bride and her friends had done that day, this woman thought she could throw a tantrum about the use of battery operated candles instead of live flame."

"No way."

"Yes way. I wasn't there when it happened, but she was working up a full head of steam when Sylvie waltzed out of the kitchen, assessed the situation, watched the bride and her mother melt into puddles, took the woman by the arm and steered her into the office. I arrived as Sylvie was telling this woman that it wasn't her day, that she was embarrassing everyone, and that Sylvie wouldn't put up with that behavior from her children and no adult should act this way and maybe the woman might want to explain exactly why she needed to throw a tantrum."

Polly's mouth dropped open, but said, "I've seen Sylvie correct her boys. She's no slouch."

"She sat down here in the office with the woman and after she'd said her piece, I watched her reach out and take the woman's hand and ask what the real reason was that she was so upset. Before I knew it, the woman was sobbing and crying and I slunk away. Who needs that?"

"So what was the deal?"

"The old lady had never been married and had acted as

decorating coordinator for all of the weddings in the family, but since she lives so far away, they assumed she wouldn't want to spend time doing this one. She was offended and so she was making life miserable for everyone."

"Oh, I love Sylvie."

"So do I! I would never have handled it so well and might have pissed off an entire roomful of people."

Polly turned around when she heard footsteps and saw Henry coming in. She smiled. It was still good to see him. Absence really did make the heart grow fonder.

Jeff stood up and put his hand out, "Welcome back, man. It's good to see you!"

"It's good to be back. But, have I missed something? Is there a new dress code around here?"

Jeff laughed, "No, a business appointment this morning in Fort Dodge and I need to get going!" He grabbed his portfolio and walked past Henry, clapping him on the back. "It's good to have you back. This one missed you," and he nodded toward Polly.

He left and Henry snickered, "It was that obvious, eh?"

"Shaddup," she said. "Do you want coffee?"

"Of course I do. And one of those cinnamon apple muffins you were baking yesterday."

"I'll gather food and drink for your majesty. You set up in the conference room."

She started to pass him and he grabbed her waist. "I had a great welcome home weekend with you." He kissed her forehead. "I'm not ready to get back to normal."

Polly broke away, her head spinning. Every time he kissed her, she forgot what came next. "Ummm. Yeah. Okay. I'll be right back."

She heard him chuckling as she walked out of the office. It wasn't fair that he enjoyed making her mind shut down each time he kissed her, but she didn't know how to change either behavior.

When she got back to the conference room, Henry had hooked the laptop to a larger monitor and pulled up a layout of her property.

"We're going to be able to bring this addition in right under the windows in your apartment," he said.

They looked over the plans for a garage on the ground level with the entrance facing the creek. A large parking lot spanned the area between Sycamore House and the main road and a small driveway broke off to enter her garage. The stage entrance door would remain in place, acting as the door into the garage. It was large enough that a section at the back of the garage would become the shed for maintenance equipment. Upstairs, a two bedroom apartment would be created and Polly hoped her young friends Doug Randall and Billy Endicott would consider renting the space from her.

One of the things she had discovered as she got older was that being an only child had its drawbacks. With both of her parents gone, sometimes she felt as if she had no family left. Her relationship with Doug and Billy felt as if it must be what having younger brothers was all about. They had moved in and slept on the floor of her offices when Sheriff Merritt worried about a murderer being loose in Bellingwood and considered themselves her Jedi Knights. The two boys welcomed her home with a puppy they'd named Obiwan after she returned from being kidnapped by an old boyfriend. Doug had been beaten up by that same man and after all of that still wanted to be her friend. Now, she encouraged them to bring their friends to Sycamore House for gaming evenings and trusted them to treat her home as they would their own.

They worked for Jerry Allen, a local electrical contractor and were young enough to still be living at home. They were best friends and couldn't figure out whether they were still boys or had become young men. If Polly could find a way for them to safely move out on their own, she knew everyone would be happy. Doug's mother, Helen, was ready for her son to grow up and move away, but didn't want to push him out. Polly had never met Billy's parents, but knew they had to be great people since he was such a good young man.

Henry said, "I'm going to start lining up subcontractors this afternoon to get this project started."

"What?" Polly asked. She focused on the screen in front of her. This was going to be an attractive addition to Sycamore House and when they started on the matching addition on the south side of the building, she was going to finally have everything in place.

"Subcontractors," Henry said.

"Oh. Right. Great," she said. "I'm ready to get this started."

Polly went out to the main office and was standing at the photocopier waiting for copies of several pages Henry had sent from the computer when she saw a police car pull up outside her office window. She waited for someone to come in and when no one did, she took the sheets back into the conference room and set them on the table.

"That's weird," she said. "A police car pulled up in front of my office, but no one has come in. I'm going to check it out."

Henry followed her out the front door and she couldn't see anyone.

"That's odd," she said. "Where did he go?"

They walked to the north side of the building and saw Ken Wallers kneeling by the back stage door.

He looked up, saw them and carrying something in a bag, strode up to greet them.

"Welcome back to Bellingwood, Henry," he said as they shook hands.

"Thanks, Ken. What were you doing back there?" Henry asked, nodding at the back stoop of Sycamore House.

"Miss Giller, do you recognize this?" He held out a piece of concrete. Polly reached out to touch it and he pulled it back.

"Umm, it looks like the chunk of concrete Harry found last week. He said it had broken off the step back there. I'd totally forgotten about it. He was going to leave it on the desk in the front office so I could find someone to fix it. Why do you have it?"

"Let's go inside. I'd like to ask you a few questions if I could, Miss Giller."

"Sure. Come on in. I've got coffee and muffins."

"Thank you, but maybe later. For now, I'd like to talk with

you."

Polly led them into office when they got back inside. Ken Wallers motioned for her to take her seat at the desk and he sat across from her. Henry stood in the doorway.

"Miss Giller, was Harry Bern a good employee?"

"He was fine. He did a good job here."

"Did you have any issues with him as an employee?"

Polly paused and thought for a moment, "Not as a worker. He really was very good at what he did. I suppose he annoyed me with his whining and complaining about things, but that didn't stop him from doing his job."

"You've been through several employees in the last two months. Is this a difficult job?"

"No, I wouldn't think so. Two of the people who left went on to different jobs, one left to go to Florida. The first person I attempted to hire for the position, though, wasn't suited to it and I had to ask him to leave the property."

"Was that Shawn Wesley?" he asked.

"It was. He insulted Jeff, called me a bitch and didn't bother to show up to work on time. While he was here, he went outside to smoke every ten minutes. I'm fairly certain he was high when I finally asked him to leave. I gave him twenty bucks and ordered him off the property."

Ken Wallers visibly relaxed in his chair. "Thank you. That's what I needed to hear from you."

"What do you mean? Did he have something to do with Harry's death?" Polly asked.

"No, but he came in on Friday to tell me that you had threatened him and that we should investigate you since one of your employees had been murdered."

"I threatened him? Well, that infuriates me," Polly growled.

"I know, I know. We've dealt with him before. That wasn't the only thing that brought me over here, though."

"What do you mean?" she asked.

"This is what was used to murder Harry." He held up the piece of concrete. "It is from your back step. Harry was in the middle of writing up a note to you, telling you where he had found it, what the condition of the concrete was and what he thought you should do to get it fixed."

"And he would have had it on my desk before I got into my office the next morning," Polly smiled. "The man drove me batty, but he took good care of this place."

"Do you have any idea who did this or why?" Henry asked.

"Not yet," Ken responded, turning to look back at Henry. "We still don't know much about the man, but we'll get there." He stood up to leave. "I'm sorry to have bothered you this morning, but I needed to hear from you."

"That's fine. I'm sorry it was my concrete that was used to kill him and I'm sorry that Shawn Wesley involved you."

"Like I said," Ken replied, "We've dealt with him before. He complains about a lot of people. Why he thinks it's ever a good idea to show up at the police station, I'll never know. One of these days we'll catch him with all of those drugs and he'll end up in jail, but until then, we let him show up and tell us what's on his mind."

He reached out to shake Polly's hand and then Henry's. "I'll let you know when we get more information."

Polly dropped back into her seat after she saw him go out the front door. "Crap! He scared me to death! I can't believe he thought that I might have killed Harry Bern."

"He really didn't think that, Polly. He just needed to hear it from you."

"But for a moment, I was a suspect in someone's death! That completely freaks me out." She sat forward and braced herself on the desk.

Henry laughed, "It's never dull around you, Pol. Never dull."

"It was dull while you were in Arizona! I promise!"

"Well, I'm back now and the first morning I'm at work, the police are here asking you questions about a murder. It's another dead body, Polly. You found another dead body."

"Oh, don't remind me," she sighed. "By the way, who won the pool at the Elevator with this one?"

"It wasn't me. I'll have to stop in there some time and see who had 'murdered employee.'"

"Oh sheesh," she said and dropped her head onto her arms. She looked up through her eyelashes. "How am I ever going to live this down?"

"I don't know, Pol," he laughed. "I'm going to enjoy watching it all happen, though."

"Hey! You're supposed to be on my side!"

"I'm always on your side, but I've never had this much fun watching someone get themselves in so much trouble."

Polly muttered, "They call that *schadenfreude*."

"I'm sorry, what?" Henry asked.

"*Schadenfreude*. Glee at someone else's misfortune."

"Then I'm planning to enjoy great amounts of *schadenfreude* because you tend to get into the middle of the craziest things!"

Polly saw the front door open and two of her favorite people walk in. Doug waved at her through the window and they came into her office.

"Hey, Henry, welcome back to Iowa. We thought maybe Polly had scared you off for good!" Doug said as he shook Henry's hand. He sat down in the other chair across from her desk and Billy stepped in and shook Henry's hand as well.

"What's up?" Polly asked.

"What's up with you? I saw Chief Wallers driving away from here. Is it about you finding your janitor's dead body?" Doug asked.

Polly nodded, "Yeah. It was. Whoever did it beaned him with a chunk of concrete from my back step."

"Cool!" Billy said. "You get involved in the best stuff around here."

"Cool? That's not exactly the word I'd use for this," Polly said sarcastically. "Someone tried to point the finger at me for killing the poor guy."

"Really? That's awesome!" Doug said.

"Why is that awesome?" Henry asked.

"Because everyone knows Polly would never do anything like

that and it's way cool that she gets herself involved in these things, don't you think?"

"Again with the cool," Polly said, sighing and shaking her head. "I'm still not ready to use that word. So what are you two up to?"

"We're supposed to be getting coffee and then heading to another work site over at Beeman's place, but we had a few minutes and wanted to stop in and ask if we could use the computer room this Friday night. I know you probably have a wedding, but we'll come in the side door and stay out of everyone's way. We'll bring in our own food and drink and they won't even know we're here."

"I don't see why that wouldn't work," Polly responded.

"I know you have those little dudes here after school. Since they'll be here until their mom is done with the wedding, they can come play with us," Billy said.

Polly smiled. "You are good guys. They will love that. I'll tell them this afternoon and talk to their mom about it as well. Do they need anything?"

"Can one of them use your laptop?" Doug asked. "We've got one, but ..."

"I will have something here for you by Friday. Thanks."

"So, since we're supposed to be getting coffee, can we raid your pot?"

"I didn't turn the big pot on this morning, but there's definitely coffee upstairs in my apartment. Go on up, I'm sure the animals would love to see you."

"Cool!" Billy said. "Obiwan is getting so big!"

The boys left and Henry grinned at her. "You were made for a big family, weren't you, Polly."

"Who knew?" she laughed.

CHAPTER FIVE

You always paid attention to sirens when living in a small town. Polly had stopped when she lived in Boston, but since she had moved back to Iowa, a siren generally impacted someone she knew. If it was important, she was confident Lydia or Andy would let her know what was going on. She was outside with Obiwan when she heard sirens screaming through town and in a moment her phone rang. It was Lydia.

"Polly. Beryl's hurt. They're rushing her to Des Moines."

"What happened?" Polly asked. She stopped in her tracks and Obiwan stopped with her.

Lydia's voice was breaking. "There was an explosion in her studio. Deena was there; she spends Tuesday afternoons there as part of a work study program. Anyway, she had gone into the house to get some tea and when it happened, she called 9-1-1 and ran back out. Beryl had managed to crawl outside after being hit with flying debris."

"Have you called Andy?"

"I can't reach her. I didn't want to leave a voice mail telling her about this. I don't know what to do."

Calm, steady Lydia relied on her friends and family to keep her anchored and Polly knew this was a lot for her to manage. She began walking back toward the front door of Sycamore House.

"How about Aaron? Is he around?"

"He's the one who called me, but he isn't here yet. Polly, should I go to Des Moines?"

"I'm going to change my clothes, get in my truck and head to your house in a few minutes, Lydia. Sit right there until I arrive, alright? I need a minute to think and when I get there, I'll have a better idea about what we're going to do next. Can you do that?"

"I'll be in the kitchen. Thank you, sweetheart."

Polly hung up and looked at her phone. It felt like every sane thought was leaping away from her neurons at the moment, so she dialed.

"Hey, Polly, what's up?"

"Henry, I need you to help me process on something because apparently my brain has shut down. There was an explosion at Beryl's studio. She was in it and they're taking her to Des Moines. Lydia is freaked out and I have to come up with a plan."

"I don't suppose you know anything yet. What do you want to do?"

"I don't know anything except that it happened. I told Lydia I would head to her house and help her decide what to do next. She can't reach Andy and I don't know if we should just go to Des Moines."

"I was going to come over to Sycamore House anyway, so I'll be there in a little bit. You get yourself out of there and head to Lydia's. I'll take care of your upstairs animals and call Mark to help me with the horses tonight. Don't worry about any of us. You get Lydia and Andy to Des Moines."

"Thank you, Henry. I'll talk to you later when I'm making more sense."

"You're doing fine. Please be careful while you're driving, alright?"

"I will. I'm outside with Obiwan right now. You don't need to worry about him, so don't hurry. I need to change my clothes and then I'll take off. Thank you again."

She hung up and whistled for her dog to join her on the front steps. He ran up and sat down beside her legs.

"Okay, a few minutes to cry. That's all I need." She sat on the steps beside him, hugged his neck, and found herself sobbing into his coat. Obiwan patiently sat there while she cried and cried. Polly finally stood up, wiped her eyes and said, "Now I need to blow my nose. Let's go inside and get me cleaned up."

She took him upstairs and washed her face. After changing into a pair of black slacks and a short sleeve blue sweater, she grabbed her purse and ran back downstairs. Henry was pulling into the lot as she headed for her truck.

Polly waited for him to park and he jumped out of his truck and pulled her into a hug.

"Thank you, Henry," she said. "But, you don't need to sit with the kids. They'll be fine for a while."

"I have work I need to do here anyway. We're laying the slab for the garage at the end of the week and I have plenty of things to deal with in order to be ready for this next project. I'll use your office if that's alright. I talked to Doc Ogden. Jason will be here after school and Mark says he's getting pretty good with the evening chores. The two of us will manage just fine."

"Oh, I forgot about Jason and Andrew! I don't mean for you to babysit those boys too. Sylvie will be here by six. Do you want me to call her? Oh, Henry, I'm sorry!"

"No." he said calmly. "Please don't. I understand what your life is like here and you have to know by now that I want to be here for you when you need me. Jason will be great in the barn with me and Andrew will be great upstairs with your other animals. I won't be babysitting them, they'll be helping me, like they help you. Now, you go take care of your girls and call me when you know something."

"I will. I can't believe this." She turned to go to her truck and Henry pulled her back into another hug.

"Polly, call me even if you don't know something. Call if all you need is to talk to me. And if you don't have time to talk, text me. Please let me know when you get to the hospital, so I don't worry about you being on the road."

"I promise to let you know as soon as I can," she replied. Polly gave him a quick kiss on the cheek and got into her truck to head for Lydia's house. When she arrived, she pulled up to the front door behind Aaron's SUV. She jumped out of the truck, walked up the steps to the porch, and was reaching for the doorbell when Aaron opened the door.

"Come on in," he said. "She's in the kitchen."

Polly followed him back to the kitchen and found Lydia sitting at the table playing with an empty mug, spinning it around on the table. Her eyes and nose were red from crying and the mug was stuffed with used tissues.

"Did you reach Andy yet?" Polly asked.

"I haven't tried again. I ran out of energy."

"Do you know anything more about Beryl?"

Lydia looked at Aaron, who said, "We don't know anything. She was unconscious when the EMTs got to her at her house. They're still en route to Methodist Hospital and I haven't heard from them."

"What about Deena? And Miss Kitty?" Polly asked.

Lydia said, "Deena took the cat to her house. She's shaken up, but her mother said she is perfectly fine. I can't believe she wasn't in the studio, too. Sometimes God takes care of the littlest things, doesn't he?"

Polly nodded and asked, "What about the studio, then?"

It was Aaron who answered. "There's water everywhere and the bathroom or storage room or whatever it was is completely destroyed."

"Have you seen it?" Polly asked him.

"No, I haven't been there yet. I'll go over after you two leave for Des Moines."

"All of her work and her supplies!" Lydia cried out. "What will she do?"

"That's the least of our worries right now," Polly said, then turned to Aaron, "Do you think we should head down to Des Moines?"

"I think you need to be there. I know Lydia needs to be there and you appear to be the sanest one in the bunch today." He smiled at her. "How do you like finally being the one to take care of everyone else?"

"It's a new experience," she said, smiling back at him.

"But, are you okay to drive, Polly? I should stay in town."

"Oh, sure. I'm fine," she said, "but, if I could get hold of Andy, I'd like to take her with us."

Lydia held her phone out to Polly, "Try her again. It's not like her to miss phone calls and not return them right away."

Polly waved her off, "I've got it. Just a second." She moved out into the living room and dialed Andy's phone number from her own phone.

It rang twice and she heard the woman's voice, "Hello, Polly, how are you doing?"

Polly took a breath and decided to blurt it all out in a hurry, "Andy, Beryl's studio exploded and they've taken her to Des Moines. Lydia and I were about to leave to head down and I wanted to see if you would like to go with us."

She heard a sharp intake of breath and then nothing. "Andy, are you still there? I'm sorry to have shocked you like this."

"Beryl? She's hurt?"

"Andy, Lydia and I are coming over to your house. We'll be there in a few minutes."

"I ... I'm not at the house."

"Oh. Well, we're heading to Des Moines. Do you want to go down to the hospital with us?"

"Are you sure something happened to Beryl?"

"Yes, honey. I'm sorry. Beryl."

"I have to go be with her. I'm her emergency contact and next of kin. I have to be there to make decisions for her. How am I going to get to Des Moines? I can't drive in this state, but I have to go."

"I will drive and take both you and Lydia. Where are you?"

"I'm at a friend's house. I need to get to Des Moines."

"I know you do, sweetie. Let me come get you." Polly wasn't

prepared for her friends to be this distraught and realized she had to be the calm one today. She was glad she'd had that little emotional breakdown with her dog so nobody needed to pay attention to her. It wasn't about her today at all. "Tell me where you are and Lydia and I will be there to pick you up in a few minutes."

Polly poked her head back into the kitchen and said, "Lydia, are you ready to go?"

With that question, Lydia shook her head and stood up. "I'm fine and I'm ready." Polly watched Aaron take a deep breath and smile at his wife. He looked at Polly and nodded as if to say, "She's back now."

Andy asked a question of someone in the background and then came back to the phone and said, "521 Walnut. It's a brown house. My car is in the driveway. I'll be outside waiting for you," and she hung up.

Lydia came out of the kitchen and handed Polly a set of keys. "I'm fine, but Aaron says you are driving. We should take my Jeep. It will be more comfortable, don't you think?"

"I suppose," Polly said.

"Come on, then. Let's go." Polly followed her friend downstairs and out the back door. She felt uncomfortable driving Lydia's Jeep, but when Lydia began to take charge, there wasn't much anyone could do.

"We're going to 521 Walnut," Polly said.

"What's there?"

"Andy's there."

"Who lives at 521 Walnut?" Lydia screwed up her face as she thought. Then she shook her head, "I have no idea!"

"We're going to find out soon. She said we'll recognize her car in the driveway."

Lydia's eyes lit up and she laughed out loud, "Polly! Of course! That's Len Specek's house! Do you suppose our girl was having a lunch date with him? Oh my!" Lydia rolled her eyes, "You don't think? She wouldn't. No." She dropped her head to her chest and laughed. "Surely. No, I can't even think that way."

"What are you talking about?" Polly asked.

"If Andy is at Len Specek's house on a date, and she wouldn't answer the phone when I called ..." Lydia shook her head again. "No, I can't even think about that. I'm going to assume they were in the middle of a very deep conversation over lunch." She shuddered. "Oh, this is going to kill me, I'm sure."

Polly giggled, "Because your friend is a widow and not supposed to get to know another man again?"

"That's part of it. But, more than that, it's because my friend is a widow and I haven't allowed her to be a woman. Promise me you won't bring any of this up?"

"I'm not promising anything," Polly laughed. "If she's having fun, we're getting in on that story."

They pulled into the driveway behind Andy's car. She was standing on the front stoop and ran over to the Jeep, climbing in behind Polly.

"Before either of you say anything about me being at Len Specek's house, you have to tell me what is going on with Beryl. What happened?"

Lydia turned around in her seat and reached her hand out to take Andy's. "We don't know anything yet. She's probably at the hospital by now. There was an explosion at the studio. Deena was inside the house when it happened. She heard it and called 9-1-1, then ran back out as Beryl stumbled out the door. Beryl fell down on the path and was unconscious. Bless their hearts; Sarah and Austin were there in only a few minutes. They loaded her up in the rig and took her away."

"How is Deena?"

"She's fine," Lydia assured her. "I spoke with her mother and they took Miss Kitty to their house. They will take care of the cat until Beryl is home."

"She's all alone," Andy lamented. "I need to be there with her. This drive takes forever."

Polly looked at the speedometer. She wasn't comfortable driving too far over the speed limit, but pushed to sixty-six and set the cruise control. "We're going as fast as I dare," she said.

"I know," Andy said. "You're fine. I'm just worried. Does anyone know what happened to cause the explosion? Did someone do this to her? Who would hurt Beryl?"

"We don't know anything yet," Lydia responded. "Aaron will tell me as soon as they know."

Polly turned a couple of corners and pulled onto Highway 17. Traffic wasn't awful and she was able to keep moving quickly as they traveled south. "I'm not sure how to get to Methodist Hospital," she said.

Lydia programmed the GPS and chuckling, asked, "Will this help?"

"You don't know how to get there without a gadget?" Polly asked.

"Of course I do, but this is better, don't you agree?"

"Fine," Polly said. "I'll use it. How are you doing back there, Andy?"

"I'm feeling a little thick in the head. All I can think about is Beryl lying there bloody and broken. It breaks my heart."

"We have to believe that she's going to be fine. Anything else isn't an option," Lydia said.

Silence took over in the car as Polly continued to head south, then Lydia said, "What was I thinking? I need to get some ladies on this right now."

She pulled her phone out and made a call, "Lorna?" She listened. "Yes. You're right. It's Beryl. Can you get the prayer chain started on this? No, we don't know anything more than that." She paused. "No, you're right." Lydia looked at Polly and rolled her eyes, "Would you rather I call Pastor Boehm?" She pulled the phone away from her ear and visibly gritted her teeth. "Thank you. It's the right thing to do," and hung up the phone.

"What in the world?" Polly asked.

"Sometimes there are women with more time on their hands than sense," Lydia growled. "Beryl doesn't go to church and since she's a little wild and free-spirited, Lorna thought maybe she should manage some of the information about Beryl's soul, in case she died. She asked me if the woman was saved so she could pass that information down the line. I don't want to curse, but are you freakin' kidding me?"

Polly chuckled to herself and avoided eye contact with Lydia. Andy swore in the back seat, then said, "You know it's just her, don't you? The rest of the women in that group aren't so judgmental. They'll just want to pray for her to be well."

"I know that," Lydia said. "But, she is supposed to be in charge of the prayer chain. I don't know who ever thought that was a good idea. It certainly wasn't me! That woman thinks she is in charge of all the souls in the city. I'm pretty sure St. Peter is going to trip her when she approaches the pearly gates, just to see if she can make it in without falling backwards into hell."

Lydia clapped her hand over her mouth, "Oh! That doesn't make me sound any better than her, I guess. I'm sorry!"

They all laughed as Polly pulled onto the interstate and began the drive around Des Moines to Interstate-235 through the heart of the city.

"Now that you're feeling better, Andy, what do you have to say for yourself?" Lydia asked.

"What do you mean by that?"

"I mean, what were you doing at Len Specek's house in the middle of the day?"

Polly glanced in the rear view mirror and watched as Andy wrinkled her face, trying to figure out what to say next.

"Go ahead, Andy," Polly laughed. "Explain it. We're waiting."

"I'm an adult. I can have lunch with whomever I want. I don't have to explain myself to you," she announced.

"Really?" Lydia laughed. "That's how you want to play this?"

"Well, if I can get away with it, I do." Andy said, a bit petulantly. Polly saw her friend's lips turn up in a smile and then she quickly turned to look out of the window so no one would catch her.

"You can't get away with it, trust me," Polly said. "You can't get away with anything around here. I've tried and failed."

"So?" Lydia pressed.

Polly turned onto Keosauqua Way and saw the medical

complex in front of her. "I hate to interrupt, but where do I go from here?"

"She has to have been taken to the Emergency Room. Let's go there first and we'll find her," Andy said.

Lydia turned back around in her seat to face the road in front of them and began pointing directions out for Polly. She glanced back at Andy and said, "Don't you dare think I'll forget about this. You have some 'splaining to do."

She guided Polly into a parking lot and the three women walked into the Emergency Room. Lydia marched up to the receptionist and asked for Beryl Watson.

"Are you Lydia Merritt?" the woman asked. "And Andy Saner?"

Andy joined Lydia at the desk. "That's us."

"Beryl is in with doctors now. She has given you two permission to receive information and make any decisions for her should she be unable to do so. If you will please have a seat, as soon as we can, a doctor will be out to talk with you."

"She's alert?"

"Oh, she was very alert," sighed the receptionist, then she smiled. "I'll let the doctor fill you in on the details when she knows for certain what is going on."

They sat down in the waiting area and Polly drew her phone out to text Henry. It occurred to her that she probably needed to let a few more people know what was going on, so she stood up and walked away from her friends. She turned around as Lydia wrapped Andy in her arms and pulled up Henry's number to call him, watching Andy's shoulders shake.

CHAPTER SIX

Fumbling in her pocket for change, Polly wandered over to the vending machines. She could use a Diet Mountain Dew and was glad to see they carried those in the machine. The doctor, a very young woman, had come out and taken Andy and Lydia into a consultation room. She opened the bottle of soda and sighed at the first drink, then smiled as she thought about her life.

For a moment, she felt a little chagrined that she wasn't as accomplished as the young doctor. Why was it that people thought it was better to be a doctor than anything else? Her friends believed it was doctors and lawyers who achieved the greatest success in life. Sal Kahane's mother was constantly pushing her to find a nice, young physician to settle down with and Drea's parents weren't at all happy that she enjoyed living as a single woman and not delivering multiple babies to them with the help of a nice, young lawyer.

She sat down, leaned back and stretched her feet out in front of her. The waiting room had ebbed and flowed with people and right now there weren't many around. She shut her eyes and thought about why she'd bothered measuring herself up to a doctor she'd never met before. That was silly. Polly's life was exciting and filled with people who loved her. Every day uncovered something new and she was actually finding success in doing business in small town Iowa.

As she mused, she shut her eyes. She wondered if the young doctor ever relaxed. Since the horses had come into her life, Polly didn't get many opportunities to stop working, but since they were responding so well and were becoming healthy again, there was very little stress involved in caring for them. In fact, as she thought about it, spending time with them was quite relaxing. Demi had a place on the back of his left ear that when she rubbed it, he seemed to cross his eyes in joy and turn into mush. She loved knowing that about him. Nan's favorite moment of the day was when Polly opened up the stall door and she could run into the sunlight. Every morning she would circumnavigate the entire pasture before returning to push Nat out of the way in order to get to the hay. He was so easy going, he just moved to another area and left her alone. Daisy was the only one who wouldn't let Nan get away with running the place. She had a tendency to push back. Polly usually let her out last, but took those extra moments to stroke the girl's forehead. That area right above her nostrils was like velvet and Polly couldn't believe she got to spend time with those glorious beasts.

"Polly?" Lydia's quiet voice brought Polly up out of her drowsiness.

She sat straight up, pulling her legs back underneath her. "Is everything alright? Tell me what's happening! Is Beryl going to get into a room? Can we see her?"

"She's going to be fine," Lydia assured Polly and sat down beside her. Andy sat down across from Polly with red-rimmed eyes.

"What's going on?"

"The water heater in her back room exploded. She was on her way out the door, so the back of her legs are badly scalded. The upper part of her body was protected from the hot water by all of the weird clothing she wears out there while she's painting," Lydia said. "But, there was a bad gash in her scalp from a piece of the metal that flew across the room. The rest of her back has also been cut up pretty badly by flying shrapnel, too."

"Her water heater exploded?" Polly gasped.

"Yep," Lydia nodded. "Here, look." She pulled out her phone and showed Polly pictures. "Aaron sent these to me. I can't believe our girl is alright at all after seeing these."

Beryl's studio was a mess. It looked as if a tornado had spun itself out from the back to the front, disrupting and destroying everything.

"Aaron says he thinks that Beryl got knocked to the floor and then managed to pull herself up and out of the building where Deena found her," Lydia continued.

Polly glanced at Andy. She had crossed her arms over her chest and shut her eyes. Polly got up and moved over to sit beside her, put her arms around Andy's shoulders and said, "She's going to be alright. If Lydia says so, I believe it. Do you?"

"I feel so guilty for having fun while she was lying there, hurting and bleeding all over. She was by herself. She shouldn't have been by herself. How am I going to live with this?"

Lydia crossed over and sat on the other side of Andy, "You stop it right there, Andy Saner. That's poppycock and you're being more than a little overdramatic. She had Deena there, so she wasn't by herself. If Beryl had any idea you were feeling guilty because of a dalliance with a man, she'd swat you up the backside of your head. You've had plenty of time to be all weepy and upset today and it's time to start dealing. Beryl doesn't need weak, scared friends; she needs us to step in and get her back to normal."

Andy gave her friend a sideways glance, "You can be a real bitch sometimes, you know that?"

Polly couldn't help herself and snorted with laughter. "The woman's not much for pity parties, is she?" she said through the laughter.

"Pity is for those who have no hope," Lydia said. "Not for those who want to feel sorry for themselves."

"Can it be for those who have had the life scared out of them?" Andy asked.

"Not any longer," Lydia snipped. She looked over at Polly. "They'll let us know when she gets into a room and we can see her. The doctor said that the scalding was bad enough on her legs, they're going to keep her here for a while to make sure that no infection sets in as they blister. Oh, that woman is going to be miserable."

A nurse came to tell them what room Beryl was in and Lydia made them stop in the gift shop for a hot pink balloon and an arrangement of colorful carnations before getting on the elevator.

The three approached the room and found the door cracked open. Lydia knocked and pushed it open, "Beryl, honey?"

"Go way," Polly heard Beryl say.

"We're not going to go away unless you mean it. We're desperate to see your face," Lydia responded.

"Face is a mess. Aw shit, come on in."

Polly hung back, allowing Lydia and Andy to get close to their friend. Beryl was lying on her stomach, her bruised face turned toward the door.

"You look awful, Beryl. Is there anyone we can punish for this?" Lydia asked.

"Thanks for the support. Knew I could count on you. Is Deena alright?"

"She's fine. She's a little worried about you, but now she has great stories to tell her friends. It isn't every girl who has to rescue her unconscious teacher."

"I'm gonna hurt like hell, aren't I?"

"I think you are. But, you're going to live and that's all we care about today, right?"

"Whatever," Beryl sneered, then she smiled. "I didn't want to be another one of Polly's bodies."

"My bodies!" Polly exclaimed. "Stop it!"

"I don't want to be a statistic."

"Oh, you are a crazy woman!"

Beryl laughed, "They told me that my water heater chose today to destroy my livelihood. Did you know appliances were so cruel? Will you kick it for me?"

"We're on it. Anything you want."

Beryl lifted her head. "Anything I want? This is a good time for me to suck you people dry, isn't it? I'm pathetic and can get away with murder."

Polly watched Andy as her shoulders began to shake again. She must have allowed a few quiet sobs to escape because Beryl said, "No you don't. Get over here and hold my hand, but no crying. You don't get to cry. If I was more than half alert, I should be the one in tears."

Lydia backed up and pulled a chair in close to Beryl. Andy sat down and placed her hand on the bed beside Beryl, so Beryl could lay hers on top.

"I'm sorry, Beryl. I'm so sorry."

"Why are you sorry? Did you do something bad?"

"I can't get the image of you lying on the ground out of my head."

"Well, I can't get the image of you and Len Specek snogging in front of his house last week out of my head, but you don't see me crying," Beryl said.

"What's snogging?" Lydia whispered to Polly.

"Kissing and making out," Polly whispered back.

"You were making out with Len Specek?" Beryl asked Andy. "When were you doing that?"

Polly looked sideways at Lydia, who shrugged her shoulders. Beryl's drug-induced haze wasn't helping her stay in the moment. Either that or she was teasing Andy and no one else was following her train of thought.

"Stop it," Andy giggled. "It's not like that."

"Oh, it's exactly like that. You were lucky I didn't pull in behind you and start honking the horn."

"I'm worried about you," Andy responded.

"Well, so am I. When they start taking me off this happy juice, my life is going to suck."

"Do you remember what happened?" Lydia asked.

"Sleep now," Beryl said and shut her eyes. In a split second, she was breathing deeply.

"Well, that was rude," Lydia giggled.

Polly sat down in the window sill, attempting to avoid the air vents. Lydia sat in the other chair in the room and there was silence.

"You people should talk so I can sleep," Beryl mumbled and began breathing deeply again.

"None of you are going to let me get away with feeling sorry for myself about this, are you?" Andy asked. She turned her chair around so she could see everyone and slipped her other hand under Beryl's.

"No, we're not letting you get away with that and, oh, by the way, we're not letting you get away with avoiding the question on Len Specek any longer." Lydia announced.

"Yeah. Are you ashamed of us?" Polly asked. "Is that why we don't get to know about him or why you won't let us be around you two?"

"No, that's not it at all," Andy said. "We've been spending time together for a little while. It's nothing very serious yet."

"Snogging," Lydia turned to Polly and said, "Is that right?" Polly nodded and Lydia went on. "Snogging in his driveway isn't hanging out a little. How have you managed to keep this hidden in a town the size of Bellingwood?"

"Well, it's not like we're trying to keep it hidden. Apparently, you have been too busy to pay attention," Andy huffed.

Lydia looked perplexed. "Too busy for you? I'm sorry if you felt that way. Honey, I'm never too busy for you."

"I know," Andy sighed. "I shouldn't be like this. I probably have been hiding it from you and I suppose I might feel a little guilty about that. I haven't told the kids anything either."

"Is it that serious?" Lydia asked.

"I don't know," Andy's shoulders dropped, then she looked up and smiled, "But it sure has been fun! I feel like I'm in high school all over again. And maybe we have been sneaking around. I didn't want to say anything because then I might have to figure out where this relationship is going and so far, it's been fun letting it be what it is. We go down to Ames for dinner and sometimes to a movie. We even ended up out in the country on a back road one night talking and watching the stars."

"Just talking?" Lydia raised her eyebrows.

"Can't you let me get away with my version of the story?" Andy asked.

"Okay, go ahead. So, you're not telling us, you're not telling your kids, who are you telling?"

"She didn't tell me," Beryl's voice came up out of a fog and she raised her head. "Keep talking, girl."

"I'm not telling anyone and I probably wouldn't have told you for a long time. This has been a bit unexpected." Andy responded. "We, well, maybe I, didn't want it to become a thing. I'm not ready to share this with the whole world. I don't want to go out on couple's dates with people, I don't want to have to take him places with me because I don't want people to look at us and wonder what old lady Saner is doing with a new man. So far, I've wanted to have fun getting to know him, all by ourselves."

Polly nodded. "It's not easy having a relationship around here."

"Will you marry the carpenter and shut up?" Beryl said.

"Go back to sleep, you. Of all the people in this room, you're the last person I would expect to be pushing me into marriage," Polly said. "You, with all of your independent girl life out there."

"When you're right, you're right," Beryl replied and dropped her head back down.

"Is it nice having Henry back in town, though?" Lydia asked Polly.

"It is. I did miss him. We went out on a great date Saturday night. I had tickets to a show at the Civic Center here in Des Moines and he took me to an Italian restaurant on the east side. He loves driving that car of his. I think it will be fun this summer when we can have the top down."

"You know you just used the "we" word, don't you."

Polly shrugged, "I know. I can't help it. We fit together nicely. I don't think I've ever felt so safe and comfortable around someone before. He treats me wonderfully; I can count on him to always be there. Today, when I couldn't think for myself, all I had to do was hear his voice and I settled down. And then, he came over and took care of everything so I could drive down with you two."

"Sounds like marriage," Lydia laughed.

"Please don't do that. I'm going to kick you out of the group if you do," Polly laughed. "Me and Andy. We want to enjoy the relationship, not plan our future, right Andy?"

"Umm, sure. Right."

"Wait, don't tell me you are planning the future." Polly demanded.

"What? Oh, for heaven's sake, no!" Andy protested. "There's no future. There's only right now. Isn't that good enough?"

"Yeah. Isn't that good enough?" Polly echoed.

Lydia looked back and forth at the two of them and said, "Fine. If you don't want a future with a man, I don't care. Maybe it's better that way for you. My life is pretty good with my man, but I don't suppose it works that way for everyone."

Polly said, "Sometimes I feel like I always have to make excuses for the fact that I enjoy being single. People always treat me weird, too. Women get all possessive around their husbands because the single girl threatens them. Single women are threatened by me because for some reason they think I must be attracted to the exact same person they're hitting on. Single men are threatened by me if they aren't looking for a relationship and sometimes married men are lechers. They think they can leer at me and get away with it because they are safely married. It's not a fun world sometimes."

She chuckled, "I had a boss at the library who took me into his office one day and sat me down to tell me we couldn't have a relationship because we worked together. I must have looked a little surprised and he went on to inform me that he knew I had been paying extra attention to him and that since I was single, I was probably looking to find a husband. He assured me that he wasn't going to be able to be that person for me."

When Polly saw that both Andy and Lydia were looking at her with their mouths open, she laughed. "Yeah. You got married when you were young. You didn't have to face the world as a single person. It's a different world out there."

"What did you say to that man?" Lydia asked.

"Oh, I batted my eyes at him," and she demonstrated for them, "and then told him that I wasn't interested in a forty-five year old bald man since I had two hot Italians waiting for me every night."

"I also told my supervisor about his concern, she wrote it up and they moved him to a different department the next week. I think he ended up in the basement of one of the other satellites." Polly shuddered. "That was a weird conversation, though."

"If you girls wouldn't mind holding your bonding session in the hallway, I think I need a nurse to help me pee," Beryl muttered. "Have you seen a nurse? What in the hell did they give me? I think I'm going to explode!"

Andy pressed the call button and told the desk that Beryl needed to go to the bathroom.

"I could have done that," Beryl said.

"But, you didn't. You threatened to explode. I thought you might have had enough explosions for one day," Andy retorted.

"Funny. But, I'm not going to laugh or I will embarrass myself."

The nurse came in and smiled at the three of them. Polly hopped off the ledge and headed for the door.

"Where are you going?" Beryl asked. "Do I embarrass you too?"

"No, I'm just not interested in seeing your naked backside."

The nurse said, "She has a lot of bandages back there, not a whole lot of naked right now."

"See!" Beryl said, "That's not so embarrassing." She looked at the nurse. "I'm going to hurt when these drugs wear off, aren't I?"

"We're going to try to not let them wear off today. Maybe tomorrow, but not today."

"I'm in your debt. Now, I have to pee. You girls should leave for a few minutes."

"Can I help?" Andy asked.

"No!" Beryl yelled. "No one helps today. You go away and come back in a minute."

The three of them went into the hall to wait.

Andy touched Lydia's arm, "I don't want to go back home tonight. I'm going to ask if I can stay here with her. Will you come back tomorrow morning? If I give you my keys, will you bring me some clothes and things?"

"Are you sure?" Lydia asked. "She's in pretty good hands here."

"I'm sure. I won't sleep tonight and if I'm not going to sleep at home, I might as well not sleep here where I can keep an eye on her."

"She's going to be pretty well out of it and I suspect she'll need you even more in days to come," Polly said.

"Then, she'll have me even more in days to come," Andy responded. "If she'll let me, I'm staying here tonight."

The nurse opened the door and said, "She's back in bed, you can come back in."

"If she'll let me, can I stay with her tonight?" Andy asked.

"Sure. We can bring you a blanket and a pillow. It won't be extremely comfortable, but she might rest better if you're here. Let's ask her and we'll get you set up."

They walked back in and Andy went over to sit down beside Beryl again, who was looking a little more alert.

"Beryl, I'm going to stay here tonight with you. Is that alright?"

"Won't your new sweetie be jealous?"

"I don't spend nights with him. Stop it."

Beryl put her hand out and Andy took it, then Beryl said, "If you don't mind staying, I would love for you to be here. Thank you."

Lydia said, "That's settled then." She nodded to the nurse, who left and pulled the door shut behind her.

Andy dug around in her purse and came up with an envelope and a pencil and wrote out a list of things to bring the next day. When Lydia asked her about supper, Andy waved her off. "I'm not at all hungry and if I need something, I'll raid a vending machine. But, you might bring me breakfast in the morning."

Lydia bent over and kissed Beryl's battered cheek and said, "I love you sweet thing. Be good to Andy tonight, alright?"

"I can't make any promises, but I'm glad she's staying."

Polly smiled at Beryl. "Maybe you've broken my dead body jinx. You're alive and I'm glad."

"As long as Andy doesn't kill me tonight, I think we're safe. Get home safely, okay?"

"I love you, Beryl Watson and I'm sorry you got hurt today."

"Love you, too. Now go before it gets emotional in here."

Lydia and Polly both hugged Andy, and when they got into the hallway, pulled the door softly shut behind them.

"Well, it's late, but I'm sure we can find supper before we leave town. Where shall we go?" Lydia asked.

Polly pulled the keys to Lydia's Jeep out of her pocket. "Are you good to drive or do you want me to be in charge of these?"

"Oh, I'm good now. Thank you for taking care of us today." Lydia took the keys back and said, "So. Supper?"

"Well, if I admit that there is one more restaurant I haven't eaten at since I got back, would you take me there?"

"Sure. Where do you want to go?"

"I saw a Maid-Rite before we got to the interstate. Can I get a loose meat sandwich and some fried cheese balls?"

"Oh, you are a girl after my heart. Let's go. I know exactly where this place is located."

CHAPTER SEVEN

Instead of returning to Des Moines with Lydia, Polly headed over to look at the damage in Beryl's studio. She was meeting Henry and Sheriff Merritt there to see what they could do to begin cleaning up the mess and restoring the building to a usable studio.

Lydia had arrived in Des Moines and texted back that Beryl and Andy had lived through the night and were both glad for some McDonald's breakfast. Andy was going to learn how to care for Beryl's wounds and everyone was hopeful the hospital stay would be over by the end of the week.

When Polly and Henry walked around the outside of the house to the studio, Polly took a deep breath. The large windows had blown out and the back of the studio had obvious damage from the explosion. She walked in the front door and felt her knees go weak.

Grabbing Henry's arm, she said, "I can't believe she's going to be alright." The door to the bathroom was hanging loose, the toilet and sink were no longer attached to the wall, and tubes of paint and canvases were scattered everywhere. The ceiling above the separating wall was still dripping water and Polly looked at the floor where Beryl must have fallen the first time. Brown stains marred the wood floor, showing Beryl's path as she escaped her artistic haven.

"What do you think, Henry?" Aaron Merritt asked as he entered the room.

"I need to spend more time evaluating the damage, but I can definitely make something good come out of this. We'll clean it up while she's recovering, then begin reconstruction."

"She has her insurance with Conyers downtown. I called him yesterday and he's got someone coming out this afternoon."

"Do you want me here for that, Aaron?" Henry asked.

"That isn't necessary. Everyone knows the insurance company will do whatever they want to do."

Polly bent over and picked up a canvas that was upside down on the floor. She turned it over. There were swipes of yellows and greens across the top and browns, golds, and reds along the bottom. She walked across the floor to a stack of canvas panels. It looked as if they had fallen off a table top. They were damaged by water and as she stacked them on the table, she flipped through them. She recognized a couple of different scenes from around town, and there were attempts at sketching people. Polly chuckled when she saw the sketch Beryl had done of Andy. It was recognizable, but water had blotched the image.

"I feel like I'm walking through a crime scene," she said, then laughed at Aaron, "Not that I've ever done that, but this feels eerie and creepy."

"I suppose it does," mused Aaron. "Do you want to see the storage room?"

They walked back and Polly gasped. The destruction that one water heater did was enormous. "I'm so glad she's alright," Polly said.

She began taking pictures with her phone so she could look at them later. It was going to take her time to figure out what the process would be to ensure that as much of Beryl's work as possible could be salvaged. It looked as if some things were a complete loss, but even as Polly shot pictures, she could see the potential for reconstruction.

"I'm glad you're here, Henry," she said.

"I am too, but what do you mean?"

"Don't you see it? There is so much potential in this space with someone like you doing the work. All of these metal shelving units can be replaced with enclosed cabinetry and she can design drawers that are exactly the right size for her tools. We can build tall, slotted spaces for her blank canvases and over here she can have a small display area. If we put a secretary against this wall, she can have her computer out here."

Polly continued to walk around the room, talking out loud to herself as she considered more possibilities.

Henry turned to Aaron, "This one is going to keep me busy for the rest of my life."

Aaron chuckled. "She has great ideas. I think you've taught her that anything is possible, so you can't complain. It's your own fault."

"Stop talking about me, I can still hear you. I'm right here, remember?" Polly said.

Her phone rang. She looked and it was a local number, but she didn't recognize it. "Hello?"

"Hi Polly. This is Ken Wallers again. Would you have some time this afternoon?"

"Sure," she replied. "What's up? Tell me you still don't think I had anything to do with Harry's death."

"Oh. No," he laughed. "That's not it at all. We aren't finding anyone in town who knew him. This is more of a personal conversation than anything professional. Could I stop by about two?"

"I'll be in the office. Come on in."

"Thanks. I'll see you then.

Both Henry and Aaron were looking at her expectantly.

"That was Ken Wallers. He wants to come over to Sycamore House this afternoon and talk to me. But don't worry, he isn't going to accuse me of murder this time."

"That's good," Henry said. "I'm not ready to start visiting you in jail. I don't know how I'd ever explain that to people here in town."

She continued around the room using the phone on her camera but stopped when she heard Len Specek's name. "Do not tell me the two of you are gossiping. I'm so ashamed of you!"

They had the grace to look embarrassed. "We're not gossiping, are we?" Henry asked Aaron.

"I wasn't. I wanted to know if you had ever worked with him. He's a pretty good woodworker."

"That's all?" Polly asked.

"Uh huh." Aaron said and both of them bobbed their heads up and down.

"And you accuse women of being terrible gossips. You're the worst because you refuse to admit it for what it is."

She headed for the front door. "I'm finished here. Is there anything else we need to do?"

Aaron chuckled, "I think we're done. I'll let you know when the insurance investigator is through and then we can get started cleaning this place up."

"Thanks," Polly said. "Anybody up for lunch?"

"You two go on ahead. I've got plenty to do today," Aaron replied.

She looked at Henry. "Sure. Where are we going? Joe's Diner?" he asked.

"That sounds fine. I'll meet you there."

Polly pulled into a parking space in front of the grocery store and was reaching back in to get her phone out of the drink well, when she heard Sylvie's voice.

"Polly!" Sylvie called as she exited the grocery store.

"Hi there, what are you doing in town?"

"They needed some help here today and I ducked out of class early. What happened to Beryl? Is she alright?"

Polly's face flushed red. It had crossed her mind yesterday to call Sylvie, but in the chaos that followed, she'd completely forgotten.

"Oh, Sylvie, I'm sorry I didn't call you. She's going to be fine. Burns on the back of her legs and quite a few cuts on her head and back, and then her face looks awful. She must have fallen into something. It's pretty bruised up. She's so pathetic. But, I'm so sorry I didn't call."

Sylvie let out a sigh of relief. "I suppose I could have called, too, but I didn't want to bother you. Henry talked to me yesterday when he asked Jason to help out with the horses, so I knew something had happened. But I had to talk to you."

Polly stepped in and hugged her friend. "I am sorry. I was planning to call you and then there was so much going on, I completely forgot."

"Don't worry about it. You'd have let me know if something awful had happened."

Polly wasn't sure if she would have remembered even then, but was glad she hadn't been put to the test. Henry walked across the street and joined them.

"Your boy did well in the barn last night, Sylvie. I appreciated his help."

She smiled and said, "I think he loves those horses as much as you do, Polly. He talks about getting one of his own someday, but for now, I'm glad I don't have to support that habit!"

Sylvie glanced at a woman walking into the store and said, "I'd better get back in. I'll be over later this afternoon. Jeff has two weddings this weekend and I need to make sure everything is in place." She turned and walked away, "See you later!" she said.

Polly and Henry walked down the street to the diner. "I forgot to call her yesterday, I feel horrible!" Polly said.

"She didn't seem too upset with you, I'd let it go," he replied.

"Well, that was a rotten thing to do to a friend. I'm not going to say anything to Lydia, it will break her heart and right now, she doesn't have much left to break."

"Hey, Henry! Welcome back!" Lucy called out as she carried three plates of food to a booth in front of the window. He waved and guided Polly to another booth along the back wall.

"I think I've even missed Joe's food," he remarked as they sat down. "Are you having your regular today?"

Polly looked at the menu. "I had one the other day, I'm going to have to get creative. I wonder what the special is. Did you look at the board?"

He stepped out of the booth and said, "Meat Loaf plate or baked spaghetti. Oh, and the soup of the day is ham and bean."

"Maybe I'll do a tuna melt," she remarked and put her menu down in front of her.

Lucy brought water and silverware and said, "How long you been back, Henry?"

"I got in Friday night. It's good to be back."

"Did you hear about your girlfriend's latest find?" she laughed, nodding her head sideways at Polly.

Polly audibly sighed, "It's not like I killed the man."

"No, this is much better," Henry said. "We can laugh with you and not feel guilty that you've done anything terrible."

"How is Miz Watson?" Lucy asked Polly.

"I think she'll be fine. It will take her a while to get back to normal, but she was lucky."

"There certainly have been a lot of things going on around here," Lucy said. "Did you hear that Don Roberts lost about a thousand dollars of equipment? They stole it right out of his barn!"

Henry looked up at her, his brow creased in concern. "I didn't hear that. When did it happen?"

"I think it was Sunday night. Can you imagine?"

Henry huffed and said, "Who would do that? People can't work for themselves any longer, they have to steal from other folks. Drives me nuts."

"Make sure you lock up your workshop," Lucy said, took their orders, and walked back to the kitchen to hang them on the order carousel.

Polly said, "What kind of equipment would they be able to easily haul?"

"Oh, it could be anything," Henry said. "Everyone has tools and small equipment they store in their barns."

"I don't," she laughed.

"Not yet, but after you've been here for a few more years, that stuff will start building up."

After lunch Henry followed Polly back to Sycamore House. As she approached, she saw that there were several people working in the corner lot. She recognized Nancy Burroughs and Deb Waters, who waved as she drove in. She pulled into the driveway and instead of turning into the parking lot, stopped to say hello.

Henry drove on in and parked, but Polly jumped out of her truck and headed toward Deb, who was working with two men putting stakes in the ground.

"Hello there," Polly called, as she walked across the lawn.

"Hi, Polly!" Deb said and stood up to greet her. "We thought we'd get started, what with Lydia and Andy taking care of Beryl Watson."

"I'm sure they'll be glad to know things are moving along even if they aren't involved," Polly said. "Is there anything I can do to help?"

Henry walked up beside her and said, "This group of people will cause nothing but trouble. You're probably going to need a lot of help managing them."

A short, stout man with a red face and blondish, red hair that encircled a bald pate, stood up and said, "You old dog. Did you finally catch a woman here?"

Henry shook his head and chuckled. "Polly, this erudite man is Deb's husband, Louis. He's better with wood than he is with words, but he'll always find a way to embarrass me."

Deb visibly gulped, "Oh, I should have introduced you, Polly. Sometimes I get so used to having him around, I forget that not everyone knows him."

Polly smiled. "That's alright," and reached out to shake his hand. "So, what woman is this dog catching these days?" she asked sweetly.

The man stood stock still and stared at her, caught between his wife's look of admonition, Polly's apparent naiveté, and Henry's very amused countenance.

His eyes flickered back and forth between the three of them and then he broke out into laughter. "Everyone in town says she's too smart for you, Henry. You'd better be good to her."

"I make it a policy to be good to every woman I meet," Henry started and then said, "Wait. I mean. I'm always nice to women. I mean," He stopped and rolled his head on his shoulders. "I'm a good guy. Right?"

Polly leaned into him, "He's a good guy even when he's a little flustered. Thanks for doing this. I can't wait to see it as you progress."

"It's going to be a nice addition for Bellingwood," Louis said. "After all of those years of this lot barely getting any attention, we're glad to help bring it back to life."

Henry pointed to his watch and Polly, remembering, said, "I have an appointment. I'd better get inside. Thanks again,"

They walked back to her truck and Henry continued to the front door, waiting as she parked it and joined him.

Polly was working in her office when, right on time, Ken Wallers arrived. She stood up to shake his hand and gestured for him to sit in one of the chairs by her desk.

"If I'm not in trouble, what can I do for you?" she asked.

"Well, it is about Harry Bern, but you aren't in any trouble. Do you have any information from his past or did you ever hear him talk about people he knew? I can't find this man anywhere. I finally sent his fingerprints down to the Department of Criminal Investigation to see if they could find any record of him."

Polly paused to think, "I don't know. Let me ask Jeff, though. He worked with Harry more than I did."

She stood up and walked past him and then stood between the two offices, "Jeff, Ken Wallers is here asking if we knew anything more about Harry. Did he ever talk about his past or give you any names of people he knew?"

Jeff came out of his office and followed Polly back into hers, sitting down in the other chair, "He never said anything about people, but I think he was in the army at some point - maybe Desert Storm in the nineties. He said something once about hating the heat. He wasn't looking forward to July, but said it was better than being in the desert in full gear."

"We haven't found anything in his house to indicate that he served in the Army," Ken said. "There aren't any pictures out or anything personal except for things he accumulated since moving here."

"How long has he been in Bellingwood?" Polly asked.

"He rented the house he was living in a year and a half ago. He worked at the recycling plant for a while and Josie up at the convenience store said he worked for her for several months too."

"Those are the references he gave me," Jeff said. "Both of them said he was a hard worker and at that point it was all I cared about. I didn't dig too much deeper."

"Well, you've given me enough information to dig more deeply," Ken said. "I appreciate that."

"Do you have any idea who might have killed him?" Jeff asked.

"We don't at this time. The house had been tossed, but whoever did it must have worn gloves. There were no fingerprints except Harry's that we could find."

Ken stood up, "Thanks for your time. If I hear any more, I'll let you know."

Both Jeff and Polly stood up. She reached her hand out to shake his, "Ken, if he doesn't have anyone around who will claim his body, I'll make arrangements for a service and burial."

"Thanks, Polly. I'm sure the military will step in and the county always cremates any unclaimed bodies and buries them respectfully, but in this case, I think we'll wait until we know who he is and what has happened to him before we make any decisions."

He stepped out into the main office and then turned around, "Oh, by the way, how is Ms. Watson?"

"She's doing better. Lydia and Andy Saner are with her today and it sounds as if she will be home by the end of the week."

"I'm glad to hear it," he said. "Quite a few people called and reported that explosion. It could have been a lot worse than it was. Let me know if you need any help over there, will you?"

Polly smiled. Small towns were really something. "I will, and thanks."

After he left, Jeff sat back down. "So, could you have any more happening in your life right now?"

Polly glanced at her inbox and saw that a message had come in from Sal Kahane.

"Apparently I could. I remembered my friend from Boston is coming in next week. I have no idea where she is going to stay. I suppose she could sleep on my couch, but it's not that comfortable."

"You're in luck. Manfred Evans, the photographer who has been staying in the front room is leaving on Sunday. He said he was finished with central Iowa and moving on to northeast Iowa."

"Jeff, thank you. I can't believe I need more space here, but at least Henry and I are getting started on it." She sat back and said, "Really. That's the best news yet today. I hadn't started to worry about where Sal would sleep, but I'm sure it would have occurred to me at some point."

"We wouldn't want you to lose sleep over it, you have too many other things to worry about."

"What am I supposed to be worrying about now?"

He laughed. "Nothing. I have two people coming in tomorrow morning to interview about the custodian job. Any advice?"

"Tell them not to die or run away, and I'll be happy," Polly said.

"That's a little over the top. Why don't I do a normal interview and we'll go from there."

"Fine," she smirked. "I hope one of them works out. Look, why don't you offer it as a full time job. Now that spring is here, we might as well hire them to do work outside as well."

"On it. That will actually make this an easier hire."

He got up to leave. "I'm sorry about your friend. Let me know if you need me to do anything, alright?"

"Thanks," she said. "I have no idea what is happening there yet, but I will."

Jeff returned to his office and Polly opened up her email from Sal.

"It's all set! I'm flying in Tuesday morning to Des Moines and will

drive over to the University of Iowa. After two days of sparkling rhetoric with learned folk, I'll head back to Des Moines. Can you pick me up at the airport about eight o'clock on Wednesday and then put up with me until Saturday?

I can hardly wait to see you!

Have you heard from Bunny? I think she's getting married this fall. She finally met 'the one' and for some reason he likes the fact that she needs him. I've met him, he's alright. I'd probably hurt him, but he's perfect for her and believe it or not, she's happy.

Are there any gorgeous farmers out there who would like to marry a city girl? I'm always ready for anything!

Love you,

Sal"

Polly read the email twice. Bunny was getting married. That wasn't surprising. Polly figured this was the first of at least three marriages in that girl's future. She hoped he had plenty of money, because it was going to cost him when he ran screaming for his life.

She called out, "Jeff?"

"Yeah?"

"Don't let me forget. Next Wednesday I have to drive to Des Moines to pick Sal up at the airport. I'm putting it in my calendar, but if I look like I'm going to lose my mind, help me keep it together."

"Got it, boss. Wednesday. Drive to Des Moines. It's on my calendar now, too."

Polly chuckled. Yes. This was her life now. She hit reply.

"Wednesday it is. Don't eat on your drive across the state. I'll take you out when you get here. Eight o'clock might be late for the folks in Iowa, but surely you won't have lost all your citification in two days.

Gorgeous farmers, eh? I don't know what I could find for you on such short notice. Can you imagine bringing your Jewish American Princess attitude to a farm? Girl, you have to be desperate. You know women actually work hard out here, right? If you're still desperate in a year, you

can come back and we'll see what I can find for you.
Love you too and I totally can't wait. I'll see you on Wednesday!"

Sal Kahane had been the epitome of spoiled. Her father was a surgeon at Mass General and she had grown up with servants and a nanny, or governess, as Mrs. Kahane insisted the poor girl be called. Sal had graduated from Concord Academy before attending Boston University and by the time she met Polly, she was looking for something more in her life. She was long past wanting to be a mirror image of her mother, but it was impossible for her to completely set aside her background. Whomever she finally found to settle down with would have to be strong, wealthy, powerful and playful and if Sal wanted any part of her family's money, he was also going to have to be Jewish. As wonderful as her father was, her mother would have no part of her marrying anyone but a nice young Jewish boy.

Polly looked at the clock on her computer. Jason and Andrew were going to be here pretty soon and she needed to get changed to spend time in the barn with them.

"Let me know if you need anything. I'm going to be out in the barn," she said, ducking her head into Jeff's office.

"I'll be fine. Sylvie is coming over this afternoon. We have a small reception Friday night and then a big one Saturday afternoon."

She waved and went up to her apartment.

CHAPTER EIGHT

No rest for the wicked. Polly wondered what she had done to infuriate the universe. The last two days had passed in a blur. She sat at her desk with her head in her hands and her eyes shut. They had to hire someone soon. She was thankful for Jason who helped her with the horses in the evening, but between their care and having to clean the inside and keep the outside yard and driveway looking clean, she hadn't had a moment to stop and think. On top of that, she and Henry had been working to sort through the debris in Beryl's studio. They had carried quite a few of the canvases into Beryl's basement so she could sort through them at some point. She had cleaned up brushes and tubes of paint, tossed out blank canvases, filled tubs with paperwork and files and carried those into the basement as well.

The two girls who were studying with her, Deena and Meryl, had come over in the afternoons and knew enough about the layout of the studio to help Polly make sense of things. She figured they had a few more cleanup days and Henry could begin restoration.

This morning, though, Polly desperately needed to get through some paperwork in her office and make sure bills were paid.

There was a stack of paper sitting in the inbox at the corner of her desk and she couldn't take it any longer. She turned on an online music player, browsed for a few minutes and landed on a light jazz channel and began opening envelopes.

People were coming and going and she assumed most of them were preparing for one or the other wedding receptions that was happening in the auditorium over the weekend. It took all of her willpower to remain at her desk and work rather than wander around and chat with people.

Jeff knocked on her door, "Polly, do you have a minute?"

"Sure, Jeff. I'd rather do about anything than this."

He smiled, stepped in, shut the door and sat down.

"I think I might have found someone to fill the position, but it's a little outside of the box."

"What do you mean by that? Are you implying that we've been hiring normal people up until now?"

"Okay, you've got me there. But this one is going to require us to take a little bit of a risk."

Polly sat back and scowled. "Is he going to die on me?"

Jeff laughed, "You aren't going to make this easy, are you?"

"I'm sorry," she said, "Go ahead."

"I know you might be gun shy after finding out that Harry Bern's background was a little thin and yes, this one isn't much better, but I like him a lot."

"What do you mean, isn't much better?"

"Well, he won't give me much information. Said he wants to work here for a month. He asked if we could pay him in cash, and then at the end of the month, if things works out, he'll tell us everything about himself and we can do all of the background checks we want and get him on the regular payroll."

"Oh, Jeff!" Polly mocked. "That doesn't sound weird at all. Of course I want to hire someone who is living here incognito. Of course I want to have him around our guests and my house."

He shook his head, "You're right. It's too strange and too risky. I'll tell him we're not interested."

"Why in the world would you think he'd be good for us?"

"Because he's polite and his hands are calloused. He's known what hard work is. He asked about your horses and how long you'd had them and if he took the job would you consider allowing him to help you care for them. He asked about the property and talked about big gardens and knows what to do with lawns. He asked about new construction and said that he'd done that in the past and wondered if he would be able to help out with any of that."

Jeff sat back. "I didn't think that giving him a one month trial would be such a bad thing. I talked about our guests and the events that we have here. He said he didn't have a lot of nice clothes, but if you wouldn't mind providing him with Sycamore House shirts, he'd wear those whenever he was working. He told me he had scrubbed a lot of toilets in his time and that good hard work was worth doing well."

"You're kicking me in the teeth here, Jeff. He sounds perfect. Why do you suppose he doesn't want us to know who he is yet?"

"I don't know, Polly. But, if he's willing to come clean at the end of a month, why couldn't we take a chance on him?"

"Did he tell you anything at all?"

"He told me he was in the army a long time ago. I'd put him around forty-eight or so. Who knows, maybe he served in Desert Storm in Iraq."

Polly scowled again, "That's an odd coincidence, don't you think? We have two men show up in Bellingwood and they both served in the Army, probably in Desert Storm?"

"I don't know," Jeff replied. "People move around a lot. Harry came into town at least a year and a half ago. It's not like they both showed up at the same time."

"It's still a strange coincidence. He didn't say anything about Harry, did he?"

"No, but I did tell him why we were hiring. I figured I needed to be up front about the fact that the last few custodians here haven't worked out."

Jeff hesitated and continued, "There is one more thing, Polly. He's been burned and scarred very badly. I didn't ask him about it, but he doesn't try to hide it and he doesn't act like he's ashamed of it."

"Is that why you want to hire him?"

Jeff looked down, "I suppose that's part of it. He genuinely seems like a good person and I don't know why he isn't telling us who he is right up front, but I like him."

"You like him?"

"Polly, I had an uncle who was burned in Viet Nam. His scars messed him up. He never had the confidence to go look for a job and because of that, he didn't have the confidence to do anything except sit in a bar every day and drink his life away. It nearly killed my mom to watch him fall apart. There wasn't anything she could do except offer him safety every once in a while. He'd come to our house once a week, take a shower, eat dinner with us and fall asleep on the couch. The next morning he would always be gone before we got up, but during those nights with us, he came alive."

Jeff's eyes misted up, "We knew him so well that he felt safe in our house, but he wouldn't let his little sister do anything more than that for him. He'd talk about the years he was a kid with mom and they would laugh together at their memories. But, he never talked about his hopes and dreams. He had decided at some point that he didn't have a future."

"Do you think that by hiring this man, you'll give him a future? That's a lot of expectation for a custodial job, Jeff."

"I know. You're right. I thought I could give him a safe place for a while. Who knows how long he'll stay or what he'll do with it. I suppose I'm still trying to fix Uncle Dick, and I shouldn't do that."

Polly sat forward. She smiled. "No, Jeff, that's exactly what you should do. Sycamore House is about giving shelter to people who need it. We aren't here simply to provide an auditorium for those who can afford to pay for expensive weddings for their daughters or for artists to hide while they're creating. We're here for everyone. Bring him in and introduce him to me. Hire him. At this point, I hope he makes it with us the whole month so I can figure out what the big mystery is!"

Jeff looked up. "Thanks, Polly. It's moments like this that I remember why I got excited about working with you that first day I met you."

"Is he here now?"

"No, I talked to him yesterday afternoon while you were over at Beryl's. He's going to be here about eleven thirty. Will that work for you?"

"That will be great. I'm not going to be around much this afternoon. The hospital is releasing Beryl and she's going to stay with Andy. I want to be there in case they need any extra help getting her inside the house and settled."

"I'm glad she's going to be back in town. How are you coming on her studio?"

"We'll get it cleaned out and stripped down by the end of the weekend. Henry is going to be here in a little bit and we're going to go over some plans for re-building it. I want to have them almost ready to go so I can show her what we're thinking and he can get started."

"How's the plan coming for the garage and apartment?"

"The concrete is being poured today. After that, it's a matter of building the frame and getting started."

"You love this part of it, don't you, Polly."

"I do. And you know, you're going to have to keep this place busy so I can keep doing it."

He laughed. "I'm trying! I'm really trying! As a matter of fact, there's a woman who wants to start teaching some adult computer classes here during the week. We're working that all out right now. I'm still trying to think outside the box for the classroom space, but I'm sure something will come up one of these days."

He waved at Sylvie through the window as she came in the main front door. Polly turned and saw her and beckoned for her to join them.

"You didn't have anything more, did you, Jeff?"

"No, that's great. I'll leave you two." He stood up and opened the door, greeting Sylvie as she came in to Polly's office.

"I didn't interrupt anything, did I?" Sylvie asked.

"No, you're fine. Are you ready for another big weekend?"

"I sure am. Tonight will be easy. It's a small group and they're going through a serving line. The bride wanted to save money, so they'll do the cleanup afterwards, too. All I have to do is cook and serve. Tomorrow's wedding is going to be huge, though. Hannah is coming over and I've got two of the girls from school coming up to help as well."

"Sylvie, I'm so glad you and Hannah are working well together. That makes me happy!"

"She said that it's good for her. She makes enough money on weekends with me that she doesn't have to try to find a waitressing job. That way she can be home with her kids during the week. Bruce's mom takes them if he's too busy on Saturdays, but everything is working out."

"How is Bruce doing with his dad?" Polly asked.

Last Christmas, Bruce McKenzie and his new wife, Hannah, had returned to Iowa. He had run from his strong-willed father who insisted that Bruce work on the farm rather than live his own life. When things got tough, though, the best place to land was with a family who loved you even though it was difficult for Bruce's father to express that love. The old grouch had been taken to task by his wife who finally had enough of his tyrannical ways and he was learning to accept both of his sons for who they were.

Sylvie gave a slight shake of her head. "I don't think it's easy, but they're both trying. Bruce works for him in the shop and has also gotten a job as a mechanic in the shop where he worked when he was in high school. During planting and harvest, he'll work in the fields. I think that was all the extra help his dad needed, so everyone feels like it is fair."

Polly sighed, "So much has happened since I moved back here and so much has changed. Sometimes I don't know what to think."

"You don't spend much time over in Story City where you grew up, do you, Polly?"

"I've only been there a couple of times since I moved back."

"I suppose it feels different with your dad gone."

"When I finally sold Dad's house and moved his things into storage, I think I closed a little piece of my heart and then when Mary died, it felt like she took my home with her. That last time I left town, it was as if my entire history collapsed into a single moment in time. Everything was a memory and my future was somewhere else."

"Don't you have friends from high school that you want to spend time with?"

"My best girlfriends all moved away, so it feels different. All of the homes I spent time in while I was growing up no longer feel like home. We aren't the same people any longer, and sometimes I think the town and I have gone two separate ways. Like meeting up with an old boyfriend and realizing he is nothing like the boy you knew so well. All of the changes that happened after you knew him make him a very different person."

"You've changed, too, Polly."

"Exactly! I'm very different than the girl everyone knew as Everett Giller's daughter. I don't fit in."

"You haven't given them much of a chance to see if you fit in, have you?" Sylvie admonished quietly.

"You're right. I don't feel as if I fit the same way I used to. It's a lot easier to show up here and get to know everyone without knowing everything about them."

Sylvie giggled, "It's easier for us, too. Trust me." She looked at her watch, "I'd better get busy. I have two deliveries showing up and I need to make sure I'm ready for them. Talk you later!"

She was out the door before Polly could say anything more, so she took a deep breath and went back to opening envelopes and sorting paperwork.

"Knock, knock." Polly looked up when she heard Henry's voice.

"Hey there," she said.

He walked over to her and hugged her while she was still in her chair.

"Hey there, yourself." He pointed at the pile of paper on her desk. "That doesn't look fun."

Polly snarled, "It's awful. But, it's necessary, so I do what I have to do."

"Did you want to look at what I've got for Beryl's studio this morning?"

She gathered the paper into a pile, stacked it as neatly as possible, tossed the empty envelopes into the recycling bin under her desk and shoved the rest to the side.

"Yes. I do. Right now. Please!" she laughed. "I'd like to look at anything other than this mess."

Henry handed her a flash drive and said, "Would you mind?"

She inserted it into the USB port and clicked to open it. Since the obvious file was "Beryl's Studio," she double clicked it and waited for it to open. Henry pulled his chair around to sit beside her.

"You know," she said, "We could have done this in the conference room."

"But, I wouldn't have been able to sit this close to you. You smell great this morning!"

"I'm clean. That's all it is. Clean. And I'm clean every morning by the time you see me."

He shrugged. "You still smell great."

"Back away, you mad molester or I'll have to do something heinous to you."

He laughed and backed his chair up an inch, leaving just enough room between them so he could prove a point.

"I guess that will do," she said. She reached over and took his hand in hers.

The file opened and Polly enlarged the image and began to move her mouse around the screen. Henry had taken her ideas and created a wonderful space. She pointed to a confusing space in the back storage room and asked, "What's this?"

"Aaron and I were surprised at the amount of flammable chemicals that woman has. I understand that she needs them, but that explosion could have been much worse. She's going to buy a firesafe cabinet. I'll enclose it so that it matches everything else, but she isn't going to be allowed to leave them out any longer."

"Yeah. You tell her she isn't allowed to do that and see what trouble you create," Polly said.

"Oh, I'm not telling her. That's Aaron's job. He gets to deliver all of the bad news to her. She listens to him. He might be the only man in town that gets away with that, but at least there is one."

Henry had taken her quickly sketched ideas for the studio and brought them alive in his CAD program. Polly wanted to open up the walls with more windows. Between each set of windows, there were floor to ceiling cabinets to hold finished pieces and underneath each window were cabinets and drawers to hold Beryl's supplies.

On the wall facing the garden between the studio and the house, he had designed a desk which wrapped around the front of the studio. The center of the room had a large work table as well as plenty of space for several easels and chairs. Polly had thought that a nice granite countertop on the other side of the room would double as a workspace, except that there wasn't room to put legs underneath. Oh well, that would have to do.

The back storage room would have more floor to ceiling storage. Polly had sat down and thought through the number of different mediums Beryl used to paint and draw and then talked to Henry about designing drawers for each type. Rather than digging through a deep drawer to find the right color, Beryl could sort her paints by hue and the shallow drawers would make things readily accessible.

She and Henry spent time talking through what type of wood to use and as long as Beryl approved, Polly was dying to use a knotty alder for the cabinets. She loved the look of the grain and the blemishes left by the knots in the wood. The last task was to collect options for cabinet hardware and then she could show Beryl the plans.

"This is wonderful, Henry," she said. "Now we have to get Beryl's approval."

"She will love it," he responded.

"I hope so. I'm emailing this to Lydia so Beryl can see it. Thanks for all your work."

"I didn't do anything but make your ideas real, Polly. Even though Beryl is a great artist and paints on canvas, you are an artist too. The only difference is that your medium is wood and structures."

"Hmmm," she mused. "I did spend a lot of time designing my perfect house when I was young. It changed all the time, but at night I would fall asleep putting rooms in my house together. Thank you, though. That's such a nice thing to say. I would never have known this about myself if you weren't here to make it real."

"Then I'm glad you ended up in Bellingwood so we could find each other."

He stood up and pulled his chair back to the front of the desk.

"I'm glad we found each other, too," she replied. She copied the file to her desktop and ejected the flash drive, then reopened it. "I'm going to print out a couple of copies of this to take over to Andy's house later this afternoon."

"They're coming home?" he asked.

"Can you believe that Beryl is letting Andy take care of her? I only hope those two women don't kill each other before Beryl goes to her own house."

"Would you do me a favor?" Henry asked.

"Sure? What's up?"

"I've been talking to people around town and Len Specek is supposed to be a pretty good carpenter. I can't believe I didn't know this about him. Would you ask Andy if it would be alright if I brought him in to help with Beryl's studio?"

"Of course I will! Oh, I can't wait to have that conversation with her. She's been trying to hide him from us. I think we embarrass her. This is going to change all of that."

"Maybe I shouldn't do it, then."

"Oh no you don't! If he's who you want, then he's who you're going to get. Andy's world got toppled upside down the day she got caught having lunch with him. It's all out in the open now and she's going to have to live with it."

"You girls are very scary."

"Tell me about it. I've had to threaten those three with their lives so they don't have us married with children in the next six months."

Henry looked stricken. "Children?"

"Don't worry," Polly laughed. "I took care of it."

"Good," he said. "I'd like to be married a little while before we have kids."

Polly looked up at him in shock and he started to cackle. "That's the Polly I love. Do you want to do something tonight?"

"If I don't get through these bills today, I'm still going to be working on them," she lamented. "And since there is a reception in the auditorium, I'll be doing them upstairs."

Then she looked up at him, "But, if you wanted to come over, we could turn on a movie. I can work on my laptop."

"Why don't I bring a pizza. What time?"

"Can you give me until seven thirty? That way I'll have the animals bedded down for the night and maybe even have taken another shower."

Henry winked at her. "I'll see you later."

CHAPTER NINE

Done for now. Stretching her shoulders and neck, Polly glanced at the time. It was eleven o'clock. She pushed the stack of papers away from her, knowing she could do the rest tonight in front of a movie. She had enough time to go upstairs for a few minutes and play with her animals. She could tell that they missed her. Luke was more aggressive than usual and Leia had started nipping at both her and Obiwan. Crawling into bed with them each night wasn't enough time to keep everyone happy. She ran upstairs and opened the front door of her apartment.

Obiwan looked up at her in confusion and she saw that Luke and Leia were both stretching and yawning on her bed in the next room. "Hi guys," Polly said, "Have you missed having me around as much as I've missed being around?" Her dog sauntered over to greet her and followed as she went in to the bedroom. She patted the bed and he leaped up, surprising Luke, who was preparing to jump to the floor. Polly sat down and pulled Obiwan in for a hug. He gave her a large kiss on the cheek and she laughed. "Not too much of that," she said. "I still have to see people today and I don't need to be completely slobbered!"

Leia sidled up and Polly scooped her into her arms. Within

moments, the cat was purring and snuggling into the crook of Polly's arm. Luke jumped on to Polly's shoulder and nuzzled her ear.

"Wow, you have missed me. I love coming up here and getting all of this attention. I don't have a lot of time, but it's all yours," she laughed. She tugged Luke down so she could carry him and they went out to the couch in the living room.

"If I stay in there on that bed, I'll lie down and fall asleep and I don't trust any of you to wake me in time for my appointment," she said to them.

Obiwan had plopped himself where she intended to sit, so she moved to the other end and got comfortable with the cats. Leia hadn't moved, except to snuggle in more tightly and Luke climbed to the back of the sofa and perched there. She rubbed his head and watched his eyes glaze over in response. His purring wasn't quite as loud as Leia's, but if Polly placed her hand on his back, she could feel him vibrating. On the other hand, Leia sounded like a rumbling freight train and at the moment was rubbing her head against Polly, claiming her territory.

"It's nice to be quiet for a few minutes with you," Polly said. She continued to rub Luke's head for a few more minutes and watched Leia's eyes close as she fell back to sleep in her arms.

The cats had both gone to sleep and Obiwan was resting his head on her lap when Polly looked at the clock and realized it was time for her to go back downstairs. She stood up and put Leia back down on the sofa where she had been sitting.

"Come on, Obiwan. You're with me. You're going to meet someone and then we'll take a short walk before I leave again for the afternoon." She picked up the leash and he stood patiently while she snapped it on his collar. They didn't use the leash much anymore. Since the fence had gone up around what was now the horse's pasture, he was pretty good about following her out to the barn. Once the gate was shut, he had all the space he needed to run. She loved watching him tear through the pasture at a full run, knowing that he finally had freedom without her worrying that he'd dash into the highway.

He followed her down the steps and looked at the front door as they passed it and then when she turned into the office he was surprised they weren't going out the side door to the barn.

"Not yet. I have a meeting. Can you hang here with me for a while?" She led him behind her desk and looked around for a place to hook his leash. She finally opened a drawer and shut it on her end of the leash, knowing that with a good tug, he'd be free in a moment. Hopefully if it were necessary, she would have enough time to grab it and stop him from lunging or leaping out of control. Obiwan was a great dog and very friendly with people, but she didn't want to take any chances. She began one last sort of the paperwork, choosing what needed to go upstairs and stuffed the rest in a drawer.

At eleven thirty, she saw someone come in the front door. He nodded at her through the window and she knew this had to be the man Jeff wanted her to meet. He was wearing a knit cap pulled down over his ears. His hands were jammed in the pockets of a dark blue pea coat and his eyes were covered by a pair of dark sunglasses. He wore loose fitting work pants and black boots. She smiled at him as he came in the main door of the office. Jeff had heard him approach and met him, then looked at Polly as if asking a question. She stood up and motioned for them to come on in.

Jeff entered her office first and said, "Polly, this is Eliseo Aquila."

She stood up from her desk and he stepped forward to shake her hand, "Thank you for taking the time to meet me this morning, Miss Giller." She expected more of a Hispanic accent because of the name, but his was very subtle.

She motioned for them to both take a seat. Jeff moved to the inside chair and as soon as Eliseo was seated, Obiwan pulled away and rushed to greet him. Before Polly could stop him, her dog had put his paws on the man's thigh and leaned in to lick his face. She knew he was comfortable around people, but this was a little unexpected.

Eliseo leaned in to meet the dog and allowed Obiwan to lick

him, then ruffled the scruff of his neck and said, "You're a good dog."

"I'm sorry!" Polly exclaimed. "I hope you like animals."

"I do and there is no reason to apologize. He's a happy, friendly dog."

Obiwan had dropped back down to the floor, but set his head on Eliseo's leg as if waiting for more attention. The man put a scarred hand on top of the dog's head and began rubbing his ears.

"Well, it looks as if you've made a friend," Polly said. "He likes you."

Eliseo nodded and Jeff interrupted. "Eliseo, Miss Giller and I talked a little this morning and I'm sure she has a few more questions before we discuss employment."

"Yes, ma'am," Eliseo said. "I'll try to answer your questions."

Polly watched as he continued to rub Obiwan's head. Any tension he had shown when walking in the door was gone. He reached up and took his sunglasses off and she was startled by the beauty and warmth in his eyes. They were soft and brown, belying the pain that he had obviously faced in his life. The right side of his body must have taken the brunt of whatever fire had hurt him, but although the left side was scarred as well, she could see traces of the original shape of his face there.

"Jeff has told me of your request to work for us for a month before asking any questions and it's only on his recommendation that I'm even considering this," she said. "I'm a little gun-shy about hiring someone without first going through background information and references. We haven't had the best of luck with the position up until this point."

"I understand," he said. "If you don't want to consider me for the job, that's truly alright."

He began to rise out of his chair, so Jeff put his hand on Eliseo's arm. "I don't think that's what she's saying."

"Tell me, Eliseo," Polly began, "Why would you be better at this job than anyone else?"

He smiled and it filled his face. "Ma'am, other than the months I spent in the hospital and in rehabilitation, I have worked hard all of my life. The one thing that got me moving again during and after rehab was being outside and forcing these muscles to become strong again. I couldn't imagine not being able to put my hands into dirt and plant things so they could grow, or spend time with animals of all sizes and watch them become comfortable with me. I had to know that I was making the world better, so I kept moving and working. It's kept me alive and healthy for these last twenty years and I'm not about to stop now."

"Do you mind cleaning rooms and working inside?"

"No ma'am. I've done it all. There is no type of hard work that a person should be ashamed of doing. Inside work or outside work is all good work." He looked at her, "I would always prefer to be outside, but wherever there is work to be done, I'll do it."

"Jeff said you had some construction background. Can you tell me about that?"

"I spent two years working for a general contractor as a foreman and I've worked nearly every job there is on a building site. I might not be a craftsman, but I know what I'm doing and I'm comfortable with the tools and equipment."

"What do you know about regular maintenance around a place like this?"

"I can replace the innards of a toilet, if that's what you're asking, and I can learn about most anything else. I'm not afraid to try things."

Polly smiled. "You seem a little too good to be true. I don't understand why you're here looking for a job."

"If I may, Miss Giller. I make most people nervous. They find it difficult to look at my face." He rubbed the top of Obiwan's head again. "Maybe that's why animals are so comfortable with me. I relax around them because they don't care what I look like and they sense that."

"We have a lot of people who come and go around here. Will it bother you to work around so many different people? What if they stare at you, will that be a problem?"

"No, it won't. I've lived with that for the last twenty years. If I'm not being too forward, will it be a problem for you?"

Polly thought for a moment and said, "I've never worked closely with someone who has faced what you did and what you must face on a daily basis. It's not a problem for me, but I can't tell you that I'll never stare at you and wonder about the pain you must have been in," she said. "But, that's not a good reason not to employ you."

"Thank you ma'am. I appreciate that. Some of your guests might not feel the same way, though. I've lost more than a few jobs because customers or clients are uncomfortable with me around."

"We would deal with that," she said. "Not you. In fact, that would be a lousy reason to let you go. Now Jeff also told me you know something about horses."

Another smile lit his face, "Yes ma'am! I grew up with horses. My father worked as a farm hand in southern California and I started working with him as soon as I was big enough to crawl on a bucket to reach their heads. I'm not bragging too much to say that he became one of the best trainers in the region. Even the most skittish would soon discover that he was safe and they could trust him."

Polly nodded. "One month and then we can make this permanent?" she asked.

"It usually takes about a month for an employer to decide whether or not I'm good enough to keep around for a long time. I don't want to make your life any more difficult than it is." He pointed at his face. "I'm not unaware of how people look at me. If you can't keep me around, then neither of us will feel bad about it."

She looked at Jeff, "Work it out. I'm on board."

Jeff smiled back at her and stood up. "Come on Eliseo. I've got shirts and caps in my office and as soon as you are available, you can start. I'll show you around and help you get acquainted with the place."

"I'm here now," Eliseo responded. "If you'd like me to begin this afternoon, I'm ready." He rubbed Obiwan one more time and then followed Jeff out of the office. When the dog tried to follow him, he knelt down, looked in his eyes and said, "Obiwan, sit. Stay." The dog did as ordered and watched him walk away.

Polly wondered how long her dog would stay in place. He wasn't used to someone else giving him direction. And then she realized she wasn't sure what to do either. She giggled and said, "Obiwan, come here." He stood up and came over to sit beside her, wagging his tail.

After a quick walk with the dog and some lunch, Polly headed over to Beryl's studio. She left a note for Jason and Andrew, who would be there after school, asking them to spend some time playing with her animals and that she didn't know when she would be back. She didn't want Jason to worry about the horses, she'd beg Henry to help her if nothing else.

When she arrived at the studio, she walked in and saw that quite a bit of work had happened. Henry had his entire crew here today, pulling drywall and yanking the ceiling down. The dumpster outside was filling quickly.

"What have you done in here?" she asked.

"Check this out, Polly," Jimmy Rio said. He was up on a ladder tearing into the ceiling over what had been the inside wall to the back room. It was now nothing more than a frame.

"What's up, Jimmy?" she asked.

"Henry says this place would look great if we opened up the ceiling and put a loft area over the back room. What do you think?"

Polly turned her eyes to the ceiling. The beams looked to be in great shape. If they were stained a dark brown and the upper ceiling were painted, it would look really nice.

"How's he planning to get up to the loft?" she asked.

Henry came out of the back room with an armful of drywall. "It wouldn't take much to do a staircase with a ninety-degree turn right here by the door to the back room." He nodded behind to the space. I think it could look funky and she could do something fun with the loft. What do you think?"

"It's a great idea," Polly said. "I'll talk to her about it this afternoon. That will change the plans we came up with, though and I'm not taking responsibility for these changes."

Henry laughed as he walked past her. "Oh, you're always responsible for changes. It's your job and don't forget it. I'll be right back." He went outside and tossed his armload into the dumpster and came back in. Walking over to Polly, he brushed her nose with his gloves.

"Hey!" she said.

"You can't be in the deconstruction zone without running into a little bit of dust," he laughed.

"What are you doing here anyway, I thought they were pouring cement!"

"I'm heading back over in a few minutes. I need to keep an eye on these guys as well."

She put her hand on his arm and said, "Do you have a minute? Could we talk outside?"

He followed her out and they walked away from the studio.

"What's up?" he asked. "Is everything alright?"

"Yeah, everything is fine, but I have a strange request. When you go back to Sycamore House, I would like you to find a reason to meet the new person that Jeff hired this morning."

"Sure." Henry looked a little perplexed. "Why do you want me to meet him?"

Polly told him about the strange request Eliseo had made regarding his employment and the fact that he seemed too good to be true.

"I want to know what your first impression of him is. Jeff likes him and honestly, so do I," she said. "And then there's the fact that Obiwan is quite comfortable around him."

"I'll see if I can't introduce myself," Henry assured her. "Isn't there a wedding reception tonight? Will he be helping with cleanup?"

"I don't think so. Sylvie said the bride was concerned about saving money. I think her family is planning to do most of the work."

"Don't worry. I'll let you know what I think over supper."

"Thank you. I don't want to make a big deal out of this and it is important to Jeff."

Polly's phone buzzed. She looked at the text from Lydia and said, "It looks as if they're on their way back to Bellingwood. Do you need anything here?"

"We're good. What are you doing with yourself until they get here?"

"I have a list," she said and showed him an email from Lydia. "I have to go into Beryl's house and get some clothes and toiletries for her and then I'm going up to the drugstore and pick up some other things Andy thinks she'll need."

"Tell her we're glad she's home," Henry said and then he smiled and winked at Polly, "and I'm looking forward to a quiet night with you and your computer tonight."

She grinned. "I'll see you later," and walked to Beryl's back door. The key was under a rock and she let herself in. She was pulling a travel bag out of Beryl's closet, thinking about the interview with Eliseo Aquila, when all of a sudden it hit her: Eliseo had called Obiwan by name when he told the dog to sit and stay in her office. She'd never said anything about his name. How did he know that?

She shook her head. She was probably making more out of it than was necessary. He must have heard her talking to the dog or maybe Jeff told him about her animals. Yes. That was probably it. Polly filled the bag with the things on the list and went out the back door, returning the key to its spot under the rock. She needed to hurry. Lydia usually pushed the edge of the speed limit and she wanted to be at Andy's house when they arrived. Lydia assured her that Beryl was walking, but Polly needed to see it for herself.

She had enough time to get to the drug store and the florist. Spring was still trying to show up in Bellingwood and bright flowers were not only appropriate, but necessary.

CHAPTER TEN

Saturday morning and Polly had no commitments for the day. She pulled the blankets up underneath her chin, dislodging Luke who had been comfortably resting on her stomach. She turned over on her side and managed to send Leia scurrying for freedom as well. The only one who didn't bother moving was Obiwan. He pressed against her legs as she turned, ensuring that she ended up shifting further across the bed.

"It's a good thing this is a king-size bed or I'd be on the floor," she mumbled. Polly squeezed her eyes shut and attempted to go back to sleep. Both cats leapt off the bed and ran to their perches and began meowing. She figured they were telling the wildlife outside they were awake. She smiled. Yesterday had ended up being a great day. Beryl was safely ensconced at Andy's house. She'd been given plenty of pain medication in order to make the trip from Des Moines to Bellingwood and between that and the fact that she was happy to be away from all of the hospital activities, the first hour was a riot.

Beryl had regaled them with tales of her flirtations with the poor doctors who didn't see her coming and the nurses who figured it out and began setting them up simply for their own entertainment. One poor young intern had asked more questions than Beryl wanted to answer so she finally turned her back on him. When he attempted to cover her with the blanket, she yanked it down and told him that she was the moon over Des Moines and he could just let it shine. He scurried away and her regular doctor soon arrived to ask if it might be time to turn down the happy juice.

Andy had rolled her eyes and told the poor woman that Beryl didn't need narcotics to be off the wall.

After four days in the hospital, many of the smaller cuts were beginning to fade. The gash on the back of her head was better, but the bruises on her face had turned so many sickly colors ranging from red to purple, green and yellow, Polly shuddered at how badly she must have hurt.

Beryl had a lot of questions about the studio now that she was in town and had Polly close by. Polly figured that it was as good a time as any to deliver the worst of the news, but then began to talk about some of the wonderful things that could happen in the little building if Beryl would let her and Henry loose on it. At that point, the poor woman had begun to cry and within moments, she was sobbing. Andy rushed to her side and managed to finally get her calmed down enough to speak.

Polly had panicked. "I'm so sorry, Beryl! I didn't mean to move this far ahead without you. We'll stop right now and I'll pull everyone out until you're feeling better and can supervise it all."

"No," Beryl sobbed. "That's not it."

"Well, then what is it?" Andy demanded. "You're scaring the poor girl."

"I'm sorry," she said, continuing to sob. "It's just that …"

Beryl broke down again and Lydia stuffed some tissues into her clenched fists. She finally sat up and wiped her eyes, then said to Polly, "Let me see what you're doing."

Polly pulled out the copies of the work she and Henry had done and poor Beryl began crying again. "I'm sorry I'm such a blubbering mess," she said. "I'm pretty sure these drugs are making me behave like this. I have no control over my emotions."

Andy patted her shoulder and Beryl pushed her away, saying, "I love you sweetie, but if you and I are going to live together for the next week, you have got to quit hovering. I'm going to live now. Please go back to treating me like a normal person, alright?"

Andy stuck her tongue out and sat back about six inches. "Well, that's not very friendly. I've been sleeping in a chair, making nurses stay quiet so you can sleep. I've eaten crappy food and invited you here so I can keep an eye on you."

"And you'd do it again next week. You don't fool me," Beryl said. "You love me and since I've spent a lifetime making sure you aren't boring, I figure this is payback."

"Girls!" Lydia admonished. "Stop it."

She looked at Polly and stage whispered, "I don't know how to separate them if they're living together."

Beryl patted Andy's knee, "Just so you know, there is no one else in the world who would have done what you did for me this week and I owe you everything. I'll never be able to say thank you, but I'll start with thank you."

She turned to Lydia, "Is that better, mom?"

"Much."

"Alright, let me look at this stuff and I'll try not to cry again."

"Are you sure?" Polly asked.

"I'm only crying because you are taking such good care of me, not because I don't like what you're doing. I swear, a person can't be touched because people are nice to her without everyone thinking the worst."

Andy tried to scoot back in and Beryl batted her away. "I'm not going to fall apart again. It's just that I've been a lone wolf for a long time and now, here I have all of these people hovering over me and I'm filled up with drugs. I'll be better tomorrow, I promise. Now show me those plans."

The four of them spent time with the designs Henry had created. Beryl was able to give Polly a little more insight into her workflow and they jotted down changes that would make it better. When Lydia asked about window boxes, Polly caught Beryl yawning.

"We finally moved past your interest level, didn't we," she commented.

"No, that's not it," Beryl assured her, "This old lady needs a nap."

Andy stood up and said to Polly and Lydia, "Then, everyone needs to go unless you are planning to take a nap too. This house is going to get very quiet now, got it?"

Beryl rolled her eyes, "Nurse Ratched. Joy." She lifted her hands to Lydia, "If I call you and beg, will you rescue me from this place?"

Polly gathered up her things and followed Lydia to the front door, then waited as Lydia stepped back into the main room, "If this place turns into a Cuckoo's Nest, I'm sending Aaron in. Be good to her, Beryl."

"I ain't got a choice. She controls my meds. Come back soon and save me!"

Andy laughed and followed Lydia and Polly outside, "Thanks for everything. I'll see you later."

Polly found Jason and Andrew downstairs helping Doug set up for the evening's gaming session while Sylvie and Jeff were getting set up for the wedding reception.

Billy had met her in the parking lot. "Hi, Polly," he said as he got out of his car. Three more people piled out of his car to follow him in.

"You are starting early this afternoon," she said.

"We're getting set up. Mr. Adams let us off at two, said we could quit early since we worked last weekend. We're going to party tonight!"

Polly snickered. By party, they meant staying up late playing games with lots of caffeinated drinks, pizza and junk food. "What's on tap for tonight?" she asked.

"We've got a lot of people coming. It's going to be epic!" he said.

"A lot?" she asked.

"Oh, we'll stay in the classrooms until the wedding is over, that's no problem. Tonight we're going to try something different.

While some of them are playing "Sword Lords" on the computer, Caleb and I are running a role playing game in the other room."

"Like Dungeons and Dragons?" Polly asked. She'd been asked by a couple of friends to play with them when she was a lot younger, but had left her character sheets in a box long ago.

"Yeah. Like that. Only way updated since you probably played it."

"I'm not that old, Billy."

"You could come down and play with us, Miss Giller," said one of the boys, pulling out a package from his backpack. He began setting up a game board and shuffling cards.

"Thank you, maybe another time."

"Polly, this is Caleb Devins. He's running the game. Oh, and that's his sister Rachel," Billy said, nodding to a dark haired girl with purple eye shadow highlighted with green accents. "And that's Dinky Stanton." Billy nodded at a very tall, bleached blonde kid who gave her some strange hand wave as he slung himself into a chair and leaned it back.

"I hope you have a good time," Polly said. "The wedding reception should be cleared out of here by eight."

"We'll be cool," Billy assured her.

Polly popped her head into the computer room and saw Jason and Andrew chatting with Doug. She'd purchased two inexpensive laptops yesterday and had called Doug to let him know they were in her office. He promised get them back into the conference room by the end of the evening.

Jason looked up, "Are you ready to go out and work with the horses?"

"Let me change my clothes. I'll be back in a bit. But, are you sure?"

"I'm sure," he said. "They're playing all night. I don't want to miss being out there, though."

She and Jason got everyone fed and bedded down, then Polly sent him back in and walked from stall to stall. It felt good to see the horses doing so well. They were content and happy.

Henry pulled into the parking lot as she walked back up to the house. They met inside and walked upstairs together.

"Nice timing," Polly said. She went inside and said, "Give me a few minutes to change."

"Need some help with that?"

"Thanks, I've got it," she giggled, her face blushing to a deep red, and went into her room.

Henry had things set up on the coffee table, so Polly sat cross-legged on the sofa against the far arm rest while Henry took the other end. Obiwan tried to get up between them, but she pushed him back to the floor.

"Sorry, buddy. This is for humans tonight," she said. The dog dropped down in front where she was sitting and watched every piece of pizza as it left the box and landed on a plate.

Henry laughed, "That's a bit intimidating."

"Don't let him fool you. He never gets people food and we're not starting tonight," She reached down and rubbed his head, "Are we, buddy?"

Henry had harassed her until she pulled out her laptop and settled in to work. Polly chuckled. She ought to keep her mouth shut around the man unless she wanted him to keep her in line. But she'd finished all of the accounting and gotten the bills paid. Henry wasn't terribly excited to watch any of the Star Wars movies again, so he'd settled for watching the latest iterations of Batman.

"You're a strange girl, Polly Giller," he said.

"Why do you say that?" she asked.

"We never watch chick flicks. You like geeky movies better than I do."

"I like chick flicks. Any time you want to watch a Meg Ryan or Tom Hanks movie, I'm there."

He shook his head. "I'm not complaining. I swear I'm not complaining. You're weird."

Polly laughed, "I can't help it if I prefer my men leaping tall buildings or using their minds to create awesome powersuits or showing off their incredible ... ummm ... superpowers!"

"Uh huh. I'm going to have a tough time competing with that."

"Oh, you have super powers," she said. "You pull my behind out of the fire all the time and then keep returning to do it again and again. That's pretty super to me.

"I don't know if those superpowers will save the world, but I'm okay with saving you once in a while."

When she closed the laptop and said, "Done," he set it on the coffee table, then pulled her next to him and wrapped his arms around her as she snuggled in to watch the end of the movie.

"You smell great again, tonight, Polly," he said.

"I'm clean," she laughed, "but trust me; I'm never changing shampoo if you react like this every time you come close."

Polly turned her face to him and kissed him. All she could think was that he had the most wonderful lips and he tasted fabulous. They continued to kiss until Luke jumped onto Henry's shoulder and tried to find a place to sit.

She laughed and Henry said, "Your animals send mixed messages."

"What do you mean?"

"Well, I'm pretty sure they like me, but I'm also pretty sure they don't like me kissing you."

"Oh, they're attention hogs. It is pretty funny, though."

"Yes. That's what it is. Funny." He pulled Luke down onto Polly's stomach. "If anyone had ever told me I was going to have to compete with four horses, two cats and one dog for a girl's attention, I would have laughed in their face."

Polly looked back up at him, "I hope you know that if you ever want my attention that badly, I will shut the animals in the other room."

He nodded and grinned. "I might put you to the test someday."

She sat up, "So, I forgot to ask you. What did you think of Jeff's new hire? Did you stop by and meet him today?"

"I did," he replied. "He seems like a good guy. Polly, he's been through a lot. I know that he acts like everything is alright, but no one can have gone through as much as he did and not have baggage."

"But, do you think the baggage is too much for us to handle?

He's not going to come unglued and turn into a crazy man, is he?"

Henry smiled, "No, I can't imagine that will happen. I shouldn't have said anything. If it's been twenty years since he was burned, he's probably managing it as best he can."

"Do you think he'll be able to do what he says he can do? Can he help with construction and do maintenance around here? Is he too good to be true?"

"He knew what he was talking about." Henry shrugged. "I suspect he does have experience in different areas. It's not like you are hiring him forever. If he doesn't work out in a month, it's over, right?"

"I suppose so." Polly nodded. "I want this to work. I figure that as soon as I hire someone for this job, they're going to find a reason to leave and I'll be back to doing the work myself again."

"It won't hurt you to take a chance with him. I'd probably hire him if you didn't."

"Really?" she asked. "That makes me feel better."

"Tell me again though," Henry said, "how do you pronounce his name?"

"I only heard Jeff introduce him, but it's ell-ih-SAY-oh."

"I have never heard that name before," he commented. "Maybe he's as unique as his name."

They had talked about Beryl's studio. Polly could hardly wait to get started. She wanted to get things going and finished so Beryl could move back in and begin painting again. Henry had pulled her closer.

"You know it is going to take some time, don't you?"

"I know, I know. I'm just anxious to get started. She is going to love it!"

"It's a good thing you don't have more friends, you know."

"What do you mean by that?"

"I'd never be able to keep up with all of the work."

"You'd just have to keep hiring more help. I don't intend for you to ever have enough freedom to leave me for two months again."

"And I didn't think you cared whether I was here or not."

Polly elbowed him. "Stop it. I cared. I didn't realize how much. So don't be running away, alright?"

They had finished watching a second movie and when she yawned and stretched, Henry announced it was time for him to leave.

"You have to get up early in the morning and take care of those behemoths in your barn. I'm going to let you get a good night's sleep," he said.

It was dark downstairs. The wedding party had left and the kids playing games were gone as well. Polly triggered the lights on and they walked down with Obiwan.

She had kissed him goodnight at his truck and then opened the gate to the pasture so Obiwan could make one last quick run. The night sky twinkled with stars and when she whistled, Obiwan returned and they'd gone upstairs to bed.

Polly looked at the clock. Six forty-five. Good heavens, the horses would be wondering where she was! She jumped out of bed and pulled on her jeans and boots, a flannel shirt and sweater under her jacket. Obiwan followed her outside and when she got to the barn, she was surprised to see Eliseo already scooping out stalls.

"Good morning?" she said, posing a question.

"Good morning, Miss Giller. I was up early this morning and thought I would help you out here. I want to thank you for giving me a chance."

"Well, okay. Umm, I was going to say I would introduce you to the horses, but it looks like you've already made their acquaintance." They were all happily eating and Demi looked up when he heard her voice. She slipped into his stall, with fresh shavings already laid down. "Good morning, Demi. I'm not quite sure what to do with this," she whispered. "Care to give me some advice?"

Demi nickered and pushed her with his nose as if to say hello and then went back to his breakfast. Polly walked into each of the other stalls and greeted her horses. Eliseo was finishing up in Nan's stall and opened her door to the outside after Polly had stopped by. Nan went dashing out to the end of the pasture and then came back to the front and waited while he let the rest of them out.

"I don't expect you to do all of the work out here," she said to Eliseo.

"Miss Giller, you have no idea how much I've missed being around horses. These are quite a bit bigger than what I'm used to, but they are such beautiful creatures, don't you think?"

"I do, and honestly, a little help here and there is wonderful. However, the horses aren't necessarily in your job description."

"I won't do anything with them if you don't want me to, but I'd love to help you out. Like I said, I've missed horses."

Polly couldn't believe how the horses had reacted to him, or rather, how they had not reacted to him. They were very comfortable with him and it made her feel a little jealous.

"I can't ask you to do my work," she said, "but I won't stop you from doing whatever you'd like around here. Now that I've had them in my life for a couple of months, I can't imagine giving them up, so I get it. But, I'm surprised at how they are already so comfortable around you."

He looked up, a little startled. "I didn't think about that," and went back to scooping Nan's stall. Polly watched as he wheeled the cart out to the manure pile. He came back in, rinsed things down and put them away.

"I'll go up and drop some more hay down. It's getting a little low down here," he said and pulled down the ladder leading to the loft.

Polly began to follow him up the ladder, "I can help you and it will go that much faster," she said.

He stopped her, "No, you stay down here. I've got this."

She stepped back. "Alright," she called out. "I'm going to go out and work with Nat this morning."

"I'll come out later and you can show me what you do with them," he called back down.

Polly felt completely intimidated by that comment. She was doing exactly what Mark had taught her to do with the horses and not much more. Her confidence level regarding her knowledge of working with them was pretty low. When it was only her and the horse, she was fine. They didn't know what she didn't know, but she wasn't ready to prove her incompetence to someone else.

She walked outside, pulled out her phone and dialed Mark.

"Good morning, Polly!" he said. "How are things at the ranch?"

"Good morning to you. What are you doing this morning?"

"Oh, I'm sitting on a beach sunning my behind. Why? What's up?"

"No really. Are you heading out to a farm?"

"Not until later. I think most of the calves that were going to be born have been born by this point. Do you need something?"

"I'm a little embarrassed to even ask you this," she said as she walked further away from the barn. She explained about her new employee and his apparent comfort with her horses, as well as her discomfort at being thought an incompetent with them.

"Would you mind giving me a little time this morning and also check him out to see if he knows all that he says he knows?"

"Polly, I'd do almost anything for you and those Percherons. Who are you working with this morning?"

"It's Nat's turn."

"Get him ready to go and I'll be right over. This is much better than what I was going to have to do here at the office."

He turned away from the phone and she heard him shout in the background, "Marnie. I have to go over to Polly's. You get to do inventory by yourself."

When he came back, he was laughing. "You might need to bake some cookies for Marnie. She hates you now."

"I didn't mean to take you away from something important."

"I hate this part of it and generally do whatever I can to get out of it, but then she wrestles me to the ground and makes me count stuff until I forget what number comes next. This is perfect. I'll see you in a while."

Polly felt as if a weight had been lifted when she went back into the barn. Eliseo was in the feed room, stacking bales of hay as she grabbed the halter and lead rope for Nat. She called him to her and he came trotting from the tree line. Thank goodness he had decided to be obedient today of all days. By the time she had him in the pen, Mark was walking towards her.

Of all four horses, Nat loved Mark the most. He had been in the worst shape when he arrived at Sycamore House, but had responded immediately to Mark's strength and care. This morning, he waited patiently as Mark approached them.

"Let's see how our boy is doing this morning," Mark said. He leaned in to Polly. "Is your new man in the barn?"

"Yes, he'll probably be out in a few minutes. He was stacking hay bales."

"Really?"

"Yeah. And I'm complaining because?"

"No kidding!"

"He fed them and mucked out the stalls this morning before I even got here," she said. "And it was exactly how I would do it, too." Polly sounded a little disgusted.

"The jerk!"

"Oh, shut up, you." she laughed. She got Nat started at a walk and then realized Mark had left her. Eliseo had come out to the fence and he and Mark were shaking hands, introducing themselves to each other. She heard them laughing and Mark opened the gate into the main pasture and walked through. Before she knew it, the two men were hauling hay out and then walking through the pasture to talk to the horses.

She'd gotten distracted while watching them and realized that Nat had stopped and was looking at her.

"Oh, whatever," she said and sent him a signal to begin a trot. He obeyed and she concentrated on him rather than the men who were obviously out to usurp her position as top dog of the horses. Even Obiwan was following them around, panting for attention.

"Stupid men. Why do I have so many of them in my life?" She was frustrated and distracted, and shortened Nat's workout. He didn't seem to mind as she released him back into the pasture. He took off without a look back and Polly decided a little pouting was appropriate, so she went back into the barn and after hanging

Nat's halter on his hook, walked into the feed room and kicked a bale of hay, only to discover that it wasn't quite as forgiving as it looked.

With more than a little attitude, she opened the back door of the barn and called out, "I'm going back to my office since you all don't need me," pulled the door shut and stalked up to Sycamore House. When she realized she didn't have her dog with her, she was too embarrassed to go back and get him and hoped that one of them would make sure Obiwan got back to her.

Noise in the kitchen told her Sylvie was already there, so she went in and found her friend peering intently at the laptop screen.

"Hey, Sylvie, you're here early."

"I know. The boys were being awful, so I put cereal on the table and left the apartment. I told them I'd be back to get them later, but I didn't want to be around them this morning."

Polly laughed, "I swear, it must be a testosterone thing this morning. Is there something in the air? I stomped away from Eliseo and Mark because they were pissing me off."

"Who?" Sylvie asked.

"Oh, you haven't met him yet! We hired a new maintenance man slash custodian yesterday. Eliseo Aquila. He knows horses and decided to help me out with them this morning."

"And that's a bad thing."

Polly rolled her eyes. "No, it's probably not a bad thing. If I'm being totally honest, I still don't feel like I know what I'm doing with them and I might not have wanted him to watch me be inept."

"You're not inept. Don't say that about yourself."

"Anyway, so I called Mark and asked if he could come over and give me a little support and maybe check Eliseo out. Some support. All he did was make friends with him and leave me."

"That's terrible!" Sylvie laughed.

"I know!" Polly agreed. "So, I walked off in a pout, because it seemed like the thing to do."

"You tell 'em, girl."

"So, ummm, would you like me to get your boys this morning

and bring them over here? Because it sounds like you did the same thing, only you can get away with it because you're the mom."

Sylvie laughed out loud. "I did do the same thing, didn't I? No, they'll be fine for now. They'll eat cereal and watch morning television without me around to bother them, then I'll call and make sure they're ready to go and they can come over later. Are you sure you're okay with that?"

"I love having them around and even if I'm not here, I'm okay with that. I'm going into my office for a while, in case Mark wants to talk to me or someone brings my poor dog back inside. Talk to you later." Polly left the kitchen, went to her office, sat down and woke up her computer.

CHAPTER ELEVEN

Tapping her mouse to move cards, Polly looked up from her Solitaire game when Mark Ogden and Obiwan walked into her office.

"Hey," he said and dropped into one of the chairs.

"Hey back," she responded, with no inflection in her voice. She was still a little annoyed with him.

Obiwan sat down in the doorway and watched them.

"I don't know where you found him, but you have to keep him around. He knows a lot about horses and he likes yours."

"How does he know mine well enough to like them?" she asked.

Mark scowled at her. "Why does it bother you?"

"Because I barely have an understanding of what I'm supposed to be doing with them and along comes someone who is practically a professional. Aren't I supposed to be the one in charge?"

He continued to scowl. "You have got to be kidding me."

"No, I'm not kidding you. I've spent less than three months with them and finally feel like they trust me. I don't want someone to come in and usurp me."

"Polly, you need the help. You can't keep this up."

"I've got Jason," she pouted, pursing her lips.

"He's a twelve year old boy who loves your horses, but knows less than you do. Eliseo will be good for Jason, too, if he wants to keep learning."

Polly sighed. "You men drive me crazy sometimes. I think you might be ganging up on me."

"That's exactly what we're doing. Get over yourself, woman."

It was Polly's turn to scowl. "I'll sic my dog on you."

"I'm terribly worried. Come here, Obiwan."

Obiwan walked over to Mark and wagged his tail. Polly shook her head. "If I didn't have such a great thing going here, I'd say my life stunk, but I'd never get away with that, would I."

He laughed at her. "I don't think so. But, really. He's fine. He is comfortable around horses, he's already shown you that he is a hard worker and wants to please you. Don't let yourself get worked up by this."

Mark stood up to leave and Polly had a thought flit through her mind.

"Just a second," she asked. "Are you interested in Sylvie?"

"What?" Shock filled his face.

"Sylvie Donovan. Are you interested in dating her?"

"I don't know. I hadn't given it much thought."

"So you haven't like dated or anything?"

"No! Where is this coming from?"

"Nothing. I thought that you might ask her out on a date after the hoe-down. You danced a lot with her."

"Is she interested in going out with me?" he asked.

Polly shrugged. "I don't know. We haven't talked about it much. She's been busy with school and," she paused. "I'm sorry. I shouldn't have said anything."

"Did I screw something up?" he asked. "I can be dense sometimes."

"I don't think so. I had a million thoughts happening in my head and then my mouth opened up and one of them came out."

"Should I be asking her out?" Then, he spoke quietly, "Isn't she like ten years older than me? I didn't even consider it. Oh, I'm an idiot."

"No!" Polly said. "No, you're not. She hasn't said anything and I stuck my nose in where it didn't belong. Don't even think about it."

"Well, how can I not think about it now? You've put it in my head!"

"I know you well enough to know that with very little effort, you can drop it right back out of your head, too. Don't worry about it."

He chuckled. "You have a mean streak. Alright, I'm going to go back and let Marnie beat up on me, too."

Mark stepped toward her door, then turned around and said, "By the way, I don't know if you heard about the break-ins that have been happening around town, but make sure you keep things locked up for a while."

"I heard about one of them, have there been more?"

"Two other farms have been hit and Sam Lewiston's pickup was robbed. They broke his tool box open, destroying it. They knew what they were looking for."

"What are they looking for? I can't imagine I have anything they'd want around here."

"They're going for high ticket tools and equipment, things they can sell quickly. I can't believe Sam's dog didn't hear them doing all that damage, but he didn't find it until the next morning. I know you don't have a lot in the way of tack yet, but Dave Samuels lost two saddles and quite a bit of equipment."

"I'll talk to Eliseo and make sure he knows and we'll keep an eye on things."

"Tell Henry to keep things locked down at his place. That man has some serious tools over there."

"Thanks for letting me know about this. I'm surprised I haven't heard more about it."

"No problem. Give me a call if you need anything," Mark said and put his hand on the door sill to walk out.

"I will. Thank you for coming over and telling me what you

think of Eliseo."

"See you later!"

He left and Polly looked at her dog. "You're a traitor. Come on. Let's go upstairs and get me cleaned up for the day."

When Polly came back downstairs, Hannah McKenzie was coming in the front door. She and her husband, Bruce had returned to the area from Colorado before Christmas and everyone was delighted that Sylvie could use her hands in the kitchen for some of the bigger events occurring at Sycamore House. Polly had known Bruce in high school; he had dated her best friend. As she thought about it, he was the only person from home she had any contact with and that was only because he had ended up in her driveway when the deputy sheriff pulled him over for speeding. The world was quite small.

"How are you and Bruce doing?" Polly asked.

"It's not always easy, but so much better than we anticipated. It's nice having his mother around. The kids have fallen in love with her and oh my, but they love being out on the farm. They're turning into regular little farm kids. Sammy loves the tractors and even though Bruce's dad tries to be gruff and tough around him, you can tell that little boy has his heart. The other day I watched my little guy reach up and tug the old man's hand out of his pocket while they walked out to the barn after breakfast. The old man didn't know what to do other than hold it."

They walked back to the kitchen together. "How long will you live there? How are things going with all of you in the same house?"

"We're managing for now, but I told Bruce the other night that we should have enough saved to rent a place in town by June first. It will be nice to have my own kitchen again and be able to scold the kids out loud if I need to," Hannah laughed. "His mom has never said anything, but I don't want her to hear me if I ever have to completely wig out on them."

Polly laughingly agreed. "I get it. Most of my outbursts around here have been pretty public and it takes a few days before I believe people aren't staring at me to see if I'm going to grow horns. I hate it."

"What do you hate?" Sylvie asked as she came out of the storage room.

"I hate making a public spectacle of myself when I'm angry," Polly laughed.

"Yeah. You've really gotta rein that in, girl," Sylvie chuckled. "It's always better if you come off as the poor, pathetic female, right Hannah?"

Hannah looked back and forth between the two of them. "I-umm-yes-no?"

Sylvie tossed her an apron. "I'm kidding. Don't worry, I haven't lost my mind or my superhero girl points."

"Speaking of girl points, Sylvie, are you interested in Doc Ogden?" Polly asked.

Sylvie stopped in her tracks, tilted her head and turned back around to face Polly, "What? Did he say something to you? I haven't talked to him since the hoe-down and that's been a couple of months ago. I know I waved at him when he walked past the grocery store a couple of times, but I wave at everyone. I see him when he's here sometimes. Why? Does he think I'm making a pass at him?"

She sucked in a breath, ready to get started again and Polly interrupted her, raising her hand. "No! He didn't say a word. I was just asking. He'd probably die if he knew I was asking you this question. But, I thought you were crushing on him a little. You tend to pay attention to him when he's around."

Hannah had pulled the apron over her head and was poised in mid tie, her hands behind her, again watching the two of them.

"Good heavens, Polly. He's nearly ten years younger than I am. When I'm sixty, he'll still be a kid!"

"Yeah. But,"

"No buts about it. I don't play in that sandbox," Sylvie said. "Boys that age still want a hot young woman who hasn't given birth to two children and lived a difficult life. Some other woman is going to have to raise him. I'm busy with my own."

Polly put both hands up and said, "Got it. You're not

interested."

"Don't get me wrong. That is a pretty hot package to look at and he's fun to flirt with, but a man is going to have to have a whole lot of life behind him before he can deal with what I've got to manage."

Polly laughed. "Well, that does make it a lot easier, then."

"Makes what easier? Are you going to try to go out with him again?"

"Me?" Polly gasped. "Oh no, not me. My friend, Sal, from Boston is coming into town on Wednesday and my random brain processing was planning an evening out with her and Henry and," she paused, "I needed another person of the male persuasion. But, if you and Mark were playing some kind of distant, non-engaged dating game, I didn't want to intrude on it."

"Well, that's a good idea, but what gave you the notion that he and I were interested in each other?"

Polly dropped her head. "Truthfully, nothing, except a little spark of excitement from the dance. I thought the two of you were having a good time together and then I thought there might be something more if either of you gave it an opportunity."

"Oh, lord no. It was fun to dance with him because he makes it so easy, but that's all there was to it."

"Well, then, I've made a huge deal out of nothing and I'm sorry," Polly laughed.

She heard footsteps in the hallway and turned around to see Eliseo coming in from the side door. He glanced into the kitchen and then turned to head for the basement.

Polly called out, "Eliseo?"

He turned back toward her, "Yes, Miss Giller?"

"I'd like you to meet a couple of people. You'll be working with them quite a bit."

He came into the kitchen and Polly introduced him to Sylvie and Hannah.

"It's nice to meet both of you," he said, shaking their hands. "Be sure to let me know if there is anything you need." He turned back to Polly. "I was going down to the basement to see what tools you had and take a glance at some of the heating and cooling equipment. Mr. Lyndsay gave me a quick tour, but I want to spend time getting better acquainted with everything."

"Thank you, Eliseo," she said.

He started to walk away, then turned back and said. "I'll be back to begin setting up tables and chairs in the auditorium. I have the layout." He pulled a neatly folded piece of paper from his back pocket. "If there are any changes you would like to make, Mrs. Donovan, let me know."

He left and Sylvie said, "What a nice man. I hope he stays around for a while."

"So do I," Polly replied. "It would be nice to hold on to someone longer than a couple of weeks."

"What do you think happened to him?" Hannah whispered.

"I think he was burned in Desert Storm back in the nineties," Polly said. "I haven't asked him myself, but that's what Jeff said."

Hannah put both of her hands on her cheeks, "Can you imagine the horrible pain of that burn?"

Sylvie jumped in, "The worst pain had to have been the months and years it took to recover from it." She turned to Polly, "You're taking a risk. Do you think people are going to have trouble with him working here?"

"Because he's disfigured?" Polly asked, shocked.

"No!" Sylvie gasped, "Because he's Hispanic."

"What in the world do you mean by that?"

"Polly, have you ever noticed the color of people's skin in this town?"

"I didn't know I was supposed to."

"It's pretty pink. The only brown that happens comes from tanning beds and trips to the Caribbean."

"Well, that's just crap. This is the twenty-first century. Are you kidding me?"

"You're back in small town Iowa, Polly. Some of the towns that have packing plants around here have had to deal with a lot of prejudices. There are whispers that Bellingwood is lucky because we don't have to worry about having more than one language in town."

"Gah!" Polly spat, "The next thing you're going to do is tell me we have a chapter of the Ku Klux Klan here."

"We used to! There are still people in town whose parents and grandparents were members of the Klan. I read somewhere that it is trying to make its way back into Iowa small towns. People don't like the fact that the world gets into their safe, little town."

"Don't tell me you feel that way, Sylvie."

"Oh, good heavens no," she said. "I want my boys to grow up knowing there is no difference in people, but I also want you to know that you are pushing a lot of buttons with the people you are hiring here at Sycamore House."

Polly stopped and took a deep breath. "If I ever hear any nasty bigotry directed at people who work here or who are guests here, I will throw a bigger tantrum than this town has ever seen. They can keep their pre-World War One sensibilities in their own homes. That man served this country and was wounded for it. And that shouldn't even matter. But it had better."

She hit the door frame with her fist as she left the kitchen and stalked to her office. Jeff stepped out of his office to speak to her, took one look at her face and stepped back in. Polly shut the door without slamming it, sat down at her desk and took a deep breath. She took two more and shut her eyes, trying to regain control. She wasn't angry with Sylvie, who was only trying to prepare Polly for what could come, but her fury at the injustice of it was making it difficult to regain her composure.

A knock at her door got her attention and she looked up to see Sylvie standing there. Polly beckoned for her to come in.

"I'm sorry I said anything, Polly. Maybe you'll never hear a word against him and it wasn't my place to make you think twice about who you hire. Heck, you put your trust in me and the last thing I want to do is hurt you."

"No, it's alright. I'm nearly back to normal. I get worked up when I know there is nothing I can do to change bad behavior. Bigots have spent a lifetime building up their beliefs and I can't change it because I'm mad at them."

"That's why I started talking to my boys a long time ago," Sylvie said. "I don't want them growing up like my mother did. It took everything she had in her to give me the freedom not to hate, but she'd had a fear of other races ingrained in her. Even when she knew it was wrong, she would cross to the other side of the street or try to avoid people in the mall in Des Moines. Then, every night she would sit down with me and tell me that I should listen to what she said and not watch what she did. She hated that her fears caused her to do that, but she couldn't shake them."

"I wasn't angry at you, Sylvie. Please know that."

"I do, but I also shouldn't have said anything. I think both things about him shocked me enough that I was stupid and then I opened my mouth."

"We're fine. I'm alright."

"Speaking of alright, did you see Beryl yesterday? How is she doing?"

"I'm going back over there this morning. Hopefully she won't have killed Andy yet. I think this process of living together is going to last less than a week and Beryl will be back at her own house."

"Can you imagine taking care of that woman?" Sylvie laughed.

"Not really. She mooned an intern at the hospital on purpose because he was asking her too many questions."

"Oh, no!"

"Exactly."

"Tell her I love her and I'll stop by Andy's tomorrow with goodies, okay?"

"I will."

"Now," Sylvie said, "I'm going to change the subject again. Do you know where Eliseo is staying?"

"I don't. He asked if we would give him a month's trial run here before he gave us all his information, so I know very little about him. Why?"

"I was only wondering. I haven't seen him downtown much. Do you mind if I keep the refrigerator stocked and tell him that he can have some of the leftovers from these events? I might show him where things are in the kitchen. One man isn't going to eat all that much."

"That's fine, Sylvie. The kitchen is yours, you know that. You and Jeff are dealing with the budgets for these events, so as long as you know what you're doing, I'm fine with it."

"Thanks. I'm going back to work. I think poor Hannah was a little worried about us. Between you asking me about Doc Ogden and my asking you about Eliseo, she probably thinks we hate each other now. I should fix that."

"Love you, Sylvie. You're awesome," Polly said.

Sylvie walked out the door, stopped herself with a hand on the door frame, "Love you too Polly. I'm glad you're my friend. I can't imagine how boring my life would be right now. I love seeing people when they come into the grocery store, but I knew that I needed something more. You helped me find it. So, ... yeah. Thank you."

"You'd have figured something out. You're pretty smart." Polly winked at her friend, who quickly left the office.

She grabbed her keys and phone and poked her head in Jeff's office, "I'm going to be gone for a while. Do you need anything from me?"

"Are you alright? You looked pretty pissed."

"I'm fine. I hate realizing that there are some things about people I can't change or fix. Do you have everything ready to go for this big shindig today?"

"They're coming in at noon to start decorating. Until then everything will be fine, but after that, if I were you, I'd stay far, far away from the auditorium."

"Say, does Eliseo have a phone?" she asked.

"I don't think so, why?"

"Get another phone for Sycamore House and give it to him. If he stays, great, it's his, but if he leaves, stick it in a drawer until we get another custodian. Don't you think we should be able to reach him?"

Jeff smiled and nodded. "That's a good idea. I'll take care of it."

She went outside, got in her truck and pulled out of the

parking lot. It was a beautiful Saturday and she needed to be out in it. She drove through Bellingwood, not sure where she was going. At some point, she would end up at Andy's house, but not yet. She pulled into a parking space down town and texted Andy, "Would you and Beryl like me to bring something fun for lunch?"

"Lydia has already taken care of it. There's plenty. Come over any time," Andy texted back.

She heard sirens and in her rear view mirror, she saw two Bellingwood police cars fly down Elm Street. Doing something she hadn't done since she was in high school, she backed out of the parking space, went around the block and followed them. They made a couple of turns and before she knew it, they had stopped in front of Harry Bern's empty house. She hung back and watched as Ken Wallers and another young man she didn't know got out of their cars. They had pulled their weapons and were approaching the house.

Polly knew she shouldn't be there, but couldn't leave now. She watched Ken open the screen door and the other man go around to the back of the house. Ken put his hand on the door and it pushed open. He entered the house and she had no idea what happened next, so she called Lydia.

"Do you have your scanner on?" she asked.

"I'm over at Andy's," Lydia said. "Is something happening?"

"Of course. I knew that. Well, I'm a little embarrassed to admit it, but I followed Ken Wallers over to Harry Bern's house and he and another patrolman went in with their guns drawn."

"Don't you go near them!"

"I'm not. I'm not! But, if you were home and heard what was going on, I was hoping you would tell me."

"Polly get yourself away from there. I'm not hanging up until I hear you put that truck in drive and leave."

Polly sighed, "I never get to have any fun. Alright. I'm leaving."

She parked behind Lydia's Jeep and after knocking on the front door, opened it and said, "Can I come in?"

Andy rushed out of the kitchen and held the door open, "Of course. You don't have to ask. Just come in!"

"How's the patient today?" Polly asked.

"See for yourself," Andy said and gestured toward the sofa. Beryl was perched on her left hip and Polly watched as she squirmed back and forth, wriggling around.

"Has she been like this all morning?"

"Crap. No. She was fine until just this moment." Andy stood in front of Beryl, "What's wrong, honey? Can I help?"

"Good god, woman. I'm just trying to get comfortable. I think I can figure it out on my own."

"Do you need another painkiller?"

"Get away from me you mother hen. I'm fine." Beryl settled down and breathed a sigh of relief. "There. I needed to adjust a few things."

"Are you sure you don't need anything?"

Beryl looked around Andy at Polly, "Tell me the truth. Do I look like I'm going to die any time soon?"

Polly giggled and said, "I don't think so, but then I don't have all the facts."

"My dearest friend here is acting like I have a death mark hanging over my head and if she doesn't take care of every little issue for me, I will fall into some bleak stupor and drift away from the world."

Polly bit her lip to keep from laughing.

"Fine, you old biddy. You're much less sure of yourself when there's no audience. If you need something from me, tell me. Otherwise, you're on your own."

Andy stalked out to the kitchen.

Beryl whispered, "She doesn't mean it. She'll be back in five minutes to make sure I'm still alive. Trust me."

Polly shook her head and sat down in the chair next to Beryl. "Are you feeling more normal now that you've slept in a real bed?"

"I slept all night! At least Andy isn't in every two hours to take my blood pressure and jam a thermometer in my mouth. And there isn't any beeping and whirring either."

"That's so great. We're glad you're back. Sylvie says she's

stopping by tomorrow with goodies."

Lydia came in to the living room carrying a tray filled with sandwiches and fruit. She set them down on the coffee table. Andy followed with another tray which contained a pitcher of tea and glasses filled to the brim with ice.

"Why were you following the police chief this morning, Polly?" Lydia asked.

"Because I was out driving around and I didn't have anything better to do," Polly said.

"You can get yourself in trouble doing stuff like that."

"I can get myself in trouble opening up an employee's door," Polly lamented. "I don't even have to work at it and trouble gets in my way."

Beryl snickered. "Maybe the people around Bellingwood will start dumping their bodies on your front lawn because they know you'll deal with them."

"Don't even say that!" Polly cried. She looked up and said, "You didn't hear that. She didn't mean it." She turned to her friends and said, "That was me talking to the universe. Just in case."

They laughed and Polly asked, "So, Lydia, have you heard anything about the thefts happening around town?"

Lydia nodded. "Aaron is working with Ken. He's pretty sure it is someone from the area because they know the farmers' habits and schedules."

"Mark told me they broke into one of those truck toolboxes. I thought those were pretty sturdy."

"They wanted in badly enough to do some serious damage. Sam had some expensive tools in there. You're going to keep your barn locked up, right?"

"I don't have anything out there that isn't easily replaceable, so I'm not too worried, but yes, we'll make sure things are locked. Good heavens, I quit worrying about locking my truck when I moved back to Iowa. I'm not happy that people are forcing me to think about that again."

"What is the world coming to," Beryl asked, "when a little town like Bellingwood has to worry about locking things up because bad boys are trying to make an easy buck?"

"That's the thing," Andy said. "This can't be easy for them. They're expending as much time and effort trying to pull off these thefts as they would if they got a regular job. They're fools."

They talked a little longer about the thefts and Polly finally said, "I should get back to Sycamore House. I want to make sure they don't need any extra help for this big wedding reception."

"Who is getting married?" Andy asked.

"It's a couple from Ogden; I don't know their names."

"Oh," Andy replied. "I hadn't heard of anyone getting married in town this weekend. Do you want to take a sandwich or anything back with you?"

"I'm good. Sylvie is making a spread and I can always snitch from that if I get hungry this afternoon. Love you guys!"

She hugged everyone and whispered to Beryl, "Be nice to her. You know you love her."

Beryl squeezed her back and released her. "I'll be good," she said.

Polly drove back to Sycamore House and smiled as she saw the parking lot begin to fill up. A young couple was starting their life together today and they had chosen her home as the location of the celebration. A year ago, she never would have imagined her life looked like this. Change was good.

CHAPTER TWELVE

"Runners and bystanders have been hurt. Have you seen any of this?" Jeff walked into Polly's office Monday morning.

"No, what's up?"

"There were two explosions at the end of the Boston Marathon. I thought you'd want to know."

Polly didn't say anything. She couldn't say anything. All she could do was stare at him and think about her friends. Drea ran the marathon every year and her brothers always worked security. She couldn't even put names to all of the people she knew who were part of the activities at the Marathon. Last year she had taken the day off and had been there at the end to cheer for Drea as she finished.

"You know a lot of people involved in this, don't you?"

Polly nodded. She was certain that if she opened her mouth, she would vomit, so she sat still.

Jeff went to the water cooler and came back with a cup of water. He put it down in front of her. "You've gone pale. Drink this."

She shook her head and continued to stare into space, thinking about more and more people she knew who were involved. Jeff stepped around the desk to stand beside her and placed his hand on her shoulder. "I'm sorry, Polly. What can I do?"

Polly's body wouldn't move. Finally she shook herself and said, "Are you sure?"

"Do you want to see it online or would you like to go into the conference room and turn on the news?"

"No, I can't watch this on television," she said. "That would be too much. I'll read it here."

She saw that she had received email and opened the message from Sal Kahane.

"Hi Sweetie.

Have you seen the news? Copley Square is a mess. We're all pretty distraught here. Dave's brother was at the finish line and we haven't heard anything from him yet. No one knows anything and we're waiting for another one to explode. I don't even know what to think.

I'm still leaving in the morning as long as the airports are open. I figure it is safer to be in Iowa right now than anywhere else in the world, so tell me you're going to take good care of me, alright?

I can't wait to see you,
Sal"

Polly emailed right back,

"I just found out. Oh my god! Why would someone do this? It's supposed to be a fun event!

I'm glad you're still coming out. I suppose phones are down in the city with all of the runners and people trying to contact their families. Call me tomorrow morning when you hit Des Moines so I can hear your voice.

Love you girl,
Polly"

Jeff had taken a seat across from her and was watching her with a frown creasing his forehead.

"Is Sal still coming to Iowa?" he asked.

"She is. I'm glad. What a strange week for it, but I'll be glad to spend some time with her after this." Polly clicked on a new website to see pictures of people with blood all over them. She clicked through a few of the photographs and shook her head at the carnage.

"Who would do something like this?" she asked Jeff. "And why? I don't understand what makes someone think this is the way to get attention."

"I don't have any smart answers for you, Polly. The world is made up of both good and bad people and today a bad person hurt your city."

Polly went back to email and sent one off to Drea asking her to send a message as soon as she could and tell her what was happening with the people she knew.

Her phone buzzed with a text from Lydia, *"Are you alright? I saw the news and thought of you. I'm sure you have friends involved in the Marathon. Just know we're thinking of you."*

"Thanks," Polly replied and set her phone down on the desk.

She said, "I could obsess about this all day, but they're doing what they have to do out there and I'm not going to know anything more about my friends by watching the media flail about trying to break news that isn't real. Talk to me about something else."

"Are you sure?"

"Yes," she said adamantly. "I can't handle this."

"The wedding Saturday evening was a huge success. Sylvie is starting to make a name for herself. I think she got a couple of catering jobs from it."

"Really? That's awesome! Oh, she's going to be great at this."

"And we had a mom ask about a sixteenth birthday party in the classrooms. Then she asked if the kids could ride the horses. I told her that wasn't probably a good idea since they were still recuperating from neglect. Was I right?"

"You were absolutely right. I don't want to subject them to anything like that for a long time. As a matter of fact, I don't want to be subjected to that either." Polly rolled her head around on her neck and said, "I'm glad you're managing it."

"There will only be fifteen or twenty kids there. Sylvie is going to do the food for it, too. Some of the kids work here as waiters and waitresses for events and thought they could use all of those rooms for different things for the party. I think it's a great idea."

"Well, at least we won't have bouncy houses littering the lawn if they're in high school."

Jeff laughed, "Not a big fan of little kids' events, are you?"

"Every time I see one of those, it occurs to me there isn't enough bleach in the world to get them clean to the point I'd want any child I cared about in them."

"Well, that eliminates the kid's carnival I was planning for August," he laughed and pulled out his tablet.

"No!" Polly exclaimed. "I'm sorry. It's my own phobia. If you have something in the works, don't let me stop you."

"I was only kidding. There's no carnival. It's not a bad idea, but the city brings one in every year for Bellingwood Days in July."

"I missed that last summer," Polly said. "It's a pretty big deal, isn't it?"

"It is. There's a big parade and they even name a Queen. They have a street dance on Saturday night downtown and all sorts of exhibitions and contests are spread out in the buildings around town."

"We should figure out how to be a part of the festivities," she said. "Is Sycamore House open that weekend or do we have weddings scheduled?"

"No, I was smart enough to check the city's calendar and block out dates. I've left that weekend open. So, what are you thinking?"

"We've got this big auditorium and we've got Sylvie. Surely we can come up with something."

"I know Cy would love to use the auditorium on Saturday for the quilt show," he grinned.

"Cy?" Polly asked.

"Cy Leverton. He's the Chamber President and owns the General Store."

"Good heavens, you know more people in town than I do!"

Polly laughed.

"It's my job," he said. "So, do you remember all of those pie plates we got for the hoe-down?"

Polly nodded.

"What if we had a pie contest on Sunday and combined it with an old-fashioned ice cream social?"

"That's a great idea!" Polly exclaimed. "But, I can't believe they don't already have something like that going on."

"I checked. No problem. We could put the pie plates out at a few different locations. People could buy them for a dollar and that is their registration fee. All of the money will go into the prize fund. We can have door prizes and then I'll talk to Cy about bringing in enough ice cream for the social."

"You've given this a little thought, haven't you?"

"Like I said," he replied. "It's my job."

"Well, you are doing it very well," Polly smiled. "Thank you. I'd hate doing this without you."

Jeff smirked at her, "Just remember that when I ask for a raise."

"Uh huh," she said. "Got it."

Polly watched him make a few notes in his tablet, then asked, "How is Eliseo doing?"

"Polly, he's only been here for two days and I'm totally in love with the guy."

"Stop it," she smirked.

"Well, not like that," he laughed. "But, he's amazing. He had the auditorium set up and ready long before the family got here and then he was invisible. Things were cleaned up as the evening progressed and even I didn't see it happening. Within an hour after the last person had gone home, the place was ready to shut down. I tried to tell him that when he worked weekend weddings, he could take a day off during the week, but he said he had no place else to be and since there was plenty to do around here to get caught back up, he'd just work."

"He's been helping me in the mornings with the horses," she said. "It annoyed me on Saturday, but when he was there again yesterday, I decided that I didn't need to feel threatened. The horses love him and for that matter, so does the stupid dog."

Jeff laughed. "Sometimes animals know people better than we do, I guess. He's cleaning out the front room upstairs and will have it ready for your friend before she gets here."

"Thanks," Polly said, her eye drawn back to the news channel on the computer. She refreshed the window and sighed as they updated the number of wounded.

"It keeps getting worse, Jeff. They're talking about people losing limbs. What in the hell happened out there?"

"Come on," he said. "Let's go outside and you can talk to your horses. They'll take your mind off this."

Polly snagged a jacket off the back of her chair. "That's a good idea. But wait, you're going out to talk to the horses with me?"

"No, I'm going to walk you to the side door and watch as you prance your pretty little fanny down to the barn."

"You're a good friend, Jeff, even if you don't like my animals."

"I like your animals just fine, but I have a commitment to these leather shoes and I'm going to keep it."

It was a rainy, cold, miserable day. Polly had hoped it would clear up so she could let the horses out into the pasture for a while. Maybe she would put them out anyway.

"Good afternoon my lovelies," she called as she went into the barn. She went back to the tack room to grab a bag of treats. Stopping first at Nan's stall, she opened it and dropped the treat into her feed dish. "Are you ready for some pasture time? I know it's miserable out there, but if you want to go out, I'll clean you up when you come back. I promise." Polly opened the outside door and went back into the barn. She stopped in at each horse's stall with a treat and an open door. None of them galloped out to the pasture, but they all found their way to the hay piles. She stood and watched them for a while and returned to the barn. Picking up the bag of treats, she took it back to the tack room. She put it on its shelf and then peered at the bales of hay. Something blue caught her eye in between a couple of bales. She pulled it out and saw that it was a small blanket. Nothing she'd ever seen before. Where would it have come from?

Polly had the blanket in her hand when she walked out into the alley of the barn. She looked up when she heard footsteps and saw Eliseo approaching her.

He glanced at what she was holding, then asked, "Is there anything I can help you with, Miss Giller?"

"No, I needed to spend a few minutes with the horses to settle my mind down and figured they might want some time outside even though it's so ugly out there. I don't want to hang out in my office and watch the news and this is a good place to be."

"Those big beasts will take the hurts away, won't they," he said.

The two of them walked back outside. The horses had stayed under the overhang and out of the cold rain. Demi and Nat were munching hay together and Polly imagined the two of them talking to each other about the crazy woman who owned them now. She wondered if they ever thought about their old life or worried they might have to return to it. What did horses think about anyway?

"I wonder that myself, sometimes," Eliseo said.

"What? Did I say that out loud?"

He chuckled. "You might have. Either that or you were thinking very loud thoughts."

"Do you think they wonder about us?"

"I suppose they might. But, I don't think they have great big thoughts all the time. They focus on the immediate a lot better than we do. If their needs are met and they feel safe, they're pretty happy."

"That's the way most of us feel until we start thinking too hard about it," she said.

"Mazlow's hierarchy of needs, you know," he responded.

Polly looked sideways at him, "Not too many people talk to me about that," she giggled.

"I had a lot of time by myself when I was in the hospital after this happened," he gestured at his torso. "They brought me a catalog for books on tape and at least I was able to have something going into my mind all the time. I learned the weirdest stuff in there. For instance, did you know that the giraffe is considered by Jews to be kosher? That's one of those weird little things that got in my brain and I've never been able to forget it. Why would anyone want to know if a giraffe is kosher?"

Polly laughed. "I can't imagine. My friend, Sal Kahane, is coming next week. I'll be sure to ask her if she worries about going on a safari and keeping kosher. But, maybe if they're out in the desert and they need to eat, it's a good thing to know."

"She's orthodox?"

"Oh no, she's not religious at all, but I like to keep her on her toes. So what else did you listen to while you were there?"

"I got tired of fiction. After a while, I'd listened to all the classics and I started begging for something other than stories to pass my time. I wasn't much for philosophy. A little Kant goes a long way. The worst thing about listening to that was the fact that I didn't have anyone to talk to about it."

"You didn't have any visitors?"

"Not really. A few guys from my unit showed up every once in a while, but I was there by myself most of the time. I think it bothered them to see me in such a mess and realize it could have been them. Hell, I was glad it was me and not them. A couple of those boys had families and this isn't anything you want to take home to your children. They got home safely and their kids got a chance to grow up with a dad who looked normal when he took them to their soccer games."

"If you had kids, Eliseo, they would love you no matter what. You have to know that."

"It's a pretty thought, Polly. There were a lot of guys whose families quit coming to see them because it was too awful to deal with their injuries. You can hardly blame them. The poor girl goes into marriage with her knight in shining armor and before they've had a chance to get to know each other, he's an entirely different man both inside and out. Injuries like this change a person and sometimes the stuff that goes on inside your head doesn't make you easy to be with."

"You do pretty well."

"You've only known me for a few days, twenty years after it all happened. I've had a lot of time to work on getting my head together, but I still have some rough times. I try to know when they're coming and get myself out of the way."

"How bad is it for you?"

"Most of the time I get depressed and angry. I've never gotten violent. At least that didn't change in me. But, I can't stand to be around people when I'm like that. Animals are easy. They don't judge you."

Polly reached out and put her hand on his forearm. "Just let us know when you're heading down that path, okay? If we know, we'll let you do whatever you have to do to pull out of it. And there are some great big animals around here who like you a lot."

He laid his scarred hand on top of hers. "I'll try. I will. It doesn't happen as often anymore."

"That's all I can ask. So, will you tell me why you came to Bellingwood?"

He moved away from her. He ducked into the barn and she wondered where he had gone and if she had pushed too hard. Pretty soon though, he came back with a couple of brushes and handed one to her. He began brushing Demi down, so she joined him and started on Nat's neck, if only to keep the connection going between them.

"I thought I knew someone here. An old war buddy. I figured I'd ask him to put me up for a while until I found a job and could get my own place."

He stopped moving and looked at Polly, then resumed brushing. "But, he isn't here any longer, so I moved up the agenda a little faster. I appreciate you giving me this job."

Polly didn't say anything. She didn't want to stop him, but he had ceased talking so she prodded once more, "How long ago did your buddy leave town?"

Eliseo shrugged, "Not long, I guess. He didn't know I was coming. It was just luck that I found out he lived here. He certainly hadn't told any of us where he was going."

"Us? Us who?" Polly asked, trying to keep the conversation moving along.

"Guys from the unit. When everyone finally returned to the States, some of us kept in touch, but this friend ducked out of any reunions we had. You know, we met up every couple of years somewhere in the country. He never came. That was weird too. He kept in touch on the message boards but never told us where he was living and he didn't express an interest in seeing us again."

"That sounds odd. How did you find out he was in Bellingwood?"

"It became a game for some of them. They tried to interpret what he said and decipher his location over the years. They finally figured out that he was moving around the country a lot, so it became even more of a game."

"Do you think he knew they were looking for him? Was he playing their game?"

"I'm sure he did. They weren't quiet about it, but most of their conversations about tracking him down were through emails, not on the boards."

"So, did they ever find him?"

"Well, over the years, they thought they had him pinned down several times."

Polly looked shocked at his choice of words.

"Not literally," he said. "Just figuratively. However, a couple of them would travel to look for him and every single time, he had moved on, so the game continued. I wouldn't be surprised if he had as much fun as they did, dropping obscure hints and then seeing if they would figure it out."

"So, this time you thought you would be the one to look for him?"

"Not as part of the game, no. I decided I was tired of living in Texas, so I kept an eye on the boards to see if there was anyone living someplace interesting. One day, someone said something about a little town in the middle of Iowa; wondering if our buddy was there or not. I didn't say a word, packed up and came north. None of them knew about my plans. I haven't been on the boards in a while, so I'm not even sure if they know I've moved on."

"This sounds pretty strange," Polly commented.

"I suppose it does. It was mostly just entertainment." He patted Daisy and said, "I don't think the horses want to play in the rain. Should we take them back in to the barn? Jason and I will get them ready for the night later on."

While they'd been talking, he had finished brushing both Demi and Daisy down and was leading them in to their stalls.

"Sure," she said. "I suppose that's a good idea." Nat followed her in and she rubbed his nose before closing the stall door. "Thanks, I needed this," she whispered to him.

"I'll bring Nan in. You go on up and get warm and send Jason out when he's ready."

CHAPTER THIRTEEN

Edging her way past a large group of people waiting to be seated, Polly went to the bar to place a takeout order. Davey's was busier than she'd ever seen it. The bartender was flummoxed as well, but happy to watch his tip jar fill. Beryl had announced she was desperate for one of Davey's steaks, so they all agreed to meet for lunch at Andy's. Sylvie even had time to join them.

Polly tried not to stare at the people around the room, so when her eyes landed on Ken Wallers and Aaron Merritt tucked into a table in the back, discussing something pretty intensely, she put a smile on and walked over to greet them.

"Hi there. Are you keeping Bellingwood safe today?"

Both men stood up to shake her hand and she said, "No, please. Sit down and eat. I'm waiting for my lunch order. Gotta get Beryl back to normal and today she thinks steak will help."

They returned to their seats and Aaron pulled a chair from the table behind him for her.

"How is she doing?" Ken asked.

"She's doing well. She's walking more easily every day and I believe that the doctors in Des Moines were quite ready to transfer all of her records back to Doctor McKay here in town. I think everyone hopes he'll tell her she is fine to live on her own after she sees him on Friday."

Polly looked at Ken Wallers, "So, what was up at Harry Bern's house on Saturday?"

He laughed. "I thought that was you following me, but I hoped you had enough sense to stay away."

"Lydia yelled at me and told me to leave."

Aaron grinned and shook his head. "You have to be in the middle of it, don't you, Polly!"

"Whatever," she laughed. "So, what's up?"

"There was a break-in overnight. We hadn't put anything back from the day he was killed, and whoever broke in did another very thorough job of tossing the place. They tore apart walls and ripped up floorboards. They even pulled the ceiling down in the bedroom."

"How did you find out about it?"

"Whoever was in there took their time, thinking no one would notice. Honestly, no one did until that morning. Bill Wells was working in his garage and when he couldn't identify the sounds he was hearing, he realized they were coming from an empty house and called me."

"Do you think this is related to those farm thefts happening around the area?" Polly prodded.

The county sheriff and Bellingwood police chief looked at each other and smiled.

"What?" she demanded.

"Nothing," Aaron remarked. "No. We don't believe they're connected."

Polly continued to look back and forth between the two of them, not saying a word.

Aaron grinned, "You do know that we're the ones who use the silent treatment on our witnesses to wait them out, right, Polly? It won't work on me."

"So you won't tell me why you believe these instances are separate?" she asked.

"It's not a big secret," Ken responded. "Whoever tore the house apart was looking for something specific. The farm thefts are snatch and grab. And besides, Aaron here has to track those down and I'm working on the murder and subsequent break-in at Harry Bern's home."

"Because we never want to get county and city law enforcement working together. It would create a black hole," Aaron laughed.

"Do you know anything more about Harry? What were they looking for?"

"Whatever it was, they didn't find it."

"Do you think whoever did it is still in town?" she asked.

"I wouldn't be surprised. But, you never know."

"You aren't going to tell me anything, are you?" Polly said, frowning at the two of them. "Like who Harry Bern really was?"

"Oh, he was Harry Bern, alright. Born and raised in Centralia, Illinois. Parents are gone, one sibling who can't be found and no other immediate family. He served in the Army and was in the Middle East during Desert Storm. After that, his life gets a little murky. Is that enough for you?" Ken asked her.

She looked back and forth between the two of them. "Is that all you are going to give me?"

"Probably," Aaron grinned.

"Then it will have to be enough." She looked at Aaron. "You know, it's a good thing this isn't your investigation or I'd sic your wife on you."

"I'm absolutely confident of that," he affirmed. "The rest of us aren't safe when you are all together in one room."

A waitress approached with two shopping bags, "Here is your order, Miss Giller. Do you need any help with it?"

"Thanks, I've got it," Polly said.

The waitress smiled, left the table and Polly said, "Well, it's been nice seeing you both. I'll say thank you for the information you gave me and then wait until I get to my truck before I snarl at the information you didn't."

"See you later, Polly," Aaron replied.

"Tell Miz Watson to take care," Ken said as she nodded and left the restaurant.

Everyone was already at Andy's when Polly finally arrived and she walked in as Sylvie was setting up the last TV tray. Glasses, plates, silverware and drinks were set out on the dining room table and Lydia took one of the bags from Polly's hand.

"Beryl says she's going to starve to death if we don't feed her soon," Lydia laughed. "I told her she'd already put on five pounds with Andy feeding her all day long."

"Hey!" Beryl called from the sofa. "I have to get back in fighting shape after that awful week in the hospital. Those people may think they know nutrition, but they don't know what my heart likes. Did you bring steak?"

"I did. Davey said he would cook it just the way you like it," Polly said.

"That's good. My teeth feel the need for carnivorous activity. Grrr," she growled.

"So you're feeling better?" Polly asked.

"I'm feeling like a rock star. This girl has been pampering me, cleaning my wounds, and treating me like a princess. Let me tell you, if a person has to get sick, this is the place to recuperate."

Polly laughed. "I don't know whether I'd be able to choose between Andy and Lydia."

"Hah. I notice you didn't include me in your list of caregivers," Beryl huffed.

"Isn't that interesting?" Polly remarked. "I didn't, now did I? Tell me, would you be a good caregiver?"

"I'd get you drunk enough to pass out and then keep you that way until all of your symptoms cleared up. How's that?"

"Exactly what I would expect."

Andy had taken the other bag of food and pointed to a chair, so Polly obediently sat down.

"Tell me the truth. How are you feeling?" Polly asked.

Beryl smiled, "I feel pretty good. Andy's been great about caring for my legs and I suspect they'll be fine. She told me that the owie on the back of my head is healing up and the big one on my butt looks better than it should. I have a bunch of bandages on my back that she assures me are covering practically nothing and those will be in good shape before we see the doctor on Friday."

"Your face looks a lot better today!" Polly said, "At least you no longer look like you've been beaten by an angry gorilla."

Beryl poked at her cheekbone. "It still hurts a little when I do that, but Lydia told me not to do that."

Sylvie poked her head out and asked, "What would you girls like to drink?"

Polly jumped up and said, "I can get my own drink. You don't need to wait on me."

Beryl peered at her through slitted eyes, "Sit down and hush. Have you learned nothing? If Lydia and Andy don't get an opportunity to take care of you, they'll find ways. Even if they have to hurl curses at your water heater."

"I'd like water, please," Polly said to Sylvie, "and thank you."

"When do I get to have alcohol again?" Beryl called out to the dining room.

Andy stepped in, "Do you want some wine with your lunch? You aren't taking pain killers any more except at night. I've got a nice red in the cabinet."

Beryl's eyes filled, "That would be great. It's nice to feel normal again." She reached up and took Andy's hand, "I'll never be able to tell you how much this means to me."

Polly watched the two friends and felt tears at the back of her own eyes. It hit her again how lucky they had all been that the damage to Beryl was so minimal. There would be a couple of ugly weeks in everyone's memories, but hopefully they would be ameliorated by the love surrounding her.

In a few moments, the three women came out from the dining room in a procession. Sylvie carried two white linen napkins, snapped the first open and laid it across the table in front of Beryl, then snapped the other open and put it in the woman's lap. She took silverware off the tray Lydia was carrying and placed it on the table, followed by the plate with Beryl's meal. She and Lydia returned to the dining room, giggling, while Andy set the glass of wine on the table and bowing, turned and walked away.

In moments, they returned to do the same for Polly.

"What did I do to deserve such treatment?" Polly asked.

"We needed an audience," Sylvie laughed, "and since you paid for this, you deserve it!"

They were soon gathered around, laughing and eating.

"How is your Marilyn doing?" Andy asked Lydia. The baby's arrival date was in June and since Marilyn had a little difficulty with morning sickness, Lydia had been fluttering back and forth to Dayton as often as possible to spend time with the twins so their mama could rest.

"She's feeling so much better these days," Lydia said. "I think she is finally happy to be pregnant again. But, I have more news! Jill is pregnant and it looks like I might get a Christmas baby in the family."

Polly smiled, "Don't they live in Kansas City?"

"It's only three and a half hours to their house," Lydia said. "Aaron is going to just have to make sure I have good tires on the Jeep, because I'll be hitting the road as often as possible."

Polly listened as they talked about babies and children. That wasn't something she had ever given much thought to doing. Her friend, Bunny, could hardly wait to have babies and every time she saw one, she oohed and cooed. Polly liked kids when they got to be about six years old and were interesting. Infants were just strange little alien things that turned grown women into crazy people as far as she was concerned.

It had occurred to her several times over the last few years that she wasn't at all interested in being a mommy. Maybe someday, she'd be a mom either as a foster parent or through adoption, but there were plenty of women out there giving birth, she didn't need to join the ranks.

She wondered what Henry would say to that. What if he wanted children? Joey, Polly's crazy, ex-boyfriend who kidnapped her, had insisted he wanted children of his own. Having his own genetic material floating around in some child was important to him. She'd dodged a bullet there. That was some corrupt DNA. Henry hadn't seemed terribly upset when she talked about waving Lydia and Andy off regarding children. What was she even thinking though? They weren't talking about marriage and she didn't need to be thinking those things out loud in her head. "Forget it," she said in her head. "I didn't mean anything by it."

Would he laugh at her having these crazy thoughts or would he get all serious with her and expect them to talk about the future of their relationship. Good heavens, they'd only been dating each other for four months and he'd been in Arizona with his parents for two of those. Why would anyone think that it was time to push their relationship along any faster?

Wait. She was the only one thinking about this. It was all happening in her head. No one was pushing her, especially Henry. He'd been wonderful about everything. Come to think of it, she was pretty lucky. Mary Shore, the woman who had cared for her after Polly's mother died, would tell her that she didn't need to rush anything and she didn't need to feel any pressure from her friends when it came to making a decision, especially one that would change her life. Mary would have liked Henry. Polly imagined all of her family: Mary and her husband, Sylvester, and Polly's dad sitting around the table meeting Henry for the first time. He would have fit right in. Sylvester was a quiet man who worked hard for Polly's dad. Mary had quit a job in a local dentist's office to come care for Polly. She loved to laugh and when the men were exhausted from a long day on the farm, she steered the conversation so Polly was able to connect with her dad and learn about the things he loved.

"Are you here with us, Polly?" Lydia asked.

"I'm sorry," she said. "I was thinking about children, then I started thinking about Mary and my dad. Did I miss anything important?"

"Well, other than the fact that Sylvie is eloping and Andy is pregnant, no I think you're fine," Beryl laughed.

"You're kidding, right?" She looked around the room and saw that everyone maintained a straight face as they stared at her.

"You're kidding, right?" Polly asked again, looking each of

them in the eye.

Finally Sylvie broke. "Oh, lordie, I hope so. I can't imagine what sort of man would convince me to run off and get married. I haven't met one in all these years and I don't intend to meet one now!"

Polly peered at Andy. "Are you pregnant? Because I'm calling the Associated Press in the morning if that's true."

"No, I'm pretty sure that if I were to get pregnant right now, there would be a lot of gynecologists out there trying to figure out what had just happened. And I don't like any of them well enough to spend that much time with them again," Andy laughed.

"Well, were you at least talking about Andy and Len Specek?" Polly pressed.

"Yeah," Beryl said. "I haven't seen hide nor hair of that man since I've been here. How have you been able to live without him all this time?"

"Will you please stop it!" Andy sputtered. "It's not that serious. We enjoy spending time together and he's nice."

"I think he's going to help Henry do some of the wood work in Beryl's studio," Polly said. "You know that means she will have access to him nearly every day for a month or so."

Andy rolled her eyes. "Oh kill me now," she said. "That's going to be a special kind of hell for me." She turned to Beryl, "Please tell me you won't torment him."

"I'll be as sweet as possible to that man. In fact, I'll be so sweet that you might even get jealous!"

Lydia laughed.

"Why are you laughing?" Beryl asked. "Don't you think Len could be interested in a woman like me?"

"You're a beautiful and wonderful woman, Beryl Watson, but that man would run far away before he even considered being interested in you. And anyway, I think he's so taken with our Andy that he wouldn't even notice you were flirting with him."

Beryl hung her head, "I've lost my touch. I'll turn into a dowdy old spinster and start collecting cats. No more life for me."

"Shall we apply for a room at the Senior Living Center for

you?" Andy asked.

"NO!" Lydia exclaimed. "Those poor people are not ready for Beryl. The women would all want to kill her and the men would run screaming from her."

"No one is ready for Beryl," Polly muttered.

"What did you say over there?" Beryl demanded. "Are you saying bad things about me?"

"I mentioned that no one is ever ready for you."

"You're right about that and I'm proud of it. It's much more fun to be a little unbelievable than to be boring."

Polly looked at the time. Somehow the lunch hour had turned into several hours and she needed to get back to Sycamore House.

"Sylvie! I need to get going or your boys will wonder where I am."

"I could pick them up at school and you wouldn't have to worry about them this afternoon."

"No way. I like having those boys there to help with my animals. Jason is turning into a wonderful stable hand and he's having fun working with Eliseo, too."

She stood up to take her dishes and silverware to the kitchen. Andy said, "Stop it. We'll take care of this. You girls go."

"Thank you so much for a wonderful time," Polly said, handing her dishes to Andy, "and Beryl, it's good to see you back to normal. I'm glad you are better." She bent over to hug her friend. "I love you!"

Beryl patted her on the back, "I love you too, girlie. Thank you for bringing me that steak today. That should give me enough strength to go to the bathroom by myself this evening."

"Stop it, you crazy woman," Andy said, coming back into the living room. "She's been going by herself all week long. I only had to pull her off the toilet once and that was only because she was dopey from drugs and started laughing so hard she couldn't move."

"Well, I looked at my scrawny legs, all red and gross looking and thought they looked like old chicken legs and not the good fatty part. It wasn't all that funny, but for some reason I lost control. I was just glad I was already sitting in a safe place to do that!"

Andy shook her head and walked both Polly and Sylvie to the door. "Thanks for coming over. She needed to see someone else's face. And thanks for bringing lunch, Polly."

Polly hugged her and poked her head back around the corner, "Bye Lydia. I'll talk to you later! Love you!"

"I love you too, girls! Be good!"

As they walked to their cars, Polly said to Sylvie, "You don't have to come to the school if you want some quiet time at home."

"Really? That would be awesome. I have some classwork I need to do. I'll come get the boys about five thirty, then."

Polly gave Sylvie a quick hug, jumped in her truck and drove home. She passed the boys who were running across the lawn toward the front door.

She parked the truck and called out, "Hello there!" then waited as they approached her. "Do you have any homework today?"

"I have another math test tomorrow," Jason said, "and I have to write a paper about Apollo 11 by Friday. Could I use your computer to look things up?"

"Sure," Polly said. "What about you, Andrew?"

"I only have spelling words to work on tonight. But, I think I know all of them."

"What was your favorite word in the list?" she asked.

"Wreckage. W r e c k a g e." he spelled. "I want to swim to the bottom of the ocean and find shipwrecks someday. That would be cool."

"Let's go upstairs and get you started on your homework. I might have made some brownies for you."

This was the age she enjoyed having kids around. Now, how could she make that happen without changing diapers along the way?

The animals were always happy to see the boys arrive and Andrew giggled every time Luke would weave around his feet, then flop down in front of him.

"He makes it hard for me to walk, Polly!" Andrew said as he

tried to get in the living room from the entryway.

"I know. He does the same thing to me when I try to go to the bathroom sometimes," Polly said. "What do you want to drink today with your brownies?"

"Milk, please," Jason said.

Andrew rolled his eyes and said, "Duh! Milk!"

She chuckled and pulled things out of the refrigerator.

"We didn't have time to talk about this yesterday," Polly said, "how did you enjoy your gaming night on Friday?"

"Oh, Polly it was the best!" Andrew replied. He had followed her into the kitchen and took the two glasses of milk she had poured back to the table. She grabbed up the container of brownies and some napkins and followed him.

"What about you, Jason? What did you play?"

"I started out playing Sword Lords, but after Mom took Andrew home, I went into the other room and played with Billy and his friends. That was cool."

"Your mom let you stay?" she asked. "How late?"

"She came back and got me at ten." He looked up at her and grinned. "That's an hour past my bed time, but she said it would be okay since it wasn't a school night."

Polly patted him on the back. "She's a pretty good mom, isn't she?"

"She took me to the General Store for ice cream," Andrew taunted, but not too exuberantly. Neither boy was sure who had the better evening. "But I fell asleep while we were watching The Avengers. That's okay, though. I've seen it three times already."

"Some of them wanted to go out and see the horses," Jason said quietly. "Especially after they saw me come back in with you. I hope it's alright that I asked Eliseo to take us down there."

"That's fine, Jason. You did exactly the right thing. What did everyone think?"

"One of the girls, Rachel, I think, wanted to know if you would teach her how to ride."

Polly chuckled. "I'm not very good, but maybe I'll talk to Doctor Ogden and Eliseo and see what they think later this spring.

I want the horses to have as much time as they need to heal up and get used to being around all of us. They were pretty solitary out on that farm, especially after Mr. Black died. But, I think they're doing a lot better. Those are pretty big horses, though. Can you imagine riding one of them?"

"I think it would be great!" Jason said. "I can't wait. When did you get those saddles in the tack room?"

"They came in last week. Mark says Daisy is going to be my best bet to start. Did you see I also got the harnesses to start exercising them as teams? Someday maybe Nat and Nan will pull a sleigh. How would that be?"

"Can I ride on the sleigh?" Andrew asked, bouncing in his chair.

Polly quietly pushed his milk glass back on the table away from the edge. "Absolutely. This summer, we'll start exercising them together as teams and before you know it, they'll be the talk of the town!"

"People already talk about them," Jason said. "My friends at school think it is so cool that I get to help you."

"I think it's pretty cool that you want to help," Polly remarked. "You work hard out there and I appreciate it. We'll see if Eliseo can teach us both how to ride those horses at the same time, how about that?"

"That would be awesome." Jason's face beamed. Before she knew it, he got out of his chair and hugged her, then he quickly backed up and sat down in his seat again.

Andrew had watched the entire interaction and said, "Mom says that in a year when she is done with school, we can get a real house. She told me I might get my own dog!"

"The dog would belong to the whole family," Jason protested.

"But I'll bet it will love me more," Andrew taunted.

"Will not!"

"Will so!"

"Will not!"

"Will so!"

"Whoa!" Polly said. They stopped and looked at her, both with sulky faces. "Well, that deteriorated in a hurry," she commented and standing up, picked up the empty glasses and brownies, then took them to the kitchen.

Behind her, she heard whispers.

"Will not!"

"Will so!"

"Stop." she scolded. They did so and looked at her, waiting for more to come. She shook her head. "Andrew, Obiwan hasn't been outside since this morning. Why don't you leash him up and walk him around for a while. Jason, we're going to the barn early. You can work on your homework after you've had some exercise. Give me a minute to get my clothes changed and we'll head out."

CHAPTER FOURTEEN

A cat purring on her chest brought Polly up out of a deep sleep.

"You know what time it is, don't you sweetie," she said to Luke, tumbling him off as she sat up. Today would be busy and she had to pick Sal up at the airport in Des Moines tonight. She pulled on jeans and a sweatshirt, shoved her feet into her boots and tied her hair into a ponytail.

"Come on, Obiwan. We're gonna have a great day!"

She and Eliseo had settled into an easy relationship in the barn. Once she decided there was no reason to be envious of his knowledge about horses, she stopped feeling like she needed to measure up to some unwritten skill set and they both relaxed. He let her have all the freedom she needed with the horses and only stepped in to make things easier for her.

Obiwan followed her to the first gate and waited as she unlatched it and headed for the barn. She pulled the door open and saw Eliseo walking toward Demi's stall with his breakfast.

"Good morning!" she said.

"You're up early today."

"I have a lot going on and since I couldn't sleep any longer, I thought I'd get started. I'll begin in Nan's stall, alright?"

"I can do that if you'd like to finish feeding Demi and Daisy. I don't mind the work."

"Twist my arm," she replied, as she took the bucket from him and opened the door to enter Demi's space.

"Good morning, sweet boy," she said and poured the feed for him. She took care of Daisy and grabbed another rake. Demi was quite polite and allowed her to work around him as he ate his breakfast. Soon everyone was fed and heading out of the barn. She and Eliseo finished cleaning up and he hauled a bale of hay outside and broke it up for the horses.

"Miss Giller," he said, stopping her as she walked back to the feed room to get another bale.

"Yes?"

"There isn't much going on here today and I need to take care of a couple of things. Would it be alright if I took the day off?"

"That would be fine, Eliseo. Just let Jeff know that you're going to be off-site, okay?"

"I texted him late last night and he asked me to tell you this morning."

"Then, we're cool. Thanks for helping with the horses, though. Jason and I will take care of them this evening."

"Thank you. I'll be sure to be here tomorrow morning, but I appreciate not having to hurry back this afternoon."

"I hope you have a good day," Polly said.

"It will be fine. Thanks again."

Wednesday was generally quiet around Sycamore House and Polly had managed to schedule her workouts with the horses so that even they were free today. Jeff had begun coming in late on Wednesdays and usually only spent a few hours to ensure their guests were cared for. Sometimes Sylvie would show up in the afternoons to plan for wedding receptions, but otherwise there wasn't much to do.

This morning Polly wanted to head over to Beryl's studio to see how things were coming along. Henry would be at Sycamore House tomorrow to get started on the garage, but today, he was either at his workshop building cabinets, or supervising reconstruction. She thought she'd try the studio first.

Obiwan wasn't thrilled to have to go inside early, he never was, but they got upstairs and she fed him and the cats, then took a shower and dressed for the day.

When she pulled up in front of Beryl's house, there were several vehicles already there, including Doug's Grand Am. That made her smile. She didn't know why she liked him and his friend Billy as much as she did, but those boys had been with her from the beginning and had stayed at Sycamore House to protect her from the boogie man several times.

Their boss, Jerry Allen, passed her as she made her way around the house to the studio.

"Good morning, Polly! Are you here to check on the boys?"

"Should I be?" she asked.

"Well, I think they might always need a little checking. We're only here for a couple of hours this morning and I think we'll have everything wired and ready to go. I believe Henry has drywallers scheduled for this afternoon. It's going to come back together!"

"Fantastic!"

She walked on around back and was stopped again by a man she didn't recognize.

"Are you Polly Giller?" he asked.

"Yes, I am," she said and put her hand out to shake his, "You are?"

"I'm Larry Storey. I live next door. We had some damage from the explosion and I need to make sure it gets paid for. When will Ms. Watson be back?"

"She should be back this weekend. Have you contacted your insurance agent?"

"I'm not contacting my insurance agent. She is responsible for this mess."

"If you contact them, I'm sure they will work things out with hers."

"I don't want my rates to go up because of this."

Polly looked at him and took a deep breath. "I'm sure that Beryl would want everything to be taken care of. Who is your agent?"

"Well, it's Mr. Conyers downtown."

"Why don't you give him a call? He will handle it and make sure you are satisfied with the outcome. That's probably why you work with him, isn't it?"

"I suppose so. How long are you going to be working back here? Everyone is making quite a racket and there's a lot of traffic. This has always been a quiet street."

"Has anyone started making noise before eight thirty in the morning or after five o'clock in the afternoon? Because if they have, I will be glad to change their hours," Polly calmly replied.

"Well, no. It's just that they're tying up traffic."

Polly laughed to herself. There were probably only four or five cars that ever traveled the street in front of these homes and right now, most of the vehicles were in Beryl's driveway and in front of her house. The poor man obviously needed someone to pay attention to the fact that he'd been involved in the explosion, no matter how minor that involvement had been.

"I'm sorry if they are making things difficult for you. The worst of it should be over this week. Would you like to come in and see what they're doing today?"

He hesitated and then nodded, following her to the studio.

Doug and Billy glanced at her as she walked in.

"Hey Polly!" Doug said. "What's up?" He was pulling cord through the open studs while Billy was working on an outside wall.

"This is Mr. Storey from next door. I wanted to show him what we were doing in here. He had some damage from the explosion, too."

"Oh, that had to have been scary!" Billy said. "Can you imagine having that thing blow up and fling shrapnel at you? Poor Miz Watson. You never expect your appliances to go all insane on you! Is she doing alright, Polly?"

"Thanks for asking, Billy," Polly said, trying hard not to look pointedly at the man beside her, who hadn't bothered to ask about his neighbor. "She's doing a lot better. I think she'll be home on

Friday."

"Back here, Mr. Storey," Polly began and led him to the back, "is where the worst of the damage happened. We're going to enclose the next water heater in a smaller room, along with a protected cabinet for her more flammable items. This wall will be perfect for her to store canvases and right now, Henry Sturtz is building cabinets and shelves for all of her paints and brushes and anything else she uses. It's pretty cool to have a famous artist right in your back yard, isn't it!"

He nodded and walked over to a window, "I used to do stained glass work a long time ago," he said quietly.

"Really? Have you thought about doing something like that now?"

"Oh, I gave all of my tools away. It would be too much trouble to start again."

"I think there's a cool studio in Ames. Have you ever been down there?" Doug interrupted.

"No."

"You should check it out. They have classes and everything. I'll bet you could start slow and get back into it." Doug continued enthusiastically. "I thought about doing it, but haven't had time to start. I don't know where I'd work on it. My Dad's shop takes up the garage and my mom's junk takes up the basement. Dude," he said to Billy. "We have got to get out of our parent's homes. I need a place to be me!"

Polly giggled, "Have you heard from Henry?" she asked.

"He said he was going to be here about eleven," Jerry Allen said, coming in the door.

"Thanks. I'll see you later," she said. "Mr. Storey?"

He followed her back outside and broke off as they approached his back yard. "Miss Giller?" he said and she turned around.

"Yes?"

"Tell Ms. Watson that it wasn't that bad. All I need is a new window. I'll take care of it."

"She'd want you to give her the bill for it," Polly said. "When you get it finished, let her know."

"It's not a problem. Thanks for showing me the studio."

Polly went back inside the studio and strode over to Doug. "You are wonderful sometimes, you know that?" she said.

"Sure! I'm wonderful. What did I do this time?" He stood up from where he was pulling cord and ran the back of his forearm across his face.

"Well, you deflected Mr. Storey and gave him something to think about. That was pretty cool, but I also want to thank you and Billy for letting Jason and his brother play games with you."

"Oh, that was nothing. They're good kids and they might as well be downstairs with us rather than up in your apartment bothering you."

Billy interjected, "We were once little dudes. I would have loved to have older dudes let me play with them."

"They thought you were a dweeb," Doug laughed, poking his friend's arm. "And you were. But hey, they don't have a dad around right now and since our dads are pretty okay, it's good to pass that on. Besides, their mom feeds us good food."

"She does that?" Polly asked. "I'm so glad!"

"Yeah. She came in Friday night with tons of cupcakes. They were like those Ding Dong things, only better, because they were homemade."

Polly huffed, "She's never made those for me."

"Well, you should ask her, 'cause they were awesome. She told me that whenever we had a game night, she'd come up with something fun for dessert if she's around. Now, how cool is that?"

"That's pretty cool. I know she appreciates you hanging out with her boys."

"The new dude you have helping out is okay, too. Some of the kids were a little weirded out by his face, but when he started showing them the horses, he got all relaxed and it got cool," Billy interjected. "You should totally keep him around."

"I'm trying," Polly said. "I'm trying. Well, thanks for everything."

They went back to work and she headed to Henry's shop. As she approached the front door, she heard the buzz of a saw. When she walked in, there were several people working. Henry looked up from the table saw and waved. She stood in place and watched the activity. Leroy was working with Sam Terhune, assembling boxes for base cabinets. Jimmy Rio was working with a man she didn't recognize and Ben Bowen was running some wood through a planer.

Henry finished what he was doing and came over to greet her. He gave her a quick hug. "What 'cha up to?" he asked.

"I came from the studio and spent a few intimate moments with Larry Storey, Beryl's neighbor."

"Was he complaining?"

Polly laughed. "Huh. How did you know?"

"It's what he does."

"Well, I showed him the inside of the studio, and Doug and Billy chatted him up a little bit. I think he left in a better mood than he arrived. He'll be fine."

"That's my girl. You keep fixing people around here, don't you! Do you know Len Specek?" he asked pointing at the man working with Jimmy.

"That's who it is!" she said. "I remember him from the dance, but I haven't seen him since then."

"He's going to help with the installation at the studio. Would you like to meet him?"

"Sure! But, I have a quick question first."

"What's up?"

"Sal Kahane is coming in to town tonight. What do you say about going out on Friday night? I thought I'd be a little evil and set her up on a blind date with Mark Ogden if he's available. That way it's just for fun since she's leaving on Saturday. No one has to make any long term commitment."

"Oh, I can't wait to see that," Henry said. "You're not just satisfied fixing people in town, you now have to start fixing people up?"

"Whatever. I thought it would be fun to take her out for dinner so she can meet you and what better way to go out than with a date for her, too?"

"That's cool. It makes me laugh. Come on, let me introduce you to Len."

They walked over and Henry introduced the two to each other.

"It's nice to meet you again, Polly," he said, shaking her hand. "I hear a lot about you."

"From Andy?" she asked. It was an innocent question, but then she realized that she wasn't supposed to know about the two of them.

"Oh, from her, but these guys talk about you, too."

"Well, I hope it is all good."

"So far it is. You've made quite a name for yourself here in Bellingwood."

Polly opened her mouth to speak and Henry interrupted, "He's seen the chart at the Elevator."

She backhanded Henry's arm, "I'm not going to ever live this down, am I?"

Jimmy snickered and continued to work.

Len said, "It's a friendly enough pool. No one is hoping for more dead bodies and we're sure sorry to hear about your custodian."

"So was I," Polly said. "I hope the next one is around for a while, though. I'm tired of this reputation!"

Henry guided her back to the front door. "Was there anything else?"

"Nope. I'm going to go to the grocery store and then I'm heading over to Story City. I have to sign some papers. Things are quiet at Sycamore House today, so I won't be around much. I'll pick Sal up at eight o'clock tonight and we will probably find dinner in Des Moines."

"Drive safely," he said. "Will you text me today and let me know where you are?"

"Because you miss me or because you're worried I'll be dead in a ditch somewhere?"

"If I say that it's both of those things will that keep me out of trouble?"

"Maybe. Will you come outside for a minute?"

"Sure." He followed her outside.

"I have a weird question for you because I was thinking about this a lot yesterday."

"Am I going to hate this question?"

"I don't know," she said. She took a breath and proceeded to ask, "So, yesterday, the ladies were talking about babies and all that and it hit me that I don't want little babies. Is that weird?"

"For you? I don't think it's weird. It's about right."

"Does that freak you out?"

"No. Should it?"

"I don't know. Alright, then. I should get going."

She turned toward the truck, but he caught her by her arm.

"Polly. What's this about?"

"Nothing much. I was thinking all these strange thoughts yesterday and," she shrugged out of his grasp and said, "Oh hell, I don't know. I'm sorry. I shouldn't have said anything."

"I think this is a conversation we should be having in a quiet place with dinner and wine. Not here in the middle of my parking lot."

"You're right. I'm sorry."

"Don't be sorry. Honestly, it's good to know that you're thinking about these things. Kinda makes me feel like there's something for us out there in the future."

Polly reached up and kissed him on the cheek. "You're such a good guy, Henry. I didn't realize I was such an insane person about this stuff. I always figured I was going to be alone for a very long time. It never occurred to me to think there would be anything more than that. I'm not sure what to do with it."

"You don't have to do anything right now. You know that, don't you?"

"I suppose I do. But, it's nice to hear. I'll talk to you later?"

He leaned over and kissed her on the lips. She felt herself swoon a little. Every time his lips touched hers, all she could think was that he had amazing lips and he tasted so good. She pressed against him and he wrapped his arms around her.

He finally broke away and said, "This is a little public."

"Yeah. Public. You have to stop doing that to me."

"No way. I'm never going to stop doing that to you. If my kisses make you get this stupid, I'm going to kiss you as often as possible. I like having that kind of power over you."

She laughed and walked to her truck. "I'll text you when I'm not driving. Have a good day today, alright?"

Her first stop was the little grocery store downtown. There were a few things she needed for the next couple of days. She made her purchases and then took them home and spent some time straightening her bedroom. It hadn't gotten completely out of control, but if she and Sal were going to be spending any amount of time in the place, she wanted to make sure it looked fairly decent.

When she'd lived in Boston, she'd learned a lot about drinking wine from both Drea and Sal. When Sal first took her out to nice restaurants and had actual conversations with the waiter about the wines which were available, Polly had truly felt like a hick from the Midwest, but before long, her friends taught her that all she needed was a little information and a few preferences. It was okay for her to like a wine and ask for it. So, she checked her bottles of wine to ensure there were a couple of Sal's favorites. Since she'd learned from the girl, she'd learned to like the same things. Everything was set and as she stood in her entryway, she nodded in approval.

"See you later!" she called out to the animals and closed the door behind her.

Before she left for Story City, she checked the front room across the hall. It was perfect. Eliseo had gotten everything cleaned up and put back together after their guest left on Sunday. The bed was re-made and there was even a small vase with flowers on the bedside table. As nice as it was, Polly still considered this room to be unfinished. She had thrown things together in here in order to have a room available and hadn't yet invested time and effort in finishing it. Maybe when everything was in place in the middle room, she'd finally finish this one.

It was time to head to Story City. It was strange to think that she had lived most of her life there and even though it was still familiar to her, it was no longer home. The last time she'd driven past her house, waves of sadness had nearly overwhelmed her. She knew every single inch of that place. The fourth step creaked on the outside, so the nights she snuck in late, she knew to skip that one. The closet in her Dad's bedroom had a strange little cubbyhole way up high. She'd found his lock box there when she was fifteen. He caught her snooping through it and brought it out for her. They sat on his bed as he went through its treasures. There were letters that he had written to her mom when they were dating and one letter in particular was well-worn. It had been read and re-read many times. Her mom had written to him after he'd asked her to marry him. She had told him all of the things she loved most about him, everything from the curl that tucked behind his right ear, to the way he held her hand in the car. He had pulled out a jewelry box and in it were her mom's wedding and engagement rings.

"Whenever you want these, they are yours, Polly. But, why don't we wait until you get a little older," he had said.

There was another, larger, jewelry case. In it was a beautiful necklace and earring set of opals and diamonds. It had been his wedding gift to his new bride. That one he had handed to Polly. "I think you would look beautiful in these right now. I want you to enjoy them at all of the dances and concerts and fancy affairs while you're in high school and college."

She had kept those in the case. She didn't wear them as often anymore, but every once in a while, she pulled them back out of the same lockbox and smiled at the memories. Whenever she had felt lonely for her mother, she pulled down the lockbox and sat on the bed, looking through the letters and even a few photographs that had been special to her dad. Their marriage certificate and all of their birth certificates were kept in the box. She'd never asked him about his passport. There were stamps for England and France. How had she missed asking all of those questions? She had always thought they had forever together. How would she ever know everything about her parents now that they were gone?

Polly pulled into a parking space and texted Henry, *"I'm in Story City. I'll let you know when I land in Des Moines."*

CHAPTER FIFTEEN

She goosed her speed because she hadn't been thinking when she finally hit the road. The airport was on the south side of Des Moines and it was going to take her an additional fifteen minutes. Polly and Sal had already spoken on the telephone, so they both knew where they were meeting, but she hated making her friend wait.

"Get out of my way! Get into the middle lane, you slowpoke," Polly yelled at the car she was tailgating. He was in no hurry and didn't mind having her run up close behind him. Finally, traffic broke open enough for her to scoot around him and move forward. She finally saw the airport and drove up to the front of the terminal. Sal was waiting for her, bags on the ground beside her.

"I'm so sorry!" Polly said as she jumped out of her truck. "I totally messed up the timing on this."

Sal hugged her and said, "Don't worry about it. I've only been here a couple of minutes. I took the time to call home and see how things were going and then waited for you. But, I'm starving. You promised to feed me! Where are we going?"

Polly put Sal's bags behind the front seat and waited while she got into the truck, then jogged around to the driver's side and got in. "Do you want fancy and a bar or something a little more casual?"

"Casual sounds great. I can hardly wait to see your house and all of your animals."

"Cool. I think we can make it to this fun Philly steak restaurant before they close. If nothing else, we can take it with us and eat it at home. How was your conference?"

"It was alright. Being in Iowa is different, though. There are a lot of fields between Des Moines and Iowa City and an awful lot of hills!"

"I'd never thought about it," Polly replied, "but, you're right and there are even more fields between Des Moines and Bellingwood. They haven't started planting this year because it's been wet and cold, but maybe you'll get to see some of the big farm equipment. It's pretty amazing stuff."

"Polly, I had no idea that you still loved this life. I thought you were happy in Boston."

"I was happy. I was really happy. But, I think I forgot what it was like to be happy and content and peaceful and calm and quiet all at the same time."

"You can truly have all that at once?" Sal laughed. "How do you ever think without all of the sounds and excitement?"

"I think the thing that surprised me the most is how easily those feelings returned once I got here. Sal, there are nights when I hear absolutely nothing. There are no sirens or cars honking. I don't hear people yelling at each other in the upstairs apartment or footsteps on the steps. I hear nothing."

"Girl, that would drive me stir crazy."

"You'd think so, but my mind works again. I don't have distractions when I want to think, I sleep through the night and I feel like I found a part of me that had been hiding."

"I'm glad for you, Polly, but I can't imagine not having Boston's excitement available whenever I want it."

"I keep making my own excitement. In the year since I've been back in Iowa, I can honestly say there hasn't been a single day when I've been bored.

"Oh, honey, I'm bored all the time."

"Then, I'm glad you're here for a few days. There are so many things I want you to see and friends I want you to meet."

"Are you going to let me meet this Henry fellow? I can't believe you're falling for a carpenter. Tell me he reads a book every once in a while."

Polly laughed. "I'm sure he does, it hasn't ever come up."

"Did he at least graduate from high school or is he still living at home working for his dad?"

"Sal! Don't be like that."

"What do you mean?" Sal sounded shocked.

"You can't bring that east coast snobbery with you. Every one of my friends, Henry included, is a college graduate. Iowa isn't some poverty-ridden, second rate state. You have to leave that attitude at home!"

"Whoa. Sorry, Polly. I didn't know that was such a sore spot." Now, it was Sal's turn to sound offended.

"I'm sorry, too, and while this might not be everything you are used to, these people are brilliant, loving and pretty wonderful. There isn't a person here who wouldn't do anything for you, even if you are a stranger. You know, you don't have to live on one of the coasts in order to be successful."

Sal put her hands up in defeat. "Okay. You're right. Differing worldviews don't mean one is better than the other. I'll give you that. Forgive me?"

Polly took a breath to calm down. "Of course. I will never apologize for Iowa, but I will always defend it. It may not be what you are used to, but in many ways it is better than anything you will ever experience."

"I'll look for the good. I promise."

Polly smiled, "Thanks. I think you'll find it takes very little effort to like it here."

They stopped and picked up food before heading north to Bellingwood. They had considered sitting in the restaurant, but it was apparent they were closing down for the evening and Sal assured her that she wouldn't actually starve to death before they got home. They exchanged what little information they had about the bombing in Boston and it hit Polly again that there were so many people she knew who were frightened, not knowing what might be coming next.

Drea had finally emailed her and assured Polly that her family was all safe. Her brothers had been part of the team pulling people out and getting them to safety, which didn't surprise Polly at all. Drea had finished the race before the bombings occurred and had taken off with some friends to celebrate, so she'd watched everything happen from a distance.

It was dark when they pulled into the driveway of Sycamore House. The street lamps were on and threw shadows across her home. Polly stopped and turned the lights on from her phone. She triggered the lights in the front room where Sal would be staying and as the place lit up, she smiled. A lot of good work had been accomplished this last year.

"Wow," Sal said as Polly parked the truck. "You really did it, didn't you? This is great!"

"Come on in. I want to introduce you to my animals and we'll eat supper."

They grabbed Sal's bags and Polly opened the front door, pointing out her office and gesturing around the back of the stairway to the kitchen, auditorium and classrooms.

"I'll show you around tomorrow morning, but let's go on upstairs."

Polly was glad Obiwan decided to be polite. He'd been getting much better about jumping up on people.

"If you bend to his level, it helps him realize he doesn't have to jump up to your level," she told Sal, who knelt in front of him and rubbed his ears.

"We all think it's hilarious that you named your animals after Star Wars characters," Sal laughed. "No one was surprised by it, though. Do you still have your collection?"

"Everything is down in the office. It's nice to finally have it all on display. I am a little worried about my friends here. Once they saw it, I watched their minds click and figure out how to make it increase. They're going to have a great time with this from now on. Henry might have to build more shelves for me."

"Your apartment is wonderful. Did your Henry do all of this work?"

Polly giggled, "My Henry. That sounds funny. But, yes. He did everything. I think you'll like the room you're staying in, too. He did all of the woodwork and the wood on these floors is from a barn that was torn down south of here. In fact, that's where I got the cats."

"A barn?" Sal asked.

"Sure. A young couple pulled down an old barn. The wood was still in good shape, so they salvaged it and we had it milled and then Henry and his crew laid it for me. Don't you love it?"

Sal bent over and ran her hand across the floor. "I've never seen anything like it. There's so much character." She stood back up, "Only you would think of doing something like this."

"Don't give me too much credit. It's done all the time and it was Henry's idea, not mine. All I did was say yes when he mentioned it and I'm glad I did."

Sal took in the apartment, running her hand across one of the beautiful built in bookshelves. "I'd say that finding a carpenter and falling in love with him definitely has its benefits."

Polly had the decency to blush, "Wait. I haven't said anything about falling in love with him."

Sal walked toward the kitchen and held her hand up, stopping Polly's words. "Whatever," she smirked. "Are you telling me that he did all of this beautiful work and he didn't get anything extra special from you as payment?"

"Hey!" Polly said, her voice a little strident. "No! That's not how it was and it's not how it is and I'm offended by that."

Sal spun around, "I'm sorry. I was only kidding you. But, really?"

"Really! I like being my own person and having some independence. This is all mine. I'm in no hurry for all of that."

"Okay, okay. I'm sorry. I didn't mean anything by it. I don't even know why I said it. You've never been that person."

"And besides, Henry does good work because it's the right thing to do, not because I'm sleeping with him."

"I thought you said you weren't sleeping with him."

Polly dropped the bag of food on the table and ripped it open, setting the containers out, trying not to slam them. "I'm not. We aren't."

Sal grinned, "You're so easy."

"That's not fair," Polly complained.

"I know. But, you have missed me, haven't you." Sal moved in and gave her friend a hug. "I know your buttons and I shouldn't have pushed them. I'm doing that a lot tonight. You're different than you were a year ago. It's good on you, but it's ... well ... it's different."

"Well, I hope it is all good different," Polly said.

They ate supper and Polly took Sal across the hall to the front room, then showed her the spa bathrooms. They stayed up and talked until Polly's eyes were watering from yawning so much.

"You have to get up early in the morning, don't you?" Sal asked.

"I probably should. But, Eliseo will probably start with the horses, so if I don't get out there at the break of dawn, I'll still be alright."

"Well, I'm going to bed. I want to see everything tomorrow. Will you take me to lunch at the diner downtown? I can't wait to try one of those pork sandwiches you talk about."

"When I come back up in the morning, I'll wake you and then we'll go from there."

Polly walked across the hallway and gave her friend a hug, "I'm so glad you are here."

Sal hugged her tightly and said, "I'm sorry I sounded insulting earlier about your friends and especially about your relationship with Henry. I should have known better than to say anything. How could you be friends with anyone but great people? I look forward to meeting them."

"No worries," Polly assured her. "Sleep well and I'll see you in the morning."

Polly walked back to her apartment and snapped the leash on Obiwan, "One quick run outside and then I have to sleep!"

When she finally dropped into bed, she didn't bother to set her alarm, knowing that the cats would wake her with the sunrise.

The next morning, that was exactly what happened. Luke went bounding across her to get to the ledge of the cat tree so he could look out the window. Leia soon followed and they began talking to the world. Polly looked at the time on her telephone. Six forty-five. Time to get up and get moving. She got up, pulled her clothes and boots on and went outside with Obiwan. Once they got in the gate, he took off for the pasture, sniffing the ground and playing with tufts of grass.

The main door to the barn wasn't open and when Polly got inside, she was surprised to see that the horses were still in their stalls. They hadn't been fed yet and there was no sign of Eliseo.

"Eliseo? Are you here?" she called out.

He'd said he would be back this morning. She hoped everything was alright.

"Well, I'm sorry you had to wait this morning," she said to the horses. "I certainly didn't expect to find you alone. I'll get breakfast right now."

When she went back to gather the feed, she noticed spots of something on the floor leading to the ladder which had been pulled down. She didn't think they were there yesterday, so she scuffed at one with her boot. It was wet. The horses were making a lot of noise, so she hurried and dropped feed for them, then opened up the doors to the outside. When she walked back to one of the spots, she bent over and rubbed her index finger in it and then sniffed it. If she didn't know better, it might be blood.

"Oh no. I wonder," she mused and quickly went up the steps into the hayloft.

"Is someone here?" she asked. "Are you alright?"

She thought she heard something coming from the front of the barn and made her way across the bales of hay, where she came upon a hollowed out space. Looking down, she saw Eliseo, curled up with blankets covering him. He moaned as she moved toward him and she saw that there was blood covering his face and hands.

"Eliseo, what happened? Are you alright?"

"I'm sorry, Miss Giller. So sorry. Just give me a little time and I'll get to work."

"Don't worry about that. What has happened to you?"

"I'll be fine."

"You don't look like you are going to be fine at all. I need to call the EMTs."

He reached out and touched her. "No, no doctors please. I'll be alright."

"Have you been sleeping here, Eliseo?"

His eyes closed and he appeared to sink further into the bed of hay he'd created. "Yes. If you want me to leave, give me time and I'll be gone."

"I don't even know where to start right now, but that's certainly not it. Tell me what has happened to you?"

"I can't."

"Then tell me where you've been hurt."

He lifted his head and she saw that both eyes were blackened and there was a cut on his right cheek. His hands were scraped and cut up and he had wrapped some cloth around his right forearm. She pulled back the blanket and there was blood on his jeans around his knee and more scrapes and cuts were bleeding through his t-shirt.

"What in the hell? You've been beaten very badly!"

"I know," he acknowledged. "But please, no doctors."

"How did you get up the ladder?"

He chuckled and then grimaced. "Very slowly."

She sat up and puffed out air in a sigh. "I need to think a minute," she said.

"I'm not going anywhere."

"It would be a lot easier for me to take care of you if you weren't up here, you know."

"I don't expect you to take care of me. I didn't intend for you to find me."

"Well, blood drops on the floor of my barn made me curious. So, have you been sleeping up here all along? It's been pretty cold at night."

"I stayed warm enough. And when it got too cold, I moved in with Demi. He was the quietest of the lot."

"So that's why my horses liked you so much. You've been around them for a while."

He tried to smile. "They've gotten to know me."

"And that's why Obiwan knows you and that's why my stock of hay downstairs has been kept in such good shape."

"Yes."

"Well, at least that little mystery is solved. But, you won't tell me what happened to you last night?"

"I got beat up?" he said, looking up at her.

"Alright. I deserved that. But you won't tell me who did it or why?"

"I can't."

"Do you want to stay up here or would you be able to come over to my apartment to get cleaned up and let me get those cuts cleaned out?"

He tried to lift himself to a sitting position and after some struggle managed to pull himself erect.

"If I don't come to your apartment, you're going to keep coming up that ladder to take care of me, aren't you."

"Yes," Polly acknowledged.

"Will you go away and let me come down by myself in my own time?" he asked.

"Can't I please get you some help?"

"I'm not going to negotiate that ladder with you watching me."

"Then, I'll go outside and make sure the horses have hay and do a quick cleanup of their stalls."

"If I'm not down by the time you're finished, don't panic, alright?"

"It's not alright. I'm going to give you half an hour. If you aren't out of here and down that ladder by then, I'm calling for help. So, you figure it out or let me, got it?"

"Has anyone ever told you that you get a little bossy?" he laughed, then grimaced again.

"Not lately, but I'll let it go since you're not yourself."

Polly crawled back across the bales to an aisle and stood up. "Half hour, no more."

She went down the ladder and wondered how in the world he would get himself down, but set it aside and dragged a bale of hay outside. The four horses were waiting for her to get there and Nan nudged her.

"I know, I know. Everything is in an uproar. I'm going to fix it. I promise," Polly said as she broke the bale up.

She grabbed the muck rake and wheelbarrow and quickly picked up the big chunks from the stalls and scattered enough hay to keep them quiet, then went outside and dialed Henry.

"Good morning," he said.

"You know. I never know who to call when I need help, but your phone number keeps coming to the top of my list," Polly replied.

"Not even a Hello or a Hi there, hotstuff?" he asked.

She giggled. "Hi there, hotstuff. Did you sleep well?"

"That's better. I certainly did sleep well. I had a cute girl ask me about children yesterday. I think there might be something to our relationship after all."

Polly laughed until she snorted, then sighed. "I have another problem and I need your help with this one."

"Well, if you had found another body, I am confident you would call Sheriff Merritt, so did you break something?"

"I found a live body. Does that count?"

"You what?" Henry sounded a little exasperated.

"Eliseo Aquila has been beaten up and he's been living in the hayloft of my barn," she said. "He won't let me call the EMTs and he won't tell me what's going on and he won't let me help him down, but he will let me clean him up once he is down. I think I need you. Do you have time this morning?"

"Of course I have time. I'll call Sam and let him know where I am. They can work on the cabinets for the studio without me. What are you going to do with him?"

"I figure the first thing I'm going to do is get him up to my apartment and clean the blood off him, get him in some warm clothes and deal with his cuts and scrapes. Then I'll feed him and make sure nothing is broken or needs serious mending."

Henry chuckled. "You get quite the assortment of people and animals at Sycamore House, don't you! However, I'm not sure I'm comfortable with you playing nursemaid to this guy."

"Do you have a better idea?" Polly asked.

"Not really. But, I will be there to keep an eye on things. If you haven't seen my naked body, I'm not ready for you to see his."

She giggled again, "You are strange and twisted. I'll see you in a bit?"

"I'll be there."

She turned around to see Eliseo limping down the alley of the barn toward her, so she ran to him. He was carrying a backpack and she took it from him, shrugging it onto her shoulder, then slipped her arm around him, offering support. She glanced back at the horses as they walked toward Sycamore House and whistled for Obiwan. He met them at the gate and followed them to the side door, waiting patiently while she opened it, then walked beside her as they went inside.

"Are you going to be alright going up these steps?" Polly asked.

Eliseo sighed. "Can I sit here for a minute?" gesturing at a bench.

"Of course!"

Jeff walked in the front door and saw the two of them as Eliseo was lowering himself to the bench.

"What in the hell?" he asked, rushing over to Polly.

She shrugged and nodded at Eliseo, who looked up and said, "I'm sorry, boss. I'm not going to be any good today."

"What happened to you? Polly, what happened to him?"

"He got beat up, isn't it obvious?" she asked, gritting her teeth and smiling at Eliseo. "That's all he will tell me."

"You have to tell us more than that. Who did this to you?" Jeff demanded.

"I can't tell you that," Eliseo responded.

"You can't or you won't tell us?" Jeff demanded.

"I won't tell you. I don't want there to be any more trouble."

"There can be more trouble than this?" Jeff asked, pointing at Eliseo.

"There probably could be," Eliseo affirmed.

"Have you called the EMTs?" Jeff asked Polly.

"He wouldn't let me, so I'm going to try to get him upstairs and cleaned up. Henry is coming over to help. Can you deal with things down here today?"

"Well, of course I can. Good god, man. You haven't even been here a week and people are beating you up?"

"This has nothing to do with me being here. I promise you that," Eliseo said.

"Well, fine, then. Do you want some help getting up the steps?"

Polly looked up as she heard the front door open and felt relief when she saw that it was Henry.

He took in the situation immediately and joined them, saying, "Just a second. Polly, can I talk to you?"

She looked at him and he said, "Over here?" pointing to the stairway.

"I'll be right back. Don't go anywhere, alright?" she said and followed Henry.

"What is it?"

"You don't want to make him go up those steps if he is going to have to come down again. He can't stay in your apartment."

"I know that, but I haven't been able to come up with a better idea."

"Why doesn't he come to my house? I have plenty of room and he can stay with me until he decides what he wants to do."

"Are you sure? I don't know what's going on or why he was beaten and I don't want you involved if it's going to bring you trouble."

He took her arm, "Do you think I would rather the trouble show up here?"

"I didn't think about that. I wanted to make sure he was cleaned up and safe."

"I love you, Polly, but having him in your apartment isn't a good decision."

"Alright, but I'm coming over to help you get him settled."

"I knew that. Don't you have a friend upstairs you need to deal with, though?"

"Oh, I forgot! She has to be wondering what is going on."

"She really is wondering," came a voice from the stairway. "I knew you'd forgotten me!"

CHAPTER SIXTEEN

"Uggh!" Polly ran over to her friend. "I'm so sorry! I found Eliseo in the barn and he's been beaten up and I need to take care of him and I left you alone and Henry wants to take him home and you don't know any of these people." She took a breath. "I'm sorry."

Sal smiled and said, "It's okay. Tell me what I can do to help."

At that moment, Sylvie walked in the front door. When she saw Eliseo on the bench, she put her bags down and rushed to him, "What happened to you? You look terrible."

She flashed on her friends, "Why isn't someone helping him? Are you all standing around waiting for him to heal on his own?" Then she saw Sal and said, "Whoops. I'm sorry. I'm Sylvie Donovan. You must be Polly's friend from Boston."

Polly moved over to Sylvie and placed her hand on the woman's shoulder, "He doesn't want a doctor and we're trying to figure out where he'll be the most comfortable. He doesn't need to go up and down the steps and Henry thinks that it would be better if we took Eliseo to his house."

"Well, why are you all still standing here? Let's get moving. He needs to be cleaned up and bandaged. What are you thinking?"

demanded Sylvie.

"Whoa!" Jeff exclaimed. He put his hands up in defense and backed up. "We've only been here a couple of minutes. Slow down!"

"Slow down, my ass," Sylvie snapped. "Let's go."

"You," she pointed to Jeff. "Put my bags in the kitchen. There are two deliveries coming in this morning. They know where to put things, please sign for them."

"You," and she looked at Henry. "Go home and get things ready. We'll be there in a few minutes."

"Are you coming with me or not?" she turned on Polly.

Polly darted her eyes back and forth between the men who had just received their marching orders. "With you, I'm guessing?" she asked.

"What about you?" Sylvie looked at Sal.

"Sal, I'll be back," Polly interrupted. "This is Jeff Lyndsay, my assistant. Why don't the two of you get acquainted? Would you mind taking Obiwan up to the apartment?"

Sal laughed and nodded. "Sure." She turned to Sylvie, "It looks as if I'm staying here."

Henry went outside and Sylvie said, "I'm going to get my car. That way he doesn't have to climb up in either of your big trucks. Stay right here and I'll pull up front."

She left and Eliseo looked at Polly, "She scares me a little. I thought she was such a nice girl!"

"I've never seen her like this," Polly remarked with a chuckle. "I don't think there's a single person among us who isn't a little scared of her right now."

"I'm sorry I've messed up your morning," he said and grimaced as he tried to stand. Jeff came over and put his arm around Eliseo's waist to give him support.

"I'll see you later," Polly said to Sal. "Oh, the dog is going to want to be fed. Just fill his food dish with the dog food in the cabinet beside the refrigerator. There's cat food in there too, if you wouldn't mind putting some in the cat's dishes."

"On it. I can figure that out," Sal replied. "We'll all be fine. And then you have to tell me all about this!"

They got Eliseo loaded into Sylvie's car and drove over to Henry's house. He was waiting in the driveway to help them get inside. Sylvie quickly took over again and began ordering Henry and Polly around as soon as Eliseo was settled on the sofa.

She asked Henry to help her get Eliseo's shirt off and Polly tried not to gasp as she saw the horrible scarring that covered his chest and neck. Whatever had happened to him had been traumatic. Sylvie began to wipe his face, arms and chest, cleaning the blood off as gently as possible. There were more cuts than Polly could count and when Sylvie pressed on his side, he winced, in obvious pain.

"It doesn't feel broken," she said, "but I'm sure you have some bruised ribs in there. You're going to have to be careful for a while. I wish you'd let us take you to the doctor's office. Then we'd know for sure."

Henry had brought bandages and antiseptic cream and set them down on the coffee table beside Sylvie.

"You're good at this, Sylvie," Polly said.

"I've got two boys and there was a time in my life when I planned to be a nurse," she responded without looking up. "I had taken two terms and then had to stop when Jason was born."

"Okay, didn't know that about you."

"It was a long time ago, before ..." her voice trailed off and she didn't say any more.

"I'm going to need to get going, Polly," Henry said.

"Oh, umm. Alright," she responded. "What do you want us to do here?"

"Make sure he has everything he needs. There are more pillows and blankets in the closet at the top of the stairs, the bathroom is through there," he pointed to the hallway leading to the dining room and kitchen area, "and he can have anything he wants out of the fridge."

Polly walked outside with Henry. "Are you sure about this?"

"He'll be fine here. At least he won't be at your place. I can keep an eye on him after work and make sure that he's still alive."

"I hate to put you out like this."

"Oh, stop it. It's no big deal. When the whole world intrudes on you, I think I can handle one person for a couple of nights."

"Thank you," she said. "By the way, if everything returns to normal, are you good to go out with me and Sal tomorrow for dinner? I haven't talked to Mark yet, but I can't imagine he'll say no."

"That sounds great. You know that she has become part of your crazy Sycamore House story now, don't you? She wasn't even here twenty-four hours and you've exposed her to the seedy underbelly of your world."

Polly shook her head. "No one is ever going to believe that I lived a simple, quiet life in Boston."

"We don't believe it. We'll never believe it."

Sylvie stuck her head out the door, "Henry, could you help with one more thing? I want to get his pants off so I can check the cuts on his legs."

"I can do it, Mrs. Donovan," came a loud voice from inside the house.

"I think you've about reduced the poor man to nothing, Sylvie," Henry said. "Let him keep a little dignity."

Sylvie threw her head back and snarled, then went back inside and shut the door.

"I've never seen her like this," Polly said again. "She's frightening!"

"You never know what will trigger a woman's insanity, do you. Oh, wait. I know exactly what triggers yours and I do my best every day not to walk into that again."

Polly pushed his shoulder. "You're never going to let me live that down, are you?"

"Probably not, I have a long memory."

"Well, let's hope that long memory extends to your own behavior."

"Oh, it will. Of that I'm sure. And if I choose to make that trek into darkness again, I'll be fully prepared and make sure I've put my armor on, or at least have a quick escape planned."

Henry had made the mistake of telling Polly what to do in regards to an old boyfriend a couple of times and both of those instances had brought down her wrath on his head, once quite publicly. Both of them had apologized, but neither of them had forgotten.

"You'd better go. As soon as I can drag Sylvie away from Eliseo, I'll be back."

Henry leaned in and kissed her cheek. "Do you know what happened to him?"

"I don't. I hope he'll tell me pretty soon. I'd hate to think that he's prone to fighting. It doesn't seem like him, but I guess you never know."

Henry left and Polly went back inside. Eliseo had fallen asleep and Sylvie was nowhere to be found. Polly looked around and pretty soon, she heard footsteps coming down from upstairs. Sylvie was carrying another pillow, but put her finger to her lips and beckoned Polly to the kitchen.

She'd never been this far into Henry's house and wondered if he had decorated it or if this was left over from his mother. The dining room had a long trestle table with benches on either side. The windows were covered with plain white sheers. A blue and gold swag looped over the curtain rod. The kitchen was a beautiful room with hardwood floors and what Polly now recognized as knotty pine cabinets. There was a small primitive table placed up against the back wall with three chairs around it. The morning's newspaper was still open, but the dishes had been taken to the sink.

"He was hurt pretty badly, Polly. Do you know what happened to him?"

"He won't tell me, Sylvie. Did he say anything to you?"

"No," she shook her head. "He smiled a lot and let me bandage him up. I suppose he had to get used to that when he was in the hospital. Did you see all of that scarring?"

"I can't even imagine the pain that goes along with that," Polly replied.

"I can't believe he does so well!"

"I know. Can you leave him?"

"He'll be fine for now and I'll check on him today. I'm going to put a bottle of water out there and then bring lunch later on."

"We should head back to Sycamore House then, and let him sleep."

They went into the living room and Sylvie sat down on the coffee table in front of Eliseo. She touched his arm and quietly said, "Eliseo?"

"I'm sorry. I fell asleep," he said.

"No, you're fine. Here's a bottle of water and an extra pillow. I'm going to take Polly back to Sycamore House and then I'll bring you some lunch. Go ahead and sleep now. You're safe here."

"Thank you," he said. He lifted his hand and Polly could see the pain in his eyes as he did so, but put it across Sylvie's and then shut his eyes and drifted back to sleep.

Once they got in the car, Polly turned on Sylvie, "Who in the world are you?"

"What do you mean?" Sylvie asked.

"I mean, who are you? A wild and insane woman showed up at my house this morning and I've never seen her before!"

Sylvie laughed. "Oh. Her. She doesn't show up very often, but no one was doing anything and he was in obvious pain. I might have overdone it, though. Am I going to have to apologize to Jeff?"

"I think maybe you might!" Polly laughed. "He was a little shocked. We all were! Do you get like that very often?"

"It doesn't happen very often. I try to keep her in check, because she can get unruly."

"Unruly doesn't describe what I saw this morning. When was the last time you let her loose?"

"It's been a couple of years. Andrew broke his leg on the playground one summer when he was six. Some lady called me, but when I got there, she was the only adult around and she was standing there gawking at him, waiting for me to show up to make a decision. She'd done nothing to help or comfort him. She hadn't touched him or even gotten close to him. She hadn't even called 9-1-1. She asked his brother for my phone number and called me. Andrew was crying and scared and she stood there. Poor Jason was holding Andrew's hand, but he was only nine and expected the adult to handle it. I probably went a little crazy that day, too."

"That's odd. If she was a mom, she should have done something."

"You'd think so, wouldn't you! But, I think she had her own set of problems. I'm not even sure if those kids were hers."

"What?"

"They weren't in town very long, and my boys said something about her marrying this guy and not wanting his kids around. He only had partial custody, so I'm hoping their real mom took better care of them than that woman did."

"What did you say to her?"

"When I saw Andrew's leg, I called 9-1-1 myself, sent Jason to the car for our blanket and once he was gone, I stood up, got in her face and screamed at her for being a self-centered, low-life bitch and told her that she didn't have a right to even be around children if she couldn't provide some semblance of comfort to a scared, little boy. Then I told her that if I ever saw her on the playground again, I was calling the police because there was more than likely a good case for neglect."

"What did she do?"

"She ran to her car and drove away without her kids. They were running after her and she had to stop and wait for them to catch up. Stupid bitch."

"Wow! Well, all I know is that if I ever hurt myself badly, I want you around to command the troops."

Sylvie chuckled, "It's a deal."

She parked her car and they went inside. Jeff wasn't in his office, so Sylvie headed for the kitchen and Polly went up to her apartment. When she walked in, Jeff and Sal were laughing at the dining room table, with mugs of coffee in front of them.

"Have you had anything to eat yet this morning?" Sal asked. "I made breakfast."

Polly dropped her head, "I'm sorry. I was supposed to take care of you while you were here."

"From here on out, you are responsible for my happiness," Sal laughed. "But, it's been nice getting the scoop on your life from Jeff. He has plenty to say."

"Should I be embarrassed?" Polly asked.

"Only that you didn't introduce me to Henry. But, other than that, I think you're fine. Do you want something to eat?"

"No, I'm good. I can wait for lunch. What would you like to do?"

"I've met your inside animals and Jeff. How about you show me around the rest of the place and I'll put on a pair of your boots and we can go out and talk to your horses. Will you join us outside, Jeff?"

Polly snickered and Jeff laughed. "I promised Polly that I wasn't taking my leather shoes anywhere near horse crap, so no. I'll work inside while you two go out and act like cowboys."

He turned to Polly, "Did Sylvie come back with you? Is she safe to be around yet?"

"I think she calmed down. I'm glad she was here, but that was something!"

"She's not normally that bossy?" Sal asked.

"No, when I met her, I thought she was a mouse," Polly said. "She's gotten a lot more confident since she started going to school, but this was quite new!"

"I might like to meet her again now that we aren't in the middle of a crisis."

"Let me take a quick shower and I'll be ready to go," Polly said. "Do you mind waiting a few more minutes?"

"Don't mind me, I'll just clean your kitchen," Sal laughed.

"If you two are going to get all girly, I'm going back to work," Jeff said and headed out Polly's front door.

"He seems great," Sal said. "He's got your back here."

"Can you believe it? And he knows what he's doing with all of the things we have going on around here, so I can sit back and enjoy myself."

"Yeah. Like that's what you do. You are the fulcrum on which everything balances."

"I don't know about that, but there's always something going on."

Polly went into her bedroom and stripped down for the shower. The cats followed her in and curled up on the countertop waiting for her to finish. When she came out, they both jumped to the floor and rubbed themselves on her ankles while she pulled a comb through her hair and brushed her teeth.

"Did you feed the cats too?" Polly called out.

"I did. I hope it was enough. They finished what I put out," Sal replied.

"They're fine then. Thanks."

Polly got dressed and pushed things around in her closet until she found a second pair of work boots. They were still fairly new and Sal could break them in once they got to the barn.

"Let's go," Polly said as she re-entered the living room. "Time's a-wastin!"

"What are you going to show me first?"

"Let's hit the kitchen so Sylvie can redeem herself and then I want to take you outside to meet Henry. He'd normally be over at my friend Beryl's house re-doing her studio, but today he's on-site."

"How were you so lucky to find him?"

"Good, clean living is the best answer I have for you."

"Whatever. You have led a pretty clean life, but there had to be more to it than that."

"I don't know. We started out working together and then we got to know each other and then he asked me out on a date and it was the sweetest thing I'd ever experienced."

"I know. You told me all about it. I was so jealous."

"When he left to go to Arizona, I wasn't in a relationship. Everyone else around me kept implying that we were, but I didn't think anything about it." Polly stopped and said, "That's not true. I didn't think about it happening very fast. When he was gone for two months, I realized how much I missed him. He's become important to me and I can't imagine not having him around."

"That sounds nice and boring."

"Well, it's not boring when he kisses me," Polly smirked. "He makes me swoon."

"Oh, girlfriend. That's a big deal!"

"Tell me about it. My head gets all stupid and I forget to breathe."

"I can't wait to meet him," Sal laughed.

They walked into the kitchen and Sylvie looked up from her computer. She wiped her hands on her apron and shook Sal's hand. "I'm so sorry that I was rude this morning. It's nice to meet you."

"You too. Wow," Sal said. "This is a great kitchen!" She walked around and peeked inside the glass doors to the pantry cupboards.

"I love this prep area," she continued. When she got to the stove, she turned a couple of the burners on and off. "This would be a great place to work!"

"Polly did it all," Sylvie said. "It's pretty close to perfect. I don't know what else I could ask for."

"I would never have imagined you had this in you, my friend," Sally said, clutching Polly's arm. "I'm proud of you!"

Polly took her into the auditorium and showed her the cases filled with items that had been found in a storage room in the basement, then they went outside to find Henry.

"I suppose I should do this formally," Polly said. "Henry Sturtz, this is my friend Sal Kahane from Boston. Sal, this is Henry."

The two shook hands and he said, "Well, you got your first glimpse of the craziness that Polly brought to Bellingwood."

"Stop it!" Polly protested. "I keep trying to tell you that it's not my fault."

"It's never her fault," he laughed and put his arm around her shoulders, "but she keeps finding more and interesting ways to keep us entertained."

"You have done beautiful work with this place, Henry." Sal said. "Polly's lucky to have found someone with your skill. How long have you been a cabinet maker?"

"I've been doing this all my life. Did you see that table in my kitchen?" he asked Polly. "That was one of the first things I built with my Dad. I was eight or nine years old. It's seen a lot of wear and tear over the years. I would have gotten rid of it a long time ago, but Mom was so proud of it, she wouldn't let me. Now I'm glad that I still have it."

"That makes a lot more sense now. I wondered about it when I saw it. It certainly didn't fit in with the craftsmanship of the rest of the house," Polly laughed.

"It's sturdy, if nothing else. I think I used every nail and screw Dad had in the shop."

Polly took Sal out to the barn and the horses came in from the pasture to greet her. Sal had ridden in high school, so was comfortable with them. Polly left her and went in and up to the hay loft again to see if Eliseo had left things behind. The blankets were still there, but it looked as if he had gathered up all of his personal possessions. She tossed the blankets to the floor on the main level before climbing back down.

"That's a lot of horse you have here," Sal said. "It's a good thing they're good-natured or you would have a terrible time."

"Nan can be a brat sometimes. If she doesn't want to do something, she lets me know. But, I try not to ask her for much more than she wants to give me. It makes it easier on all of us."

"Are you going to hitch them up to a cart one of these days?"

"We will, but I will probably let Mark Ogden tell me when they're ready. I've only had them here a few months and after the time they had, I want to make sure they are completely healthy and feel safe. Speaking of Mark, what if I asked him to go to dinner with you, me and Henry tomorrow night?"

"What? You're setting me up on a date with someone from Iowa?"

"Let's not call it a date," Polly laughed. "Let's call it four people going out to dinner. He's terrific and I know you two will enjoy each other. That way ... okay, it's a date. What do you think?"

"I'm game for anything. Does he know about this yet?"

"No, not really," Polly snorted. "I should probably call him and ask, but I wanted to check with you before I said anything. Just a second."

She stepped back through Nan's stall and walked into the main alley of the barn to dial her phone. "Mark?"

"What's up, Polly? Is there a problem?"

"No, everything's fine. I was wondering if you were busy for dinner tomorrow night."

"Umm, aren't you dating Henry?"

"Stop it. I have a friend in town from Boston and thought it would be fun if the four of us went out to dinner."

"You are setting me up on a blind date?"

"Maybe?"

"Is this what all those questions about Sylvie were about?"

"Maybe? So, will you?"

He was quiet long enough that Polly said, "Did I lose you?"

"No, I'm still here. I'm wondering if this is as strange as it sounds."

"It's no big deal. Come on. Say yes."

"I can't say no to you. I'll go."

"Thank you, Mark. I'll text you details. See you tomorrow!"

She slipped her phone back in her pocket and walked outside. "He's on. This will be fun. So, now that I'm thinking about food, I'm hungry. Are you ready to go for lunch?"

Sal slipped out of the work boots and put her shoes back on. "What do you want me to do with these?"

"Let's leave them here. I don't know why I hadn't in the first place," Polly said.

They walked to the parking lot and got in Polly's truck. She drove around a little bit, showing Sal the little town she now called home and then turned onto the main street going through the downtown area.

"Oh, it's so quaint!" Sal exclaimed.

"Don't let them hear you say that, okay? People work in these shops and live here."

Sal pursed her lips. "I'll be good. But, this is wonderful! And why am I not surprised that nearly every other vehicle is a pick-up truck?"

"Oh, I can hardly wait to hear what you have to say about the diner. Please be good when you're in there, alright?"

Polly parked her truck and they walked across the street. When she opened the door to the diner, the warm smells of grease and food greeted them. Lucy was standing at the kitchen window waiting for an order and acknowledged them with a nod, then pointed at an empty table. Polly took Sal's arm and led her over.

"Are you going to try a pork tenderloin?" she asked. Polly knew her friend didn't keep kosher, but this was almost funny.

"When in Rome, I guess."

"Do you at least want a salad to start?" Polly asked.

"What are you having?"

"A salad. Yeah. That's what I'm having," she nodded.

"No onion rings today?" Lucy asked as she approached the table with menus and silverware.

"Okay, we'll split some onion rings and I will have a salad with ranch dressing. Lucy, this is my friend Sal from Boston. She's here to try one of your famous pork tenderloins."

"How about a nice salad for you, too?" Lucy asked.

"Sure. Do you have a vinaigrette dressing?"

"I have oil and vinegar or our house Italian."

"House Italian sounds fine and an iced tea. Thank you."

Lucy left and Polly felt a hand on her shoulder. She looked up and Ken Wallers was standing over her.

"We keep meeting in all the restaurants in town. I'm going to have to start bringing my lunch to work. People will talk," he said.

"Hi Ken," she smiled. "This is my friend, Sal, from Boston. Sal, this is our police chief, Ken Wallers. What's up today?" she asked.

"I heard your new custodian showed up with a lot of scrapes and cuts this morning. Do you know what he got himself into?" he asked, pulling out a chair and sitting at the table with them.

"He won't tell me. But, he's doing a lot better. Sylvie Donovan took matters into hand."

"There was a bad fight at Jefferson Street Alehouse last night. A couple of out-of-towners were involved. Do you suppose that was him?"

Polly put her head into her hand and sighed. "I don't know, Ken. I'll ask him later today. I'd hate to think I hired another loser for this position. I like him and he has worked so hard this last week."

"Well, make sure you are careful. You've found enough bodies for one month, okay?"

He stood up and started to walk away, then turned back. "Take care of yourself. Neither the Sheriff or I want you in any trouble."

CHAPTER SEVENTEEN

Running her finger around the rim of her glass, Sal had watched the interchange between Polly and the police chief. After he walked away, she said, "You've got some good friends in this town. People like you a lot."

"Sal, I can't tell you how glad I am to be settling in here. I don't think I ever appreciated small town Iowa until I came back to it. When I was young, I couldn't wait to go away to college and start living in the real world, but it's nice to be back. I can't imagine wanting to live anywhere else now that I'm here."

"I didn't intend to talk you into coming back to Boston, your emails and our phone calls have let me know how much you love it here, but until I saw it for myself, I didn't understand how this fits you. You know, I was serious the other night. You're a lot different now."

Polly wrinkled her nose, "Different? What do you mean?"

"I've been thinking about this. You were living someone else's life when you were in Boston. You had friends, you had an apartment, you had a job. But, it wasn't all you. I haven't been here very long, but your friends are bonded to you a little more deeply and your apartment is so your home. There are little pieces of you everywhere I looked. And you don't just have a job, you have a life here. Sycamore House is an extension of who you are. The whole town recognizes you and it's like you are a piece of their puzzle. You fit in."

"I suppose."

"No, I'm not kidding. It never occurred to you to have a pet while you were in Boston, but look at you. You have horses and a dog and cats. What's next? Sheep? Cows? Chickens?"

Polly put her hands up in defense, "Nothing! I swear. Nothing!"

They laughed and Sal continued, "I'm so glad to get a chance to experience this part of your life and see how content you are. I hope someday I will feel as satisfied with my life as you are right now. You figured this out."

"I never thought about it. Sheesh, Sal. Everything just fell together. Other than buying the building, there was no plan in place where I would uncover peace and contentment."

"Well, you found it and I'm a little jealous."

"You don't think you could find yours in the middle of Iowa?"

Sal let out a loud laugh and they both looked around the diner to see if anyone was paying attention after that outburst. People glanced up, but went back to their own conversations and meals.

"No," she laughed again. "Somehow Sal Kahane, Jewish American Princess and small town Iowa will never be the perfect blend of peace and harmony. I like a little more excitement in my life. However, when it comes to the excitement barometer, you're certainly pushing it up there. Dead bodies, beaten employees, rescued horses. We wouldn't have known what to do with you if any of that had happened back east."

"You know, Sal, you should never say never. Stranger things have happened. Who knows, maybe you'll meet the perfect man. You could always teach. There are plenty of great universities and colleges out here."

Sal had started to take a drink and set it back down. "Can you imagine what my mother would do if she thought I was going to marry someone and move to Iowa? She'd have a heart attack. Remember, she's still setting me up with doctors and dentists as often as she can."

"I can't believe that you have never gone on a second date with any of them. Where is she finding these people?"

"Oh, I haven't told you about the one she set me up with last week. He's the son of some woman she knows from her card club. She doesn't even like the woman, but when she heard there was a single male, those two biddies set us up. They made reservations for us and sent a cab to pick us both up so we couldn't bail out on it."

"How was it?"

"At first I thought it was going to be, well, not the worst blind date I'd been on. He was fairly good looking and polite. He held doors open for me and even helped me with my seat at the table. I was a little impressed."

"So?" Polly encouraged.

"We ordered our meal and when the soup came out, I thought I was hearing strange noises, but I couldn't figure it out. Then, the entree came out and when he wasn't eating, I didn't hear them, so I paid close attention. He was snorting like a pig as he chewed!"

Polly gasped. "No way!"

"I'm not kidding you! And once the food got there, he couldn't hold a conversation, he was so intent on jamming it in his mouth. I've never seen such awful table manners and I've been on some pretty bad blind dates."

"I'd have died."

"I wanted to. I was so embarrassed, but honestly, that wasn't the worst of it."

"There can't be more."

"Well, yes, there can be. He finally finished eating and wiped his mouth with the linen napkin. That was fine, but then he stuck the thing in his mouth and began rubbing his teeth clean. When that was over, I am not kidding you, he belched. Right there in one of the nicest restaurants in downtown Boston, he belched!"

"No, no, no, no, no," Polly sighed. She shook her head. "What did you do?"

"I pulled money out of my purse, put it down on the table,

stood up and walked away. I didn't say another word to him. I didn't say good bye, I just left. I called a cab, then I called my mother and told her that was the last straw. She is never again setting me up on another blind date. Ever."

"You do know that I'm nervous about you meeting Mark Ogden for a blind date now, don't you?"

"I thought you assured me this wasn't a date, girlfriend."

Polly shivered and chuckled. "Okay, it's not a blind date and I promise you that I've had a meal with him and he doesn't snort or do anything gross while he eats. He's really nice."

They were laughing when Lucy brought their meals to the table and set them down. She said to Polly, "I hear you had more excitement over there at Sycamore House this morning."

Sal's eyes sparkled as she listened. Polly knew exactly what she was thinking, but said, "It never ends, does it, Lucy?"

"Do you suppose he was part of that fight at the Alehouse?"

"I'm going to ask him. I hope not, but you never know."

"How long has he been in Bellingwood?"

"He started working for us last week, but I don't know how long he'd been in town before that. Why do you ask?"

"No reason, just wondering. Enjoy your tenderloins, girls."

She walked away and Sal snickered under her breath, "News travels fast around here, doesn't it!"

"You have no idea," Polly said. "And not only news, but before too long, they'll have names and blood types and every other piece of information about all the parties involved. They'll know motive and what the police should do about it. Now, only ten percent of it will be actual truth, but if you listen long enough, you get a few nuggets of good information."

She stopped talking and watched as Sal's eyes got big. She had pulled the fries away from the sandwich and sat up a little straighter as she attempted to take in the full dimensions of the tenderloin.

"I can't eat all of this," she whispered.

"No one can," Polly laughed. "Cut it in half, then eat what you can."

After lunch, Polly and Sal wandered up and down the main street in Bellingwood, peeking in the stores, and stopping to say hello to people who recognized Polly. Sal couldn't believe the prices on items in the thrift and antique stores.

"I could make thousands of dollars, buying from the stores here and reselling these things at home," she exclaimed as they wandered through an antique shop. "How come no one does that?"

"I'm sure they do," Polly said. "You aren't the first person who has been astounded at these prices. But, everyone makes the money they want to make, so they're all happy."

Sal picked up a stack of old photographs, flipped through them and said, "How sad. Someone's memories are here and no one will ever know who they were." She set them back down on the table and drew her finger across a small chest of drawers that was next in the aisle. "This would be lovely in my foyer."

"I don't think they'll let you carry it on the airplane, Sal."

"I know, but I love it." She turned the price tag over. "Polly it's only one hundred dollars. Are they kidding me?"

Polly pushed her friend's hand away from the chest. "You can't take it with you. Let it go."

"But!"

"Let it go. Maybe we ought to get out of here before you forget yourself," Polly laughed and began walking toward the front door of the shop.

"How can you come in here and not want to buy everything?"

"That's why I don't come in here, you nut. It's the only way I restrain myself. Besides, where would I put this stuff? I still haven't unloaded the storage unit at home."

They walked back onto the sidewalk and Sal said, "You haven't dealt with those things yet?"

"No, not yet," Polly replied.

"I figured that once you got settled, you would bring all of your memories into your home."

"I know. I know. It's just that if everything is over there, tucked neatly away, I don't have to think too hard about missing them,"

Polly said. She felt her eyes begin to fill with tears and brushed at them with her hand.

"It was one thing to live in Boston and not have them around, but I've been avoiding those feelings since I moved back to Iowa," she continued.

"I'm sorry I brought it up, then. I didn't know you were still carrying that," Sal said. "You never talked about it much after your Mary died. I suppose we all figured you were doing fine."

She stopped on the sidewalk and turned to Polly, "I'm sorry I wasn't more sensitive to your loss during those years. I feel terrible that you were holding it all in and I didn't see it."

Polly took her hand and they crossed the street. "I was fine. I loved my job and I was having fun doing things with my friends and living my life in the big city. It was okay. Some nights I would pick up the phone and think about calling Dad or Mary to tell them about the things that were happening, and then I would cry, but it happened less and less as time passed. One day it was a good memory without the pain."

The two of them stopped again in front of the Bellingwood General Store. "When I was little, the drug store in Story City had a soda fountain," Polly said. "The drug store here doesn't, but this place has great ice cream. Are you game?"

Sal grinned and hooked her arm in Polly's. "What do you suppose their flavor of the day is?"

The two went inside and sat down at the counter. A young man, replete in his soda jerk uniform greeted them. The owner had designed a throwback fountain, with sparkling glass ice cream dishes and parfait glasses standing on transparent glass shelves in front of a mirror. Neon signs at each end of the wall advertised "Ice Cream Sundaes" and "Coca-Cola." Polly pointed to a metallic sign advertising root beer floats and Sal smiled as she took in the nostalgic touches, with glass straw dispensers and a bright red and chrome milk shake maker.

Sal ordered a scoop of their daily special - peach ice cream, and Polly ordered a turtle sundae. Before long they were sharing their ice cream with each other and giggling at the stories in a book Sal pulled from its stand on the counter.

Sal sighed, "I'm going to be miserable all afternoon if we keep eating like this. Maybe I should walk back to your house."

"Oh, nonsense. It's only ice cream. You're fine. Come on. Let's go for a ride," Polly said.

They crossed the street back to Polly's truck and Sal laughed. "You don't worry about jay walking or getting hit by cars in this little town, do you!"

"Every once in a while you have to pay attention, especially after school is out and the kids are home, but it's not a bad way to live."

"Where are you taking me now?" Sal asked.

Polly looked at her watch. Sylvie's boys, Jason and Andrew would be showing up a little after three, but she didn't need to be home until around four thirty. With Jason and Sal's help, they could have the horses back in the barn quickly. There was plenty of time.

"Let's drive down to Boone. The town is so pretty. You'll love all of the homes there. I remember driving through there when I was young, astounded at how beautiful they were."

"Okay," Sal sounded doubtful.

"Trust me. It's a nice day for a drive. We'll drive past Mamie Eisenhower's birthplace and though we don't have a lot of time, I'll take you past the old train station."

"Alright. I'm trusting you."

"Look, I know it isn't Concord or Cambridge with all of the excitement of Boston's history, but ...," Polly started.

"No, I'm sorry," Sal said. "I'm sure it will be lovely. This is what I wanted to do while I was here. I wanted to see why you love Iowa so much. Onward." And she pointed to the road in front of them.

"I'm going to make a quick call to Jeff to let him know I'm not going to be there when the boys arrive. He'll make sure they get upstairs."

She dialed Jeff's phone and told him that she was taking Sal to Boone. He assured her that everything was quiet and he'd point the way for Jason and Andrew.

They drove into Boone and were promptly stopped by a train crossing the main street. Polly watched Sal's eyes flit from right to left as she tracked the cars filled with coal heading east.

"Do you ever count the cars?" Sal asked.

"Sometimes I do and sometimes I like to watch for patterns in the car numbers to see if they're in sequence. Sometimes I try to figure out what the graffiti says. It's all entertainment."

Polly pointed out some of her favorite homes, set far back from the street. There were so many big, old gorgeous homes and she loved seeing them kept in such great shape. Finally she drove down a few side streets and stopped in front of a tiny yellow home with a sign out front announcing that it was a Historic Site – the Mamie Doud Eisenhower Birthplace. It wasn't open, so they stopped for a moment.

"It's fun knowing that someone famous was born here," Polly said. "It's hard to believe that from a little house like this, a girl would grow up to become the First Lady of the United States. It makes you realize that anything is possible in this world."

Sal smiled, "You love it here, don't you. We have streets filled with homes where famous people lived back home. I never knew you to be this retrospective about those places."

"I suppose you're right," Polly agreed.

She pulled back out and started heading north. "We probably need to get back. I'm sure Jason is ready to feed the horses and bring them in for the evening. That boy loves spending time with them. I'm so glad his mom lets me have him around to help. Andrew adores Obiwan. Once it gets warmer, there's no way any of them will want to stay in the apartment. It's a good thing I have a fence up."

"You love spending time with those boys, don't you?"

"Sure I do, they're great kids."

"Are you ever going to have kids with Henry?"

Polly raised her head up and started to speak, but Sal interrupted her, "No, don't get mad. I'm not pushing you or anything. Of all my friends, you never seemed interested in having children. You've never talked about it and since you didn't have your mom around pushing you to get married and have lots of grandchildren for her, it never came up."

She relaxed and thought about what Sal was saying. She was right. Polly wasn't interested in having children. "I don't know, Sal. Henry's cool about this. Believe it or not, I asked him about it the other day."

"You what? Oh, Polly, you're a complete nut!"

"I know. But, we're too old to get into a long term relationship if we have different ideas about something that important, so I asked."

"Well, of course you did. What did he say?"

"That we should probably talk about it someplace other than the parking lot of his business and it wasn't something that was important right now. Then he kissed me and I swooned."

"It sounds like he handled you quite nicely."

"He did at that. If I could start with kids about the age of Jason and Andrew, I'd be fine. They can feed themselves and have real conversations with you. You don't have to worry if you forget they're in the next room and run outside to take care of something. They entertain themselves and make decisions all on their own."

"It will work out for you someday, I have a lot of confidence in you," Sal assured her.

"I hope so," Polly replied. "I hope I don't make some huge mistake."

"Sometimes it's in the way we look at things," Sal said. "Choices aren't mistakes unless we spend a lot of time regretting them. You could look at them as a wild adventure."

"I like the sound of that. I'm always ready for an adventure."

"What's that?" Sal pointed to a bird standing on the shoulder of the highway.

"That's a pheasant," Polly said. "Look at the red and green on his head." The bird lifted up and flew across the highway in front of them, causing Polly to tap her brakes and slow the truck. He darted into the brush of the ditch and was gone from sight before she took the truck back up to speed.

"Do you see a lot of wildlife out here?" Sal asked.

"I do! There is a lot of natural wildlife around. I hear coyotes in the creek behind Sycamore House and there are deer that travel through the area. We have raccoons and possums and lots of squirrels and rabbits. Sometimes you will see a fox, but they don't come out very often."

"It's not quite like prairie days, but after a lifetime in the city, it's close," Sal said.

"You do know that life in the city isn't necessarily real for most of the country, don't you?"

"Isn't that weird to think about? I always assumed everyone lived like we do. Lots of traffic and stores that stay open until the middle of the night. Bars that never close and everyone racing to get to their jobs. I don't know how you live without a coffee shop on every corner or delis and fast food available all the time."

"I make my own coffee and cook my own meals."

"Well, that's right. You are a great cook, but still!"

"It was an adjustment. My pantry is better stocked than ever before and I plan better for the meals I'm going to cook. I probably have enough food stocked to live through a two week blizzard."

They pulled into the driveway of Sycamore House and both Jason and Andrew were playing in the grass with Obiwan. He saw the truck pull in and ran over to Polly, wagging his tail.

She got out of the truck and leaned over to hug him, then called out to Jason, "How about we head down to the barn after I get changed."

"Okay. Do you want me to start without you?" he asked.

"No, you play here for a while. I'll be back down soon."

Sal asked, "Do you want some more help with the horses?"

"Sure, that would be fun. I left your boots down there, so pull on your old stuff and come on down."

They went inside and Sylvie met them at the stairway.

"Hi there, did you have a good day?" she asked.

"We did. How is Eliseo?" Polly said.

"I was going over to check on him and take him some supper.

When I went over for lunch, he said he had slept all morning. I'll change his bandages and hopefully get him settled in for the night. It sure is nice of Henry to let him stay there."

Sal went on upstairs and Polly said, "I don't think any of us expected you to be his nursemaid, Sylvie."

"Who else was going to do it? Jeff?"

"Well, I could have."

Sylvie patted Polly's arm. "Your friend is here and wants to spend time with you, not watch you care for an employee. I'm glad to do this. I don't think he's had a lot of attention from people in his life. I think he's been alone a long time."

Polly hugged her. "You're wonderful, you know that?"

"When I'm ready to murder my sons, remind me, will you? Those two boys make me feel like a horrible ogre some days." Sylvie looked around and asked Polly. "Do you think he was involved in that fight uptown last night?"

"I don't know. Why don't you ask him?"

"Me? I'm not comfortable messing around in his business."

"If it's natural, would you ask him?"

Sylvie drooped her shoulders, "I shouldn't have asked you about it. That will teach me to be part of the town gossip. Okay, if it comes up as part of the conversation, I'll ask. But, otherwise, you have to. Got it?"

"I'm also going to have to ask him where he plans to live after this, too," Polly said. "I can't have him living in my barn."

"I'll bet he doesn't have any money until you pay him. He isn't the type of person who carries much with him."

"This is why I wish I had better guest quarters around here," Polly complained. "I own this great big building and I have no place for someone to stay. My apartment isn't even big enough for me to have Sal stay with me."

"What if you finished a room in the basement?" Sylvie asked.

Polly stepped back and tilted her head in contemplation. "That's an interesting idea. That's an interesting idea. I'll talk to Henry about it. It's not a perfect solution, but it has possibilities."

Sylvie held up the satchel she had in her right hand, "I'd better go. I'll be back for the boys after a while."

Polly went up to her apartment and changed her clothes, then went out to feed her Percherons and get them bedded down for the night. She was thankful that tonight they chose to behave since Sal was with her. She thought they might be showing off a little and was certain of it when Demi put his head over the gate for a little attention before they went back up to the house. He usually ignored her once he spied his food, but Sal stopped and rubbed his nose, standing on her tiptoes to plant a kiss on his forehead. He dipped his head to give her access and then returned to his stall as they walked away.

CHAPTER EIGHTEEN

Enjoying a few extra minutes in before the day started, Polly stretched and looked at the time. Six-fifteen. She rolled over and got a surprised look from Luke, who shut his eyes again, trying to ignore the fact that she was moving. Leia was curled up in a ball, tucked in between Obiwan's front paws and his chest. It was so cute, she snapped a quick picture with her phone, then pushed at her dog's back end with her foot. He raised his head, looked up at her, and settled back in.

"We need to get moving, kiddos. Today's going to be fun for me and I can't wait to get started. Up, up, up, up, up!" she said as she flung blankets over the top of all of them. Luke crawled out and stretched, his back arching, then sat down and began cleaning his left shoulder, a sure sign that he intended to ignore her. Obiwan slid himself off the bed, trying to avoid disturbing Leia, but to no avail. She ended up on the floor and when she jumped back up onto the bed, she was more than a little startled at being so abruptly awakened. She padded over to her brother and, leaning against him, lay back down.

"You're slugs," Polly said. "But you two can get away with it. Obiwan, you have to come with me. Let's get going."

She pulled her jeans and sweatshirt on, slipped into her boots and headed out her door into the living room, chuckling as she saw the mess. Last night had been fun. Sal had begged Polly to cook for her, so they stayed in after Sylvie picked up the boys. Polly had offered to drive down to Ames and find something fun to do, but Sal insisted the reason she was in Iowa was to spend quality time with her friend in her home, not traipse all over the countryside.

Fortunately, Polly had the ingredients for a nice, homey dinner and whipped together a meatloaf. She sliced potatoes and tossed them in a mixture of flour with her homemade Moroccan seasoning and while things were baking, put together a quick asparagus gratin and soon, supper was on the table. They'd laughed their way through two bottles of wine and when Polly pulled out her drawer filled with games, they stayed up late playing Scrabble Slam and laughed until they were in tears.

Polly opened the gates for Obiwan and he ran to the barn door, waiting for her to open it.

"You've been inside all night long and you want to go in here first?" she asked, pulling it open.

Eliseo was coming down the alley of the barn with a bucket of grain, headed for Nat's stall.

"Good morning, Polly. I'm moving a little slower than usual, but we'll get them fed," he said.

"What are you doing? You shouldn't be here this morning!"

"I'd rather be here than laying around. Your friend, Henry, doesn't need me in his house any longer. He was gracious enough to put up with me on his couch last night."

Polly felt her phone buzz with an incoming text.

"Eliseo there?" Henry asked.

She smiled, *"He's here and working. So, I hope you aren't this stupid."*

"What do you mean by that?"

"Thinking you have to be all macho when you've been hurt."

"Don't worry. I'll whimper and whine and let you nurse me back to health."

201

"Blech," she texted back. *"None of that, please."*

"Well, what do you want from me? Macho man or helpless human?"

"Get moving. You have to work today."

"Yes ma'am. I'll be there in a jiffy."

She looked up at Eliseo who was coming back again with another bucket and heading into Daisy's stall and asked, "Where are you planning to stay? Now that I know, you can't live out here in the barn."

"I'll sort something out," he said. "I always do. Don't you worry. I've been taking pretty good care of myself for a lot of years and I didn't forget how to do that because I got into a fight with some lowlifes."

"Was that the fight everyone is talking about at the Jefferson Street Alehouse?" Polly asked him, as they walked back to the tack room together. He grabbed the wheelbarrow and she picked up two muck rakes.

He nodded and said, "I'm sorry you had to hear about that."

"I'm going to assume you won't tell me what happened."

"I don't want to," he replied, taking one of the rakes and walking into Nan's stall. He opened the outside door and said, "I already hauled hay for them. You don't need to worry about that this morning."

"Eliseo. I could have taken care of this today. You have to be hurting."

"Ma'am. I've had much worse pain than a few bruised ribs. This is the last thing that's going to slow me down for longer than a day. Please don't worry."

"Well, I can't help but worry. Oh, and by the way, don't call me ma'am. The last person who did that had a mug of coffee poured on him. I'd prefer it if you would call me Polly."

"Yes ma'am, I mean, yes Miss Giller." He chuckled, then grimaced and put his hand on his side, "It might take some time for me to get used to calling you Polly, but I'll try to stop using ma'am."

They went to work in the stalls and soon the place was cleaned up and the horses were outside.

"Are you going to work with them this morning?" he asked her.

"They get a day off," she said. "I promised Sal that I would make breakfast and then we're heading over to see what is going on at Beryl Watson's studio before she returns to her own home today."

"Would you mind if I spent some time with them? I know you've been busy this week and they could use the exercise."

"I hate to ask that of you. You already have so much going on here."

"Miss Giller, these horses give me a little bit of peace. Would you mind?"

Polly smiled and shook her head and felt tears threaten again. She wondered if maybe she needed to look for some Midol or something while she was out today. Her emotions were running fairly high these days and she was certain it had to be her hormones.

"Eliseo, feel free to spend whatever time you want with them. Thank you."

"Then, you go in and enjoy your friend and I'll be in later to do my own work. It looks as if Mr. Lyndsay has quite a bit scheduled for the weekend, so it will be busy around here. I appreciate the work, you know."

Polly wanted to reach out and touch him, to extend a little human contact, but he turned away and walked outside. She watched him lean his head against Nat's shoulder and stroke the horse, then he ducked under Daisy's chin to get over to Nan, who pushed at his shoulder with her nose. He had definitely bonded with the one horse Polly couldn't reach. The two of them stood quietly together for a moment before he made a clicking noise with his teeth and walked away from her. She followed him and he began to pace around the perimeter of the pen with her walking beside him. Polly watched until her stomach grumbled and then went inside to clean up and get breakfast ready.

She was in the kitchen cleaning up from the night before when she heard her front door open.

Sal peeked around the corner of the entry way and said, "Are you up and moving?"

"Girlfriend, I've been up since six thirty. Breakfast is in the oven, I'm cleaning the last of the mess and we're waiting for you to show!"

"I don't know how you do it," Sal complained. "I might have had a little too much wine last night." She sat down at the dining room table and slumped over, laying her head on crossed arms. Polly poured a cup of coffee and put it in front of her.

"I quit a lot earlier than you did. While you were drinking, I was sipping," Polly laughed. "You drank most of that last bottle by yourself."

"Why didn't you stop me?" Sal whimpered.

"Maybe because you're a big girl."

"This big girl might need a nanny."

Polly opened her cupboard and pulled out some aspirin, then drew a glass of water and placed those in front of Sal as well. "Drink that whole glass. You need to rehydrate. Take the aspirin. You don't get to have a hangover on me today."

"I know," Sal said. "It's my own fault." She put the aspirin in her mouth and took a drink to swallow them.

"The whole glass," Polly reminded her.

"In a minute!" Sal whined.

Polly laughed and put her hand on Sal's back, rubbing her friend's shoulder and neck. "You're going to live. I promise."

The oven timer rang and she went in to retrieve the French toast casserole she'd baked. She checked the pan of bacon and it still had a few more minutes before they turned crispy, so she began pulling out dishes and silverware and set the table.

Sal finished the water and began sipping her coffee. "That's the stuff," she said in a moan, then looked up at Polly. "I'm useless, aren't I?" cradling the cup in her hands.

"It's alright. You're the guest. You get to be whatever you want to be. When I come stay with you, it will be your turn to take care of me."

"Deal. But you know I can't cook so we'd either have to hire someone or eat out a lot."

"If you hire a cook, he has to be young and hot."

Polly put the bacon on a plate, cut the casserole and put several squares on another plate and took them to the table.

"You're going to make a great wife to Henry someday," Sal said as she took a bite of the casserole. "Oh my. This is good!"

"Don't you dare start with that, too," Polly warned. "I'm not marrying anyone for a while. I like my life just the way it is."

Sal waggled her finger at Polly, "Methinks you doth protest too much."

"I'm not protesting. And stop it! I'm simply reacting to the fact that everyone wants me to behave in a certain manner and I'm not ready for it."

"Simmer, girl. Obviously, this is another of your hot buttons."

Polly giggled, "Apparently it is. But, I'm not getting married, got it?"

"Just know I'll come out for the wedding."

"Whatever," Polly said.

A knock at her door made them both jump and before Polly could get there, Henry stuck his head inside and said, "Good morning! Is everyone decent in here?"

"We were just talking about you," Sal said, looking up from her breakfast.

"I don't even want to know." Henry looked at the food on the table and said, "Would you feed me if I told you I hadn't eaten breakfast yet?"

Polly laughed, "You're pitiful. You've been up for hours. What have you been doing with yourself?"

He didn't wait for her to invite him in, but headed for the table. As he passed her, he gave her a quick peck on the cheek and whispered, "Good morning, sunshine."

Polly brought out another plate and silverware and set them down at the place across from Sal. "So what have you been doing this morning?"

"Don't I get coffee?" he asked.

"Oh, good heavens!" Polly exclaimed. "Get it yourself."

She sat down in her chair and he laughed, but got up and

obeyed, saying, "I met Len in the workshop this morning. They're going to start hauling the base cabinets over to Beryl's studio so they can begin assembling them. After that I met Ruby Lindahl at her house to look at an old built-in hutch she has. It's beginning to pull away from the wall and she's worried it will fall on her. That thing isn't going anywhere, but I need to spend some more time there. I think the floor is sagging. I told her she was fine, it's been like this for years, but I'll get started on it next week. Then, I ran over to Beryl's place to make sure it was unlocked and ready to go for the day and now I'm here."

He gave Polly a puppy dog face and said, "And I knew you would be making breakfast, so I thought I'd beg from you."

She shoved his arm and laughed. "Where are we going tonight for our big double date?"

"Oh!" he said. "I figure Mark knows Ames as well as I do, so he might have a good idea about where we could eat. Or, we could head over to Story City. Have you taken Sal to your home town?"

Sal looked at Polly with wide eyes and said, "That sounds interesting. I haven't been there since that spring break of our junior year."

"There isn't much fun to do there, everyone always leaves town on Friday nights. Let's go to Ames," Polly replied.

Henry glanced back and forth between the two of them. "Sure, that's fine. Are you up for barbecue, Sal?"

"Anything is great."

"Hickory Park is a tradition around here," he began and Polly interrupted him.

"And you can get ice cream, too!" she laughed.

Sal shrugged. "Really. Whatever you want to do, I'm ready for it. I'm here for the experience."

"I'll text Mark, then," Polly said. "Henry, can you drive?"

"My truck?" he asked.

"Well, it's either your truck, my truck or Mark's truck. Yours has the easiest access for four people and is probably the cleanest of all of them."

He looked a little bemused, "Sure. Tell Mark to meet us here and I'll drive my truck."

Polly texted Mark with the details and he wrote back, *"And here I thought this might not happen."*

"Why would you think that? I never cancel plans," she wrote back.

"You're right. I should have known better. I'll dress in my best overalls and see you later."

"Brat."

"And you love me for it."

"We're set," she said to Sal and Henry.

They had finished eating and were cleaning up when another knock was heard. Before Polly made it past the kitchen peninsula, Sylvie stuck her head in. "Did I miss breakfast?" she asked.

Polly looked guilty and said, "I should have brought it all downstairs, shouldn't I!"

"Oh stop it, you crazy girl! I caught the scent when I opened the door just now and it smells heavenly."

"It was," Henry laughed. He handed Polly the dish towel and said, "I need to get downstairs and move people along or you will never have a garage."

He touched Sylvie's arm as he passed her and was out the door and gone before Polly could say anything more.

"What's up, Sylvie?" she asked.

"I was coming up to say good morning and see if you heard anything about Beryl. Will she go home today? I thought I'd take food over for her."

"The doctor's appointment is at ten thirty and both she and Andy are pretty certain he will tell her that she's fine. We're meeting at Davey's for lunch if you want to join us."

"I don't have time for that today, but thanks," Sylvie said.

"Did you know Eliseo was working this morning? He beat me to the barn," Polly said.

"He told me last night that he wasn't going to be able to lie around any longer than a day. I'm not surprised. Did you talk to Henry about a room downstairs for him?"

"Darn! No I didn't. And I should do that right now. Maybe we can get something in place yet today."

"Do you have any extra beds around?"

Polly thought for a moment and shook her head. "I don't. And it takes so long for them to deliver something up here. Shoot, I should have spent more time thinking about this yesterday."

"We'll come up with something."

"You know, he told me this morning that he would manage. I don't know if he'd particularly like a couple of women trying to figure his life out for him," Polly said.

"He can get over that," Sylvie snapped. "Stupid men. They think they don't need anyone and then they end up in a little town in Iowa all by themselves with no place to live. There isn't a woman I know who would put up with that crap."

Polly laughed and heard Sal snickering behind her. "You're right! You know what? You go talk to Henry, will you?"

Sylvie looked at her in confusion. "Me? He works with you."

"No, you go talk to him because Sal and I are going to haul ourselves down to Boone and buy a bed. They'll load it up in my truck and before Eliseo even knows what happened, we'll find a way for him to stay here until he gets his own place."

Polly turned around and said, "Are you okay with this, Sal?"

Sal put her dish towel down on the counter and said, "Wherever you want me to go, I go. I'm ready."

Sylvie left and Polly made sure the coffee pot and oven were all turned off. Sal went across to her room for a jacket and they headed downstairs. Henry met them outside by her truck with a handful of rope and bungee ties.

"Make sure they strap things in tightly. I know it isn't a long trip back, but you don't want to lose anything. Be safe, okay?" He put the items in Polly's truck behind her seat and said, "We'll be ready when you get back, but you know he could have stayed with me for a while."

"He wasn't going to stay with you. I don't even know if he'll let me do this for him. I think he'd rather sleep in my barn than allow people to help him, but that changes today," Polly announced.

"You go get 'em, girl," Henry said. "We'll clear the space and be ready."

Polly and Sal made their way to the furniture store in Boone and went inside. Of course, they wanted to sell her more than she was willing to buy. Fancy was not what she wanted. She finally settled on a simple frame and headboard and a comfortable mattress. She chose a bedside table and lamp as well as a rug to put on the concrete floor.

Sal asked, "Do you have bedding?"

"No!" Polly cried. "I'm glad you remembered."

With the bed tightly strapped in, they made one more quick stop to pick up bedding, then hurried back to Bellingwood. She pulled up to the front door and Jeff and Henry came out to meet them.

"I told Eliseo what you were doing," Jeff said. "I figured you wanted me to deal with him. Is that alright?"

Polly said, "As long as he isn't upset with me, it's perfect!"

"He's surprised and not too pleased, but I told him you're this way with everyone."

She laughed, "Maybe a little. I'll give you that. Let's get this inside and set up. Sal and I are going to lunch at Davey's and I want this to be done before we leave."

Sal pulled the bags of bedding out of the cab of the truck and Polly reached in to grab the lamp. Sylvie showed up and took that from her, so Polly waited for the bed of her truck to be unpacked. As soon as the box springs were out, she was able to muscle the mattress enough to get to the frame and grabbed parts of it and headed inside and down the steps.

Henry and Jeff had cleared out one of the back rooms. She set down her load and went back up to help bring the rest down. Soon, it was unloaded and she and Sylvie unrolled the rug. It filled the room and they arranged the bedframe on top of it. When everything was set into place and the lamp was turned on, the room actually looked quite warm.

"This will be fine for the short term," Polly said. "Thank you."

Jeff said, "Eliseo is avoiding us. He's in the auditorium setting up for this evening's reception."

"Would you send him down," she asked. "I want him to hear

from me that he has to accept this with grace."

Jeff smiled and rolled his eyes, "I'll tell him. He won't like it, but I'll tell him."

Sylvie said, "I'm out of here. I don't want to be around for this." She grabbed some of the plastic wrapping and headed for the stairs.

Henry and Sal did the same. Sal turned around and said, "I'll be playing with your animals. Come find me, okay?"

"I'll be up in a bit," Polly acknowledged. After they left, she sat down on the bed and looked around. This would work.

In a few moments, she heard footsteps on the stairs and soon, Eliseo walked in. Before she could speak, he said, "Miss Giller, this is too much. I would have figured it out on my own."

She didn't move, just sat on the bed and looked at him, then said, "You know. I've had it pretty easy all my life. I didn't have to do things I didn't want to do in order to make a living. When I bought this building, one of my dreams was to be able to make it possible for other people to find relief from the things that stopped them from being creative. I'm not an artist or an author; I don't shoot beautiful photographs or design homes. I can cook, but I'm not a chef. I'm just Polly and I've been fortunate. But sometimes people have to kill themselves in order to live and when they have a few free moments, they use themselves all up trying to create beauty they can share with the world.

"So, I fixed this place and as we grow, I hope people will come here for a short time and feel like we took care of them so they could be creative without worrying about all those things that make life stressful.

"At the same time, though, I want this to be a safe place for the people who work with me to make that happen for our guests. I like you a lot. I want you to be here for a long time. You are good with my animals and this morning I watched Nan react to you in a way she never has with me. She loves you. Jeff likes you and Sylvie reacted to your pain yesterday like I've never seen her react to anyone before. In a short period of time, you've created relationships with both my animals and my staff and you're doing a great job around here.

"I can offer a lot to my guests and my friends and Eliseo, you have to let me give this to you, even if you find your own place and move out in a few weeks. I don't feel sorry for you and I'm not giving you charity. This is how I live around the people who are in my life. It's not a big deal unless you make it into a big deal. You have to trust me on this.

"Sycamore House isn't only about me or about the guests; it's about whoever needs or wants a place of safety and shelter. Does this make sense to you?"

He had stood in the doorway while she spoke and finally said, "Then I will assure you that you'll never have reason to be disappointed in my work. I will be out of here as soon as I can afford it, but for now, thank you."

Polly stood up, crossed the room and took his hand to shake it. "Thank you for not making this difficult for me, Eliseo. I didn't want to have to get pushy."

He laughed. "One of these days I'll find a way to repay you for this generosity."

"Don't do anything for me," Polly said. "Take care of someone else who needs it and we'll be square."

She moved past him through the doorway. "I don't know what you have brought with you, but this room is yours, so feel free to settle in. I'm sorry there aren't bathrooms or a shower down here, but you know where they are. Bring a chair down from the conference room if you want a place to sit."

Polly went upstairs to her apartment and before walking in, she stopped and took a breath, looking around her home. Then, opening the door, she went inside, ready to start the next part of her day.

CHAPTER NINETEEN

It was later than she'd hoped when Polly finally rushed out of Sycamore House with Sal to meet up with her friends for lunch at Davey's. Beryl's appointment with her doctor was finished, stitches removed, and she was ready to return to her own home.

When they walked in, the hostess greeted them and said, "They're waiting for you, follow me."

Sal leaned in and whispered, "She knows who you are. Do you eat here a lot?"

Polly giggled. "I probably do. But, remember, it's a small town. Everyone knows everyone and Lydia would have told her to keep an eye out for us."

The hostess showed them to a round table in the back of the main room where Lydia and Beryl were seated.

"Where's Andy?" Polly asked, surprised to see that she was missing.

"She's probably run over to my place to have a quickie with her boyfriend," Beryl smirked, then said, "Hi. You must be Sal, I'm Beryl Watson, the invalid. Here. Sit down by me and you can tell me all about Polly's lurid past."

Sal looked at Polly, who shrugged and said, "If you sit by her, I will not take responsibility for what's to come."

Lydia had stood and reached across the table to shake Sal's hand. "I'm Lydia Merritt. It's nice to meet you. Have you had a good time in Bellingwood so far?"

"It's been lovely," Sal replied and sat down beside Beryl. "Now I have a better understanding as to why Polly will never come back to live in Boston. She's told me why she loves it here, but after seeing the way she has become such a part of this community, it all makes much more sense."

"We love her," Lydia said, "and probably wouldn't let her leave anyway. Has she given you the ten cent tour?"

Sal nodded. "We had lunch downtown yesterday and wandered through a few of the stores. Then we drove around Boone in the afternoon and made another trip back down this morning."

Lydia looked at Polly, "Because it's there?"

"No. I needed to buy a bed."

Lydia was perplexed. "A bed? Do you have someone coming in before the bedroom set I ordered arrives?"

"Oh, not for upstairs, for the basement."

"Sure," Beryl interrupted. "For the basement. Because your basement needs to sleep."

Sal grinned, "It's a roller coaster of events over at Sycamore House. I'm almost ready to return to my quiet life in Boston. Polly has more going on than one person should."

"No kidding," Beryl laughed. "We just sit back and wait for the bodies to fall."

"Stop it!" Polly protested. "I put together a bedroom in the basement for my custodian. He doesn't have a place to live and he had been sleeping in the hayloft of my barn. It was either this or Henry's house and he didn't want to bother Henry."

"So you made a room for him." Beryl poked Sal. "We love her, we really do, but she won't be happy until everyone has moved into Sycamore House. I will protest loudly and with most foul language if she makes me leave my home again. I don't want to live with her!"

Polly rolled her eyes and shook her head. "It's only temporary until he can find his own place. And besides, it has been bothering me that I don't have a place where people can stay if they show up."

Sal picked up on Beryl's attitude, "So you would have put me in the basement?"

"No!" Polly said. "Oh, forget it. I'm not going to win with this, am I? I bought a bed," and she stopped because Sal interrupted.

"And a lamp, and a rug and a bedside table and if we're not careful she'll find a way to put in a shower and bathroom down there, too."

"You're going to walk to Des Moines tomorrow if you aren't careful, you brat," Polly said.

Sal pursed her lips and sat back in her chair.

"Anyway, I bought a bed. So there." She picked up her menu and began flipping through the pages.

Andy walked in and joined them. Introductions were made and Polly asked, "Beryl said you were meeting Len for a nooner. How was it?"

Beryl looked appalled and Andy's mouth dropped open in shock. "I wanted to make sure that things were ready at her house. I picked up her mail and took things inside, then ran out to the studio to check on their progress," Andy responded, then said, "Beryl!"

"Those are not the words I used!" Beryl laughed. "Not exactly, at least. I might have implied it, but I certainly didn't call it a nooner. That's a terrible word."

"Right," Polly said, "because quickie is much better."

They laughed and told stories on each other through lunch. Andy described Beryl's morning walks to the cemetery behind her house. One morning, she had snuck up on a poor man who was replacing the flowers at his wife's headstone. He didn't hear her coming and when she had wished him a good morning, he fell over and rolled partway down the hill before he could catch himself. Beryl insisted that he was in his eighties, Lydia assured them that he was only a few years older than Beryl and Andy. The worst part of the story was that when he fell, he had knocked his toupee off his head. Beryl had quietly picked it up, shook it off and before he could stand up, placed it back on his poor, bald pate, adjusting it for him until it looked as it always did.

"He's going to be glad she has gone home," Andy said. "He's there every Thursday and I'm certain that next week, he will approach with great trepidation."

Not to be outdone, Sal pitched into a story about one of Polly's study dates in college. Polly wanted to crawl under the table, it was one of her more horrendous evenings, but she listened as Sal began.

"He was in your American Lit class, wasn't he?" Sal asked and Polly nodded her affirmation, then Sal asked, "Why was he even in there?"

"Because he'd registered late, I think. Go on and tell the story."

"Well, he called Polly in a panic one evening because there was a paper due on some author,"

"Henry James," Polly interjected.

"Anyway, he hadn't done any work and wondered if Polly could sum up his writing in a few sentences so that he could get the paper written the next day. Didn't he give you two days' notice?"

Polly nodded.

"Oh, I didn't tell you that this kid was gorgeous. Drop dead gorgeous. Big brown eyes and soft, curly hair that hung to his shoulders. He was a knockout. Poor Polly couldn't turn him down, so she told him that if he would commit to six hours the next day, she'd take him through the process and help him get a paper written.

"He was living off-campus in an apartment and invited her to come over. She dressed up for him and packed her backpack with books by Henry James and books about Henry James, tossed in her laptop and headed over."

Beryl snickered, "I can see this one coming."

"She walked in and the place was a total dump. He hadn't even bothered to pick up his dirty underwear."

Polly shuddered at the memory.

"It didn't occur to him that it might be offensive, so his filth stared at Polly all evening. He invited her to sit at the dining room table, which was covered with dishes and empty food trays. When she looked at him he shoved it all to one end and picked up a chair, shaking the stuff off it to the floor. She told me she was scared to sit down because she was afraid she'd stick there forever. So, she asked if he had a clean towel anywhere in the apartment. He went to a drawer beside the kitchen sink and said, 'I think Mom left me some towels,' and pulled out an unopened package of dish rags. Polly ran some water over one and scrubbed the chair as clean as possible, then wiped down the table where she was going to work. He asked her if she'd like some supper and what did you say to him, Polly?"

"'No, I'm not feeling very well.' I thought that if I ate a single thing in that apartment, I would vomit."

Sal continued, "He started drinking beer as Polly pulled out her books. They were talking about one of the books and why James wrote from the point of view he chose and the next thing she knew, this kid left the table, walked over, sat down on the sofa and turned on the television. When she asked about his paper, he told her he was dropping the course and asked if she wanted to make out."

"What did you do?" Andy asked Polly.

"I put my books back in the bag, packed up my laptop, tossed the dirty wet rag at his head and left. That was one of the worst nights ever!"

"I wonder what ever happened to him," Sal mused.

"Hopefully he hired a maid or else he probably died from his own filth."

When they finished lunch Andy said, "We're going to Beryl's house. You two ought to come over and see the progress on the studio. I think you'll be pleased, Polly."

"That's a good idea," she agreed. "We'll follow you."

They all made their way to Beryl's and while Andy and Beryl went inside the house, Lydia, Polly and Sal walked around back to the studio. Polly could hear noise coming from inside the little building and when they walked in, were greeted by several of Beryl's friends. Her art students were there and the place had been decorated with balloons and flowers. A cake was set out reading "Welcome Home," and festive paper plates, napkins and cups were neatly arranged.

"Nice," Polly remarked as she glanced around the room. She recognized a few of the people, but others simply smiled and nodded. Once again, she knew they recognized her. One day she hoped to be able to put more faces and names together at the same time.

It didn't take too long before they heard Andy talking to Beryl as they walked from the house to the studio and when Andy opened the door, they all yelled "Surprise!"

"Dammit," Beryl said, "You should have made me pee before I left the house. You know I don't handle things like this well."

Deena, the young girl who had been at Beryl's the day of the explosion rushed over to hug her mentor. "Look around," she said, "This is going to be wonderful when it is finished!"

She pulled Beryl into the room and Polly watched as the girl pointed out some of the new features of the cabinets they were building. When they approached the back room, Beryl stopped and turned on Polly.

"You cleaned up the blood. I was looking forward to showing that off to my guests."

"Sorry about that," Polly laughed. "I couldn't leave those ugly brown stains. They bothered me."

Deena looked up and said, "That was one of the worst things I'd ever seen, Ms. Watson. I was so scared for you."

"I know you were, dear. But, you handled yourself like a professional. I'm lucky you were around."

They disappeared into the back room and within moments, Beryl came out laughing.

"Whose great idea was it to lock up all of my flammables? Did y'all think that one explosion was enough or what?" She strode over to Polly, "You know that all of this perfect organization is going to mess with my chaotic flow of creativity, don't you."

Polly shook her head, "I am completely confident that within a week of you getting back in here, things will be as chaotic as you desire."

Beryl poked her in the arm, "Think you know me pretty well, do you? Maybe I'll surprise you."

"Maybe the only reason you ever keep this place organized is because your students put your things away between sessions," Polly smirked.

Deena stood behind her mentor and giggled. Beryl spun around, "Don't you laugh at me, sweetling. You're the one I'm going to hold responsible for keeping this place up to snuff."

"Yes ma'am."

"Such deference," Beryl laughed. "I don't know what I'm going to do when she decides to go to college."

Polly recognized the man who had stopped her earlier in the week, "Mr. Storey!" she called out. He looked up and caught her eye, then made his way over.

Putting his hand out to shake Beryl's, he said, "Welcome home, Miz Watson. I'm glad you are doing alright."

"Thank you!" she said, "I'm sorry my water heater's explosion broke one of your windows. You will be sure to stop by some morning and give me the bill. Bring your sweet wife and we'll have coffee."

"That's alright," he responded. "I've already had it replaced and it wasn't that much money."

"Well, you should come over and have coffee some morning anyway. We've lived beside each other for so many years and have never done that. Why don't we plan on it next Thursday. Will you come?"

He stood there, speechless. "Well, I would need to talk to Vanessa..."

"Tell her that I will be expecting the two of you next Thursday at nine thirty. You don't need to bring anything except maybe the receipt for the window. I'll have coffee and rolls for us. Now, if you will excuse me, I see someone I need to speak with."

Beryl turned away and walked toward another cluster of people. Polly watched as Beryl's neighbor tried to comprehend what had just happened.

"Nice to see you again, Miss Giller," he said, then walked out the front door and left.

Polly chuckled and said to Sal, "Well, that was hilarious."

"What just happened?" Sal asked.

"Beryl ensured that he would never complain about anything around here again. And I'll bet she has also ensured that he'll keep a pretty good eye on her safety."

"She wasn't letting him say no to coffee."

"And she also didn't let her invitation be set aside. That was fabulous!"

Len Specek, who was handling the installation of the cabinets for Henry, was standing in a corner, waiting for the party to die down so he could go back to work. Polly watched him eyeing Andy and sidling up to her, said. "Go talk to him. He doesn't look comfortable."

"If I go anywhere near him, Beryl is going to say something awful, I just know it!" Andy replied.

"Sheesh," Polly said. "Come on." She grabbed both Sal and Andy and approached the poor man.

"Hi, Mr. Specek," Polly said. "I'd like you to meet my friend, Sal Kahane from Boston."

He reached out and shook her hand. "Welcome to Bellingwood," he said. "I hope you are enjoying your stay."

"It's a wonderful community," Sal replied. "I can see why Polly loves it so much."

Polly could barely hold back her laughter as she watched Beryl sneak up behind Andy. She glanced at Len Specek, who had absolutely no idea what was about to transpire.

"Who's the hot dish?" Beryl said directly in Andy's ear.

Andy jumped and then clutched her heart.

"Careful dear, you'll bloody my nose if you keep flinging your head around like that. Then, there will be blood on my floor again and Polly won't be happy." Beryl laughed. "So, is this the hot thing you've been hiding from all of us?"

Andy looked at Polly with a scowl on her face. "See, I told you."

Polly shrugged and smiled.

"Hey! You! I'm right here. Are you going to introduce me or am I going to have to embarrass you?"

Andy took a deep breath, stepped to the side and said, very graciously, "Beryl Watson, I know you have met Len Specek since it isn't like he is new in town. So, please, I'm begging you, be polite."

"Why, Len Specek!" Beryl said, "You look fabulous! It's so good to see you again. It has been absolutely years since we've seen each other."

"Months," Andy muttered. "You saw him at the hoe-down. Now you're being obnoxious."

Beryl continued gaily, ignoring the obvious discomfort of her friend. "I'm so glad that you and Andy are finding time to be with each other. It's wonderful when old friends reconnect, isn't it? She has spent this last week telling me absolutely ..." Beryl paused, "nothing about you and it's making me crazy. So, I think that you and she should come over for dinner next week sometime. Let's make it Sunday noon. I would love to reconnect with you and since Andy has been such a wonderful friend this last week, maybe I can tell her thank you all at the same time!"

"Oh no," Andy said. "You don't have to agree to this, Len."

"Yes he does!" Beryl insisted. "Don't you?"

The poor man obviously had nothing to say, but finally responded, "Dinner would be nice." He took Andy's hand, "I'm sure it will be very nice. Don't worry, Andy. It will be fine."

Polly heard Sal giggle, then Lydia stepped in and said, "Beryl, you have to be nice."

"I am being nice. I invited them over for dinner. How is that not nice?"

"Don't you want some cake and maybe some punch?" Lydia asked, taking Beryl's arm and moving her away.

"That's why you wouldn't let me eat dessert at Davey's. Is everyone waiting for me?" Beryl spun around and said to Andy,

"Look what you made me do. I got all interested in you and your friend here and everyone had to wait for cake."

Deena rushed over to the cake table and handed the knife to Beryl, who made the first cut, then announced, "Let them eat cake!"

Soon, plates were handed around the room and Beryl wandered over to heft herself up on a cabinet under a window. Polly and Sal made their way to her.

"Sal and I are going back to Sycamore House. I'm glad you are back where you belong and I can't wait to see you working out here again.

"I know that you did most of the design for this place, Polly and I love it. Thank you."

"Please be good to Andy," Polly pleaded.

"Nope. Not gonna. She doesn't get to have a new boyfriend and hide him from us. If she'd been upfront about this from the beginning, it would have been far less painful for her."

"Alrighty then," Polly laughed.

She leaned in and hugged Beryl, then turned to wave goodbye to Andy and Lydia. Sal followed her out to the truck and they drove back across town.

"This has been a crazy day, Polly," Sal said as they went in the front door of Sycamore House. "Is it like this all the time?"

"Oh, heaven's no. If there was this much excitement every day, I'd be exhausted all the time!"

They moved aside as three very young men rushed to the front door, followed by several children who were chasing each other out into the parking lot.

"There's a wedding reception tonight. I'm sure they're decorating the hall," Polly remarked as they headed up the steps.

When they got to the top, Sal moved toward her door and Polly said, "Come on over whenever you're ready. The door will be unlocked."

She went on into her own apartment, sat down on the sofa and was immediately joined by two cats and a dog. As she leaned back, Obiwan attempted to curl up on her hip, sprawling himself out on the rest of the couch, while the two cats finally perched, one on her chest and the other behind her head. She shut her eyes and woke up when all three animals jumped off and came to attention.

Polly had enough time to sit up and rub her eyes before Sylvie's boys came barreling in.

"Oh. Hi, Polly!" Jason said. "I didn't expect to see you here."

Andrew chimed in, "You're never on the couch when we get here!"

"I know," Polly replied. "But, I'm here now. Did you stop and say hi to your mom?"

"She was busy," Andrew said. "But she gave me this!"

He showed her a zippered bag of cookies. "She said we could eat them all!"

Polly watched as he counted the cookies in the bag. When he looked back up, he announced, "There are seven in here. Would you like one too?"

She stood up and headed for the kitchen, with the boys following her. "I would love one. Who wants milk?"

Jason stood in front of the cupboard which held the glasses. "I know Andrew does and I do, too. Should I get a glass for you?"

"That would be great, Jason. Thank you." Polly pulled out the last gallon of milk. She hardly ever drank the stuff, but since the boys had started coming to her house every day after school, she made sure to have plenty of juices and milk on hand.

Andrew had placed napkins out for each of them and when he began counting out the cookies, he hesitated. "Would you like two cookies, Polly?"

She giggled to herself and said, "No thank you, Andrew. I've had plenty to eat today and I'm going out to dinner tonight. One cookie will be perfect."

"Cool!" he said as he split the cookies up. She nearly choked, though, when she realized that he had carefully chosen the largest cookie and placed it on her napkin. He was climbing into his chair as she wrapped her arms around him and kissed his head.

When she released him, he brushed his hair back into place and said, "What was that for?"

"You're a great kid. You're both great kids."

Andrew dramatically rolled his eyes at his brother and got down to the business of eating his cookies.

Polly took a bite and said, "Hey, what kind of cookie is this?"

"Mom calls them monster cookies," Jason said. "She says the original recipe called for cookies that were this big."

Polly laughed as he spread his arms open wide. There were M&Ms, chocolate chips, peanut butter and oatmeal exploding in her mouth. "These are great cookies," she said.

"What do you boys plan to do this afternoon since you don't have any homework?" she asked.

Andrew grinned, "It's my turn to choose the game today. We're racing!"

"I always beat him, but he still wants to race me," Jason said.

"Someday I'm going to win," Andrew declared. He jumped up, slugged down the rest of his milk and ran for the entertainment center. He pulled out a game and plugged the controllers in and sat down on the floor.

"Come on, Jason!" he said. "Come on!"

Jason's attempt to be dignified as he walked over to sit beside his brother touched Polly's heart. She smiled as she picked up their glasses and napkins, wiping the crumbs from the table into her hand.

Jason said, "We'll play one game and then take Obiwan outside. Is that alright?"

"That sounds great," she said. Polly began cleaning up, assuming that after dinner tonight, if they wanted to settle somewhere, they might come back to her apartment.

Jason and Andrew, true to their word, took Obiwan outside and when they returned, Jason said, "Eliseo asked me to tell you that he and I could take care of the horses tonight. Would that be alright? And Mom said to ask if we could stay later because the reception gets over at ten o'clock."

"Sure, both of those are fine," Polly said, while she tried to wrap her head around finishing a double date in her apartment with two young boys. She had looked forward to spending her last evening with Sal having fun, maybe playing games or watching classic movies, something both she and Sal did a lot of when they were in college. Polly fancied herself in love with Cary Grant, while Sal was a swooning fan girl in love with Gregory Peck. It mattered to neither of them that those men were old enough to be their grandfathers and were both dead, it was enough that they were gorgeous, suave and debonair on screen.

She shrugged it off. They would figure something out.

Jason was out in the barn with Eliseo when Sal knocked at Polly's door and came in. Andrew was sitting on the couch curled up with the animals, writing in one of his many notebooks. His mouth dropped open and he didn't say a word, but simply stared at the tall, dark-haired beauty that walked in. She was dressed to kill in three inch sparkling black heels with legs that went up to the middle of her thigh, where they were suddenly interrupted by a skin tight red dress. Sal had piled her dark hair on top of her head, adding to her height and her makeup was designed to light up her eyes. She wore simple diamond earrings, which Polly recognized as a gift from an old boyfriend in college and a diamond chain around her neck.

"Umm. Wow." Polly said. "I haven't seen you dress up like this in years! We're going to have to change our plans for tonight."

"Too much?" Sal asked, grinning as she spun around.

"For Hickory Park it is," Polly laughed. "Let me make a couple of quick calls and oh, for heaven's sake, it's going to be a riot getting you up and in the pickup truck while you're wearing that dress!" She started to laugh out loud and looked down at Andrew. He was still a little star struck.

She quickly called Henry and said, "We have to go somewhere nicer than Hickory Park tonight and you have to dress up."

"Why?" he whined. "It's been a busy week."

"Just do it. You'll see why."

"I'll be over in a while, then. I have to pick out what to wear now!" He laughed and they hung up and she made her next call to Mark Ogden.

"Absolutely no overalls tonight. We're dressing up!"

"But, I ironed them and everything!" he laughed. "Okay, that's no problem. How dressed up are we doing?"

"A lot dressed up," she laughed. "Trust me."

"I look forward to it. You always look gorgeous when you dress up."

"Tonight you won't even notice I'm in the room," Polly laughed.

"Well, you've done it," she said to Sal. "Now you have to come help me find something to wear that doesn't make me look like your lowly stepsister."

CHAPTER TWENTY

Nodding toward the boys on the sofa, Sal grinned, "It looks like they're impressed with you." She turned to them. "What d'ya think, boys?"

Jason said, "She looks beautiful. You both do!"

Andrew turned to his brother, "We haveta find a man for mom so she can dress up like that."

Jason poked him and the two boys laughed.

Henry and Mark knocked, then walked in Polly's front door and both of them grinned and gaped at the two young women.

Mark elbowed Henry and said, "You didn't tell me she was so hot."

"You've seen her before," Henry commented. "You know how hot she is."

They laughed and Polly said, "Mark, I'd like to introduce you to my friend, Sal Kahane from Boston. She'll be your date this evening."

Mark stepped in, took Sal's right hand, lifted it and tipped his forehead to it. "I assumed a friend of Polly's would be bright and fun, but I didn't dare make the assumption she would also be stunning; that would have been too much to ask. You both look beautiful this evening." He took her hand and tucked it into the crook of his arm.

Polly looked Henry up and down and whistled. "Stop it woman," he said." You're making me blush."

"You look pretty good for someone who has been working outside all day," she commented. He looked wonderful, wearing a charcoal jacket over a black, high-collared shirt.

"Hey!" Mark protested.

"You look fine," she said.

Sal smiled and said, "Really fine."

"That's better."

"We should get going. I left the truck running so it would stay warm," Henry said.

Polly turned to the boys who were sitting on the sofa watching things unfold. "Thanks for taking care of the dog tonight. I'll see you tomorrow, okay?"

Sal and Polly grabbed coats as they walked to the hall and Polly pulled the door shut behind her.

When they got to the truck, they found that Henry had placed a step stool on the ground so the girls could easily enter the truck. "I'm sorry this isn't fancier, ladies," he said, "but I hope you will be comfortable."

Mark helped Sal get in to the back, shut her door, and moved the stool for Polly to step up into the front seat. He picked up the stool and walked around to the other side of the truck as Henry got in and waited for them to all belt in.

"We decided that no matter how fabulous you looked, we were going to Hickory Park," Henry said. "It's not often you can cause an entire restaurant to turn and gawk at your dates, so that's our plan for the evening."

Polly smiled, "Sounds good to me. Are you going to take us dancing after dinner?"

She turned around to Sal, "Mark is practically a professional dancer. His mother owns an Arthur Murray studio in the Minneapolis area and he's amazing."

"Really!" Sal said. "I might be a little intimidated by that and now I'm a little worried about my high heels."

"I'll be kind," Mark laughed. "I've danced with women in higher heels than those and managed to keep them from hurting either one of us."

Henry put his right arm on the console beside him and opened his hand. When Polly didn't do anything about it, he poked her leg and then returned his hand to the console. She looked sideways at him and grinned, but ignored the obvious invitation.

He poked her once more and she said, "What?"

Henry raised his eyebrows and waggled his fingers.

Polly crossed her arms and giggled, then turned in her seat so she could see her friends in the back and said to Sal, "Mark is the one who has been trying to teach me everything he knows about how to work with the horses. I'm awfully glad he's been around to help out while they recuperated." She turned to Mark and continued, "You know, you've never told me how it is that you love those animals so much when you grew up in the city."

Henry shook his head at her obvious attempt to ignore him and put his hand back on the wheel. As soon as he did so, Polly put her left hand on the console. Without waiting a moment, he set his on top of it and lightly squeezed her fingers.

"It was my grandpa," Mark responded. "My dad's father. He had a farm out in Watertown. It was only about a forty-five minute drive and I spent every bit of free time I could with him. As soon as school was out in the summer, I moved out to the farm with him and Grandma. When I was in high school and got my driver's license, I went out every Friday night and came home on Sundays every chance I had. I liked that way better than having a social life. I worked hard, but it was fun."

"Did your brothers and sister do the same thing?" Polly asked.

"Not really," he mused. "Mom always sent them out for a week or two in the summer, but none of them liked it as much as I did. They spent more time at the dance studio, covering for me, I guess."

Sal asked, "So, you'd rather be a country boy than a city boy?"

"Absolutely!" he said. "When I found the practice here in

Bellingwood, I couldn't believe my luck. It's close enough to home that I can get there in a few hours, it's near a couple of nice cities and every day I'm surrounded by farmland. Pert' near perfect," he drawled.

"What's the strangest thing that has happened to you on a farm?" Polly asked.

"I'll tell you the most embarrassing thing, but this happened when I was still a kid." He grinned and began his story. "So, grandpa and I were pulling pigs one spring ..."

Sal chuckled. "Why were you pulling pigs? Do you have to do that when they won't go where you want them to go?"

Everyone in the truck laughed and after Mark regained his composure, he apologized. "I'm sorry. I shouldn't laugh. I forget that most people have no idea what some of the things I say actually mean. No. Sometimes we have to help the sow give birth."

"You what?" Sal exclaimed. "That sounds awful. Like a gynecologist?"

"Umm, sure. But, it's definitely not in a doctor's office. Anyway, I knew this poor sow had a bunch of piglets in there and she was doing everything she could, but nothing was happening. So, I did what every young man does, I stuck my hand in there to find the piglet, but then I couldn't find anything."

Polly caught Sal shuddering out of the corner of her eye. She looked at Mark and saw his eyes twinkling. However much embarrassment he had felt at the time had obviously passed and this was now a great story.

"You stuck your hand up her ..." Sal started quietly, then stopped.

"Yes. That's what you're supposed to do. Well, I finally had to call grandpa over to give me an extra hand ..."

"Because yours was stuck up this poor sow's hoo hah?" Sal giggled.

"Apparently not," he laughed.

"What?"

"Well, the reason I couldn't find any piglets in there was

because I'd stuck my hands in the wrong hole. Grandpa laughed and laughed and then pulled the piglets while I tried not to think about what I had just done."

"That poor pig!" Sal exclaimed. "Not only did you assault her, but you really assaulted her! I can't imagine she liked you very much after that."

"She might have been the sow who chased me out of the pen one day.

"Is this a true story?" Sal asked.

"It sure is," he said. "It was one of my most embarrassing moments on a farm, but grandpa told me not to worry about it, those things happened."

Henry chuckled. "That's not a story you should be telling girls on a blind date, my friend."

"Probably not," Mark laughed. "But, she asked for a weird story and I don't know why it occurred to me to tell that one. I have a lot of stories from being out on the farms around here. That's one of my favorites, though. Most of the good stories are those like Polly's horses. There's nothing I love more than seeing beautiful animals return to health. Okay, and I love helping out with the births of new animal babies."

"Even after that pig experience?" Sal asked.

"Especially after that. I watched Grandpa pull those little piglets out and then watched the sow relax as they lined up to feed and it was the most beautiful sight. I still get excited when a new foal is born and the mother begins to clean it up or when I get to watch a calf come up on its wobbly legs for the first time. I have a great job. And I get to be outside all the time."

"I can't imagine having this much fresh air every day," Sal laughed. "I'm pretty sure it would mess up my lungs, not to mention force me to be outside instead of under the protective cover of steel and glass."

"Have you always lived in the city?"

"I always have and I suppose I always will. It's my natural habitat. I have to be able to get to the stores and restaurants and clubs and, well, all of that!"

"I don't miss it," Polly said quietly.

"Well, of course you don't," Sal responded. "You grew up out here and don't forget, you have Mr. Hunk over there to keep you company when things get boring."

"That's right," Henry laughed. He grinned at Polly, "She thinks I'm a hunk," and then chortled with laughter. "No one has ever called me that before, but I'll take it."

"You're alright," Polly said and winked at him, squeezing his hand. "You don't offend me."

They were laughing as he pulled into the lot of Hickory Park. He pulled up front and Mark tapped him on the shoulder, "I'll get it," he said and jumped out. He helped both Sal and Polly out of the truck and shut the doors, then escorted them to the front door of the restaurant and they waited inside for Henry to join them.

Henry had been right. As they were escorted to their booth, most of the people they passed looked up and watched them go by. They were completely overdressed and Polly was having the time of her life. She was certain that Sal garnered most of the attention, but felt pretty confident she wasn't shaming their small group. She hadn't worn heels in a while and was quite proud of herself for being able to stride along behind her friend, even if she didn't have the courage to wear, much less purchase, stilettos as high as Sal was used to wearing.

They were seated and menus brought to the table. The poor waiter couldn't keep his eyes off Sal's cleavage, but since she had her back to him, she was completely oblivious to his attention. Polly smiled. Mark and Henry enjoyed the attention and when Henry remarked that he hoped no one thought they'd purchased escorts for the evening, Polly poked him in the side with her index finger.

"Be careful," she said, "Or the entire place will know that we're on a date and I'm not making any money on this evening."

"Got it," he laughed.

The food came out and Polly tried to be dainty, but soon gave in and picked up her sandwich. "If I drop any of this in my lap, I'm going to be annoyed, but here we go!"

They laughed and told stories and just as they were ready to look at the dessert menu, Polly's phone rang in her purse.

"I should have left this at home," she muttered, but pulled it out. It was Jeff Lyndsay calling.

"Hey Jeff, what's up?"

"I'm sorry to bother you," he said, "but there is something going on out in the barn. The horses are making a lot of noise. One of the guests who was outside having a cigarette noticed it. Jason started to go out to see what was going on, but his mother wouldn't let him. What should I do?"

"Where's Eliseo?" she asked.

"Well, duh. That's a good idea. He's down in his room in the basement waiting until the reception is over."

"Just a sec," she said, then put her hand over the phone and said to Mark, "Jeff says the horses are making a lot of noise. Sylvie wouldn't let Jason go check it out and that means she thinks it is a big deal."

"Ask Jeff if either he or Eliseo would go out and see what's going on and we should probably head back to check on them."

"Jeff?"

"I have my leather shoes on, Polly. I'm not going to be happy about this, am I?"

She chuckled in spite of her concern. He had sworn to never dip those shoes in horse crap, but she knew he would help her out. "Take Eliseo with you to check it out. We're going to head back. We'll be there in less than thirty minutes."

"I'm sorry about this," he repeated.

"No worries. At least I got to eat my meal tonight."

Henry had already flagged the waiter down and asked for the check.

"One of these days we're going to make it through an entire meal here without any incident," he said.

"I'm so sorry. Jeff wouldn't have called if it wasn't a big deal," Polly apologized.

They paid for the meal and Henry brought the truck up. When they were on the road again, Polly apologized again. "I can't believe this. The last time we were at Hickory Park, I got scary phone calls about one of my guests. This time, it's my horses."

She turned to Henry, "It's takeout from now on if we want their barbecue. I'm not risking it again!"

Sal quietly said, "I was looking forward to ice cream," and then she giggled. "I'm kidding. We need to make sure everything is alright. I totally get it."

"If the horses are fine, I will make sure you have ice cream before the evening is over. How does that sound?" Mark asked her.

"That sounds nice," Sal responded.

Polly turned around. Her friend's voice had gotten lower and sultrier. If she didn't know better, she would have thought Sal was seriously flirting with Mark.

She heard him say, "Why don't I check out the horses with Polly and you go upstairs and get into something more casual and comfortable and then we can find a little something sweet. I know of a couple of places where we can wet your whistle and end the evening quite nicely."

"I'd like that. A lot." Sal said. She bent forward and asked, "You don't mind, do you?"

She was flirting with Mark! Polly tried not to think too hard about it. She'd wanted them to enjoy each other so that Sal's last evening in Bellingwood would be fun, but she wasn't sure what to do with this at all. She checked herself. Was there a hint of jealousy in her feelings? Yes, actually, there was. But that didn't make any sense. She didn't want a relationship with Mark Ogden. He wasn't her type. And if Sal could have fun with a nice guy, well, she should be fine with that. Then she decided she was absolutely fine with it. Anything else was stupid and selfish. She smiled to herself. This had the potential for disaster or fabulousness. Or it could be nothing in the long run. And besides, it was a little cute.

"Polly, do you care if we go out for a while?" Mark echoed.

"No," Polly replied. "We don't care at all. We'll hang out. No problem." She squeezed Henry's hand and he squeezed back, neither of them looking at each other. She was a little afraid of giggling until she couldn't stop herself, so she bit her lip and kept her eyes straight ahead.

When Henry pulled into the parking lot of Sycamore House, it was full, so he drove up to the front door. All of the outside lights were on, as were the lights in the barn. Mark helped Polly and Sal out and then, both men shrugged out of their jackets and headed down to the barn, while the girls ran upstairs.

Polly said, "I'm sorry about tonight, but it sounds as if you two are going to redeem it."

"I hope so! You go get changed and I'll talk to you later. Leave the light on if you want me to knock when I come in."

"Cool!" Polly laughed and ran for her door. Jason and Andrew were watching a movie when she entered.

"Hi," she said. "Do you know anything yet?"

"Eliseo told me to stay up here," Jason said. "I don't know what's going on. Are you going down? Can I come with you?"

Polly was pulling her heels off as she went into the bedroom. "Let me find out what's happening first, okay?" She shut the door, unzipped her dress and dropped it to the floor. Pulling jeans and socks on, she opened the dresser for a sweatshirt, pulled the bobby pins out of her hair and shook it out. She pushed her phone down into her back pocket, ran to the entryway, slipped into her boots and took off for the barn.

She ran through the gates and into the opened doors. Mark was in Demi's stall, checking his forelegs, Henry was standing there as if on guard and Eliseo was seated on the bench between Nan and Nat's stalls. He was bent over with his head in his hands. Jeff was sitting beside him with a stricken look on his face and his hand on the man's back.

"What's going on?" she asked.

"Everything is good, Polly. The horses are alright."

"Why are you checking Demi's legs then?"

"He kicked at the wall and I wanted to make sure he hadn't hurt anything. He's fine. No worries."

She looked down at his shoes. They were filthy. "I might owe you a pair of shoes."

"They'll clean right up. At least they aren't leather."

Jeff looked up at her, shook his head and smiled.

"Will someone tell me what in the hell happened out here, then?" she asked.

Mark walked out into the alley of the barn and pulled the door shut behind him. "I'm no longer needed here. This is your deal. I have a gorgeous date to pick up and take away from your world. See ya."

"Be sure to have her home in plenty of time for a good night's sleep," Polly admonished.

"Yes, Ms. Giller. I'll be honorable."

"You'd better!"

He left and Polly spun on the other three men in the barn. "Okay. Now, who is going to tell me why my horses got so agitated tonight and destroyed yet another of my dates?"

Eliseo looked up at her. Misery filled his eyes. "It's my fault, ma'am."

Jeff patted his back and said, "It's not your fault. You couldn't have stopped them."

"Stopped who?" Polly gasped. "Who in the hell was in my barn tonight upsetting my horses? And why didn't you call the police?"

Ken Wallers walked out of her tack room and said, "They did, Polly. I'm afraid you've been hit."

She dashed back and looked at the room. All that was left was feed and hay. Her brand new tack was gone; the saddles, the harnesses, everything."

"Damn it," she cursed. "They actually did this when there was a party going on up at the main house? Are they nuts?"

"Apparently they thought that would help them get away. It worked out for them," Ken responded.

"And no one saw anything?"

Eliseo had come up behind her. "It's my fault. I wasn't feeling great, so I went down to my room. I should have stayed out here tonight. I knew this was going on around town."

Polly spun around, "Stop it. I'm not blaming you. It's no one's fault but the smarmy, sneaky thieves. They're the ones who are in trouble, not you."

"Have you talked to any of the wedding guests, Ken?" she asked.

"No, not yet. I was waiting for you to get here before I interrupted their party. Would you mind doing that with me?"

"I sure can, but I think they know Jeff better. I'd rather stay here with Eliseo and make sure the horses are calm."

"That's fine with me," Ken said. "Jeff?"

The two men walked out of the barn and Polly said, "You shouldn't feel guilty about this, Eliseo. The horses are fine and the rest of it is only stuff."

A playful grin passed across his lips. "If you had let me sleep in the hay, this wouldn't have happened."

"I think it still would have happened," she replied. "That would have been an opportunity for you to get hurt again. It was better this way."

She opened Daisy's stall door. The horse was snorting and Polly could tell she was edgy. She stroked her neck and began talking to her, "I'm sorry you had to deal with that this evening. It's not much fun having strangers in your space when no one is around to tell you it's alright."

"Polly?" Eliseo called from Nat's stall.

"Yes?"

"What about poor Jason. I know he wanted to be down here."

"You're right. Let me run up and get him. I'll be back in a minute." She patted Daisy once more and shutting the stall behind her, ran up to Sycamore House and her apartment.

She was panting when she got in the door and Jason stood up, "What happened? Did one of the horses get hurt?"

"No," she said, leaning against the door. "I decided to run up here and tell you that you could come down with me. Everything is okay. The thieves who have been breaking into barns and trucks around the area hit my barn and stole my tack tonight. It upset the horses and I think we could use you to help out."

"Really?" he asked.

"Sure," she said. "I know you love them and I get it that you want to be with them after something like this. Go on down. I'll be there in a minute."

Andrew was sitting on the couch. His ever present notebook and pencil were perched on top of the cat in his lap while the other cat was nuzzling his neck from the top of the sofa.

"Are you okay with staying up here, Andrew? If you want to come down to the barn, you can."

"It's cool," he said. "They don't like me as much as they like Jason. I think I'm too small. They scare me. Maybe when I'm bigger."

"You're a good kid, Andrew Donovan. Thanks."

She went back downstairs and as she passed by the offices, Ken beckoned for her to come in. He was standing in the outer office with two young people dressed for the wedding.

"Polly, this is Debbie Siffel and her boyfriend, Terry Danour. They've given us our first good lead in the case. They saw an old green, pickup truck leaving when they went outside to have a cigarette and have given us a pretty good description of the people inside the truck."

"It wasn't someone from the party?" Polly asked.

"No, ma'am, it wasn't," the young girl said. "Terry and I know most everyone here. They weren't with us. We figured they worked for you since they drove down to the barn."

"Did you see them come in?" Ken asked.

"No, they were getting in the truck and drove away when we went outside."

"So, you don't know how long they were there."

"No, like I said. We ran out to have a quick smoke and a little peace and quiet for a minute. We didn't think anything about it. They acted like they knew what they were doing and then drove away."

The young man interrupted and scowled at the girl with him, "We don't know if they acted like they knew what they were doing. We wouldn't have a clue about that, but they weren't in a real hurry. They drove off and headed back toward downtown."

Debbie sneered and said, "We don't know if they went downtown, they turned north out of the driveway."

"Whatever," the young man remarked.

"That's fine," Ken said. "I appreciate your help this evening. I think I have everything I need from you right now, but if I have any more questions, someone from my office will give you a call. Will that be alright?"

"We're glad to help, sir," the young man replied and escorted his friend out of the office and back to the party.

"Are they from Bellingwood?" Polly asked.

"No, they're in town for the wedding. That would have been a lot more helpful, but at least this gives us some good information."

"So, you don't have a list of fences around here?" Polly asked. "You know, like on the cop shows? Somewhere these people will try to get rid of the items they are stealing? Surely they're doing it for the money."

Ken laughed with her. "No, we don't have anything like that. These items will probably end up on an online auction site. I don't have the manpower to keep an eye on all of them, but if you see any of your things, let me know."

"It wouldn't have even occurred to me to look."

"That's about the only place they're going to sell all this stuff. I can't believe they keep doing this. They have to know that every time they steal, it puts them one step closer to my jail."

"They've gotten away with it this long, they probably think they're invincible."

"Could you email a list of what you've had stolen to me tomorrow, Polly?"

"Sure. Eliseo and I will work on it in the morning."

"How are things going with him? Is he doing alright?"

"He's doing great here and is alright physically. I'm hoping that one of these days he'll open up and tell me what's going on and why those guys beat him up the other night. I know the horses would hate for him to leave and at this point, so would I."

"Let me know if you need something from me or if you find something out I should know about."

"Thanks for coming out tonight."

Polly headed back down to the barn. Henry, Eliseo, and Jason were standing in the center alley talking when she entered. "Is everything okay?" she asked, looking into Daisy's stall. The horse was nibbling at an itch on her side and swung around at Polly's voice. She came over for a head rub, then turned back to her hay.

Jason was the first to speak, "I'm sorry you lost your stuff, Polly."

"I know, Jason. So am I." She gritted her teeth. "Stealing incenses me. I don't know why people think it is easier to take from others rather than do a little work."

Eliseo quietly said, "Sometimes it isn't as easy as all that."

Polly forced her shoulders down and took a breath. "You're right. I would have been a lot more tolerant if they hadn't chosen to steal my brand new saddles. And Mark was talking about starting to work the horses as teams this next week. That's going to be a little difficult to do without the tack, now, isn't it?"

She was starting to work up another rage when Henry put his hand on her forearm. "You can order more tack, Polly."

"I know! I'm going to start checking some of the auction sites tomorrow. Maybe my own stuff will show up and I can freakin' buy it back!"

"Well, that would just be wrong, now wouldn't it!" Henry laughed. "But, what a good idea!"

"It was Ken's idea. What I want is for them to be stupid enough to put it up on one of those online Buy/Sell sites and I can show up with the cavalry and shut their little operation down. I'm only going to feel guilty if they are doing this to feed a family. If they're doing it to feed an addiction, I'm going to have their heads!"

Jason and Eliseo had been quietly talking as they walked to the end of the barn, heading back to the main house. Jason stopped, turned around and looked at Polly, horror on his face.

"What is it Jason?" she asked.

He shook his head. "Nothing. It's nothing."

"Something freaked you out, Jason. What is it?"

"It's nothing, Polly. Sorry. I'd better get upstairs and check on

Andrew." He took off at a dead run for the house before she could say anything more. Eliseo and Henry both looked at her in surprise.

"What was that all about?" she asked.

"I have no idea, ma'am ... I mean, Polly," Eliseo responded.

They walked together back to the house and he went in to the kitchen to check on the evening's progress with Sylvie.

"Are you ready to call the evening off?" Henry asked.

"I feel as if I should go upstairs and push Jason a little more, but I hate to do that. He'll tell me what's on his mind as soon as he can. So, no. What were you thinking?"

"I know this quiet house where there is a comfortable sofa, movies, popcorn and maybe even a little ice cream in the freezer."

"That sounds perfect. Let's go."

CHAPTER TWENTY-ONE

"Two-thirty in the morning. Seriously. Are you kidding me with this?" Polly sat up. Henry had brought her back to Sycamore House after midnight and she had curled up on the couch to wait for Sal. She wanted to hear everything about the rest of her evening with Mark Ogden. Polly had left the lights on and unlocked her front door so Sal could just come in, but so far, nothing. She'd finally fallen asleep about one o'clock and knew better than to worry. Both Mark and Sal were adults and could take care of themselves, but what if there had been an accident?

Polly chuckled to herself. When she was in high school, she had promised her dad that she would always let him know where she was, even if it was after curfew. If he knew where she was and she didn't have something going on early the next morning, he told her to call again when she was leaving and come straight home at that point. That way he wouldn't worry about whether or not she was dead in a ditch somewhere. While her friends were constantly grounded for staying out late, she was smart enough to play by the rules of the house.

One Friday night, though, she'd stayed out much too late with a boy and didn't have a way to call home. They'd been out parking on a country road and when she came rushing in the front door, her dad had been sitting in his recliner reading a book. She'd apologized and showed him that her watch had stopped. He simply smiled and told her to go on to bed. The next morning, however, there was a note on the kitchen table beside Polly's breakfast plate. When she opened it, there was two dollars for a new watch battery and instructions to meet her dad in the barn at nine o'clock. Mary had smiled at her and told her to wear her sloppiest jeans and oldest boots.

Polly had spent the rest of the day scrubbing down tractors. Her dad had told her that after church the next day she needed to wash both cars and as soon as they were dry, she would sweep out the garage so that they'd stay clean for a while. That was the last time she'd lied about where she was. It was much simpler to make a quick phone call. Sylvester had been quite proud of his clean tractors, even asking her to pose on one for a picture.

She got up and went into the bathroom, where she washed her face, changed into an old baggy t-shirt, and pulled her robe off the back of the bathroom door. Then, she realized she could check across the hall to see if her friend was back. Maybe she'd come in to the apartment and had seen Polly sleeping. She pushed her feet into a pair of slippers and headed for the front door. There was no light coming from Sal's room and she didn't know what to do next. If Sal was sleeping soundly, she hated to wake her, but Polly knew she would worry all night without knowing. Finally gathering her courage, she knocked on Sal's door and waited. There was no response. She knocked a little more loudly. Still no response. Finally, Polly ran back to her apartment, grabbed her phone and brought it back to open the door electronically. There was no one in the room.

"Well, hell. Now I'm going to worry," she said out loud.

"About what?"

Sal's voice behind her made Polly jump and yelp.

"You scared the crap out of me. How did you get in here and up those steps without me hearing anything?" Polly demanded. "And where have you been until nearly three in the morning!"

Sal smirked. "You turn into quite the mother hen at this hour, don't you!"

"Maybe a little," Polly giggled. "Sorry. I was starting to worry."

"Don't tell me you've been waiting up all night for me to get home!"

Polly shifted her eyes back and forth. "No, I fell asleep. I woke up a few minutes ago."

"Whew. I'd have felt terrible. I assumed you were sleeping, but I suppose I should have texted you anyway."

"Yes, you should have. You're a bad, bad girl and I should probably ground you for that."

"You mean you won't let me fly back to Boston tomorrow? I could probably live with that."

"You had that much fun with Mark? Oh, come on back to the apartment and give me all the details. You can't hold anything back!" Polly said and grabbed her friend's elbow.

"I've never had so much fun," Sal replied. "We had a great night."

"Where did you go? What did you do?"

Polly shut the door to her apartment and the two of them landed on the sofa. Sal kicked off her shoes and tucked her legs up underneath her and faced Polly, who did the same. Polly pulled a blanket off the back of the couch and threw it across the two of them.

"He took me to Des Moines. We stopped at the Dairy Queen in Boone and got some ice cream and then headed on down. He said he'd heard about a club where we could dance and that's exactly what we did, Polly. That man is like a dream on the dance floor. I didn't want the night to end."

"Oh, Sal. He is, isn't he! That night he taught me how to dance last January was like heaven. I felt like such a princess."

"Yes! That's the word for it. He made me feel like a princess. Now, tell me why he hasn't been caught by some young, hot thing here in the Midwest, because I'm thinking about stealing him and making him come back to Boston with me."

"You can't have him unless you move out here. If you try to

take him away, I'll make your life miserable."

"Oh, he'd never leave Bellingwood. He's so happy here, it's sickening."

"I knew you two would get along. He spent enough time living in the city that he gets you."

"And he's spent enough time living in rural Iowa that he gets himself too. Seriously, why is this man not taken?"

"He's been pretty busy with his practice, you know. I don't think it's been easy and he just brought on a partner this year. He's been doing it all by himself. That probably hasn't left a lot of time for a social life."

"I'm not complaining, but I still don't understand."

"Did he take you down in his pickup?" Polly asked.

"Yeah. Why?"

"How did you find room to sit? The thing is a dump!"

"I didn't think it was that bad. Maybe he cleaned it up or something. It wasn't like there was stuff on the floor or my seat."

"Oh, then, he cleaned it up. Huh, maybe he does like you. He could barely make room in there when I tried to get in."

"No. It was fine. I didn't pay too much attention to it, though. We talked all the way down and all the way back."

"And he took you to Dairy Queen?"

"Well, he promised me ice cream. It was fine. Actually, it was pretty good. Too many more trips and I will know how to get around Boone all by myself!"

"How much do you like him, Sal?"

"I like him a lot, but it isn't going to do either of us any good. After tomorrow we're going to be fifteen hundred miles apart and neither of us is planning to uproot our lives. This was a just lot of fun."

"You know, if you ever decided to write all of those story ideas you have tucked away on your hard drive, you could probably live anywhere."

"Can you imagine me telling my parents that I was going to move to a little town in Iowa, marry a veterinarian and write books? They'd toss me in the ocean!"

"They'd love Mark."

"You have to stop this. I can't think about it. It's not going to happen and I'm not going to build something up in my mind that will end up breaking my heart. Because that boy could break my heart."

"It's been one date and you're already talking like this?"

"Polly, we had barely gotten down to Boone and he was holding my hand. When he brought me back here, we stopped out back and kissed in the truck for a while. Neither one of us wanted the night to end, but he has to work early in the morning and I knew you had to get up with the horses. I'm sleeping in, though, since I don't have to be at the airport until two o'clock."

"I'm sorry. You said you were making out in my back lot?" Polly giggled.

"A little bit. Not for very long. But, it was sweet and romantic. I've never done anything like that either."

"One date with the man and this is what happens. I'm impressed, Sal Kahane. You found something to like about the Midwest after all."

"Hey! I like it all. I think this place is wonderful!"

"I know, I'm only kidding."

"What happened with the rest of your evening? Mark said the horses were alright."

"Not much else happened. Ken Wallers, the police chief, was down at the barn and he interviewed a couple of kids from the wedding reception who saw the truck drive off. After that, Henry and I went to his house and watched a movie."

"Nothing else?"

"No, nothing else. Okay, maybe a little kissing. But, nothing too steamy."

"Good heavens, Polly. You two are like an old married couple."

"That's not true! I like that things are going slowly. I want to know everything about him before ..."

"Before what? The end of the world? Girl, you two need to get over yourselves. The whole town knows you are together. Hell, even most of Boston knows you're together. Whenever you finally admit that you're a couple, you'll have a lot more fun."

"We know we're a couple. But, there's a lot going on in my life right now and if I lost Henry as a friend because I screwed this relationship up, I'd have to move. Let me go slowly, okay?"

"You can go as slowly as you like, but this turtle and molasses thing is a little bit much, don't you think?"

"It's working for us. Just because I don't go out on a blind date with someone and end up making out in my friend's parking lot doesn't mean I'm doing something wrong."

Sal smiled. "Well, it doesn't mean I'm doing anything wrong either." She fanned herself, "Whoa, am I not doing anything wrong."

Polly giggled.

Sal got serious and said, "I have a question for you, Polly. Would you be upset if Mark took me down to the airport tomorrow?"

Polly cocked her head, "No. I don't suppose I would. Really?"

"I feel like the girl who drove off from a party with a boy, leaving her friend to get another ride home. Are you sure?"

"It will be fine, but I get it. Hot boy trumps girlfriend every time."

"Oh, now you're trying to make me feel guilty."

"Maybe a little bit," Polly giggled. "No, it's fine."

"Thanks. He's going to take me out to lunch and then to the airport, so we'll leave about eleven."

"You'd better get to bed so you can get your beauty sleep. I need to get a couple of hours before the morning gets here, too."

Polly followed Sal to the entryway. "I'm glad you had so much fun tonight. I was worried that I'd screwed the evening up," she said, "but it seems like I sent it in another direction."

"And what a nice direction it was. Goodnight, Polly. Thanks for a wonderful week. I'll see you in the morning before I leave, okay?"

"Love you, too, sweetie," Polly said and hugged her friend. She stood in her doorway and watched Sal practically skip across the hall to her room, unlock the door and slip inside. The cats were already asleep on her bed, so she patted it for Obiwan to jump up, tossed her robe on the floor, crawled in between the sheets and was asleep within moments.

Her alarm went off at 6:30 and Polly rolled out of bed and hit the floor. "Crap," she said. "I didn't even have anything to drink last night. Oh, this is going to be a long day." She moaned and groaned as she pulled her jeans and a sweatshirt on. Fumbling with her phone, she checked the temperature outside and when she read that it was only 39 degrees, she moaned some more. She pulled the sweatshirt back off, yanked a flannel shirt out of her drawer and then after making sure the buttons were all in the right place, tucked it in and drew the sweatshirt back on. She patted the hair on top of her head and figured it would have to do until after she'd had a shower. Her boots and jacket were beside the front door and she pulled a pair of work gloves out of another drawer.

Eliseo took one look at her and laughed out loud, then grabbed his side. She didn't see him laugh like that very often, so she smiled and said, "I look that bad, do I?"

"No, of course not," he said. "Did you get any sleep? I heard your friend come in and wondered if you two had stayed up after that."

"Oh, I'm sorry you heard that. I didn't think about you putting up with the noises from upstairs."

"I was up for a few minutes. I wouldn't have heard anything if I'd been asleep."

"Yes. We stayed up far too long talking. I need more than three hours of sleep a night to be able to function like a normal human. Either that, or I need a quart of coffee." She looked at him. "I'm bringing a coffee machine out here."

He chuckled and grimaced as he held his side.

"Should you be out here working?" she asked. "I can do this."

"This morning, it will probably take both of us to finish the job. Neither of us is in any shape to be doing it by ourselves."

"Why don't we do what's necessary and finish up tonight," she offered. "I swear I'm taking a nap this afternoon."

"It's a bit chilly right now, but today is going to be a beautiful day. I think we can feed them and get them outside. It won't be too hard to clean up after them once they're gone. If we do it together, it will be finished and you can enjoy your evening. Besides, there's a pretty big wedding happening today."

"Oh, you're right. I wasn't thinking," she said.

Polly walked back to the feed room and saw that they were getting low on hay. There was enough for the day, but more needed to be dropped down out of the loft. She turned around and walked back into the alley as Eliseo was leaving Nan's stall.

She put her hands on her hips and said, "You listen to me. You are not going up in that loft today. I will be out here this afternoon and will climb up there to bring down more hay. If I see that you have done it, there will be a lot of trouble and you won't like it."

"If my ribs didn't hurt, I'd argue with you, but when I came down from there the other day, I knew I wasn't going back up for a while. I'm sorry to make you do this," he apologized.

"Don't you apologize to me, mister," she laughed. "These are my horses and my responsibility. That you are helping me out is one of the nicest things you can do for me, but it doesn't change the fact that I should be doing more than I am. I can't believe how much I've come to rely on you in such a short amount of time. If you're not careful, I'm going to be a lazy slug. It's good for me." She went back into the room and hauled out a bale. "See, I've still got it. Now, make sure I don't lose it."

He laughed and before long, they had the horses fed and outside. When they were finished mucking out the stalls, Polly sat down on one of the benches and Eliseo sat across the alley from her.

"This is no good," she laughed. "I could go back to sleep right here."

"It might get a little chilly."

"Well, you seemed to make it work," she said and then stopped herself. "I'm sorry."

"No, that's alright. I did make it work."

"Eliseo, is that why you didn't want to give us your

information? Because you were sleeping in my barn and didn't have another address?"

"That's most of it. I figured by the time I had worked here for a month, I would have enough money to get a room for rent."

"What's the rest of it? I know a month hasn't passed, but a lot has happened in this last week. Can't you tell me yet what is going on?"

"I don't want to drag you into my troubles. They are either going to work themselves out or not. If they work out, then no one will have any trouble. If they don't, well, then, only the good Lord up above knows what is going to happen."

"I can't believe that after the time you have spent here, you don't get it that it's always better to have people on your side."

"Miss Giller … Polly … I've always taken care of myself. People don't spend a lot of time on my side. Now, you might think you're different and maybe you are, but it's not easy for a man like me to trust people. You've done some mighty nice things for me and I appreciate it. I appreciate it more than you know, but in my experience when the bad stuff shows up, most everybody finds somewhere else to be. They don't stand by your side."

"I wish I could convince you that things are different now, Eliseo, but I understand your hesitation. Just do me a favor. Before you get to that bad stuff, would you consider talking to me or Jeff? If we can't help, we might know someone who will."

He shook his head, "I can't make any promises. Sometimes things happen when they happen. You all have been nicer to me than anyone has in a lot of years. I'll try to remember that."

Polly stood up and reached her hand out to him. He shook it as she said, "That's all I can ask. Let's head back and get cleaned up for the day. You know you can use the showers upstairs, don't you? Since you clean them, you can definitely use them."

"Thanks, Polly. I'll be up in a while. I want to spend some time with the horses."

She walked out and turned around to watch. He walked over to Nan and touched her shoulder. She nudged him and Polly watched as he spoke to and touched each of the horses. She hoped he would figure it out soon.

After a quick shower and two cups of coffee, Polly felt a little better about being awake. She was sitting at her table with her hand wrapped around a third cup of coffee when there was a knock at her door and Sal poked her head in the entry way.

"You're alive!" Sal said. "I was so afraid you wouldn't get up on time this morning."

"I'm barely alive. You look a whole lot better than I do."

"That's what healthy living gets ya!" Sal laughed. "Now, do you have some coffee for me?"

"Sure, I can make breakfast. I haven't had anything yet this morning, just started sucking down caffeine."

"Toast would be great. Don't you have some of your famous homemade bread around here?"

Polly laughed. Even when she was living in Boston, people knew that she preferred baking her own bread. She kept thinking that one day she would experiment with artisan breads, but every time she opened her bread machine, the same favorite ingredients fell in and the same favorite bread ended up in the oven.

"I do. Sit down and I'll hook you up."

"This has been a great break for me, Polly. I love your home and all the people you've added to your life."

"It's a good place to be," Polly responded. "When I sit back and think about it, I can't believe that I waltzed into town and expected my life to come together, but it did!"

"You would have made anything work out. I remember the day I met you. Before I'd even unpacked my first box, you were settled in and ready to go. Before I knew what had happened, you had me traveling all over the city. Do you remember the first time my mother had you over for brunch?"

Polly laughed. "Uh. Yeah. Did I do something strange?"

"No! My mother loved you! She couldn't believe you had grown up on a farm in Iowa. She thought you were the most well-mannered, proper young girl she'd ever met. You figured out how to adapt and fit into that environment so rapidly, I was stunned."

"It was just brunch," Polly protested.

"You're right. It was. But you fit in with all of those ladies, telling the right stories so they would laugh with you, but never make fun of your background. You knew instinctively what they wanted to hear."

"Oh. Well, I pay attention, I guess."

"You guess. Girl, you are so comfortable in your own skin that you make everyone around you comfortable."

Polly blushed as she set plates with toasted bread on the table. She returned to the refrigerator for a couple of jars of jelly and poured more coffee for both her and Sal.

"I've enjoyed having you here, Sal. It's been a lot of fun to show off my world."

"It's a really good world. I might come back again this fall if you have time for me."

"I'd love that!" Polly gave her friend an evil grin, "But, will you stay with me or will you be offered lodging elsewhere?"

"We'll see!" Sal laughed.

Another knock on Polly's door and Henry stuck his head in. "I hear there's coffee."

"Where did you hear that?" Polly demanded.

"Eliseo said you were in rough shape, so we both assumed you had made a pot. Are you sharing?" He looked at Sal, "Good morning, bright-eyes. Did you have a good evening after you left us?"

"I did," Sal said demurely.

Polly got up to get another cup and drained her coffee pot into it. Filling it with water, she replenished the filter and coffee and re-started it.

"She didn't get back until nearly three. They went dancing in Des Moines."

Henry sat back in his chair, surprised. "Des Moines! That boy is looking to impress!"

"I think he did exactly that," Polly laughed. She winked at Sal and went back into the kitchen. "Would you like some toast, Henry? I'm cooking!"

"Thanks. That would be great," he said. "What time does your flight leave today, Sal?"

"Not until three thirty. I scheduled it so I wouldn't have to get up early this morning."

"What are you doing here this morning, Henry?" Polly asked.

"I told Jeff I wouldn't get in the way, but the weather is going to get bad this next week so I wanted to start working on the walls of the garage today. I want that to be finished before winter sets in again, you know."

Polly chuckled. The toast popped up and she slathered some butter on, put it on a plate and brought it over to the table. "Anything else?"

They both shook their heads and she sat down again.

"Polly, what does your bedroom look like?" Henry asked.

Sal laughed. "Her bedroom? That's the worst come on line I've heard in my life."

Polly smacked her friend's arm and said, "Why?"

"I might be doing some demolition in there this next week."

"I like my bedroom! I know that I don't keep it very clean, but it doesn't need to be demolished!"

"It's gotten bad again, hasn't it," he said.

"Maybe," she said, hanging her head. "I was going to do laundry today. That will help. So why do you want to wreck my perfectly good bedroom?"

"You aren't going to believe it, but I think there is a flight of stairs back by your closet."

"I assumed that was blocked up ductwork or something."

"So did I, but I've been thinking about this being a school and there couldn't have been only one set of stairs in and out of here. I asked Sylvie about it the other day and she didn't know, so I called Andy. She said there were stairs in that classroom when she was in high school here in the seventies. She doesn't remember when they were boarded up, but I thought maybe you might like a private exit down to your garage."

"Henry! That would be so cool! When do you think you're going to want to tear this place up?"

"I can wait until Monday if you want to clean things up first. I'll start down in the supply room. If it's not what I think it is, we can replace the wall. But that will give us something to do when it's raining outside."

Polly shook Sal's arm. "I'm going to have my own entrance! I can sneak in and out of here and no one will know!

Sal chuckled. "You're fifteen again! You'd better keep him around so he can keep finding new ways to make you happy." She winked at Polly and then said, "I should probably finish packing. Mark will be here in a little bit."

She stood up and Polly followed her to the door. Polly hugged her and said, "Don't leave without saying goodbye, alright?"

"I wouldn't dream of it."

When Polly turned around, Henry said, "Mark? You're not taking her to Des Moines?"

Polly ran back to the table and sat down beside him. "Can you believe it? They were making out in the back parking lot last night before she came upstairs. It was only supposed to be a fun time with my friends and they're making something of it."

Henry heaved a sigh, "Well, at least I don't have to worry about him stealing my girl, now."

"You never had to worry about that," Polly said.

CHAPTER TWENTY-TWO

Her friend waved good-bye as Mark's truck pulled away from Sycamore House. Polly leaned against the door frame and watched them leave. Sal had been a part of her life for many years while she lived in Boston. From college roommate to best friends, they had lived through each other's ups and downs. There might have been a little guilt at uprooting her life so quickly and leaving her friends behind, but this week with Sal had been a good reminder that friends didn't necessarily rely on geographic area. All that it took was common memories and a lot of love. Polly smiled. Her life was all filled up with love some days. It was almost more than she could fathom.

She was still standing there when Ken Wallers pulled up in his squad car.

"Good morning!" she called when he got out of the car.

"Good morning, Polly. How are things today?"

"Oh, they're fine. I've decided I have too many other important things to think about than losing some stuff out of the barn. What do you know today?"

"I turned everything over to the Sheriff, since he's running this case. I wanted to talk to you about Harry Bern, though."

"Do you want to come inside? Sylvie came in this morning and started the coffee maker. I'm sure she has made something sweet back there as well."

"No, this won't take a minute, but thank you."

"What do you need?"

He had come up to the stoop and was standing there with her and said, "I need to hire someone to clean his stuff out of the house. I hate to leave it to poor Dave Steery to clean that place up, but hopefully his insurance will cover the damage that has been done to the house."

"You haven't found any of Harry's family?"

"No, there's no one that we can find. The military doesn't have anything more on him and I hate to say it, but we're going to have to stop looking."

"You aren't going to stop looking for whoever killed him, are you?"

"Oh no. That's still an open case."

"Well, then let me clean his things out of there. I can put personal things in storage in the basement here, we can give the rest to Goodwill or the Salvation Army and if you give me Dave Steery's phone number, I can talk to him about what he owns and what needs to go."

"I know he didn't work for you very long, Polly. That's a lot of effort you're putting into this."

"It's the right thing to do, Ken. I'd hate to think that anyone's life meant nothing to the world. Even though the man drove me out of my mind, Jeff and I were the last people he worked for and I think we can extend a little effort. I'll make some calls today and try to get over there tomorrow afternoon."

"Let me know if you need anything and thank you."

Polly watched him drive away and shook her head at herself as she walked back inside. Sure it was the right thing to do and there wasn't anyone else who would do it, but what was she thinking? It was time to see if she could round up some help to dig through his stuff tomorrow. She pulled out her phone and dialed Doug Randall.

"Hey Polly! What's up?" he asked when he answered the phone.

"I need a favor," she said. "I told Ken Wallers I would clean out Harry Bern's home and I need some help. Is it too late for me to call on some of your gaming friends to meet me there about one o'clock tomorrow? I'd even feed you all pizza when we're done."

"Just a sec," he responded and she heard him say in the background, "Hey, Billy. Polly wants to know if we're free tomorrow at one to help her clean out some dude's house. Yeah?"

He came back, "Sure, we'll make some calls. They will always show up for pizza."

"Thanks, Doug. I knew I could count on you."

"Hey, we all owe you. But, maybe you could let us use the computer room next Friday night?"

"You know you can, Doug. I'll put it on the calendar. Thank you!"

She hung up and dialed Andy Saner.

"Hello?"

"Hi Andy, it's Polly."

"What's up? Aren't you driving your friend down to the airport?"

"Would you believe that Mark Ogden is doing that? I might have created a little somethin'-somethin' there."

"I don't believe it. That's terrific. So, what can I do for you today?"

"Ken Wallers asked me to clean out Harry Bern's house and I have a bunch of kids helping me tomorrow at one, but I think I'd like another normal person there to help me keep things organized. Are you available?"

"Well, I, umm. Sure. I can be available."

"Andy, if you have something else going on, I can do it without you."

"No, that's not it. Beryl made a big deal out of me bringing Len over for lunch tomorrow, but I can make sure we're done before one o'clock."

"I didn't even think about you having a date. I'm sorry. Don't hurry on my account."

"I'm glad to help you out. Don't worry if I'm late though, I'll be there."

"That sounds fair. Thank you!"

They hung up and Polly wandered through the auditorium to the storage room where Henry was supposed to be working.

When she opened the back door, she saw four men, including Henry, lifting the side frame of the garage. She stood and watched while they anchored it into place, attaching it to the concrete and another wall. The garage was actually going to happen! Polly waved at Henry when he looked up and caught her eye, then pulled the door shut and went back in. She peered at the walled up space in this room and wondered at the stairway that might be there, giving her immediate access to the laundry room and the garage. She grinned. Henry was her hero and she might not have to make too many more embarrassing treks down the main stairs with baskets full of her underwear again.

That thought made her laugh aloud. Her relationship with Doug Randall had been cemented in stone the day he startled her into pouring her basket full of laundry down the main steps of Sycamore House. One look at her bright purple undies had embarrassed both of them and allowed an entire community of women to get to know her because of that humiliating moment. It was something she and Doug never talked about, but that communal embarrassment was a joke they shared with each other.

A glance at the washing machine had her running for the stairs up to her apartment. She needed to get started on that now. She could not let her bedroom get so far out of control again that people weren't allowed in the apartment. The rest of the place always looked pretty good, but for some reason, Polly hated managing her clothes. They ended up in piles all over her room until she finally broke down and washed things before putting them away. She had to admit to herself that the bathroom counter wasn't much better. She didn't have an issue scrubbing down the shower or washing the toilet, but putting things away she used every day didn't make sense, until there was a worry that someone might show up and see her slovenly behavior.

She stripped the bed, piled all of her clothes in the baskets, grabbed the dirty towels and dragged things to the hallway. While she was at it, she figured she would also strip Sal's bed and check the bathrooms for dirty towels. Piling the towels on top, she opened the room where Sal had been staying. The bed was already stripped and the sheets and a couple of towels were in a pile on the floor beside the door. Everything had been put back in order and there was a note under the flowers by Sal's table. Polly walked over, picked it up and sat down on the bed to read it.

"Polly, I can't tell you how much I've missed you this last year. I don't suppose I even knew myself until I spent these last few days with you. You are a lightning rod and I mean that in the very best way. Things happen around you and you find ways to make them work out for good. I've always known that but never appreciated it. Your heart has led you home and you followed it, listening because you trust it. I hope you always trust your heart ... it's smarter than most people's heads. Thank you for your friendship and for allowing me to be part of your world for a short time. I can't wait to do it again. I love you, Sal."

Polly smiled and folded the note so it would fit in her back pocket. She was going to miss having Sal around, but it was time to get on with her day. She took the first basket down the steps, left it in front of the stairs and ran back up for the second. It occurred to her that maybe Henry could install a laundry chute so at least one end of the trip would be easier.

Sylvie had arrived and was working in the kitchen, preparing for the evening's meal, so Polly stopped in to say hello.

"How was the date last night?" Sylvie asked.

"Other than the interruption with happy little thieves stealing my tack, it was a great evening. Did you hear that Mark took Sal down to Des Moines to go dancing? I think he made her fall a little in love with him."

"No way!" Sylvie replied. "Well, you don't have to worry about whether or not we have a thing for each other."

"Oh, Sylvie, if I even thought that you did, I would have never set this up. I know better than to tempt fate."

"Well, I'm glad they had fun. What did you and Henry do?"

"We went over to his place and watched a movie. So, did Jason say anything to you last night?"

"No, why?"

"Well, when we were down at the barn and were talking about who might have been stealing things, he got a look of horror, like he might know who did it. But then he quit talking to me and avoided the subject completely. That's so not like him and it was odd."

"He didn't say anything to me, but I was so tired I didn't pay any attention to what his mood was."

"If he says anything, let me know. But, you don't have to make a big deal out of it. Are the boys coming over today?"

"If you don't mind. I was going to go back and get them about three o'clock. I hate making them stay cooped up in that little apartment all the time."

"I don't mind at all! You know I love having them here."

"Thanks. Someday I'll be able to afford a nice, big home for them, but for now, I appreciate that they have a safe place like this to hang out."

"What are you doing tomorrow afternoon?" Polly asked.

"I have two papers to write this week along with all the rest of the classwork, so I'm going to hide in my room with the laptop."

"Ken Wallers asked if I could round up some people to clean out Harry's house. Would you want me to pick up the boys a little before one o'clock? I've asked Doug Randall if he could get some of the gamer kids to help us and Andy is going to be there."

The look of relief on Sylvie's face was Polly's answer.

"Sunday afternoons are the worst with those boys. That's when I know I should be out doing things with them, but with everything that is going on, all I do is make them hang out at the apartment."

"Then I'll pick them up and we'll work for a while. When we finished I planned to bring everyone back here and serve pizza. I will text you and let you know when the boys are coming home."

"Thank you, Polly. I couldn't do all of this without you. Well, I couldn't do any of it well without you, that's for sure. I'll tell them to bring any homework over tonight so they can make sure it is finished and won't have to worry about it tomorrow night."

"Cool. So, do you have any boxes back here that I can use tomorrow?"

"I'll empty the boxes I have and you can take those. There are probably five or six there. Let me call the grocery store. They always have a few that can be picked up."

"Thanks. I'll be around. Gotta do laundry and get things cleaned up, you know!"

Polly headed for the barn. While the washing machine was doing its thing, she could be busy pulling down hay. It was always best to get the difficult tasks completed as quickly as possible so she could move on to something else. She climbed up into the hayloft and breathed deeply. She loved this smell. Hefting the first bale, she slid it down the ramp Henry had built for her after listening to her complain. She sent three more down before following them and stacking them in the feed room. Back up she went over and over again. Polly hefted a final bale and something glinted and caught her eye. She tossed the bale down and went back to look more closely.

Tucked behind one more bale of hay, which she pulled out of the way, was a large, ornate vase. Polly took a deep breath and peered at it, wondering where it had come from. Did Eliseo put it up here? She pulled the vase out and looked at it. It looked to be ancient, with intricate painted details and lettering Polly couldn't identify. There was a mark on the bottom of the vase and it felt very heavy. She looked inside and was astonished to see that there was paper stuffed into its base. She reached in and pulled out a handful of hundred dollar bills.

"What in the hell?" she exclaimed. Polly pushed the vase back into the space she had discovered it, knowing that she didn't want anyone else to know about this until she'd done some checking. Then, she had another idea, pulled the vase back out and snapped a picture of it with her phone. She pressed it back one more time and went down the ladder, stacked the hay bales and pushed the ramp up to the ceiling, where its magnets caught to hold it.

She was distressed and distracted as she went up to Sycamore House. Her first stop was her office. She uploaded the photo and did a Google image search to see if there was anything that it might compare to. She became even more distressed when the only comparisons were vaguely similar pictures of vases that had been stolen from several museums in Basra. The only two people she knew who had access to her barn and who had been in Iraq were Harry Bern and Eliseo Aquila. One was dead and the other had just been beaten. Was this what those people were looking for? Did Eliseo know it was here all along?

Her phone beeped at her, reminding her that laundry needed to be transferred around. She sighed, shut the browser window on her computer and went through the kitchen, nodding at Sylvie, to the back room. Her work automatic, she quickly moved laundry around and went back through the kitchen to head upstairs to her apartment.

Polly knew she should call someone, but it didn't feel like today was the day to do that. The vase had obviously been in the barn for a while, and there was no reason for anyone to be up in the hayloft since she had spent time refilling the feed room, so things could stay as they were. She spent the next half hour scrubbing her bathroom clean and hanging clothing up so her room was more presentable. Another quick trip downstairs and she had sheets to remake her bed. When that was finished, Polly hadn't yet come to any good decision on what to do next. She changed into a pair of tennis shoes and grabbing Obiwan's leash, she called him to follow her. Before going outside, she and Obiwan snuck into the laundry room to start another load, then left through the side door, waving at the men who were still working. Instead of heading to the pasture, she crossed the road to the swimming pool and tennis courts and into the wooded area that separated them from the newer subdivision in town.

Agitated, she picked her pace up to a slow jog so Obiwan could stay with her and before she knew it they were both running along the path. A tug on the leash reminded her that he was still attached and as he slowed down to smell the brush and mark his territory, she stopped, bent over, placed her hands on her knees and caught her breath. Obiwan came close to her, sat down and licked her face.

"Thanks, bud. I suppose I know what the right thing to do is, but give me until Monday, alright? If I'm going to lose another custodian, I don't want to screw up an event for Jeff hours before it happens. Monday will be soon enough, right?"

With his tongue hanging out, Obiwan simply wagged his tail. Polly sat back on her haunches and rubbed his head.

"And what am I going to do with Jason? He knows something and doesn't want to tell me about it. That surprises the heck out of me. Who is he protecting?"

She looked at her dog and though he cocked his head back and forth, listening to her voice, she knew he didn't have much to say.

"Since you're being such a good listener, would you mind terribly if I whined a little bit more?"

Obiwan licked her face again, then sat back down in front of her. "I know it's not fair, but I wasn't expecting Mark and Sal to hit it off like that. She's my friend and if she comes to Bellingwood, I want her to come spend time with me. Now, if she comes back here, I won't know whether it is to see me or the next new love of her life. I didn't even get to take her to the airport today because some guy is all of a sudden important to her. She doesn't know it, but that kicked me in the teeth."

Polly sat all the way down on the path with her knees bent, pulled Obiwan in close to her and he sat between her legs so they were face to face.

"Here's the deal, bud. Sometimes I get tired of being strong and creative and I want to sit down and cry. But, I don't want anyone else to know that, so don't tell, alright? Sometimes I want to be totally selfish and scream that I don't want to have to be the one who figures out how to take care of my custodian and then drive to Boone to buy a room full of furniture. I don't want to have to call people to go over to Harry Bern's house and clean it up. I don't want to have to be Sylvie's other parent for her boys and I don't want to have to pay the bills and make all the decisions."

Tears filled her eyes and she buried her face in Obiwan's neck. "Sometimes I want to go back to being a stupid girl who doesn't have to think about anyone but herself."

The tears flowed for a few moments until Obiwan pulled back and barked. Polly quickly dried her eyes with the sleeve of her sweatshirt and stood up and began walking away from the direction he had barked. Pretty soon, she heard footsteps behind her and moved to the side as a young couple jogged past, nodding and smiling on their way around her.

She bent back down and rubbed Obiwan's neck. "Thanks, bud. You're a lifesaver. And by the way, don't you ever tell anyone that I melted down, okay? It's not as awful as all that. In fact, I'm pretty lucky and I know it. Maybe a good cry was what I needed. Though sometimes I wish Mary or Dad were around so I had someone to talk to."

They ran back to Sycamore House and went in the front door and up the steps. She met Lydia on the way up.

"There you are," Lydia said. "Do you have a few minutes?"

"Sure. Come on in." Polly raised her eyes to heaven in thanks for having done at least some straightening up and cleaning in her apartment."

They went inside and she released Obiwan, who took off at a dead run for the kitchen, then spun around and ran for the bedroom.

"I think he's letting everyone know he's back," Polly laughed. "Can I get you something to drink and some brownies or something?"

"What do you have to drink in the refrigerator?" Lydia asked.

"Well, there's milk for the boys and look, I made iced tea the other night. Yeah me!"

"I'd love a glass of tea. Thank you"

"So, what's up?" Polly asked as she pulled down two glasses and set them on the peninsula. Lydia put them on the table and Polly brought the pitcher. They both sat down and she filled the glasses.

"I thought maybe I should check on you. I stopped by to see if Sylvie needed me to do anything with her boys while she was working this evening and she told me that Mark Ogden had taken your friend back to the airport in Des Moines. That escalated quickly, don't you think?"

"It did. I was a little surprised, but what are they going to do? With nearly fifteen hundred miles between them and neither of them planning to move, I suppose it is what it is."

"The world gets smaller every day, though, doesn't it? Do you know that I talk with my daughter in Kansas City on the computer? I can see her and when she holds that little one's face up to the camera, my heart about bursts."

"That's pretty wonderful, isn't it? Henry and I communicated that way when he was in Arizona. I'm glad you can connect with your family."

"Was it hard for you to let her leave with Mark?"

Polly ran her index finger around the rim of her glass and said, "It was. I shouldn't be jealous, but she's my friend and I haven't seen her in years."

"You're jealous of Mark spending time with Sal, not the other way around?"

Polly laughed at that. "I'm not interested in Mark and I'm glad they had such a good time together. It was a little surprising to know that my time with her was cut short because she wanted to spend more time with him."

"That's what I wanted to hear you say to me."

"Why?"

"Because I wanted you to say it out loud."

"It sounds silly now that it's out there, doesn't it? What did I lose, four hours? Not even that. And to be honest, I'm so tired that it was probably just as well I didn't drive to Des Moines and back today."

Polly thought about telling Lydia about the vase in her barn, but looked back down at her glass of iced tea and decided to ignore the impulse. No use getting anything else started.

"Andy also called me and told me that you were cleaning out Harry Bern's house tomorrow. Do you need any more help with that?"

Polly chuckled. It didn't surprise her at all that Lydia was up to date on everything that was happening. "I'd love help, but you don't need to. Doug and Billy are going to round up their friends who come here to play games. I called Andy because I knew she could manage a bunch of kids and keep us all organized. I didn't want to bother you. You have so many things going on all the time."

"Alright, then. I'll let you handle it. Aaron and I will head over to Dayton to check on Marilyn."

"Is she still feeling good?"

"She sure is, but I'm the mama and I want to be there as much as possible for her."

"You're a good mama," Polly sighed.

"Do you ever think about how much you miss having your mother around?" Lydia asked.

Polly looked at her friend. Was she psychic?

"It isn't my mother so much, but sometimes I miss having Dad or Mary here. Sometimes I feel really alone."

Polly's face screwed up, her eyes filled and she began to cry again. "I'm sorry," she got out before the tears came.

Lydia scooted her chair closer to Polly and wrapped her arms around her. "It's alright. I know. I can't imagine doing everything you are doing and taking care of all the people you take care of and then coming home and crawling into bed by yourself with no one to hold on to you."

"I have to either be hormonal or very, very tired," Polly giggled through the tears. "I don't usually do this."

She pulled away and Lydia pushed her chair back and said, "Or you could be handling a lot of things right now. Ken Wallers called Aaron about your theft last night."

"Wow. Was that just last night?" Polly asked. "It feels like it happened a week ago."

"Aaron is going to find who did this, you know that, right?"

"I know. And then I'm going to make them hurt. It's my present goal in life."

Lydia smiled. "Of course you will. By the way, you do look tired. Are you getting sick?"

"No, I only got three hours of sleep last night. I'm exhausted and I don't think I've quit moving since I got up this morning."

"Why don't you take a nap? I'll pick up Sylvie's boys and we'll spend time in Beryl's studio this afternoon. She is starting to go through her paints and brushes. She told me this was a perfect time to get rid of things she never used. I figure she's been in that studio for thirty years. If we can get her a fresh start, it will be another thirty before we have to worry about cleaning her out again.

"She'll be nearly ninety!" Polly laughed.

"And?"

"And nothing. I'll be there to help!"

"Perfect. I'll bring the boys back here around six o'clock. Sylvie said they needed to work on homework tonight and they can do that here."

"I need to go back downstairs. I have to finish my laundry before everyone shows up for the wedding reception."

"Don't worry about a thing. You go to bed. I don't want to hear that you are awake before five thirty, alright?"

Polly yawned. Her body agreed with Lydia.

"Thanks for mothering me today, Lydia. I don't know how you knew to show up, but I needed you."

Lydia stood up and headed for the door and Polly followed her. She turned around and hugged Polly, "Sometimes I know when my favorite girl needs a little extra love." She left and Polly kicked off her shoes, turned off all the lights and went into her bedroom. She dropped on top of the bed and promptly fell asleep.

CHAPTER TWENTY-THREE

Eyes opening to small slits, Polly saw daylight and felt lost. What time was it? Was it morning already? Why was she still in her clothes? What day was it? She shut her eyes again and tried to think. Everything was fuzzy. Finally it hit her, she'd taken a great nap. She stretched and shook her head to rid herself of the last bit of fuzziness. Obiwan stretched beside her, his front paws reaching up beyond her head. She turned over and rubbed his belly and he rolled over so she could reach all of it.

"That's much better, now, isn't it? I feel more rested. At least I'm no longer worried that my emotional life is going to crash and burn any time soon. Lydia was right, I did need that nap."

She pulled herself upright and tossed her legs over the edge of the bed, then looked at the time on her phone. Five-fifteen. Not bad timing.

"I woke up on my own and I feel much better. Thanks for the push," she texted to Lydia.

In a few moments, Lydia returned the text, *"That's great. I am feeding the boys and we'll be there around six."*

"Thank you! I didn't expect that. See you later."

That meant she should probably figure out what to eat for

supper before they got here. As soon as she thought about food, her stomach growled. She hadn't eaten anything since toast this morning. That needed to be fixed soon. But first, Polly had to run downstairs to at least bring up the laundry that was finished. She opened her front door and just outside the door were two baskets filled with folded laundry. She pulled them into the apartment, carried them into her bedroom, and set the baskets on her bed. She looked for the guest towels and sheets, but found nothing in the baskets except her own clothing. Shaking her head, she knew that things had been neatly put away where they belonged. Lydia and Sylvie paid close enough attention to what was happening around Sycamore House, she knew better than to worry.

Taking a few minutes to put everything away and stow the baskets back in her closet, she felt better about everything.

Her phone buzzed with a text message from Henry. *"I'm standing outside your front door with supper. Will you let me in?"*

Running to the front door again, she opened it to see him standing there with a shopping bag. Polly hugged him and reached up for a kiss.

"Thank you!" she said. "This is perfect timing. I was about to forage for supper."

"Don't thank me," he laughed. "This was Lydia's idea. She stopped by while I was working outside, told me you were exhausted and would be awake by 5:30 and that if I wanted to gain your undying gratitude, I should show up with supper for the two of us. We have half an hour before the boys arrive, may I come in?"

"That woman is a planner!" Polly laughed. "I guess it makes sense to go along with what she has happening in that conniving little brain of hers. It always works out perfectly."

"I'm learning that," Henry said. He followed her to the dining room and set the bag on a chair.

Polly went into the kitchen and pulled two plates from the cupboard.

"Oh no," he said. "Put those back. We've got everything we need in here."

He lifted out two plates, two wrapped silverware packets and two glasses. Polly recognized them from the kitchen downstairs. Then he began pulling out containers filled with green beans, mashed potatoes and gravy, sliced roast beef and sliced ham. A bag filled with rolls and butter and another with cookies finished the meal.

"Sylvie shared," he said. "I'm supposed to take the dishes back down later and she'll wash them with everything else."

The last things he pulled out were two small votive candles and a lighter. "She told me I should be romantic," he laughed.

He lit the candles and began opening the containers of food. Polly sat down and helped and before long, they had devoured everything he'd brought upstairs.

She sat back in her chair, "That was perfect," she said. "Thank you for listening to Lydia."

"I told you long ago that she was a force to be reckoned with. I much prefer listening to her and obeying. It works out pretty well," he laughed. "Now, tell me why she was managing your world this afternoon."

"I might have melted down on her."

Henry's eyes grew concerned as he wrinkled his forehead. "What's wrong?"

"Nothing's wrong. I was exhausted. Sal got in late last night, and then I was up at six thirty to take care of the horses ... The horses! I have to get them bedded down!"

"No, Eliseo's got it. He told me it was no big deal and he had plenty of time between getting the hall set and cleaning things up. So. Exhaustion, was it?"

"Exhaustion was the biggest thing. Because I was so tired, I started thinking about missing Dad and Mary and then I felt sorry for myself because I didn't get to take Sal to the airport and then because of all that I decided to feel put upon by the whole world. But, a nap fixed most of it. The rest is a matter of fixing my attitude."

"I'm sorry," he said. "Can I help with anything?"

"You already do so much," Polly said. She stood up and took

the dishes into the kitchen.

"What are you doing?"

"I'm not sending these downstairs filled with gunk. I'm rinsing them off."

"Isn't that what a dishwasher is for?"

"Whatever," she said. "I'll run some water over them and make sure the big chunks are gone. Here, hand me those containers, too."

With an audible sigh, Henry picked up the containers and carried them to the sink. "This is nuts, just so you know."

Polly pursed her lips and looked up at him. "I'm rinsing the dishes and you aren't going to give me any trouble about it."

"Yes ma'am. The silverware, too?"

"No, you can drop those in the bag unless you left food on them. When these dry off a bit, we'll put them in the bag and take them downstairs."

"So, you didn't answer me. Is there anything I can do to help you?"

"What are you doing tomorrow afternoon?" Polly asked.

"I don't know. I hadn't made any plans yet. Do you have something fun in mind?"

"Not so much. But, I could use your pickup truck. I have a bunch of people showing up at Harry Bern's house to clean his stuff out. I'm going to bring some of his personal things here and store them in the basement for a while, but I'm sure there will be things that need to go to the dump and other things that need to go to a thrift store or Goodwill. If you came by about 2:30, we could use you."

"I'll be there. Anything else?"

Polly turned the water off at the sink and dried her hands on a towel. She walked over, stood in front of him and wrapped her arms around his waist, leaning her head on his chest. "This. This helps."

He pulled her in tightly and held on. "Then you can have *this* whenever you like."

They stood there for a minute until the animals perked up and

Obiwan walked over to the front door. He released her and stepped back as Jason, Andrew and Lydia came in. Both boys dropped their backpacks on the floor and Andrew dropped down to hug Obiwan.

"Eliseo is in the barn. Can I go out and help him?" Jason asked.

"Sure!" Polly replied. "Here, take this bag of cookies out to him." She handed him the zipper bag that had come up with their dinner and looked at Henry. "Okay?"

He shrugged as Jason ran over to snatch the bag from her hand. "I'll be back when we're done," he said and ran out the door.

"How was dinner?" Lydia asked.

"It was wonderful. Thank you for organizing all of this."

"Oh, it's what I do," she said as she waved Polly off. "We went to Davey's for dinner and these boys were great. She ruffled Andrew's hair and he looked up at Polly and winked. She nearly burst out laughing at his behavior, but contained herself.

Lydia headed back for the door, "Aaron's downstairs, waiting for me in the Jeep. We might go see a movie!"

Polly laughed. "That sounds fun."

"It does! I've had the television turned on to the news stations for the last week watching all of the tragedy in Boston unfold and he thinks I need to be distracted."

"He doesn't know you very well, does he?"

"What do you mean?"

"You find plenty in your life to distract you from tragedy. Look what you did for me today," Polly remarked.

"We don't need to tell him all my secrets," Lydia smiled. "I like it when he gets all husbandly and tells me what to do. It doesn't happen very often, so I let him get away with it."

"You go take care of your husband and thank you for everything." Polly hugged her and held the door as Lydia walked out and down the steps.

She shut the door and turned around. "Well, what homework do you have tonight, Andrew?"

"The usual," he commented, his voice drooping. "Will summer ever get here? I'm tired of homework."

"I know what you mean, bud. Let's get started and maybe we'll play some games later on this evening. Henry, are you staying?"

"I'd love to stay. I want to look at your bedroom anyway. Since the door is open, I assume you got a little cleaning done?"

"Yes, I did. You are welcome to it."

"What's he looking at?" Andrew asked.

"He thinks there is a stairway that has been walled up. It will lead down to the new garage."

"Do you think there are any more dead bodies in there?"

"Oh, Andrew, I hope not. I don't think my reputation can stand any more of those."

"I think it would be cool. What if they walled that staircase up because there were zombies trying to break into the old school and that was the only way to stop them?"

"Well, I hadn't thought of that. Maybe we shouldn't let Henry open it up. You never know when zombies might come back to life."

Andrew shuddered and then said, "What if the staircase actually leads down through the floor downstairs to the underground and there are tunnels that go everywhere in Bellingwood and a long time ago, they used to smuggle slaves."

"The school wasn't built until the 1920s, but maybe they built it on top of those tunnels and this was the main house people stayed in before they moved on."

"Yeah!" he said. "And all of those tunnels underneath the town are still there and maybe rat people live down there and have a completely different life than we do up here. They don't know there are people on top of the ground either."

"Or maybe that boarded up stairway was a time transfer portal and they lost too many students through it because they didn't know how to use it and got caught in the vortex," Polly encouraged.

"Yeah! Maybe it was a portal to a whole 'nother universe!" Andrew was getting excited. "I gotta write this down!"

He dug in his backpack and pulled out his notepad and a pencil and began scratching things on a blank page. Polly watched as he concentrated, chewing on his lower lip. He was writing as quickly as he could and then shut the notebook.

"There," he said. "That is cool stuff."

"I'm glad. Why don't you pull out your homework and get started. I'll talk Henry out of breaking into that wall until Jason gets his work done and then maybe we can see if there are any real mysteries hiding inside it."

"Cool!" Andrew pulled out a couple of books and opened the first one, sliding a folded piece of paper out and opening it. "I need to do math problems and then read this chapter and answer questions. It shouldn't take me long."

He settled in and Polly headed for the bedroom. "Henry?" she called.

He poked his head out of her closet. "I'm trying to figure the best way to knock this wall out without destroying everything you have. I don't even know which way these steps go downstairs."

"Would you mind waiting until Jason and Andrew are done with their homework? I promised they could watch you cut into the wall."

"Why not?" he said, "I'll go in from the front anyway. I need to get some tools. I won't open the whole thing up today, I want to see what I'm looking at."

"That little boy out there has a creative mind. He had all sorts of ideas as to why this was boarded up."

"Oh to be young and have an imagination that hasn't been squashed by reality," Henry lamented. He came out of the closet and sat down on the bed. "You know, they always ask young boys if they want to be a fireman or a cowboy. I always wanted to be an astronaut. I thought for sure we would be traveling back and forth between earth and colonies on other planets by now."

"Me too!" Polly said. "I wanted to live in space and fight aliens and sail past galaxies. Maybe that's why I became a librarian. Books are so much more exciting than real life."

"This real life is pretty exciting," Henry said as he pulled her down on his lap.

"But, you aren't piloting a ship called Serenity and fending off evildoers and I'm not stopping the Empire from taking over the universe."

"Not today we aren't. But who knows what is going to happen tomorrow?"

Polly kissed him on the cheek, "Thanks."

Henry placed his hand on the back of her head and pulled her back in so he could kiss her lips. "Any time, Princess," he said.

"Whoa!" she whispered as she broke the kiss. "We've got a kid out there and you make my head spin."

Henry's silly grin filled his face. "The head spinning I like. The kid, well, okay."

She stood up and headed for the door, then turned around. "I like the head spinning too, and I like thinking about you in a ship traveling from planet to planet."

"Because I'd wear leather or something?"

"Sure, that's it," she giggled and went out into the living room.

Andrew looked up and said, "Is he gonna wait for us?"

"No problem. I had to talk him into it. He was excited about opening that wall, but then he remembered he needed some tools to do it."

"I do need tools," Henry echoed. "I'm going to my shop. What if I came back with some ice cream treats?"

"Yeah! Jason better hurry back so he doesn't miss out," Andrew said and went back to his homework.

Polly walked him to the door and kissed him goodbye then stood there waiting since she heard footsteps coming up the stairs. Henry held his hand out for Jason to slap as they passed in the hall and Polly held the door open for the boy as he entered.

"Henry's getting ice cream and some tools to tear into the wall in my bedroom, which will all happen after you two get your homework done," she said.

"Cool!" Jason replied. "The horses are ready for bed. Eliseo told me tonight that he liked working with me."

"I'm glad," Her heart gave a thud as she hoped Eliseo was still going to be here after Monday. Then she realized she needed to set it aside and enjoy her evening.

Jason and Andrew worked on their homework until Henry returned with treats.

"How close are you to being done?" Polly asked while Henry unloaded the bag of goodies into the freezer.

"I have one more section and I'm done," Andrew announced.

"I'm nearly finished with my math and then I'm done." Jason said.

"Alright. Finish your work and when I see your books back in your backpacks and the packs by the front door, we'll have ice cream." Polly said.

Henry winked at her and went back into the bedroom with a saw and a tool belt.

She followed him in. "What was that wink for?"

"You like having kids around, you can't deny it."

"I love having kids around. It's babies and toddlers that make me nuts. If I could figure out how to have kids this age without all that other messy stuff, I'd do it right now."

"Right now?" he teased.

"Well, okay, not right now. But, I wouldn't hesitate."

"You know there are other options."

"Yeah, but ..." Polly paused. "I'm walking right into this one, aren't I?"

"Without a doubt. Should we stop here?"

"Can we please?" she laughed.

"I'm done!" Andrew called out. She heard him carrying his bag across the room and as she walked out into the living room, Jason shut his book and began pushing things down into his own pack.

"Alright! Let's see what Henry brought us."

Polly opened the freezer and nearly snorted with laughter. There were popsicles, ice cream sandwiches, ice cream bars and cones. It seemed as if he had bought out the freezer.

"Well, it looks as if you have plenty of choices. Come on over, boys and tell me what you'd like.

Andrew stood up on his tip toes to see inside the freezer and pointed at a frozen candy bar ice cream treat. She pulled it out and handed it to him, while Jason asked, "Could I have an ice cream sandwich please?"

"Those are my favorite, too," Polly said.

"Oh, you can have this and I'll choose something else."

"No, look. He bought two of them. We're set." She pulled the second one out and then said, "Henry, what about you?"

"One of those ice cream cones would be perfect. Thanks."

"No, thank *you* for getting these!"

Polly looked pointedly at the boys, who were both too busy opening their packages to pay any attention. She grabbed some napkins and joined them at the table.

Handing off Henry's cone to him, she said, "We appreciate you picking these up for us, don't we boys."

"Thank you!" Andrew said, brandishing his frozen treat on a stick. "This is great. Mom never buys these."

"Thank you," Jason responded and took a bite of his sandwich, giggling as the ice cream pushed out on the sides. "I hope I can eat this fast enough so that it doesn't melt."

Polly gathered up the paper wrappings and napkins when they finished, and said, "Wash your hands and then follow Henry in to the bedroom. Do what he says and stay where he tells you to stay so no one gets hurt, alright?"

"Cool!" Andrew said. He ran to the kitchen sink and turned on the water. "What do you think we'll find in the wall, Jason?"

"Stairs?" Jason said.

"I mean other than stairs. You know there were bodies in the bathroom ceiling. Do you think there will be anything like that in there?"

"Maybe ghosts will pour out when Henry opens the wall," Jason said, then wobbled his fingers at his brother, "Oooooh, and they're gonna haunt you and follow you home and scare you every night when you try to sleep."

Andrew looked up at him and said sarcastically, "Dude. There are no such things as ghosts." Then he got excited, "but there might be zombies."

Jason rolled his eyes at Polly and shrugged his shoulders as if to say, "What can you do?"

Polly nearly swallowed her tongue as she attempted to hold back her laughter. She couldn't believe the little boy's attitude, but it was perfect.

The boys went into the bedroom and displaced Luke and Leia who were snuggled up at the end of the bed.

Henry shook out a tarp and said. "Can you help me throw this over Polly's bed so the dust doesn't make too much of a mess?"

He pulled the closet door closed and nodded to the bathroom door, which Polly closed. He tossed another tarp over the cat tree and said. "Are you ready?"

Both boys nodded and Henry lifted the saw and began cutting through the plaster. After a few cuts, he pushed and pulled and the section fell to the floor of Polly's bedroom.

"Oops, maybe I should have put something down," he laughed.

"I'll bring you a broom," she said.

He looked down into the hole and said, "Hmmm, it's awfully dark down there. Do you boys want to come look?"

Polly watched the boys approach the hole with more than a little trepidation and she tiptoed up behind them. Just as they peered in the hole, she jumped at them and yelled, "Boo!"

Andrew yelped and Jason looked at her in shock, then both crumbled into laughter.

"That was funny, Polly!" Andrew said. "You scared me. Did she scare you, Jason?"

"Yes. A lot." Jason said, trying to regain his composure. "I didn't see anything. How can we make it lighter in there?"

"I have a flashlight," Polly said and pulled it out from under her bedside table. "See if this helps."

Henry shone the light in the hole and said, "Yep, stairs. But, I don't see anything else. What about you boys?"

"Do you think they're safe? Can you open this up so we can go down?" Jason asked.

"No, we aren't going down these tonight. I don't want anyone on them until I open up the lower level and can figure out why they closed this stairway off."

"Look!" Andrew said, "There is something down there on the floor."

Henry pointed the flashlight toward the lowest step. "You're right, there is. But, it looks like boxes, not a body."

"Shoot. Boxes are boring," Andrew replied.

"Those boxes might tell the story about the portal to other planets, Andrew. You never know what's in them."

His eyes lit back up and then he slumped. "It's probably kids' school work. Nothing exciting."

"What's going on in here?" Everyone spun around at Sylvie's voice. She was standing in the bedroom door.

"I thought I heard something weird up here. I was in the storage room and nearly wet my pants when you broke through that wall, Henry," she laughed. "At least now I see what was making all that noise. I didn't know what to think!"

"We thought there might be zombies in there, mom," Andrew said. "But, it's only some stairs and boxes."

"Stairs? That's fabulous. Polly, you'll have another exit!"

"I know! I can do laundry without bothering you in the kitchen and you can sneak up here when you're tired of all of your employees," Polly laughed.

"Did you get your homework done so you can help Polly tomorrow?" she asked.

Both boys nodded yes and she said, "Then we should go home. I'm all done here and I'm beat."

Jason and Andrew slowly walked out of the bedroom, following their mom.

"I wish we could stay and watch Henry open up that stairway," Andrew lamented.

"I'm not going to do anything more tonight, boys. I wanted to make sure that was actually a stairway. You can rest easy. I'll let you know what's happening when we open the whole thing up."

"Cool!" he responded.

Polly laughed to herself. It was wonderful to watch a little boy's emotions jump all over the place as he learned to process his environment.

"Tell Polly and Henry thank you," Sylvie commanded.

"Thanks Polly. Thanks Henry." Andrew said.

"Thank you," Jason echoed.

"I'll pick them up tomorrow about ten 'til one and then feed them pizza after we're done. I hope you get a lot of studying done."

"Me too, otherwise, I'm going to be very stressed out and we don't want that, do we?"

"No, because when she's stressed out, I have to hide in my room," Andrew said. "She's no fun."

Sylvie giggled and shook her head. "Let's go."

They left and Polly leaned back on Henry. "They're such good boys."

"It's still early. What would you like to do?" he asked.

"What I want to do is finish knocking that hole in the wall and see what's down on those steps."

"We're not doing that. I'm not letting you head down those steps until I know they're safe and I'm not going to know they're safe from up here. Got it?"

"Whatever," she grumped. "We could watch a movie, I suppose."

"We did that last night. Don't you have any games around here? Maybe some cards or something? Turn on some music and we can dance. Something. Anything."

"No dancing. But, I have games." She opened one of the cabinets along the wall and pulled out a backgammon board. "Care to play, carpenter boy? I'll whip you."

"Bet me," he laughed. "I was a backgammon master in college."

"So was I. It's on."

They set up on the dining room table and began to play.

"So, Henry. If I told you I found something strange in the barn, what would you say?"

He rolled his dice and said, "I don't know. What do you think is strange?"

"I found a very old vase up in the haymow this afternoon. I haven't said anything to anyone because it scares me to death that

Eliseo has something to do with it and I didn't want to lose another custodian before tonight's wedding reception."

Henry laughed, "Of course that's the way you thought about it. You are a nut, Polly. What if he has nothing to do with it?"

"He's the only person other than me who has been up there. And he was living up there."

"It's not like you lock the barn. Anyone could have stowed it there, thinking it was safe."

"But it wasn't safe. I found it today. And Henry, it was filled with cash!"

He stopped and looked at her. "Cash? How much cash?"

"A lot of cash. I didn't count it, but it was hundred dollar bills."

"Alright, you probably should have told someone about this. When are you going to do that?"

"I was thinking that I'd call Aaron on Monday. He's never surprised to hear from me anymore."

"No, you're right, he's not. At least it's not a body," he chuckled. "What if it's gone on Monday?"

"Then, I screwed up and we're the only ones who know."

"This doesn't sound like you, Polly."

"I know, I can't stand the thought of getting Eliseo into trouble. I like him and I want him to be a good guy."

"Yes, you do and I love that about you, but avoiding the truth won't help him."

"Will you support me through Monday?"

"Polly, I would support anything you did, you know that. I'm not going to tell anyone about this. It's your story."

"You won't make me feel guilty?"

"Nope, I won't even do that. I think you're feeling guilty enough already."

"That's helpful," she sneered.

"Oh," he chuckled. "Sorry. You'll be fine until Monday morning. Call Aaron and tell him that you found something in the barn and he'll show up and everything will work out."

"Thanks," she said and rolled double sixes. "Hah. Take that."

CHAPTER TWENTY-FOUR

Both boys were standing outside their apartment building when Polly arrived to pick them up on Sunday.

"Hi," she said as they climbed in the truck. "Did your mom kick you out of the apartment?"

"She was grouchy this morning," Andrew said. "I'm glad we're leaving.

Jason nodded, "It was bad. She dropped her cup of coffee and cried. I tried to help her clean it up, but she yelled at me and told me to go do my homework. I thought she knew I finished it last night."

"Your mom is tired," Polly assured them. "She's been working at Sycamore House and the grocery store and going to school. I'll bet she doesn't get much time to sleep."

"We didn't go to church this morning either," Andrew said. "I hope I still get my attendance pin."

Polly couldn't believe they still gave those out. She had an entire set from her elementary and junior high years. At some point in high school, it was no longer important, but when she was a kid, that ceremony every fall was pretty special.

"I hope you do, too, bud."

She pulled up in front of Harry Bern's house and smiled when she saw police tape across the bushes. Apparently, no one was in a hurry to clean up. Doug Randall's car was parked in the driveway and two other vehicles were parked in the street. When she began walking across the lawn, kids began flowing out of the vehicles. She counted nine people besides herself and the boys. When Andy and Henry showed up, there would be more people than the house could manage.

"I brought some boxes, Polly," Doug said. "Mom saves these things in the garage. I brought packing tape, too."

"That's great, Doug, thanks! I have some in the bed of my truck, but I don't know how many we'll need."

Andy pulled in and parked. She got out of her car carrying a large tote bag. "Don't say anything," she commented. "We're going to need markers and maybe paper to make signs. Trust me."

"Alright, then. You're the boss!" Polly laughed. "Where shall we start?"

"It looks like you have a great crew. Let's go in and I'll take a look around to see what our plan of action should be. Maybe everyone here could unload boxes and bring them to the front stoop."

Polly opened the front door and went inside. There was still a stain on the living room carpet where poor Harry had died.

"Is that his blood," Andrew asked in a loud whisper.

Polly swallowed and took a breath, then looked down at his face. Rather than having a look of concern, she could see excitement in his eyes. Oh, to be young and interested in everything again.

"Yes, it's too bad that this had to happen, isn't it."

"I can't believe you got to see a dead body. That's so cool."

"Right. Cool," she responded.

Jason had hung back and was watching the kids pull boxes from her truck. She watched for a moment as he paid close attention to two boys who were laughing together. Then, he shook his head and wandered over to where she and Andrew were standing together.

Andy came back out onto the porch and announced, "Alright, it looks as if there isn't a lot of stuff, but it is all over the place. I need two of you to go into the kitchen. I've placed three trash bags in there. Empty the refrigerator and any opened food from the cupboards. If there are unopened dried goods, put those into a box."

She pointed at one of the boys, "Would you mind pulling out the large stack of newspapers I have in the back seat of my car? We'll use those to wrap the dishes."

"Two more of you can go into the back bedroom and begin packing up his clothes. I know it sounds nasty, but you will have to toss his dirty clothes into one box and label it, then anything that is still in the dresser or hanging in the closet should be neatly folded and placed in another box," she said.

Kids came forward and grabbed boxes, then took markers from her tote as they passed her. Polly couldn't believe what she was seeing. A little good will from some gaming sessions was certainly paying off.

"Polly, you and I and the boys will work in his office. We need to go through his desk and make sure there isn't anything that needs to be handled. If there is, you can work that out with the Sheriff on Monday."

Andy assigned tasks to the rest of the crowd and set up stations for depositing bags of trash and boxes on the front lawn. Before much more time had passed, everyone had settled into their work.

Polly sat down at Harry's desk. All of the drawers had been emptied out onto the floor, creating chaos in paper. She bent over, shuffled a pile of paper together, set it down in the center of the desk, then reached for some more.

"We can do that, Polly," Jason said. He and Andrew began collecting stuff off the floor. Jason straightened the paper into stacks and they sorted out office supplies.

"Should we give you blank paper and stuff?" Jason asked.

"No, that's cool. Make another pile for notebooks that have nothing written in them," she replied.

Andy was picking up books and looking at them as she placed them into a box. Andrew sidled over to her and pulled out one of the books she had dropped in. He opened it up and flipped through a few pages.

"This is cool," he said.

"What do you have there?" Polly asked as she separated bank statements from utility receipts.

"It's a book about Alaska. And look, here's another one about California." Andrew sat down with his back up against a wall and got lost in the pages of the travel guides he was holding.

Jason muttered, "He'll read anything. Mom says he will read the back of the cereal box over and over just because there are words on it."

"I was that way too, Jason," Polly said. "It's good for him. Don't you like to read?"

"I like to read good books. He'll read anything, though."

She giggled. It was fun being around these two boys.

Andy found a couple of other travel books and set them down beside Andrew and continued to gather up the rest of the books from around the room. They'd spent nearly forty-five minutes working when one of the kids stepped in.

"Mrs. Saner?"

"Yes"

"I think we're done in the kitchen. Would you come check it out?"

"I'll be right there." She turned to Polly, "Good kids! I'll be back in a minute."

Polly heard Jason make a huffing sound.

"What's up, Jason?" she asked.

"Up? Oh, nothing."

"Did you disagree with Andy?"

"No, it's nothing."

He went back to sorting out the different receipts and stacking them in piles on the desk.

"Jason, you've had something going on in your head since Friday and you won't tell me about it. Why not?"

"Really, Polly. It's not that big of a deal."

"Polly, look at this," Andrew said. "And this! And look at this!"

He held a couple of pieces of paper in his hand and then fluttered the pages of the book he was holding. A few one hundred dollar bills fluttered out along with some other currency.

She stood up from the desk and walked over to him. "What in the world do you have there, Andrew?"

"I was looking at this travel book of ..." he turned to the cover and continued, "Utah, and I found this stuff. There's a lot of money here. Is it real? And what is this money?"

He held up the odd currency and she didn't recognize it. "I have no idea, Andrew. What else do you have there?"

He picked up a newspaper article that had fallen out and handed it up to her. There was an advertisement for a furniture store on one side, but the article on the other side was about a soldier who had been arrested for theft.

"That's odd," she said.

"Do you suppose there is money in any of these other books?"

"I can't believe that they didn't find this when they were tearing the house apart," she said.

"That's because the pages were glued together. Not like really glued, but just a little bit on there so they wouldn't fly open," Andrew said.

"Do you two want to look through the rest of the books, even the ones Andy has packed up to make sure we don't miss anything?" she asked.

"Like a treasure hunt," Andrew said.

Polly sat down at the desk again and began rapidly going through the rest of the piles of paper. She didn't care about receipts and if she needed to worry about the man's bank statements, she'd have the sheriff ask the bank to reprint them. He didn't have that much money in the bank anyway. Just enough to maintain what she assumed was a debit card. She'd take all of this to the recycler on Monday so no one could get their hands on it and be done. She found some personal letters and emails he had printed off and slid those into a manila folder. She'd look at them later to see if there was anyone that she could contact about his life and death.

He had collected a lot of information about Mesopotamian artwork. She began sorting those into another manila folder.

"We found another one, Polly," Jason said. He brought the book over to her, thumbing the pages free as he walked.

Polly turned it upside down on the desk in front of her and riffled the pages. A few more bills and foreign currency fluttered out, but nothing else.

"Keep looking. Though someone at the thrift store might think it was cool to get this, I'd rather hand it all over to the Sheriff, just in case. Something about this doesn't feel right. And we'll keep the books that you find this stuff in separate, too, alright?"

She picked up a small box and dropped the two books and other items into it, then began gathering the paperwork from Harry Bern's life into another box. When it was full, she flapped it shut and marked "Recycle - Paperwork" on the top. She'd kept the last copy of his statement and the latest bills out so that she could work with Ken Wallers to close the accounts. When that was finished, she gathered all of his unused office supplies into a box, filled it, labeled it and set it outside the office door. Finally, she pulled paintings off the wall and stacked them on the floor. There were a few knick knacks and candles around that she set on the desk.

"I'm going to wander around the rest of the house, boys. When Andy comes back in, tell her what's going on. You can set any other books you find like these two on the desk."

She walked into the main room and saw that boxes were beginning to fill the lawn outside. Henry's truck was parked on the lawn and several of the boys were filling the bed with junk. Polly moved around the room, lifting paintings down to the floor. She went into the bedroom and found several more and carried them into the living room, stacking them all together.

"How are we doing, Polly?" Henry asked as he entered the front door.

"I think we're doing great. We've had some good help today."

"My truck is full and I'm going to run this load to the dump. I should be back in about forty-five minutes. Will you still be here?"

"Thanks," she said. "Yeah. I think I'll still be here. Hopefully most everything will be done by then, though."

"See you in a bit," he said and left.

"Yeah," she muttered, "see you."

She turned back to the hallway, walking toward the kitchen. She was surprised to see that it had been cleared out completely and heard voices coming up from the basement. Polly followed the sound of the voices and found Andy down there with several young people.

"He collected weird junk, Polly," Andy said. "This looks like an old carburetor and I know that this is part of a flue from an old coal stove." She turned on the kids who were standing there. "Don't you dare ask me how I know that either. I'm not that old."

They laughed and one of them took it out of her hand.

"I think we'll box this up and take it out to the Homer Brothers junkyard. Brandon here says he goes out there all the time with his brother to get parts for his brother's truck. He'll take it for us."

"That sounds great. So, there's nothing interesting down here?"

"All of this stuff was tossed around, so if they found anything interesting, they took it," Andy responded.

"Have you been in the garage?"

"There's an old mower and a nice snowblower out there. I found a tent and a bunch of camping supplies," said one of the kids. "You should totally put that stuff up for sale. It would go really fast. So would the furniture."

"That's a good idea," Polly said. "A one day, take it all sale. Maybe we could donate the money to the library for their computer lab. What do you think about that?"

The kid shrugged, "Their computers suck. Anything would be an upgrade."

"I'll call Ken Wallers and if he says it's okay, we might do that next weekend. Maybe you should drag all the stuff that can be sold into the garage."

"If that's what you're doing with the furniture and household things, we're pretty close to done," Andy said.

"Great. I'll go back into the office and help Jason and Andrew finish up and we'll be out of here. Remember, food at Sycamore House."

Doug Randall came down the steps, "Did I hear someone talking about food?"

"But, don't you think it's a bit early?"

"What if you bought pizza for us on Friday night instead of tonight," he said.

The kids in the room nodded their heads. "That would totally work."

One of the girls piped up, "Mom thinks I should be home anyway. She says I've been gone too much this week and I need to clean my room. Seriously, why does she care? It's not like anyone is ever in there but me. If she goes in there, it's only to nag me about cleaning it."

"Kelly, if you clean your room it makes her happy. If she's happy she lets you go out and do things." Doug popped himself in the forehead. "I don't understand why it is so hard to figure this out."

Andy gestured at the junk in the basement, "Let's get this upstairs and we can call this part of the house finished."

Polly ran up the steps and made her way back into the office. Jason and Andrew had found another book and placed it on the desk.

"Did you open this?" she asked.

"Yeah. We peeked. There's more money in there," Jason said.

"How close are you to being finished?"

"We've gone through every book except what's in this box," he said, pointing to a box Andy had taped shut. "We were just getting to it."

Andrew ripped the tape off and opened the box. "Whoa," he said, "The mother lode."

"What?" Polly asked.

"Check this out!" he exclaimed.

She looked down and chuckled to herself. His idea of the

mother lode was a series of Time Life books about ancient civilizations. She had the same set in one of her boxes at the storage unit in Story City. It had seemed like such a great idea, but after the first book arrived and she had spent time looking through it, with the arrival of each new book, she simply unwrapped them and placed them on the shelf.

"Would you like to keep this set of books, Andrew?"

"Wow, could I?" he said.

"I tell you what. We'll take them back to my place and then we'll ask your mom about them. If she doesn't want to store them in your apartment, you can keep them on my bookshelves. They're yours, though, not mine. Okay?"

"Thank you! Mom will let me have them, won't she, Jase?" he asked.

"You already have a million books. Where are you going to put them?"

"Well, we could move some of your junk off the shelves."

"Hey. That's not junk, it's important stuff."

"Really, boys. We'll talk to Sylvie and if she says yes, they go to your apartment. If it stresses her out at all, they come to my place. It's not like you aren't there all the time anyway, right?"

"Right!" Andrew said. He picked up the book on Egyptian Pharaohs and sat down again.

"See?" Jason said. "Useless."

Polly laughed. "Let's finish this box and then we'll head back to my place."

They didn't find any more books that contained currency or articles, so she repacked the box. The only thing in it other than the series of books was a hard copy of a world atlas. The maps were beautifully printed and she figured Andrew would enjoy that as much as the books, so she tucked it in and flapped the box shut.

Polly dropped the last travel guide into the small box with the other items they'd recovered and shut it as well.

"Andrew, would you carry this box out to the truck and put it in the back seat?" she asked. "You can hang there for a few minutes while I close things up here. Jason, can you get this box?"

"Sure, Polly. I've got it." he said.

The two boys left and she gathered up the folders filled with items she wanted to spend more time with. She flipped the light off and walked into the main room. The two cars out front had gone and Doug and Billy were talking to Andy on the front lawn.

"Is everyone done in here?" she called out.

"I think so," Andy replied.

"Cool." Polly closed the door behind her and joined them.

"Doug, your friends were a great help today. You know that means I owe you all a lot now."

"Oh, we figure it's payback, but as long as you want to feel that way, we'll keep using the computer room. We love it there."

Polly smiled. "That's great then. I'm glad you're using it."

She reached in and hugged Andy, "I couldn't have done this without you today. I didn't even think about packing paper. You're so organized. This wouldn't have happened if I'd been in charge."

"It went faster than I expected," Andy acknowledged. "But, I don't think he had as much stuff as I thought he would."

"He hasn't been here that long," Polly said. "If you move around a lot, you don't have time to accumulate much."

"It's a pity they damaged so much of the house when those thieves were tearing through here. It's a cute little place for a single person. I'm glad I don't have to fix it up."

"Hopefully the owner has insurance and once we get everything out he can gut it and fix it," Polly said.

"Maybe we should rent it," Billy said to Doug. "We could totally live in a place like this if it was all fixed up."

"Dude! That's a great idea! We could have great parties here too."

Billy looked sideways at Polly. "He didn't mean anything by that. Don't tell our moms."

She laughed. "I wouldn't tell your moms anything anyway. But, do me a favor. Don't be renting anything anywhere for a while, okay? Give me a couple of months. I might have something even better for you."

Doug wrinkled his eyebrows. "Seriously?"

"Seriously," she said. "But, I don't want to talk about it until I know for sure that it's going to work out. Do you think you can wait two or three months?"

Doug shrugged, "I've waited this long and hadn't even thought about when I was going to move out. I think I can wait three more months. But, seriously?"

"Seriously," she laughed.

"High five!" Billy said and the two boys jumped in the air, bumping their chests and clapping their hands together.

"We'll see you later! Remember, Polly. You're serious. Right?" Doug said.

"Right," she acknowledged and watched as they got in his car and backed out, then drove away.

"Thanks again, Andy," she said. "You were a lifesaver today."

"No problem. Do you want help with the sale this weekend?"

"You know I do. I might make Lydia help us out with that too."

Andy got in her car and Polly walked over to her truck. She pulled her phone out and texted Henry. *"We're done. If you want pizza you can come to my apartment. The boys and I are headed there now."*

Polly pulled into the parking lot at Sycamore House and saw that Henry's truck was already there. He met her as she opened her door, "Surprise!" he said. "I was driving into town when you texted, so I just came here. Can I help with anything?"

Andrew smirked from the back seat. "He can carry this."

Everyone laughed and Polly took it out of his hand, "It appears we have a little bit more mystery surrounding Harry Bern."

"Really!" Henry replied. "I can't wait to hear about it."

He watched Jason pull the box of books out of the front seat. "I can get that, Jason," he said.

"I got it," Jason assured him.

Henry looked at Polly and she shrugged. "Alright then, I'm feeling a little useless," he said. "Should I go get pizza?"

"Nah, it's only four thirty," Polly said. "Come on up and we'll show you our treasures."

"I got some great books," Andrew said. "You're gonna love 'em!"

They went up the steps and by the second level, Henry took the box from Jason who was struggling a bit.

"I've got it," he said and then dropped his arms as he felt the weight. "Jason, these are heavy. You should have said something, but good for you!"

"They weren't that bad until the steps," Jason said.

"Well, I'll get them in the apartment. There must be bricks in here."

"Just my books. Polly says I can keep them here if Mom won't let me bring them home."

"Well, Polly has plenty of room for books. I made sure of that," Henry smiled.

When they got into the apartment, he put the box on the coffee table and Andrew pulled the flaps open. "Look at these," he exclaimed.

"Those look great, Andrew. You'll have fun with them." Henry turned to Polly. "I think I had a set of those at one time."

"Me too!" she said. "Mine are in a box somewhere. Did you ever read them?"

"Just the first one," he laughed, "but it would be great if Andrew could enjoy them. So, what do you have in there?" Henry pointed at her box.

"Come on over and see," she said.

Polly, Jason and Henry sat down at the dining room table and she began pulling items out of the box. Jason gathered the US currency into a stack in front of him and began counting. Henry sorted through the foreign currency. Polly put her hand over her mouth as she read the words in English.

"That's Iraqi," she said.

"And that's Hussein." Henry pointed at the picture on the currency.

Jason was ignoring them and then looked up, "There are forty-three of these," he said. Polly picked one up and looked at the date on the bill. Nineteen eighty-nine. She looked at two others. They were from nineteen ninety-one.

"This is strange, Henry."

"What's strange, Polly?" Andrew asked. He was carrying one of the books and set it down beside her as he took a seat at the table. Polly glanced at the opened book and stopped breathing.

"What's strange, Polly?" Henry asked again.

"This," and she pointed to a picture on the page. "This is strange."

Everyone looked at her.

"What's going on Polly?" Henry asked.

"Remember what I talked to you about last night?"

"Yes. Why?"

"Look at this picture. See that image in the left there?"

"Okay."

"It's the same image on that thing."

Henry pulled the book closer and looked at it again, then he shut the book and read the title out loud, "Ancient Mesopotamia."

"Polly," he said.

"I know. Now what do I do?" she asked.

Then, she started scrabbling through the other items that had been hidden in the books. There were a few pictures and some newspaper articles. She set them out in front of her.

The articles were about a few soldiers who had been arrested for stealing antiquities from Saddam Hussein's palace. Other articles talked about how many of the museums in Iraq had been looted. She pushed those over in front of Henry.

"What in the hell?" she asked, then clamped her hand over her mouth when she realized the boys were watching her. "Sorry."

"It's okay, Mom has said a lot worse," Jason assured her.

"Polly, I think you need to call Aaron right now. If this is what you think it is, he needs to know."

"They're over in Dayton. Do you think that I should bother him?"

"Do you have Ken Wallers' number?"

"Yeah. In fact, I think this is his case instead of Aaron's. They were talking about it at the restaurant last week."

Polly pulled out her phone and scrolled through her calls, landed on the right one and pressed the send key.

"Polly Giller, I don't know if you should consider it an honor that you are now a contact in my phone. Please tell me you don't have a body."

"No, I call Aaron with those, but I think I need you to come over to my place if you have time."

"What's up today, Polly? I was enjoying a nice relaxing afternoon."

"Well, I found something in my barn and I found something in some books at Harry Bern's house and you might want to know about those things. But, if you want to wait until tomorrow, that will be fine."

"You're a cruel woman, Polly Giller. Let me get changed and I'll be over. Do I need to bring anyone with me?"

"I don't think so. None of this is particularly heavy, but then again, there's a lot of money involved."

"Money?" he asked. "Never mind. I'll be there soon."

CHAPTER TWENTY-FIVE

As they all sat at Polly's table waiting for the police chief to come over, Polly's mind began whirring.

Suddenly she jumped up and said, "I'm going to the barn to get the vase. That way it will be here when Ken arrives." She opened a cupboard in the kitchen and grabbed a large brown paper shopping bag with handles, then dug around in a drawer and came up with several towels.

"I'll be back in a few minutes," she said, heading for the front door.

"Do you want any help?" Henry asked.

"No, it's nothing. Stay here and wait for Ken. There are ice cream treats in the freezer from last night. Have one and we'll get supper after he leaves."

She headed out to the barn. When she opened the door, she ran back to the feed room and up the ladder to the haymow and began digging for the vase. It was exactly where she'd left it. She drew it out and looked at the designs. Now that she knew what she was looking at, it was obvious that it had come from an ancient Mideast civilization. She wrapped it in the towels and gently set it in the bag, then wrapped her hand around the handles and headed for the ladder. As long as she didn't drop it, she'd be set.

Polly clambered back down the ladder and took a breath. Now, to get this into Ken Wallers' hands. She should have called him when she found it, but honestly, until today, she hadn't been ready to accuse Eliseo of stealing something like this. However, with all the information she had, it looked as if Harry had been the one to hide the vase in her hayloft. Eliseo probably hadn't even realized it was there. Surely if he'd known there was this much cash lying around, he wouldn't be working for her.

She turned the corner into the alley of the barn and stopped at the sight of two strange men approaching her.

"Who are you?" she asked. "Can I help you?"

"What do you have in that bag, miss?"

"Nothing. Just some things to take back up to the house. Who are you and why are you in my barn? This is private property."

"We're some old friends of Harry Bern. He didn't have what we were looking for and might have met with a little mishap when he wouldn't tell us where it was. After a little investigating we discovered his last job was working here for you. Did Harry hide something up in your hay loft?"

"I don't know what you're talking about," Polly said, "but I do know you shouldn't be here."

"No, miss. You're the one who shouldn't be here. We saw you at Harry's house today and we saw you take a couple of boxes away. Did you find something there, too? Maybe we should go up and grab up those two little boys who were with you. They might tell us where to find what belongs to us."

They continued to slowly walk toward her and Polly found herself backing into the feed room. She knew better than this. Every badly scripted chase scene had the poor, benighted victim backed into a small room. Well, at least she knew she wasn't going to go up the ladder. She couldn't understand why movie directors always sent people up to the roof or up the steps. There was never going to be a good end to that situation.

Polly glanced around trying to find a weapon or something to protect herself with then realized that she carried a priceless vase in her hands and it wasn't going to be destroyed on her watch.

"This is a small town. I'm going to start screaming and someone will come. You might want to get out of here before that happens," she said. "And besides, my horses aren't any too happy with you in here either. I'd hate for one of them to come crashing through a stall door because they were worried about me." Then she remembered that the horses were still out in the pasture. That wasn't going to do her any good.

The larger of the two moved in a little faster and grabbed her. He spun her around and clamped his hand over her mouth. She opened it enough so that she could bite the skin, but he refused to budge even as she ground her teeth into the meat of his hand.

"You shouldn't have done that. I don't like to hurt pretty little girls, but if they piss me off enough, I'll do what it takes," he said.

The other tried to rip the bag out of her hand, but Polly refused to release it. She wrapped her hand around the handles and the top of the bag. He grabbed her hand and began to squeeze it together, rubbing bone against bone. Tears spurted from her eyes as the level of pain increased and then she got mad. She kicked him in the shin and reached up with her free hand to smack his nose with the base of her palm as he bent over.

The fury in his eyes warned her in time to flinch as he smacked her across the face. The man holding her mouth released her in time for her head to fling to one side. Polly let out a screech and kicked again. This time the one in front of her punched her in the stomach and she doubled over.

Then she heard a voice say, "Get the hell away from her. Why does it take two of you to attack one little girl?"

They released her and she dropped to her knees to see them rush back out of the room. She took a breath and looked around for a hiding place for the vase. Somehow she made her way to a cabinet on the other side of the room, opened the door and shoved the vase in, closing the door behind her. She didn't want that antiquity to be a casualty of the fight. She'd heal, the vase wouldn't.

Still panting, she put a hand to her cheek. It felt hot. Damn, she was going to have a black eye, she was sure of that. She looked out into the alley and saw that Eliseo had been her savior and he was dealing with both of the men. They nearly had him down.

She pulled her phone out of her pocket, hit re-dial and when Ken Wallers answered, all she said was, "Help me in the barn," and hung up.

Then, she looked around the room again and her eyes lit on a shovel. Grabbing it, Polly ran out into the fray and as soon as she got a chance, lifted it up with both hands and with all the strength she had, brought it down on the head of the closest man. He dropped to the ground. It was the man who had punched her.

Polly figured that turnabout was fair play and kicked him in the balls, then said, "Stay where you are unless you want more of that."

He didn't move.

Eliseo and the other man were grappling in front of her. Dropping one of the intruders out of the fight had given Eliseo an advantage.

"Come on, Seo," the other man said. "You don't want to fight me again, do you?"

"I already am, Dover, and this time things are a little more even. You don't come into my territory and beat up women, you asshole."

"You're a pansy-assed moron. Just give up. All we want is the vase and the cash and we're out of here. Hell, we'll even give you some of the money if you stop fighting us."

"Not now, you won't. I told you to get out of town the other night and you didn't listen. I should have gone to the cops."

Dover punched Eliseo in the side. Polly knew that more damage to those ribs had to hurt like hell and she gasped in shock.

Then she heard a click. "Stop right there."

Polly looked up and saw Ken Wallers with his gun drawn, striding into the barn. She heaved a sigh of relief.

Neither man stopped what they were doing.

He approached a little more closely and looked over at Polly who was standing behind the man on the ground with her shovel poised to hit him again if he so much as twitched.

"Stop," he said and aimed the gun so that the man called Dover could see it. "I'm the Chief of Police in Bellingwood and you are finished with this fight."

Dover released Eliseo, who slumped over, breathing heavily.

Ken said to the man, "Drop to your knees, put your hands behind your back and link your fingers." The man did so and Ken pulled a zip tie out of his pocket and whipped it shut around Dover's wrists.

"Stay," he said. "Don't you dare move."

He walked over to the man who was lying on the ground and said to Polly, "What in the hell did you do to him?"

"He punched me. I felled him," she said. Yeah. That was a good word.

"You certainly did. Why is he all curled up?"

"I might have taken a little revenge. He hit me in the face, then he punched me in the stomach and when he threatened Jason and Andrew, I got mad."

Ken shook his head as he bent down and turned the man over so he could pull his hands behind him and zip-tie them together. "I am not going to ask any more questions and I am certainly not going to ever make you angry. I have to say, though, Miss Giller, Aaron Merritt worries about you a lot. After this, though, I'm not sure why. I think you did pretty well by yourself today."

Polly smiled and then felt a few tears begin to leak out of her right eye. She brushed them away and said, "Sorry, that doesn't do much for my reputation as a tough girl."

He laughed and pulled her in for a side hug. "You're fine, Polly. I can't believe what you've done here today."

Eliseo stood up and said, "I can't believe it either. You should have seen her. She was a little ferocious."

"Are these the two men who were in a fight with you the other night? Do you know them?"

"Yes I do, sir. I thought they would leave town, but they didn't."

"Do you want to press charges for the fight the other night?"

Dover looked up at Eliseo with venom in his eyes.

Eliseo nodded in the affirmative, "I think I do, sir."

"I have two patrol cars that should be here right about now," Ken looked up as three of his men walked into the barn. "Yes, here they are. They'll take these two down to the station and maybe we'll wrap this little mystery up today. I can't wait to hear which of you two murdered Harry Bern."

"Oh!" Polly said. "Just a second. I can tell you why they did it, too!"

She ran back into the feed room and opened the cabinet, pulled out the paper bag and carried it out to the crowd of people in her barn. She pulled back the towels and showed the vase to Ken.

"I'll bet these guys were in the army with Harry Bern and they stole this vase and this money when they were in Iraq. Am I right?"

She looked at the one kneeling on the ground and he was silent.

"This thing is priceless," she said and tipped the vase so Ken could see the bundles of cash in its belly. "And not only that, I have no idea how much cash is in here, but the articles say that millions of dollars were stolen. This is probably only a very small part of it."

Two of the three men who had joined them had brought the two thieves to their feet and were walking them out of the barn. Ken called the last of his men over and handed him the bag with the vase and then spoke to him in low tones.

Polly said to Eliseo, "I'm sorry you got hurt again, but I was very glad to hear your voice when you came in the barn."

"I'm sorry I didn't get here more quickly, ma'am."

"It's Polly. Even more so now, it's Polly."

"Yes ma'am." he smiled.

"I'd like to hear what the two of you have to say," Ken said. "Then tomorrow you should come to the station and make a statement and we'll get these men dealt with."

"Why don't you come on up to the apartment," Polly said. "I

want to put some peas on this eye and I think Eliseo could use a little TLC.

"Peas?" Ken asked.

"For my face. Frozen peas. Because they form themselves to the hills and valleys and I can't bear to use a steak for something like this."

"Don't you have an ice pack?"

"I like peas. I have plenty of them in my freezer. Eliseo, are you with me on this?"

"Peas it is," he laughed.

"Henry and Sylvie Donovan's boys are upstairs. I'll bet they're getting worried. I was going to run out here and get that vase and have it ready when you got there. It was Andrew who helped me figure this out. Maybe I should call Sylvie to come over."

"That would be fine," he said. "I'll be up in a few minutes."

"I'm going to be alright, Polly," Eliseo said. "I can go down to my room."

"You need to come with me. I think Ken is going to want all of the parts of the puzzle and you have a little more information than you've let on," she commented. "Come on up and let me take care of some of that blood, too." She pointed at his cheek and he touched it, then laughed as he saw it was covered in blood.

Polly pulled her phone back out and dialed Sylvie.

"How are you doing with your studying?" she asked when Sylvie answered.

"It's been a wonderful day!" Sylvie responded. "I even got a little nap. How are the boys?"

"They're fine and I'm glad you got a nap. They were awfully glad to get in my truck today!" Polly laughed.

"Oh, I'm sorry. I was a bear this morning. I was so tired and stressed out over all the work I had to get done for my classes. You're such a good friend. Thank you for taking them."

"Did you get most of your homework done?"

"I am all caught up. All I needed was some quiet time and some focus, so thank you again."

"That was no problem, but, umm, Sylvie? It's been a crazy day and Ken Wallers is here and I think I would like you to come over while we all talk. The boys have part of a story to tell and they'd be more comfortable with you there."

"What happened? Did they do something?"

"Oh, nothing like that. We've solved the murder of Harry Bern and a lot of that was because Andrew stumbled on some books at his house. Can you come over?"

"I'll be right there. You're up in your apartment?"

"Almost. Oh, and don't panic. Eliseo and I were in a fight with two men and we might look a little rough, so you'll probably want to tend to his wounds again."

"Oh, Polly, what have you done? Are you alright?"

"Just come over. I'm fine and you probably need to see this for yourself so you can be assured we're going to live. We're almost inside and I just want to stumble up the steps."

Polly and Eliseo went in to the apartment and Henry looked up from a game of cards he was playing with Jason at the table.

"What happened to you two?" he exclaimed as he jumped up and rushed to Polly.

"It's a long story," she said. "Can you wait to hear it until Ken Wallers gets up here?"

"I guess," he said. "Have you been in a fight?"

"Maybe," she winced.

"You've been in a fight?" Andrew exclaimed. "Did you win?"

"She definitely won," Eliseo said. "Henry you never want to cross this woman if she's got a weapon in her hand. And from what I've seen today, anything she can get her hands on is a weapon."

"Can I please get some peas?" Polly asked. "This is going to get worse before it gets better." She pointed to the side of her face.

"Peas?" Henry asked.

"In the freezer," she responded. "I want a bag of peas for me and get me a Dew out of the refrigerator." She turned to Eliseo. "Anything to drink? I think there's some iced tea."

"I'd love a glass of ice water. That's all," he said.

"Come on in and get comfortable," she pointed to the sofa.

"We're about to have a crowd."

"Who hurt you, Polly?" Jason asked. He had followed Henry into the kitchen and came back to her carrying a bottle of Mountain Dew. He twisted the top to break the seal and handed it to her.

"Thanks, Jason. Sit down. I'll tell you the whole thing when Chief Wallers is here. Is that alright?"

"Sure. I'm sorry you got hurt, though. Did you really hurt a bad guy? Were you scared?"

Polly looked into his fear-filled eyes. They'd had a conversation much like this after she had a run-in with her ex-boyfriend, Joey Delancy. Jason was trying desperately to grow up so he could take of his mother. Something had happened in their past that frightened him and he needed a little more reassurance that she could take care of herself.

"I did, but I called Chief Wallers so that he would come help us and I knew that Eliseo had my back, too."

"Okay," he said.

There was a knock at the door and Henry nodded to Jason who ran to get it. He placed a bag of peas in Polly's hand and handed Eliseo a glass of ice water.

Sylvie and Ken Wallers came in together. She hugged both of her boys then took a look at Eliseo and Polly and sighed. "What did you two do?" she asked.

"They beat up some bad guys, mom." Andrew said. "Polly did too, can you believe it?"

Sylvie's eyes crinkled. "You did?"

"Uh huh," Polly said.

"Oh, Eliseo, you've been hurt again. Polly, do you have a first-aid kit?"

Polly rolled her eyes, "I'm fine, thanks. It's in the bathroom underneath the sink."

Sylvie hadn't even heard her and rushed into the bathroom. She came back out with the first aid kit and said to Henry, "I know Polly has some rags in the kitchen drawer. I need a bowl of warm water and some of those as soon as possible, please."

Eliseo put his hand out to stop her. "Miz Donovan, I'm fine. Please don't hover over me today."

"I'm cleaning up those wounds and you aren't going to stop me. Henry?"

Henry slunk into the kitchen and Eliseo slumped back on the sofa.

"Think I'm the tough one now?" Polly asked.

With a bowl of water in one hand and towels in another, Henry came back into the living room. He set them on the coffee table and sat down beside Polly, "Are you hurt anywhere other than your face?" he asked.

"He punched me in the stomach, but I'm pretty much over that. Eliseo took most of the damage."

Ken Wallers looked around at them and finally said, "I'm sorry, but I need to find out what has happened here today."

Sylvie was startled and looked up, holding a warm, wet cloth to Eliseo's cheek. "I'll only be a minute. But, you can start."

"Thank you, ma'am," he said and tipped his head toward her, smiling.

"So, Polly. Tell me what you know."

"I found that vase in my hay loft and didn't know what it was. I probably should have called you last night, but I had no idea where it had come from."

"I get it. Go on."

"When we were cleaning Harry Bern's house out this afternoon, Andrew opened a book to look through it and things fell out. There were one hundred dollar bills and some Iraqi currency and a few articles. Those are over on the table. Jason?"

He got up and went over to get the box of items they had recovered.

"We found a few more books with money and articles in them. Harry had put some light glue on them so they wouldn't spill out unless someone worked at it."

"I worked at it," Andrew spoke up. "We went through all of his books and found the ones with stuffing. Jason counted and there were forty-three hundred dollar bills!"

"Hmmm," Ken said.

"Andrew also found a set of Time Life Ancient Civilization books and we brought those back with us as well. Sylvie, we need to talk about that."

Sylvie nodded as she put a bandage on Eliseo's cheek.

"He was looking at some pictures in the Mesopotamian book and happened to set it down in front of me and I realized that the patterns were the same as what I had seen on the vase. Then, I began looking at the newspaper clippings and realized they were all about these soldiers who had stolen things from Iraq during Desert Storm. There were some arrests, but not everything was recovered. The hundred dollar bills were dated from the late eighties and some from nineteen ninety-one and it occurred to me that it was probably part of the money they had stolen from the palace."

Polly flipped through a few of the articles and landing on one, handed it to Ken Wallers. He glanced at it and said, "Okay, keep going."

"Well, then I called you. But, I figured I would run out and get the vase so that I could show you everything at once. I put it in a bag with those towels because I had to bring it down the ladder. When I got to the bottom, those guys were in my barn and they attacked me. I kicked and bit and got one in the nose, but they were getting serious when Eliseo showed up. They let me go and probably thought I was a stupid woman."

"But, you're not," Jason interrupted.

"But, I'm not. I grabbed a shovel and dropped the one who punched me. Then, not long after that, you showed up. But, Eliseo. You and that Dover guy knew each other."

Ken turned his body to face Eliseo. "I think it's your turn now."

"I did know those two fellows. We were in the same unit together with Harry Bern. Because of my accident I got out of there before they did, but I always wondered what they were up to."

"Is Harry the man you were telling me about who traveled around the country and didn't let anyone know where he was?"

Polly asked.

"Yes," Eliseo said. "It wasn't a game. They wanted their part of the money. He had gotten it out of Iraq and it seemed like he enjoyed taunting them on the message boards. They'd show up in a town a few days after he had left. When I figured out he was living here in Bellingwood, I came up to try to talk some sense into him. I didn't tell any of the others what I was doing, just dropped off the message boards and headed up here. I thought I would beat them, but I came into town the day he was killed."

"You moved into my barn," Polly said.

"I did and I'm not sorry," he smiled.

"Go on," Ken encouraged.

"I knew those two were around the area and that one of them had killed Harry. I saw them downtown and thought I would take the day off and talk to them, see if I could convince them that he was gone and his stash was probably long gone. We did fine until they started drinking that night and then they got mad and accused me of stealing the money and using it myself. I couldn't make them see the sense in that. I was working and living in a barn. If I had the money, I would certainly be living better than that. Everything deteriorated and we got into a fight."

"How did you know I needed you today?" Polly asked.

"I had come up to get a glass of water when I saw their car pull into the parking lot. I saw them run down to the barn and decided to give them enough time to do whatever they were going to do. I didn't know you were there until I heard you scream."

Polly felt Henry shudder beside her. "I'm fine," she said. "Let it go."

"Then I ran into the barn and distracted them and now we're here."

"Did either of them tell you that they had killed Harry Bern?" Ken asked.

"One of them told me that he met with a little mishap," Polly said. "Is that close enough?"

"That will be close enough for me to get started."

"What now?" she asked.

"Well, now, we get the process started down at the station. I'll make some calls to find out what to do with the vase and the money. I'd like the two of you to come down tomorrow morning and make a statement and we'll see from there."

"What about this money?" Polly asked, holding up the small box.

"Well, I suppose that I asked you to deal with all of Harry Bern's stuff and you were planning to bring his things back to your house. I'll take the articles, but this money was part of the books, so it's yours to deal with."

Polly smiled, "I know exactly what to do with it." She counted out twenty of the bills and handed them to Sylvie. "Here. Your boys found this stuff. You should do whatever you want with it." Then she took out three more and handed those to Sylvie as well. "One for each of you. Do something fun with them, okay?"

Sylvie looked at her with her mouth open, then she began shaking her head. "I can't take this."

"Oh yes, you can," Polly said. "Ask Eliseo. I'm a dangerous woman."

Sylvie took the cash and looked at her boys, neither of whom knew what to say. They stared at the money and then at their mom.

"Thank you, Polly. This helps," she said.

Polly handed the rest to Eliseo. "You're going to find a place to stay this week. This will get you started."

He pushed the money back at her.

"Really?" she asked. "You've been part of this longer than any of us. Take the money, say goodbye to Harry and let this chapter be over for you. And besides, I'm ferocious, remember?"

He breathed through his nose a couple of times. "I'm not sure what to say here."

"Thank you is all you need to come up with. Oh, and be at work tomorrow morning. That would be nice," she laughed.

Ken Wallers stood up and said, "I'll see you tomorrow. Thanks for a very exciting afternoon. Now, I have work to do."

Henry walked him to the door and shook his hand. Polly heard them speaking in low tones, but had no idea what they were talking about.

Ken left and Henry said, "I could use some supper. What do you think?"

Sylvie tried to hand a hundred dollar bill back to Polly, who simply ignored her.

"Would you mind picking up pizza?" Polly asked him.

"I'd love to do that. Boys, you wanna take a ride with me?"

Andrew was up and out of his chair before Henry had finished his question.

Jason stood up and said, "Thank you Polly." He reached over and hugged her, then whispered in her ear, "I want to talk to you tomorrow after school, okay?"

She hugged him back and winked at him.

CHAPTER TWENTY-SIX

Releasing Polly so that he could go home had been difficult for Henry after everyone left. He had gone home quite late and hadn't let her do anything. When Eliseo and Jason went out to bed down the horses, he went out to help them, insisting that Polly stay in. Sylvie thought it was sweet; Polly figured she'd let him get away with it for one evening.

He had cleaned things up and made her stay on the sofa while he said good night to everyone, then after they were finally alone, he pulled her close, looked into her eyes and said, "You nearly killed me this evening. I didn't even know you were in trouble. If anything truly awful had happened to you, I don't know what I would have done, Polly."

She had patted his hand and said, "But, nothing did. I'm alright."

He took her hands in his and she watched his eyes fill, "I was so shook up when you two walked in and I realized you had been beaten. If those boys hadn't been here and Ken hadn't already sent those two away to his jail, I don't know what I would have done. It took everything I had to force my fury down and be pleasant. You scared me to death."

Polly had leaned in to his chest and said "I was pretty scared, too. But, it all worked out and I'm here and I'm okay."

She'd fallen asleep while he watched a movie and then taken Obiwan out for a final walk. After he came back with her dog, she had come awake as he was trying to lift her from the sofa.

"What in the hell?" she'd asked.

"I was going to put you to bed."

Polly had laughed out loud and sat up. "Oh, Henry. You're wonderful. I'm not that breakable and I'm going to be fine." She had kissed him and then said, "But, you're right - it is time to go to bed. Tomorrow morning is going to come whether I've been punched or not and you need to go home and get some sleep. The bad guys are in jail and I'll be safe."

"Are you sure? I can sleep on the sofa again."

"I'm absolutely positive. But, thank you for taking care of me."

She had walked him to the front door, kissed him good night, swooned a little as he walked down the steps, then had run back inside and to the kitchen window to wave at him as he got in his truck and drove away.

"There's a man worth keeping around, Obiwan," she had said to her dog as he followed her into the bedroom and jumped up on the bed.

The next morning, she and Eliseo were cleaning out stalls when she said, more to herself than anything, "Huh. I wonder if that would work."

"What's up, Polly?"

"Well, I was thinking about Harry Bern's house. The man who owns it has a big mess to clean up with all the destruction your buddies did in there. He saw Henry last week at the diner and asked about someone to do the work. All of Harry's stuff is still there. I wonder."

"What do you wonder?"

She stepped into the stall he was raking and leaned against the wall.

"Doesn't it make sense for you to move in, trade labor you can do in your free time for rent until it's fixed up? You could use

Harry's furniture and household stuff until you want to replace it. Then I wouldn't have to hold a sale, you wouldn't have to buy much, you wouldn't have to look for a place to live and if there was anything you needed help re-building or fixing, Henry is around."

"You never stop thinking and plotting and planning, do you?"

"Tell me that doesn't sound like the perfect way to manage everything," she grumped.

"Do you think the owner will go for it?"

"Before I ask, are you on board?"

Eliseo nodded, "It's not a bad idea. I could do the work."

"Then I'll call him when I get to my office. If he doesn't have someone else interested, it should be perfect."

"I'm not comfortable with you doing all of this for me. You know that, don't you?"

"But, if it makes sense, why would you fight it?"

"It does make sense, in a strange way."

"Then let me make the initial call and you can do the rest. When I finish speaking with him, I'll email you the details and you can contact him later on today."

"Fine," he agreed. "I'm going to spend some time working with Nan this morning. Jeff said there is a delivery of furniture scheduled this afternoon for the middle room upstairs and there's a dancer from Dallas coming in on Wednesday to spend time with Mark Ogden's sister and her dance school as they prepare for the end of the year."

"Really!" Polly said. "No one tells me anything."

Eliseo pulled his phone out and showed her the calendar. "It's all on here," he laughed.

Polly pushed his hand away. "Crap. I was supposed to get the Computer Room scheduled for Doug and his gang Friday night. I forgot."

Eliseo looked at the calendar again and said, "It's been taken care of."

"I'm afraid Doug knows me too well," she laughed.

Polly looked at the man she had hired to work with them at

Sycamore House. He was more than a custodian. He had begun to insinuate himself into the family she was creating; loving her animals, protecting her from the bad guys and now he was even keeping her on track with their schedule. She still saw his scars every time she looked at him, but they were part of who he was.

"If we get you a home address today, will you fill out all the paperwork for Jeff so we can make everything legal and keep you around for a while?" she asked.

"Even if I have to use this address, I'd like to do that," he replied. "I look forward to settling down in Bellingwood for a long time. Thank you for the opportunity."

"You earned it and it didn't even take us a month to get to this point. I'm glad." Polly walked up to him and put out her hand. He took it in his scarred hand and looked down at them.

"Thank you," he said again, looking up into her eyes.

Polly went back to her apartment, took a quick shower, dressed and headed to her office. She looked out and her parking lot was filling up with vehicles. That was exciting. She went outside and looked around. There were ten or fifteen people working in the corner lot on the garden. She walked to the side of the house and saw walls going up on the garage. Henry had told her it would be ready for interior work in a few weeks. She could hardly wait. Then, she saw a large truck come in, loaded with trees.

The driver pulled up and jumped out. "Polly Giller?" he asked, peering at her a little strangely.

She wasn't sure what was up, but said, "That's me. Are these my sycamore trees?"

"Yes ma'am. We have the plan you discussed with our manager, would you check this out to make sure we do what you expect?"

She looked at the plans and watched as another truck with equipment on the back pulled into the lot. She signed off on the paperwork and stepped back as he re-entered his truck. Jeff came outside and joined her.

He looked at her, wrinkled his forehead and finally said, "This is a big deal day, isn't it!"

"I didn't realize they were showing up today to plant the trees. I suppose they need to do it while they've got the weather."

"When did you plan on them being here?"

"Later in the week, but the forecast looks terrible for Thursday and Friday. It's supposed to rain; maybe even snow. I'll be glad to have these in."

"What's up with all the gardeners over there?"

Polly giggled. "They're more excited about that park than I am, so I'm going to let them have fun. I have no idea what is happening today. I suppose I should make sure there's plenty of hot coffee."

"I already turned the pot on. It's brewing as we speak."

"I'll be back," she said and walked across the lot.

"Good morning!" she called as she approached.

Nancy Burroughs looked up and her mouth got big, but she said, "Hello, Polly. How are you this morning?"

"I'm fine. You look as if you have a big crew today!"

"We are finishing the hole for the pond. Deb's husband is installing it tomorrow. I'm mapping out the pathway, so they can excavate that next. We have grass pavers to install. It will be so pretty."

"I'm excited about watching the progress. This is fun!"

"It is fun and they enjoy working together." Nancy nodded at the group behind her.

"There is a big pot of hot coffee in the kitchen. Please feel free to come in and warm up or take a break. Would you let everyone know?"

"Thank you, Polly. We'll surely be in. I see your trees are here today! That will change the look of this corner."

"I know that Eliseo won't think that picking up all the sycamore leaves is a great deal of fun in the fall, but one day this will be beautiful!"

"Now ..." Nancy pointed at the side of the building, "what are you building there?"

"I'm putting a garage in with an apartment overhead on this side and then later on, we will build a matching structure on the other side which will offer me four rooms, at least two of which will be accessible."

"You've got quite the venture here, don't you? I hope that everything goes as well as you hope."

"I can only do what I believe to be the right thing and hope for the best."

"You are certainly the talk of the community. Actually, you're the talk of several communities around here. I think people are a bit envious and astonished that you are investing so much effort and money into this place."

Polly recognized an interrogation when she was in the middle of one and decided it would be easier to answer the woman's questions. If she could get good information out there, then at least they might not make up strange stories about her.

"The investment is already beginning to pay off. The auditorium is filling up with quite a few events and I know that Jeff is getting requests from artists who want to spend time at Sycamore House. Once we have activities to fill the classrooms on the main floor, we're going to be busy around here. Sylvie Donovan is creating a name for herself as a caterer and there's no reason to think her business won't grow. I have great people who are working here with me to make this place successful."

"There is some talk that you have hired a new janitor and he was involved with the one who was murdered."

"They knew each other back in Desert Storm, but Harry was killed before Eliseo got to town. He is going to fit in very well with the family here at Sycamore House. It's pretty wonderful to see it continue to grow. Now, please let everyone know they are welcome to come in any time for coffee. Thank you so much for all your work here. It is going to be beautiful and a terrific addition to this corner," Polly said and turned around to walk away before she had to answer any more questions.

Back in her office, she looked up his phone number and dialed Dave Steery, the owner of the home Harry Bern had been renting.

"You've got Dave. Go," he said when he answered the phone.

"Mr. Steery? This is Polly Giller from Sycamore House. How

are you today?"

"Hello, Miss Giller. Ken Wallers said you were cleaning out your employee's things from my house. Thank you. When do you expect to have that finished?"

"Well, that's what I wanted to speak with you about," she said. "I have an idea that might benefit you."

"Is it going to fix my walls and my ceiling?"

"Yes, in fact, I think it will."

"Then I'm listening."

"I have an employee who needs a place to live. He has some skill with carpentry and is a very hard worker. Would you consider allowing him to live there for one year rent-free in return for his labor as he renovates the house? You would provide all the supplies he'll need. He would do the work in his off hours and would have support from Henry Sturtz when necessary."

"Would Henry provide him with tools?"

"How about you provide the pneumatic nailer, dry wall knives and pans and Henry will make sure he has a saw."

"I won't pay for the utilities and I'd like him to pay for the property taxes on the place each month."

"Can I tell him this is the deal you will make?"

"It sounds reasonable to me. But, if he leaves before the house is fixed, I'm not going to be very happy with either him or with you."

"I can't guarantee anything like that, Mr. Steery."

"I suppose you can't, but I'm still not going to be happy."

"You can discuss that with him. His name is Eliseo Aquila and I will have him call to make an appointment with you to fill out paperwork."

"Yes, ma'am. That sounds good."

Polly hung up and emailed the information to Eliseo, leaving it to him to finish the deal. She then emailed Andy to tell her the sale was off, since he would be able to use the items they'd packed into boxes.

She sat back and shut her eyes so she could think. That was one thing off her list. Trees and garden, garage and apartment.

Furniture for the middle bedroom was coming in and Lydia was going to take care of getting the linens for that room. It would be ready to go before week's end. When the guest rooms upstairs were full, she was going to appreciate having a back entrance to her home. This was going to be a busy summer; she could hardly wait.

Jeff walked into her office and said, "Alright, I can't stand it. What in the hell happened to you?"

Polly peered at him and asked, "What do you mean?"

"I mean ... your face. What happened over the weekend?"

Polly's hand flew up to her face and she said, "OH! That's why everyone is looking at me so strangely. Yeah. I got beat up last night."

He sat down and placed his hands on the arms of the chair, "You what? By whom?"

"You wouldn't believe me if I told you that Henry did this, would you?"

"Hell no. That man is so head over heels in love with you, he'd lay down in front of a freight train before hurting you. So, who did this to you?"

She grinned. "It's nice having you live out of town. If you were a resident, you'd already know by now through the grapevine."

"My tentacles apparently don't reach out that far yet. Spill."

"We discovered who killed Harry Bern last night, but in the middle of it, they smacked me around a little bit and got into a terrible fight with Eliseo. I also found a priceless ancient vase from Mesopotamia that was filled with hundred dollar bills."

He sat back in his chair and then chuckled.

"What?" she asked.

"You're going to want to wait a minute. The troops are here and if you are telling the story, you may as well entertain us all." He pointed outside and Polly turned around in her chair. Jeff was right. Lydia, Beryl and Andy were coming in and they looked as if they were quite serious about something.

"Oh no," she said. "I'm going to be in such trouble."

"Shall we go into the conference room?" he asked.

"Yes, and would you mind bringing in some coffee? I'm going to have to offer up something to placate them."

Polly stood and followed him into the outer office. He was on his way to the kitchen when the three women entered, planted their feet and stared at Polly. No one said a word.

"I'm fine," Polly finally said.

They continued to stare at her.

"Oh, come on!" she pleaded. "I'm fine!"

Beryl pointed at Polly's face. "That's a most creative makeup job. Purple, green and black and only on one side."

Lydia and Andy continued to stare silently.

"I didn't do anything wrong and I'm fine. What more do you want from me?"

"March," Lydia said and pointed to the conference room. Polly marched and the women followed her in, taking seats around her when she sat down.

"Now tell me why I had to wait until this morning to find out that you had been beaten up?" Lydia asked.

"I don't know! I would have assumed that you heard the activity on your police scanner or Aaron would have told you," Polly countered.

"I should have heard from you. If I had heard it on the police scanner I would have worried all night long."

"So it's better that you didn't hear anything until this morning, right?"

"Wrong! Polly, we're your friends. Even if you don't need us to take care of you, we want to know what is happening. Especially when someone hurts you!"

"And leaves a mark," Beryl interrupted. "That's gonna be glorious!"

Jeff came in with the coffee and quietly set it down on the table, then pulled up a chair. He looked around at the group of women and said, "I want to hear the story, too. Can I stay?"

Polly chuckled. "First they have to beat me up a little, then I'll tell the story."

"Oh, I want to watch this, too. Sometimes you're my greatest entertainment."

"We aren't going to beat you up, Polly," Andy said. "We're sick that you were hurt."

"I'm fine," Polly assured them. "I promise. Now, if you will pour yourselves some coffee and sit back and relax, I'll tell you what happened yesterday so you don't have to hear exaggerated stories from anyone else."

Polly began her story by admitting to finding the vase on Saturday and hoping to wait until the weekend was over to tell anyone in case Eliseo was involved. She had a great deal of fun watching her friends react to her retelling of the events and made sure to emphasize Eliseo's heroic intervention. When she described being hit in the face and punched in the stomach, Lydia's face fell and she could see that the woman was near tears, so she rushed ahead to recount her superheroine actions with a manure shovel and then the delivery of a good, swift kick to the poor man's privates.

Beryl interrupted, "That's the second time you've kicked a man when he's down, Polly."

"And if someone threatens me again, it won't be the last time," Polly announced. "He certainly didn't care how much he hurt me and I was going to insist that he remember that came with a price."

Andy shuddered. "I don't think I would remember to do any of those things in a crisis. I hope you're around if I ever have to face that," she said to Polly.

"Ladies," Jeff said, "you can never allow Polly to own a gun. It's bad enough she aims down there with her foot, but if she ever got angry enough and aimed a gun at a man, she wouldn't aim for the heart, she'd aim much lower. That's frightening!"

Polly gave him an evil grin and continued, telling of Ken Waller's arrival and the arrest.

"Eliseo and I need to go to the police station today to give our statements, but I think this chapter is finally closed," she said.

Lydia was shaking her head, "Why would you have gone out to the barn alone?"

Polly was taken aback. "Why not? It wasn't dark. I had no idea that anyone was around. It's my barn and this is Bellingwood, for goodness' sake. That would be like telling you not to go out to your garage alone, or telling Andy she couldn't walk over to the cemetery."

"I know. You're right. It's just that in hindsight ..."

Polly interrupted her. "In hindsight, everything is clear. In hindsight, I would have called Ken or Aaron on Saturday, but I didn't know then what I know now and I didn't make any poor choices. In fact, given what has happened, I think I made great choices all around. I have friends who love me, a boyfriend who cares about me. I've hired great people - I hired one man who played the hero last night. I trust law enforcement here and know that when I call they will show up and help me out and I think that the good far outweighs the bad in this scenario."

Lydia sighed. "You're right. I keep thinking of you as my daughter and you're my friend. I was so upset when Aaron told me what had happened and when I saw your face it devastated me."

Polly wheeled her chair closer to Lydia and reached out to hug her. "I love you very much. You know that, right?"

"I do know that," Lydia said.

"Me too?" Beryl asked.

"Oh, I love you girls so much. I'm sorry I scared you. I will try to be better about telling you things so that you don't hear them from someone else. I can't make any promises, but I will try."

"That's all we can ask for," Lydia assured her.

Polly sat back. "Are you going to be here this afternoon when the furniture is delivered?"

"Jeff said he'd call me, right?" Lydia responded.

Jeff nodded yes.

"Then I will be here."

"If I'm finished with my statement and whatever else Ken Wallers needs, Eliseo and I will be here as well. I can hardly wait to see this come in!" Polly exclaimed.

"This room will be as beautiful as the Walnut Room," Lydia

said. "Do I get to work on the front room next?"

"You sure do and by the end of September, Henry thinks there will be four more rooms to decorate in the addition on the south side of the building."

"That's a lot of guest rooms. Are you going to be able to keep them filled?" Andy asked quietly.

"It may take a while, but when I realized that we didn't have anything available that was accessible, I panicked," Polly said. "It was also difficult for me to sort through the fact that I didn't have room in my apartment when Sal came to visit and then I didn't have a place for Eliseo to stay while he was waiting to have enough money to afford an apartment. If this is supposed to be a place of hospitality and safety, I needed to get a few more options in place so everyone feels welcome."

"You don't have to take care of everyone, Polly," Jeff chided.

"Why not? Sycamore House should be available for everyone from Queen Elizabeth to Mother Teresa's poorest children." Then she giggled. "They can't all show up at the same time, though. I would run out of room."

CHAPTER TWENTY-SEVEN

"Noooo! Watch out below!"

Polly jumped back as a hammer fell out of Ben Bowen's hand. She wasn't sure why she jumped; he was across the room on a ladder.

"Sorry, Miss Giller," he said. "I must have taken clumsy pills this morning instead of my regular suave and debonair medication. My wife mixes 'em up all the time."

She waved and turned back to Henry. She had returned from the police station after giving her statement and was surprised to see him, but he had stopped by to check on the progress of the garage after having been at Beryl's studio for most of the day.

"Are you going to get her back in there in two weeks?" she asked him.

"The base cabinets are installed, the floor to ceiling cabinets are going in. Len is cutting shelves and drawer pieces tomorrow. All he has left is the doors and the countertops. That's most of it. There will be quite a few odds and ends, but before spring has fully arrived, she'll be back in her space."

"I didn't tell you about my brainstorm with Harry Bern's place yet," she commented.

He looked sideways at her, "What have you gotten into this time?"

"I don't think it should be too bad. I negotiated a year's rent for Eliseo if he provided labor to fix the damage and renovate the place."

"That's not a bad idea," Henry agreed. "Steery talked to me about the house last week, but I'd rather see your custodian living off site and he sounds as if he has the skills to do the work. It will be a good deal for both of them."

"You know what that means, don't you?"

"I'm almost afraid to ask," Henry said, "What does that mean?"

"When we're done with everything out here this summer, I'm going to ask you to look at possible renovation plans for the basement."

"Of course you are."

"It's dry and clean."

"You're right, it is and there are quite a few things we can do down there to make it more useful."

"See," she said and nudged his chest with her shoulder, "I knew you'd be positive about it."

Henry shook his head and smiled, "It's either that or think you are insane. I prefer the idea of being positive."

"So, what are you thinking about the stairway in here?" Polly asked and walked in the side door to the storage room situated behind the auditorium's stage.

"You're going to lose your closet," he began.

"I'm what? I already have trouble keeping things clean."

"We'll figure something out, but the stairs come up to your back wall and you need a hallway. I'm going to leave the walls up down here and put a door at the end. I'll knock out all of the walls that have been built upstairs and I'm sure you'll design a beautiful railing. There's also another window hidden in there."

He walked back outside and pointed up. "See, it's been covered. We can expose that and add even more light to your room."

"So I'll have even more light to see my mess," she lamented.

"I'm confident you will get past this and see what a good idea it is."

"Henry, it is going to be a great idea, but I'm a slob."

He chuckled. "It's good to know you have a couple of faults."

"Oh, I have plenty of faults. Lydia, Beryl and Andy came over this morning to harass me because I didn't call them last night."

"Oh, I should have thought of that," Henry said as he clapped his palm to his forehead. "I'm sorry."

"It's not your fault!" Polly exclaimed. "You'd think that after this long, I'd be more aware of my responsibilities. I'm not. I felt horrible."

"Did they forgive you?"

"What do you think?" she smirked. "But, not until they'd thoroughly guilted me."

They walked around the outside of the structure and watched as another tree was being planted. The tree spade was simply immense and Polly was fascinated as she watched them work.

She was thankful for a nice day. So far there had only been a few of those.

"Hey Polly!" she heard and looked to see Andrew and Jason crossing the highway. They ran across the lawn to where she and Henry were standing.

"You look funny," Andrew giggled.

She couldn't help it and reached up to touch her face again. "It's pretty ugly isn't it?" she asked.

"No, it's not ugly," Jason assured her.

"Do you want to go up and get Obiwan?" she asked Andrew.

"Yes! Do you think he'll be glad to see me?"

"He'll be very glad. He's been cooped up in that apartment all day long. I bet he would love a nice long walk today."

"I've been cooped up too. We had a substitute teacher and she got mad at our class so we didn't get recess today," Andrew complained. "And it wasn't my fault. But some kids thought they would talk when she was talking and then wouldn't answer her questions. We all got into trouble."

"Then it sounds as if a walk would be good for both of you,"

Polly said. "Why don't you take your things upstairs and then, Andrew, you can take Obiwan all over the property."

The boys ran inside and Polly said to Henry, "Jason told me he wanted to talk to me. I don't know what's up with him, but he's been off for a few days. Would you keep an eye on Andrew out here?"

"Sure. We'll watch them plant some trees and help in the garden and we might even make some more holes in the plaster. Text me when you're ready for him to be back in your world."

Polly took his arm and pulled him close, "I'm a lucky girl. Don't ever let me forget that."

She was walking to the front door when Andrew came tearing out with Obiwan on a leash. He pulled up short in front of her.

"Jason has a secret he wants to tell you," Andrew whispered. "He won't tell me what it is, but he's upset about it."

"How do you know this?" she asked.

"I'm his brother!" Andrew announced. "I know these things."

"We'll see if we can't fix it all now. You and Henry and Obiwan are going to hang out here watching trees get planted. Is that alright?"

"Cool!" he said and took off at a dead run for the side of Sycamore House, pulling on the dog's leash until he caught up and trotted along with the little boy.

Polly went inside and found Jason sitting on the main stairs.

"Do you want to come in and sit down in my office so we can talk?" she asked.

He raised his shoulders as he took in a deep breath and said, "I may as well get this over with."

Jason stood up and began walking dejectedly to her office. She caught up with him and put her arm around his shoulder as they walked. Jeff was standing at the copier and looked up when they entered, but saw Jason's demeanor and said nothing, just turned back to his work.

Polly followed the boy into her office and shut the door as he slumped in a chair.

"Alright, Jason, what has upset you so much?"

"This isn't easy for me," he said. "It's going to change everything and just about the time things were starting to go good, too."

She could tell he was serious, but couldn't imagine what had happened to make things so dire.

"Why don't you dive in and start somewhere," she said.

"After I tell you this, Doug and Billy are never going to want to me play games with them again. I hate being a snitch. And I'm the little kid in the group, too."

"Doug and Billy?" she asked, very confused. "What do they have to do with this?"

"I know you like them a lot and you trust them ..." he started.

Polly's heart sank. If those two boys were involved in something that had Jason this upset, she was never going to be able to forgive herself. This was nearly more than she could stand, but she kept quiet so he could continue.

"Last week when we played games here, everyone wanted to go down and see the horses and you said it was okay."

"I remember," she said.

"While we were down there, I showed them the new saddles and the collars and harnesses that had come in. I was so excited about the possibility of hooking up teams. Eliseo has been talking about it and he told me that I could help him. So, I was bragging on the horses and talking about everything.

"I should have known better," he said. "Mom always tells me that I'm not supposed to brag about things, but they were talking about their cars and their trucks and I wanted to talk about something in my life that was that cool."

"It's alright, Jason. You have a right to be proud of the work you are doing with my horses. Not very many kids your age spend time doing something like that. Go on."

"I didn't think anything about it until the other night when you talked about the truck that had driven off. Polly, I know whose truck that was."

Polly came fully alert. "You do? How do you know?"

"Because his brother was at the school that night bragging

about how he was going to get the truck when he turned eighteen. He was helping his big brother fix it up and then he said that his brother about had enough money to get a new truck."

"Are you sure, Jason?"

"It's the same truck. His brother picked him up in it that night. I saw it."

"But don't you suppose there are a lot of trucks that look like that?"

"Nope. They are painting it themselves. Doug is going to be so mad at me for tattling on his friends."

"I'm pretty sure Doug would be proud of you for stepping up, Jason. He's not going to be mad at you."

"But the other kids will know that I've snitched. That's the type of thing that never goes away."

Polly knew exactly what he was going through. This was the age where peer pressure began to chew a kid up and she had to help him get through this with his integrity and his reputation intact.

"Here's the deal, Jason. I'm going to call Sheriff Merritt. This is his case. You know him and trust him, don't you?"

"Yes, ma'am."

"I'm also going to call Doug. I want him to tell you that what you are doing is the right thing to do and we'll see what he says about it all. How does that sound?"

"Not great, but okay."

"In fact, I'm going to call him first and see if he'll be here when the Sheriff comes. Sit still and we're going to take care of this."

She placed the first call to Doug Randall.

"Hey Doug," she said. "Where are you?"

"Hi, Polly. I'm headed back into town. We were over in Stratford on a job today."

"Who is we?"

"Me and Billy. Duh. Oh, I texted Jeff this morning about Friday night. I heard about your big fight last night and figured that you had better things to deal with than my game night."

"That's cool. I did remember this morning, but it was late, so

I'm glad you took care of it."

"What's up?"

"I need you and Billy to come be Jedi Knights for me and Jason. Could you stop by here when you get into town?"

"Do we need our light sabers and robes?" he asked.

She chuckled. "Nope, just your noble selves."

"We'll be there in ten minutes."

"Thanks."

She hung up and dialed again.

"Polly Giller, if this is about another body, I'm going to lock you up in my attic," Aaron Merritt said when he answered.

"Nope, no body this time, but I think we might have solved your farm theft mystery. Do you happen to be in Bellingwood?"

"Really!" he said. "I'm not in town right now, but I'm on the road. I could be there in fifteen or twenty minutes. Can I stop by your office?"

"That would be terrific. I appreciate it."

After they hung up, she said to Jason, "Do you want me to call your mom? Would you like her to be here while you talk to Sheriff Merritt? You haven't done anything wrong at all, but I want you to feel completely comfortable."

"No, it would just upset her that I haven't already told you about this," he said.

"I'm not upset about it. Are you sure you don't want to call her?"

He looked at her, pleading with his eyes, "Can we please wait until this is over? She's going to be disappointed in me and it's hard enough."

Polly's heart broke for him. He had turned this event into an immense problem in his mind, not understanding how easily it could be fixed. Time was so compressed for these kids. She sighed. "It's going to be alright, Jason. I promise."

He didn't say anything, just stared at the floor.

Polly beckoned to Doug and Billy to open the door and come in when they arrived.

"Hey little dude!" Billy said to Jason when they came into

Polly's office. "Are you gonna play with us again Friday night? You were rockin' and rollin' last time."

Jason turned pale and didn't say anything.

"Doug," Polly said, "Could you grab a couple of chairs and come in and shut the door?"

Doug pulled two chairs into the office and sat down in one of them.

"You two look pretty serious, is something wrong?"

"Well, Jason thinks he knows who has been stealing from the farms around here and who took my tack the other night."

"Dude! That's good stuff!" Billy said, clapping the younger boy on the back. Jason continued to look miserable.

"He's pretty sure they're associated with your group of gaming buddies," she said, dropping the news on them.

"Oh little dude. That's freaky weird. Are you sure?"

Doug spoke up. "That makes sense," he said.

"What do you mean?" Polly asked.

"Oh, a few things that have been going on. Crap. I can't believe I was so dense. Billy. Dude. Think about it. Just think about it."

Billy cocked his head, then he shut his eyes and when he opened them, they were huge. "You're right. We totally should have figured it out!"

"What are you talking about?" Polly demanded.

"Every farm that was hit?" Doug said.

"What?"

"There's a kid that games with us. Why didn't I put that together?"

"Are you kidding? Every one?" she asked.

"Pretty much. And you are the last to have been hit. That makes me mad," Doug said. "What were they thinking? You don't crap in your own nest."

Doug turned to Jason, "It's Dinky Stanton's brother Roger, isn't it?"

Jason nodded, still silent.

"That jerk. Of course it is."

"You know him?" Polly asked.

"Yeah. He works construction ... sometimes. Dinky isn't much better, but I was hoping he'd figure it out."

A knock at the door and Aaron opened it, "Can I come in?" he asked.

Polly pointed to the empty chair and said, "Sit down. I think we have a story for you."

Doug looked at Polly in surprise. "How did he know to come here?"

"I called him when Jason told me what he knew," she said. "But if we can keep Jason out of this, that would be my preference. I think it would be his as well."

Jason nodded rapidly.

The Sheriff said, "Jason why don't we start with what you know and then we'll determine whether or not I can use what Doug and Bill here, can tell me instead."

Jason quietly repeated what he had told Polly, doubling his regret that he had led Dinky Stanton to the barn in the first place.

Aaron didn't speak until he was finished, and then turned to Doug, "Now, tell me what you might know about this."

"Sheriff, Billy and I just figured out what morons we are. Every single family that has been hit has a kid who comes to our gaming nights. Dinky Stanton has to be the connection. And Jason is right. The truck that was here at Sycamore house the other night sounds exactly like Roger's truck. Dinky has been talking about it for months while they've been working on it. They go out to the junkyard every weekend to get parts."

"Was that Dinky Stanton in the basement of Harry Bern's house yesterday?" Polly asked.

"Yep. He was probably going to take that junk out to trade for something for the truck."

"They haven't sold the stuff they've stolen yet?"

"I dunno," Doug said. "If Roger sold it, he's holding the cash until he can get enough for a new truck. Dinky has been talking about that a lot, too."

"Have you ever been out to their place, Doug?" Aaron asked.

"Sure. We used to go fishing there all the time. They have a shed out by the lake where they keep a couple of old boats and some motors. Hey! I'll bet that's where they're keeping the junk until they sell it. It's big enough."

Aaron nodded and said, "Jason, there's no reason you need to be involved in this. I think I can get a warrant to search based on what we know. I'll pull the license information on that truck and I suspect it will line up with what you've told me."

He stood and stepped to the door. "Thanks a lot, Polly. People are going to feel better when we get this stopped."

Jason visibly relaxed when he left and Polly said, "Doug, Jason is a little worried that you might think he's a snitch."

Billy's eyes got huge. "No way, dude. You were a hero instead. Nobody wants to hang around a thief, especially when they're stealing from friends."

"Really?" Jason asked, his eyes brightening.

"Really! Buddy, you did a good thing today. It's what a Jedi Knight in training would do. You always have to be truthful to be on the light side."

"I didn't want to screw up your group. I'm only the little kid."

"Even little kids know when you have to tell the truth. You did good."

"Don't tell anyone, please?" Jason begged.

"If you don't want anyone to know that you were the hero, we'll keep quiet. I totally get it that people might not appreciate the light side of the force," Doug said. "So you'll ask your mom if you can come Friday night?"

"Yes!" Jason exclaimed. "Thanks, guys."

Billy winked at Polly.

"Thanks," she echoed.

Jason saw Eliseo walk past her inside window and asked, "Can I tell him what happened today?"

"Sure, invite him to come in.

"How did it go?" she asked Eliseo when he came into her office.

"We worked out a good deal. Thank you for that. I'm moving in tomorrow."

"Where are you gonna live?" Jason asked.

"I'm moving into Harry Bern's house and I'm going to fix it up again."

"That will be cool!" Jason said. "Your own house. Someday we're going to get a house. Whenever mom is ready."

"If you need any help with electrical, Billy and I are available," Doug said. "We don't have our certificates yet, but we can help."

"I'll keep that in mind."

"Eliseo, you should know that these three just solved the mystery of the farm thefts. I think there should be a big celebration tonight after all that has happened this weekend. We deserve it. What do you think?"

He looked around the room and saw the expectant looks on three young faces. "It sounds like a good idea."

Henry, Andrew and Obiwan came in the front door and he peered at her through the window. Polly nodded for him to join them.

Eliseo backed out of the office so Henry and Andrew could enter. Andrew jumped to the vacant seat.

"Did you tell her everything, Jason?"

"What do you know, runt?" he asked.

"I know that you were upset about something and that you had to tell Polly. That's what I know," Andrew said, sticking out his lower jaw in defiance.

Doug laughed. "He told her who had been stealing things from farms. He's a hero."

"He did?" Henry queried.

"He did. Doug and Billy figured it out too. It's the brother of one of their gaming buddies. The Sheriff has gone off to investigate and if I'm lucky I might get my stuff back before it's sold," she said. "And we're thinking there should be a celebration tonight. Don't you agree?"

"Why don't I go get my grill and bring it over? It's a nice day and we can pull chairs and tables out onto the new garage floor. Polly, do you want to go get food? Make some calls. Invite your friends."

Jeff stuck his head in and said, "Eliseo and I will set up chairs and tables."

Polly turned to Doug and Billy, "Ask your parents to come too. Why don't we plan to eat about six fifteen? Jeff, can you pull out some of those battery candles and lanterns?

"On it," he said.

Later that evening, as sixteen people she had grown to know and love sat around tables laughing and enjoying themselves, Polly thought about the last few weeks. It seemed as if she had been uncovering treasures. From the priceless vase to the stairway which would give her freedom; to the people she continued to add to her family. Each time she turned a page in her life, something new and wonderful popped up amidst the chaos and stress.

She looked at Eliseo and couldn't believe how fortunate she was to have listened when Jeff begged her to give the man a chance. She watched as he sat there with his hand on Obiwan's head, laughing at some story Andrew was telling the adults gathered at his table.

Sylvie and her boys had become so much a part of Polly's family; she couldn't imagine them not being around every day. Doug and Billy didn't know it but when she finally got the apartment done and they moved in, she was looking forward to having them around as often as possible.

She smiled at the women in her life. They continued to love her no matter what and she couldn't believe how much Jeff had become a part of all that was happening even outside of Sycamore House.

Henry was closing up the grill after finally serving the last hamburger and hot dogs. He was a treasure she continued to discover and was making it easier for her to consider settling down. Where would she be without him? She didn't want to think about that, so she smiled and sat back. Tomorrow they would all go back to their busy lives, but for now, her treasure was right here and she was thankful.

THANK YOU FOR READING!

I was sorry to leave Bellingwood this time, how about you? I've begun writing Book 4 and everyone is back for more fun. The summer festival – Bellingwood Days – brings strangers into town, the Percherons will be in the parade and a woman who knew Polly's parents well reaches out with a mystery from her past. It will be published in October 2013.

Check out the Bellingwood Facebook page:

https://www.facebook.com/pollygiller

for news about upcoming books, conversations while I'm writing and you're reading, and a continued look at life in a small town.

Recipes and decorating ideas found in the books can often be found on Pinterest at:

http://pinterest.com/nammynools/

And, if you are looking for Sycamore House swag, check out Polly's CafePress store:

http://www.cafepress.com/sycamorehouse

CHARACTER LIST

Polly Amelia Giller
    Parents: Everett & Barbara (Mahoney) Giller – deceased
    Relatives in Story City: Clyde & Ivy Giller
    Caregiver / Farmhand: Sylvester & Mary Shore
    Animals:
        Obiwan - German Shepherd / Labrador mix
            (gift from Doug Randall & Billy Endicott)
        Luke & Leia – cats (gift from Brad & Lee Giese)
        Nan, Nat, Demi, Daisy – Percheron horses (black)

Henry David Sturtz
    Parents: William & Marie Sturtz (Arizona)
    Sister: Lonnie, Graduate work – Univ. of Michigan, Ann Arbor

Polly's Bellingwood Girlfriends:
Aaron & Lydia Merritt (County Sheriff)
    Children: Marilyn & Brian Erikson (Dayton, IA)
    Jill & Steve Redman (Kansas City)
    Daniel Merritt (Des Moines)
    Sandy Merritt (Minneapolis)
    James (Jim) Merritt (ISU, Ames)

Beryl Watson - Artist
    First husband: Stewart Lanier (divorced)
    Second husband: Scott Watson (deceased)
    Cat: Miss Kitty
    Students: Deena, Meryl

Andy Saner – Retired Teacher
    Dating Len Specek?
    Children: Bill Saner, Junior
    John Saner
    Melanie Saner (ISU, Ames)

Sylvie Donovan – Chef at Sycamore House
    Children: Jason – age 12
    Andrew – age 9

Polly's Boston girlfriends:
Drea Renaldi - Professor at Boston College
    Two brothers: Ray & Jon

Bunny Farnam

Sal Kahane

Henry's Employees:
    Jimmy Rio
    Sam Terhune
    Leroy Forster
    Ben Bowen

Sycamore House Employees:
    Jeff Lyndsay
    Eliseo Aquila
    Sylvie Donovan

Bellingwood Friends:
Mark Ogden – Veterinarian
    Partner – Seth Jackson
    Employees – Marnie Evans, Dena Harrison, Leanne Malloy
    Siblings:
        Jack – IT – Mayo Clinics (Rochester, MN)
        Robert (Robbie) – Portrait & Wedding Photographer (Mnpls)
        Devin & Ellen – Interior Design (Austin, MN)
        Evan (Devin's twin) – Journalist (Duluth, MN)
        Lisa & Dylan Foster – Dance Studio & Pizza Pizzazz
          (Bellingwood)

Doug Randall – Electrical Apprentice for Jerry Adams
    Parents: Helen & Frank
    Sister: Tracy

Billy Endicott – Electrical Apprentice for Jerry Adams
    Parents: Marcus & June

Occasional Characters:
Bruce & Hannah McKenzie
    Bruce – Mechanic & sometimes farmer (went to high school with Polly)
    Hannah – works with Sylvie Donovan at Sycamore House
    Children: Sammy, Emma, Tyler
    Bruce's Parents: Lyle & Shirley
    Bruce's Brother: Kevin

Brad & Lee Geise
    Farm south of Boone, IA
    Provided barn wood for flooring
    Gave Luke & Leia (cats) to Polly

Rev. Del & Angela Boehm
    United Methodist pastor & wife

Jerry & Marian Allen
    Electrical Contractor

Doug Leon
    Former custodian at Bellingwood Schools

Shawn Wesley
    First of several awful custodians at Sycamore House

CPSIA information can be obtained
at www.ICGtesting.com
Printed in the USA
LVHW080941040122
707785LV00031B/721